FOLKTALES OF *Mexico*

 *Folktales*
OF THE WORLD

GENERAL EDITOR : RICHARD M. DORSON

FOLKTALES OF
Mexico

EDITED AND TRANSLATED BY
Américo Paredes

FOREWORD BY
Richard M. Dorson

THE UNIVERSITY OF CHICAGO PRESS
Chicago and London

International Standard Book Number: 0-226-64571-1
Library of Congress Catalog Card Number: 79-107225
The University of Chicago Press, Chicago 60637
The University of Chicago Press, Ltd., London
© 1970 by The University of Chicago
Published 1970
Printed in the United States of America

For Julie,
who will never read it;
And for Amelia,
who has made it easier than it
might have been

Contents

V   FORMULA TALES

Foreword

Mexico is deeply and passionately a land of folklore. One authority has said that over half of her people live folkloric lives.[1] In this country of striking contrasts, the first of consequence in the New World to feel the European conqueror's heel, the folklorist finds his ideal laboratory. Here he sees within one nation the uncertain balance between the high civilization and the village culture, and he recognizes that no observer can comprehend the whole without knowing something of both parts. In lands where industrial technology has produced a mass culture, the folk traditions are driven into dark, stagnant corners. In nonliterate societies where modern ways have barely penetrated, no broad line divides the folk from the elite, and this is the domain of the anthropologist. In Mexico the folk communities flourish twenty kilometers off the highways, and extend into the mestizo populations of the cities. British folklorists of the nineteenth century peered hopefully into village customs and usages seeking survivals of pagan rites. They would have had a field day in Mexico, where pagan continuities are brilliantly visible within the institutions of Christian Europe.

Although Mexican folklore differs greatly from the folklore of the United States, both can be considered under the "Theory for American Folklore" that I have elsewhere developed.[2] This thesis might better be called a theory for New World folklore. In es-

For valuable suggestions in the preparation of this foreword I am indebted to my colleagues Robert E. Quirk and Merle E. Simmons.

[1] Frances Toor, "Mexican Folk Dances," in *Renascent Mexico,* ed. Hubert Herring and Herbert Weinstock (New York, 1935), p. 179.

[2] Richard M. Dorson, "A Theory for American Folklore," *Journal of American Folklore* 72 (1957): 197–212; and idem, "A Theory for American Folklore Reviewed," ibid., 82 (1969): 226–44.

sence the argument runs as follows. The Americas, because of European colonization in modern times, possess a blend of imported, indigenous, and American-historical traditions very unlike the long-established, homogenized folk cultures of Europe. In Asia and Africa imperialism did not substantively alter the traditional cultures, but superimposed a thin overlay of European intellectual culture. In the Americas and Australia colonization did set in motion historical forces that would shape a new folklore. Four centuries later we can see distinctly New World customs.

The "Theory for American Folklore" gains some support from Herbert Bolton's thesis of a common North and South American history, which met with great success in his classes but failed to arouse the historical fraternity. Bolton's concept does suggest a unitary approach to New World folklore, by stressing certain large common factors, such as colonial and revolutionary phases. But Bolton's vision of an all-American history carries his premise too far, and the corollary of a common folklore does not follow. Few family resemblances link the folk traditions of Mexico and the United States, or of Jamaica and Surinam. A distinction needs to be made here between process and product; the folklorist can see the same historical process determining traditions, but he also perceives that the end products sometimes vary considerably.[3]

For each nation of the Americas, the same variables are shuffled in different combinations. We observe the clash of rival races, the impact of a formidable environment, and the struggle for racial identity. In the United States, the main factors molding folk traditions appear to be colonization, the westward movement, Negro slavery, immigration, regionalism, the rhetoric of democracy, and the technology of the mass media. The Indian, although a vital figure in the colonial period, is virtually eliminated from consideration by the twentieth century. English middle-class Protestants bring with them a relatively weak folk spirit, more than compensated for by later waves of immigrants and enslaved blacks. In the folklore of Chile, the only Latin American

[3] Lewis Hanke, ed., *Do the Americans Have a Common History? A Critique of the Bolton Theory* (New York, 1964).

country previously represented in the Folktales of the World series, the Araucanian Indian makes a secondary contribution; the
immigrant, chiefly the German, a minor one; the African Negro
virtually none; and regional variation looms large.[4] Now we
turn to Mexico.

The central fact of Mexican folklore is the Spanish-Indian synthesis. Instead of the slow drama of colonization, we should
speak of the concentrated epic of conquest in 1591–21 that led
immediately into racial and cultural confluence, heralded by the
Aztec identification of Cortés with the white god Quetzalcoatl,
and abetted by Franciscan and Jesuit missionaries sympathetic to
the natives. Slavery involves the Indian rather then the Negro, although there are pockets of Negro influence, for instance in Vera
Cruz and Oaxaca. Immigration is of small account, save that the
Spaniard continues to come even after New Spain declares her
independence as Mexico, and renews the tradition of the Spanish
upper class, the *gachupines,* and of the creoles, the American-
born Spaniards. Even the affluent mestizo slides into the master-
servant relationship that divides two social classes living under
the same roof.

Regionalism is certainly a factor in Mexican folklore, even if
it is a regionalism that develops outward in radial spokes from
Mexico City rather than falling into place in the course of a
steady western trek, as in the United States. With its two sea-
coasts and its variety of climates, from humid tropics to icy
mountain altitudes, Mexico does exhibit the diversity of land-
scape that stimulates the folk imagination. Large, distinct regions
are the plateau of the Valley of Mexico with its populous centers
and Aztec memories; the thumb-shaped Yucatan peninsula, hark-
ing back to Mayan glories; the empty highland forests of Chiapas in the south peopled by such isolated Indians as the Chamu-
las, Lacandónes, Tlotzil, and Zoques; the vast cattle-ranch grass-
lands of Chihuahua on the Texas border, where Pancho Villa
made his mark and Apaches and Comanches roam; Lower California jutting into the Pacific on one end and hooked onto *gringo*-land on the other. Yet these differences all fit into the Span-

---

[4] Richard M. Dorson, "Foreword" to Yolando Pino-Saavedra, *Folktales
of Chile* (Chicago, 1967), pp. vii–xxxvi.

ish-Indian spectrum; there are not, as in the Unites States, plural-istic cultures of Louisiana Cajuns, Pennsylvania Dutchmen, and Utah Mormons. I recall the vivid pageant of "Mexican Folklore" presented in Mexico City during the New Year's week of 1960; by folklore the sponsors meant dance, music, and costume, and by Mexican they meant the *regional* Indian dances of pre-Colum-bian ancestry refined and stylized by European influences.[5]

Another way of looking at Mexican folklore is to consider the parallel traditions of status and class, divisible into the Spaniard (*gachupín*), creole, mestizo, and Indian viewpoints that often clash in allegiance to rival images and heroes. Cortés the con-quistador, revered by the Spaniard, has been anathema to mestizo and presumably unknown to the remoter non-Spanish speaking Indians. In his place the leaders of the revolution exalted his Aztec victim, Cuauhtémoc, actually hated by other subjugated Indians as an Aztec oppressor.[6] One can draw a line from the tribal mythologies of mountain and jungle Indians, like the Lacandónes of Chiapas and the Tarahumaras of Chihuahua, to the creole Catholic legends of Mexico City, as presented by Thomas A. Janvier. These legends deal with Catholic miracles and punishments: of a pious nun who in death shrinks to fit her coffin; of the blacksmith who shoes a priest's mule at the re-quest of two blacks pummeling the mule, only to discover next day the priest's housekeeper shod and beaten; of a cursed church bell rung by the devil in a Spanish town, whose alcalde orders that its tongue be torn out and shipped to Mexico; of the priest summoned to hear the confessions of a man dying in a deserted house which, he learns the next day, has not been inhabited for a lifetime—but who on returning finds his handkerchief there, al-beit no trace of the dead man; of the sentry who turned up on 25 October 1593 in the Plaza Mayor of Mexico City, having been suddenly transported (it was said by the Devil), from Manila where, he claimed, and events later proved, the governor had the

<hr>

[5] Regionalism in dress is handsomely illustrated in Donald and Dorothy Cordry, *Mexican Indian Costumes* (Austin, Tex., 1968).

[6] Lesley Byrd Simpson, *Many Mexicos,* 4th ed. rev. (Berkeley and Los Angeles, 1967), pp. 263–64.

night before been murdered.[7] Yet the extremes of the Spanish-Catholic and pagan Indian lores fit into a continuum linked by a strong supernaturalism, with the mestizos, by far the largest population element, at the center. At one end are Indian peoples still close to their pre-Conquest legacy, known to us in such artistic mythological records as the *Popul Vuh, the Sacred Book of the Ancient Quiché Maya,* containing legendary history from the creation of the world to the growth of the great family houses of the Quiché, and in biographies of Aztec kings reconstructed from "oral, written, and carved history." [8] Thus the Lacandon Indians who perpetuate Mayan rites in the jungles of east Chiapas revere as their second deity the god Yanto, who is guardian of all foreign peoples, animals, and objects such as cats, dogs, oranges, and knives, and who dresses like a white man.[9] In the mountains of Chihuahua, teams of Tarahumara Indians vie with each other in fiercely competitive races in which victory depends not on their tremendous stamina but on the efficacy of their shaman-managers, who bury human bones in the path of the opposing team, throw herbs in the air, and make offerings to the dead. In 1926 the outside world discovered the Tarahumaras and their running ability, and two years later they easily won the marathon Olympic trials in Mexico City. Two of them were sent on to Amsterdam for the Olympics, not without dread at crossing the "wide river"; they finished three minutes behind the winner, and complained not of black magic used against them but of the shortness of the distance.[10] At the opposite pole, the urban so-

[7] Thomas A. Janvier, *Legends of the City of Mexico* (New York and London, 1910). Although these legends are somewhat overwritten, Janvier does name informants and append some corroborative notes, and he was a member of the English Folk-Lore Society.

[8] *Popul Vuh,* English version by Delia Goetz and Sylvanus G. Morley, from the Spanish translation by Adrián Recinos (Norman, Okla., 1950); Frances Gillmor, *The King Danced in the Marketplace* (Tucson, Ariz., 1964), p. xiv (quotation); idem, *Flute of the Smoking Mirror* (Albuquerque, N. Mex., 1949).

[9] Howard Cline, "Lore and Deities of the Lacandon Indians, Chiapas, Mexico," *Journal of American Folklore* 57 (1944): 114 and insert table.

[10] Frances Toor, *A Treasury of Mexican Folkways* (New York, 1947), pp. 277-81.

phisticates of Mexico City relate the legend of La Llorona, the
wailing woman in white seeking her children who died in childbirth. Originally an Aztec goddess who sacrificed babies and disappeared shrieking into lakes or rivers, La Llorona usually appears near a well, stream, or washing place. The Hispanicized
form has La Llorona murdering her own children born out of
wedlock when her lover married a woman of his own station.[11]

Besides the post-Conquest merger of Spanish and Indian lores,
two other historical factors have left a lasting impress on Mexican
traditions. The revolution of 1910–20 created a set of heroes and
villains celebrated and castigated by the mass of the people, who
saw in the revolutionary movement their chance for liberation
from political, economic, and social vassalage. In place of the
beckoning frontier in the United States, Mexico has suffered
from a reverse situation, the loss of her exposed lands through
annexation, conquest, and purchase by the northern bully. An
anti-*gringo* lore is one consequence of this unneighborly behavior. When President Lyndon B. Johnson restored 630 acres to
Mexico by dynamiting the Rio Grande back to its course, a mestizo muttered, "The goddamn *gringos* took a mountain and now
they give us back an anthill!"[12] Not yet as rife as in the United
States, but looming, is the pseudolore or fakelore promoted by
the mass media.[13]

SPANISH AND INDIAN FOLK SYNCRETISM

One famous example illustrates the merger of Spanish-Catholic
and Aztec Indian heritages that produced Mexican folk nationalism.[14] This is the apparition of the Virgin of Guadalupe,

[11] Janvier, pp. 134–38, 162–65.

[12] Enrique Hank Lopez, "Mexico," *American Heritage* 20 (April 1969):
5.

[13] Vicente T. Mendoza, "Current State and Problems of Folklore in
Mexico," *Journal of American Folklore* 61 (1948): 367.

[14] American anthropologists have strenuously debated the question of
Spanish origins of Mexican folktales. The position of Franz Boas, that
Hispanic had replaced indigenous themes, was vigorously challenged by
Paul Radin, speaking for syncretism ("The Nature and Problems of
Mexican Indian Mythology," *Journal of American Folklore* 57 [1944]:
26–36), and George M. Foster ("The Current Status of Mexican Indian

the central symbol of Mexican history. "The Most Holy Virgin Mary, Our Lady of Guadalupe, Queen of Mexico and Empress of the Americas," one North American writes, "is so much an inextricable part of Mexican life that it is almost impossible to describe contemporary Mexico, or explain its history, except as it refers to Her." This observer boldly states that "the one factor that has created and preserved Mexico as a nation has been the apparition and veneration of Our Lady of Guadalupe." An anthropologist notes that the "Virgin of Guadalupe, with the universally known story of her miraculous apparition to an ordinary Indian, is the religious common denominator of Mexico." A lady traveler from the States remarked that the "most ignorant Indian may not know of the President, Congress, or machinery of government, but he is sure to be well informed as to the merits of 'Our Lady of Guadalupe.' " [15]

The apparition of the Virgin was first seen on the dawn of 9 December 1531 by Juan Diego, an Aztec recently converted to Christianity, on Mount Tepeyac, as he was walking to mass at the Franciscan monastery of Tlatelolco from his native pueblo of Quahutítlan, four leagues from Mexico City. The Virgin bid him relay to the bishop of Mexico her desire to have a church built on that spot. Juan made his way to the bishop (actually the bishop-elect), Fray Juan de Zumárraga, a Franciscan and the new appointee of Charles V, Emperor of Spain, who endeavored to protect the Indians from the freebooting conquistadors while replacing their heathen orgies with holy Catholic worship. Three times, spurred on by the Virgin, Juan Diego had to seek out the busy and dubious prelate. On the third encounter, 12 December, the

Folklore Studies," *Journal of American Folklore* 61 [1948]: 368–82) in two articles of exceptional interest. Radin suggests that syncretism was aided because the Spaniards specialized in tales of humans, the Indians in tales of natural objects, while both possessed, and ultimately shared, animal tales.

[15] Donald Demarest and Coley Taylor, eds., *The Dark Virgin, the Book of Our Lady of Guadalupe* (Freeport, Maine, and New York, 1956), pp. 2, 36; Robert Redfield, *Tepoztlán, a Mexican Village* (Chicago and London, 1930), p. 196; Fanny Chambers Gooch, *Face to Face with the Mexicans*, ed. C. Harvey Gardiner (Carbondale and Edwardsville, Ill., 1966), p. 128.

Virgin commanded Juan to pick for the bishop roses that he would find at the top of the hill, where only cactus was growing, and promised that his uncle, seized with typhoid fever, would be cured on the instant. Juan took the roses in his *tilma* (a kind of poncho) to the bishop's palace, and after some rude jostling from the servants, gained his audience, and showed Zumárraga the fragrant roses of Castile, quite out of season. But yet more wonderful, as he opened his *tilma* to display them, those present saw a glorious portrait of the Virgin drawn on the coarse cloth. Soon it was learned that Juan's uncle had indeed been cured, and that he too had seen the Virgin.

Such is the essence of the event, covering four days, but its impact has endured through more than four centuries of Mexican history. A church was built on the site where Juan had seen the apparition, and the image on the *tilma* enshrined; it can be seen there today. Reports of the Virgin of Guadalupe (why she took this name became the subject of much speculation, usually hinging on a like-sounding Náhuatl word) spread electrically among the Indians, who flocked into the church for mass baptisms that taxed the strength of the clergy. Pagan temples gave away to Christian ones, usually on the same location. But it would not be correct to say that Catholicism replaced the old polytheism. Rather the two systems fused on common ground: ceremonialism and processions, the veneration of saints and deities, the emphasis on pain, suffering, bleeding wounds, and human sacrifice[16]— even though the Catholic priests and friars were horrified at the sacrificial slaughter of thousands of Aztec captives to the god Huitzilopochtli, whose Indians priests plucked out the hearts of their living victims on stone altars. The hill of Tepeyac had held the shrine of an Aztec goddess, Tonantzin, particular patron of the Totonoqui Indians, protectress of earth and corn, whose worshipers easily made the transition to the Virgin painted in the

---

[16] A point often made; see, e.g., Henry Bamford Parkes, *A History of Mexico* (Boston, 1960), pp. 9–10; Robert Redfield, *The Folk Culture of Yucatan* (Chicago and London, 1941), chap. 4, "Spanish and Indian: the Two Heritages"; Anita Brenner, *Idols behind Altars* (New York, 1929), *passim.*

likeness of an Aztec princess, speaking Náhuatl to the Aztec
Juan Diego, and appearing to him as a dark-skinned compatriot.
Pre-Conquest Indians called Tonantzin "Our Mother," and mod-
ern Indians speak of Tonantzin as "The Virgin."

The fame of the Virgin of Guadalupe continued to grow. A
whole series of miracles was attributed to her. When a plague of
typhus struck Mexico in 1534, the Franciscans arranged a procession of boys and girls to the shrine at Tepeyac, and the deaths
dropped overnight from more than a hundred to three. For a five-
year period, from 1629 to 1634, the image was transferred to
Mexico City to ward off floods threatening the lake-encircled capital. Over the centuries thousands of ex-votos have testified to the
miraculous cures she has effected for her believers. Armies of the
revolution carried her banner into the wars for independence
against Spain, from the first utterance of 1810, the celebrated
Grito de Dolores issued by the priest Miguel Hidalgo, "Long
live the Virgin of Guadalupe, down with the bad government,
death to the *gachupines!*" It still echoes in the present century,
giving rise to the comment that "throughout the long emerging
Indian revolutionary struggle 'Long live Our Lady of Guadalupe!' has been inextricably blended with 'Long live Independence.'"[17] The royalists countered with their own banner of the Virgin of the Remedies, whose image was supposedly
brought to New Spain by one of Cortés's men, and lost on La
Noche Triste (30 June 1520) when Cortés had to abandon
Tenochtitlán (later Mexico City). When one army captured
the banner of the enemy, its troops shot the rival Virgin for a
traitor. The powers of the Dark Virgin are still evident. In 1921
a bomb was set off in her church during a high mass. Although
a heavy painting behind the altar was smashed, a large bronze
crucifix twisted into a bow, and marble torn from the altar,
the image was completely unharmed, not even the glass in
the frame being cracked, and none of those in the crowded
church, including many distinguished prelates, received a scratch.
During the anticlerical period of Calles's presidency, commencing
in 1926, the priests struck for three years, but the Indians main-

[17] Demarest and Taylor, p. 8. This documentary anthology brings together many source materials about the Virgin of Guadalupe.

tained their saints' festivals and village fiestas, and excited throngs converged on Guadalupe in response to the report that the Virgin had abandoned her shrine and sought haven in a tree nearby.

The institutions of Indian tradition—family legend, temple offering, ritual song and dance, picture paintings, codex, fiesta—all contributed to the maintenance and deepening of faith in the Guadalupan Virgin. How firmly the accounts of the apparitions and miracles entered Indian oral history can readily be seen in the Vatican-sponsored Inquiry of 1666, which took depositions from grandchildren of Juan Diego's contemporaries, themselves octogenarians and even centenarians, testifying that they had heard of these happenings directly from their elders. Andrés Juan, between 112 and 115 years old, recalled that his family had taken him to the chapel over a hundred years before, and that he had seen the painting, now housed in the new church his people had helped build; he believed the Virgin of Guadalupe had spared him that he might give this testimony.

Another witness, Juana de la Concepción, eighty-five, daughter of a *cacique,* spoke of the detailed picture chronicles drawn by her father, one setting down the miraculous history as he had heard it from Juan Diego himself. Pablo Xuárez, seventy-eight, governor of Cuautitlán, said the matter was so well known that the children sang about it in their games.

Of special interest is the evidence given by Becerra Tanco, a scholar of Aztec culture and one of the earliest chroniclers of the miracles, whose narrative was published in the 1666 Proceedings. Tanco drew from a variety of sources for his crisply written, explicit relation. One source was unbroken oral tradition.

> I assert as a witness, that which I heard from people worthy of entire faith and belief, and very well known in this City of Mexico, very respectable Ancients, who understand and speak with elegance and perfection the Mexican language: who, speaking soberly, reported the tradition just as I have written it down, certifying to have heard it from those who had known the Indians to whom the Most Holy Virgin appeared, and also the most illustrious lord, Don Fray

Juan de Zumárraga and other people learned and sage who
lived in that first century of the dominion of our Catholic
monarchs in this New World.[18]

Besides what Becerra heard himself he gleaned from docu-
ments, such as pictorial annals with texts of Indian words in
Spanish characters, that recorded the traditions. Then there were
cantares, or chronicle songs, along with *mitotes,* the ritual dances
dramatizing historical episodes, which for centuries had served as
popular records of births and deaths of great *caciques,* of war and
pestilence and epic matters. Now these story-songs and story-
dances had incorporated the great days of Juan Diego and the apparitions, along with battles of the Conquest and wars in Spain.

On their part, the Spaniards equally adopted the Virgin of
Guadalupe into their religious institutions of shrine, mass, processional, adoration, and coronation. A full-panoplied processional
carried the painting on Juan Diego's *tilma* on 26 December 1531
from the bishop's cathedral in Mexico City to the new hermitage
at Tepeyac, and within six weeks Bishop Zumárraga had built
the church requested by the Lady of Guadalupe. Thenceforth it
promptly assumed the status of the first shrine in Mexico, and a
site for special sermons and ceremonies important to church and
state. The miracles continued to accumulate; in 1565 storm-tossed
sailors of a Spanish ship returning from the Philippines vowed to
carry their remaining sail to the Virgin of Guadalupe if she saved
them, and the sail (in stone, since the original sail was destroyed
in a 1916 earthquake) can be seen on the hillside by the chapel. In
1666 a special commission of painters and physicians examined the
painting on the *tilma* in the presence of the viceroy, and agreed
that no natural explanation could account for the marvelous composition on so coarse a fabric. An expert painter, Miguel Cabrera,
analyzed the portrait in an essay of 1756 and concluded that no
human hand could have mixed four such distinct media as oil,
tempera, watercolor, and fresco on a single surface. A skeptic of
the painting had a copy made on a similar fabric and placed in
the chapel of the Pocito in 1789, but saltpeter and humidity

[18] Ibid., p. 171.

caused it to peel, mildew, and turn greenish black, and after seven years it was removed.

United States citizens will recall the Treaty of Guadalupe Hidalgo, signed in 1848 to end the Mexican-American War. Apparently the American commissioner, Nicholas Trist, suggested Guadalupe as a likely meeting place because of its associations, and he and the Mexican commissioners repaired to the church after their negotiations for thanksgiving. The victory of the Mexicans over the Americans at Monterey is credited to the Virgin, who hovered over the battlefield and advised the Mexican officers where to strike.[19]

The climactic recognition of the shrine came on 12 October 1895 with the coronation of the Virgin of Guadalupe in a splendid ceremony, at which a poem written by Pope Leo XIII "to the Virgin of Guadalupe" was set to music and sung at the offertory. On the fiftieth anniversary of the coronation, 12 October 1945, Pope Pius XII sent a radio message to the international convocation, "Hail! O Virgin of Guadalupe," that celebrated the tradition:

> And so it happened, the sounding of the hour of God throughout the spacious regions of the Anáhuac. These had hardly been opened to the world when on the shores of Lake Texcoco there flowered the Miracle. On the *tilma* of humble Juan Diego—as tradition relates—brushes which were not of this earth left painted an Image most tender, which the corrosive work of the centuries was marvellously to respect. . . . From that historic moment total evangelization was an accomplished thing.[20]

Spokesmen for the European-Spanish-Christian inheritance minimize the role of the Aztec goddess in the emergence of the Guadalupan wonders. Poets, dramatists, novelists, artists, and composers have avoided the apparitions, but the folk have embraced her in cheap *corridos,* lucky amulets, household images, circus acts, crude *retablos,* and joyous fiestas. Great crowds gather

[19] Charles M. Skinner, *Myths and Legends beyond Our Borders* (Philadelphia and London, 1899), p. 225.
[20] Demarest and Taylor, pp. xiv–xv.

for the annual fiesta on 12 December in Guadalupe, spilling into
the streets and hills. Frances Toor writes of the fiesta in the present century:

> Many a time I have seen the dawn at the Basilica on De-
> cember 12, heard the mañanitas to the Virgin and seen the
> dancers perform reverently for the Virgin in the dimly
> lighted church. Afterwards I have followed them to the top
> of the hill to see them put up the three huge, freshly-painted
> crosses and dance around them, blow incense at them, and
> then offer it to the four cardinal points as in the days of the
> Aztec goddess.[21]

The market that accompanies the fiesta is a kind of folk fair, at
which all kinds of amulets, ex-votos, and medallions of the Virgin are sold. Throughout the year the pilgrims come to drink,
bathe in, and bottle the brackish water from the well that opened
beneath the Virgin when she stamped her foot at the bishop's
delay in building her church. They eat the mud around the holy
well to be cured of ills.[22]

Another and more caustic report of this fiesta is given by Ernest Gruening, who observes, "Intoxication is an invariable feature of Guadalupe Day, December 12, as anyone who has witnessed the ceremonies, as I have, can testify." He then cites Alta-
mirano writing in the nineteenth century.

> After the twelve o'clock mass, a most solemn ceremony
> with music, at times celebrated as pontifical, and with the
> presence of course of the canons of the basilica and the
> reverend abbot of Guadalupe, the Indians clad in the
> bizarre raiment of ancient days, that is, with feather plumes
> and fantastic garments of shrieking colors, perform their
> dances. After communion and the other ceremonies of the
> cult, the crowd climbs the Tepeyac hills to eat, according
> to the custom of that day, goat's milk . . . with a red *chile*
> and *pulque* sauce, commonly called "drunken sauce," and
> washed down with copious draughts of *pulque*.
> By six in the evening all these pilgrims are in the same

[21] Toor, *Mexican Folkways*, pp. 176–77.
[22] Ibid., p. 176; Skinner, p. 242.

state as the sauce, and the Holy Virgin witnesses the abom-
inable acts and crimes which are common in the religious
festivals of Mexico.[23]

A remarkably vivid and impressionable account of the festival
of Guadalupe from the 1880s was rendered by an American lady,
Fanny Gooch Chambers, who resided for a period in Mexico. To
capture the scene would require, she acknowledged, the pen of a
Dickens and the brush of a Hogarth, but she has conveyed a
sense of the discordant, prayerful, tumultuous throng in their various activities of gambling, cooking, vending, drinking, singing,
and, at the center of it all, performing the ceremonies.

> What a scene! The wildest, most fantastically decked be-
> ings that mortal eye ever beheld were in the inner space. The
> old men, adults, and boys, with their immense panaches of
> variegated colors that towered to startling height; their curi-
> ously wrought dresses that were strongly marked with the
> national colors, somewhat resembling the kilt of the Scottish
> highlanders; their ornamented moccasins; the women and
> little girls with their curious masks of coarse gauze, in black
> and white, crowned with immense wreaths of feathers, of
> every variety, intermingled with flashing tinsels, with tawdry
> dresses of many colors, and in fashion not unlike the kilt of
> the men and boys, made a scene that was grotesque and fan-
> tastic beyond description.
>   Then the dance! They formed circles—the men on the
> outer circle and the women on the first inner circle—and
> again other circles of the younger Indians of both sexes,
> forming one within the other. The everlasting jangle and
> trum-trum of the ghastly jarana [a stringed musical instru-
> ment] covered with the skin of an armadillo, looking like an
> exhumed skeleton, with the finery of flaunting ribbons float-
> ing around it, its harsh notes mingling with the drowning
> wail of the wild musician who played as though in a frenzy,
> were in keeping with the whole scene. The circles, with all
> their varied colors, danced in opposite directions with a slow,

[23] Ernest Gruening, *Mexico and Its Heritage* (New York and London,
1940), p. 251. A 1925 photograph of a dance performed on Guadalupe
Day faces p. 233.

bouncing step that was half a waltz, half a minuet, and as
they proceeded they grew more excited—more frenzied—
the musician seemingly more infused with his awful duty,
and the dancers stepping higher and higher, the circles
wheeling more rapidly, until the ear was overpowered and
the eye confused with the endless changes of faces, colors,
and sounds. It was the wildest, most mournful dance that
mortal could invent; and it seemed as if the souls of the de-
votees were in the movement. It was a sort of paroxysm of
physical devotion, and seemed to exhaust its votaries.[24]

Following the dance honoring the Virgin, the worshipers
moved into the church to continue their devotional singing and
praying. In unison they hymned a praise song to the Virgin.

> From Heaven she descended,
> Triumphant and glorious
> To favor us—
> La Guadalupana.
>
> Farewell, Guadalupe!
> Queen of the Indians!
> Our life is Thine,
> This kingdom is Thine.[25]

Commentators interpret the apparitions and the painting according to their lights. The historian Henry Bamford Parkes
simply observes that no one has yet presented a naturalistic explanation of the portrait, and drops the thought that Zumárraga
might have committed a pious fraud.[26] Defenders of the faith accept the traditions as indisputable evidence of the powers of the
Lord, the Virgin, and the Church, and dismiss Tonantzin as in-
consequential.[27] Skeptics have castigated the Mexican clergy for
manipulating the Dark Virgin to suit their purposes, whether
through a pretended miracle to take credit for ending the epi-

[24] Gooch, pp. 132–33.
[25] Ibid., p. 134.
[26] Parkes, p. 108, note.
[27] Demarest and Taylor, p. 31.

demic of yellow fever in 1737, or inciting in her name the murder of union organizers in a mining town in 1922.[28] The folklorist is intrigued by the rise to national prominence of a widespread tradition. Throughout Spain, Italy, Greece, Latin America,
villagers relate the legend of a vision or dream of the Virgin,
followed by a miracle and the building of a church on the site of
her appearance. I have tape-recorded from a Greek family in
northern Michigan a circumstantial account of a miraculous apparition of a picture of the Virgin Mary beheld halfway down a
mountainside by a shepherd in Greece. He reported this sight to
the bishop and priests, who lowered a man on a rope down the
cliff to secure the icon. But the next morning it was back in its
original spot, 150 feet down from the mountain top. "Well, then
they find out it was the will of Virgin Mary the church should
be there." So construction workers commenced blasting out the
side of the cliff. A bricklayer laying a cornerstone slipped and fell
a hundred feet to the bottom. The other bricklayers went down
with a basket to pick up the pieces, but found him whole, walking up with the stone on his shoulder. When the Elona Monastery was completed, a Turkish general sought to destroy it, but
was blinded by a flame of fire that darted out from the church
door. The blind general pasha returned to Istanbul, sold all his
possessions, and returned as a Christian monk to spend the rest
of his days in the monastery. Many healing miracles are told
(and were told to me) of persons healed at that church by Saint
Mary.[29]

However one interprets the Guadalupan episode, no one denies
the potency of the Dark Virgin as a symbol for the Mexican people. Drivers of buses, taxis, and trucks suspend her image before
them for protection. Ballad-singers regularly invoke her name.

¡Madre mía de Guadalupe;
que no me vaya a matar!

[28] Vernon Quinn, *Beautiful Mexico* (New York, 1938), p. 190; Gruening,
p. 222.

[29] Richard M. Dorson, "Tales of a Greek-American Family on Tape,"
Fabula 1 (1957): 138. The main informants were John and George
Corombos of Iron Mountain, born in Bambakou, Greece.

> My Mother of Guadalupe;
> Don't let me get killed.

All the farmers listening doff their hats at the mention of the Virgin. The *corrido*-singer strums his guitar and continues with the tragic story of the drunken miner who beat his mother, received her curse, and then, remorse-stricken, appealed in vain to the Virgin to stay the curse.[30]

Politicians and intellectuals as well as the folk reverence Our Lady of Guadalupe. When Huerta seized power from Madero in 1913, the minister of foreign affairs and president pro tem, Pedro Lascurain, called on the upstart dictator. "I beg of you," he requested, "to give effective guarantees that the lives of Madero and Suárez [the deposed vice-president] will be spared." Huerta pulled from under his shirt a scapulary with medals of the Virgin of Guadalupe and of the Sacred Heart of Jesus on a gold chain. "This was hung around my neck by my mother," said Huerta. "By her memory, before these sacred images, I swear to you that I shall permit no one to make an attempt against the life of señor Madero." And he kissed the images. Satisfied, Lascurain handed over the resignations of Madero and Suárez. Next day they were shot.[31]

Today, as I write this, the gifted Mexican novelist Carlos Fuentes reviews a biography of Zapata and invokes the Virgin in a moody speculation on his country's search for identity: "From what does legitimacy spring in a country that denies its rapist Spanish father and condemns its treacherous Indian mother? . . . the image of the dark-skinned virgin, Guadalupe, saves us from the fear of being sons-of-a-whore: we now see our Mother pure and enshrined. . . ."[32] Here Fuentes speaks from a deep-seated emotional tradition arraying the Aztec concubine of Cortés, Malinche, symbol of Indian betrayal to the white invader, against the Dark Virgin. On the folk level Malinche ap-

---

[30] Merle E. Simmons, *The Mexican Corrido as a Source for Interpretive Study of Modern Mexico (1870–1950)* (Bloomington, Ind., 1957), pp. 4–5.

[31] Gruening, p. 306.

[32] *New York Review of Books*, vol. 12, no. 3 (13 March 1969), p. 5, col. 4.

pears regularly in Mexican Indian dance dramas as a lone female figure among the warriors, sometimes specifically as Cortés's wife; on the intellectual level she represents *malinchismo,* the sell-out by Mexicans to foreigners.[33]

Willa Cather has paid tribute to the Guadalupan tradition in *Death Comes for the Archbishop* (1927). A padre in the New Mexico territory tells his bishop in Sante Fe he has promised an audience with the bishop to a native priest. "He has just been on a pilgrimage to the shrine of Our Lady of Guadalupe and has been much edified. . . . During your absence I have found how particularly precious is that shrine to all Catholics in New Mexico. They regard it as the one absolutely authenticated appearance of the Blessed Virgin in the New World, and a witness of Her affection for Her Church on this continent." The mission priest is granted his audience, movingly recounts the story of Juan Diego to the bishop, and describes the golden painting he has seen at the church in Guadalupe, fifteen hundred miles distant, marveling that paint could stay on the coarse cloth. He had brought back medals carrying on one side a relief of the painting and on the other the legend in Latin. "She hath not dealt so with any nation." [34]

How thoroughly the Virgin of Guadalupe permeates Mexican folk belief and custom can be seen in one village, Tescospa in the Valley of Mexico, where descendants of the Aztecs have evolved a culture blending Spanish and Indian elements in every phase of their existence. Speaking of this fusion, William Madsen, ethnographer of Tecospa, comments, "The Virgin of Guadalupe is a symbol of Indian genius for combining the old and the new." [35] And he titles his book *The Virgin's Children,* the name the Te-

[33] Octavio Paz, "The Sons of Malinche" in *The Labyrinth of Solitude* (New York and London, 1961), trans. by Lysander Kemp, esp. pp. 84–87; Lopez, p. 7; Frances Gillmor, "The Dance Dramas of Mexican Villages," University of Arizona Bulletin, vol. 14, no. 2 (Humanities Bulletin No. 5) (1 April 1943), pp. 18, 25; Eric R. Wolf, "The Virgin of Guadalupe: A Mexican National Symbol," *Journal of American Folklore,* 71 (1958): 34–39.

[34] Willa Cather, *Death Comes for the Archbishop* (New York, 1940), pp. 52–58.

[35] William Madsen, *The Virgin's Children: Life in an Aztec Village Today* (Austin, Texas, 1960), p. 231.

cospans give themselves. His low-key, simply written portrait of the Tecospans, illustrated with drawings by a ten-year-old village child as he sees the culture, and with realistic photographs, is a splendid miniature of the Christopagan syncretism and folk supernaturalism typical of Mexican life. These villagers, living in the district of Milpa Alpa within a morning's drive to Mexico City, descend from the Aztecs who battled Cortés. By the Virgin they refer both to the Lady of Guadalupe and to Tonantzin, "Mother" in Náhuatl.

In their creation myth, clearly showing influences of the Franciscan fathers, the Virgin intercedes with an angry God, her son, to save mankind, whom in the Aztec fashion he recurrently destroys. They quarrel, and she outwits him by saying, "All right, I will let you kill my children if you will give me back but one thimbleful of the milk with which I nursed you. I do not want cow milk. I do not want goat milk. I want a thimbleful of my own milk." God asks, "Where can I get that?" So, since the Virgin controls the supply, he loses this round. But finally she agrees that men are evil and lets him send a mighty rain that covers half the world with water. God saves ten people in a boat built by Christ and captained by San Francisco, patron saint of Tecospa, and lets pairs of animals find refuge in a second boat. When the flood subsides, God causes the boats to reach a place where they can float, and so they come to the floating gardens of Xochimilco. The boats in these canals today are of the same type as the ones Christ built. The myth continues, bringing in Adam and Eve, witches, and Judgment Days. In the debate between God and the Virgin, the Aztec principle of opposites—male vs. female, hot vs. cold, north vs. south—is maintained. God destroys, the Virgin protects.

Pulque, the exhilarating drink that accompanies every Mexican fiesta and revelry, is known as the Virgin's milk. The goddess Tonantzin fed those of her children who had survived God's flood with pulque. She then created the sturdy, broad-leafed maguey plant at the foot of a mountain, and after three centuries a gopher gnawed out the top and let man see its juice, called "honey water." Pulque is sacred today as it was to the Aztecs. Tecospa has a reputation for fine magueys and pulque.

Godparenthood is an institution introduced into Mexico by the Spaniards which found so congenial an environment that it developed its own extensions. Not only do the Tecospans appoint godparents for every *rite de passage* but also for buildings, trucks, and prized possessions. Altar images of female saints must have godmothers, and those of male saints, godfathers. So a family that purchases a picture of the Virgin of Guadalupe, as most Tecospan families do, selects a godmother to bring it with her to dinner and place it on their altar between two candles, while incense burns. On the eve of the Virgin's feast day the godmother brings flowers and a candle for the holy picture, which in the morning she decorates with crepe-paper bows and carries over her heart to church; this is said to be "taking the Virgin to Mass." The Virgin's godmother serves also as godmother to any other pictures of female saints the family acquires, and her husband as godfather to the pictures of male saints. Through the rituals and obligations of godparenthood a family magically insures the safety and welfare of its members.

In the Tecospan synthesis of Aztec and Christian beliefs in heaven and hell, the Virgin again has her role. Women who die in childbirth ascend to the sky world and are sent to the Virgin, who asks them, "Where is the hair I lent you?" If they have cut their tresses and failed to save the cut hair, the Virgin commands them to return to earth as spirits until they have collected their hair. Hence the women of Tecospa keep their hair cuttings in pillows, to be placed beneath their heads at burial and offered to the Virgin. They pity the sophisticates of Mexico City who bob their hair and so can never enter heaven. The Virgin of Guadalupe also cares for dead children, who are dressed in saints' costumes (as once they were dressed in the regalia of the gods), and put in coffins with toys and a bottle of mother's milk to relieve their trip to the otherworld. Once in heaven the Virgin nurses them with her own milk in the Garden of Flowers until they can be weaned, and raises them as if they were her own. They are now angels, and their parents should not mourn unduly for them, or the Virgin will order a dead child to rejoin his parents. Then the child must leave heaven, but being dead he cannot return home, and suffers greatly before he can reenter the sky-world.

In dire exigencies the villagers of Milpa Alpa have recourse to the Virgin. When a *pingo*—the Aztec demon—showed up in a village in Morelos, dressed as a *charro* (horseman) in the likeness of Ramón, who had died a year before, a rash of suicides followed. Ramón appeared daily at five P.M., whereupon half a dozen people killed themselves, until a whole *barrio* was emptied. In despair the town built a chapel to the Virgin of Guadalupe in the empty *barrio,* and effectively discouraged Ramón from further visits.

In sum, the Aztec mother goddess Tonantzin, or Coatlicue, has undergone a radical transition to the Catholic Virgin of Guadalupe. Physically she has changed from a flabby-breasted, clawed, and snake-entwined ogress wearing a necklace of hearts, hands, and a skull, in token of her relish for corpses, to a serene protectress and benefactor. Both are mothers of gods who created men, and both receive offerings from their worshipers, but the one in a spirit of dread and the other in a spirit of affection.

The major folkloric form of Mexico can best be described in a series of synonyms: pageant, spectacle, entertainment, procession, fiesta, carnival, festivity, celebration. No one word completely fits the need to cover a variety of events, partly religious, partly secular, sometimes civic, sometimes tribal, embracing such varied phenomena as an auto-da-fé of the Inquisition, a bullfight with associated acts and comic routines, an enactment of the Passion, a mock drama-battle of the Moors and Christians, a performance by *charros* and their trained horses, a mass pilgrimage to Guadalupe, a ritual seeking and drinking of peyote. Yet common elements bind these activities, for they are all highly visual and sensual, ceremonial in their structure and folk in their variability. The senses are vividly appealed to, through gorgeous costumes and masks, bunting and drapes, candles and incense, flowers and instrumental music, images and charms, firecrackers and gunpowder, delicacies and strong drink. Action, often strenuous and violent, involving or suggesting bloodshed, is characteristic: dancers swirl and circle, horsemen gallop, soldier-actors charge. The line between the real and the simulated is continually crossed; living persons were crucified in some village Passions, and bulls went free in mock bullfights. So too does the line between the sacred and the worldly waver; the faithful dance in church, and athletes invoke spirits against their competitors. The rites of magic are present in all these engagements. Much time, energy, and money go into fiestas and ceremonies, to which many village men devote the bulk of their efforts.

This especially Mexican folk behavior results directly from the fusion of Spanish and Indian cultural elements. Early in the post-Conquest years, the Church realized the predilection of their new Indian converts for the spectacular, and obliged them with ever more numerous and splendid functions, such as the *máscara* or *mascarada,* transported from Spain and quickly adapted to New Spain.

> It was, essentially, a parade of persons dressed in varied costumes and wearing peculiar masks, who promenaded about the streets by day or night, on foot, or mounted on horses or other animals; if after dark, they carried lighted torches, giving the city an unaccustomed illumination. They represented historical, mythological, and Biblical personages, gods of primitive religions, astrological planets, allegorical figures of Virtues, Vices, and other abstractions, and almost any bizarre creature, real or imaginary, was a welcome novelty.[36]

All classes and races participated in and enjoyed *máscaras,* which rapidly became a regular feature of life in New Spain. Some were serious and reverential, some satirical and facetious, and most a mixture of gravity and jollification. A minute portrayal by a creole writer of a typical *máscara,* held in 1680 in Querétaro, thirty leagues northwest of Mexico City, records both the brilliant pageantry of the hours-long procession and the mixture of Hispanic and indigenous traditions: magnificent tableaux of Aztec monarchs, of the emperor Charles V of Spain, and, in the

[36] Irving A. Leonard, *Baroque Times in Old Mexico* (Ann Arbor, Mich., 1966), p. 119.

most glorious float, of the Virgin of Guadalupe, her image resting on a throne set in the midst of an imitation ship covered
with streamers and bouquets, around which Indians danced their
famous *toncontines,* an ancient royal dance, while old men in-
toned devotions to the Virgin and tribesmen played on drums
with rubber drumsticks, on wooden fifes, on timbrels and on
other native instruments. The motive of this celebration was
to honor a new church in Querétaro built for the Virgin of
Guadalupe.[37]

The appeal of the Dark Virgin lies not in her uniqueness but
in her typicality. Her fiesta is merely the most celebrated of a
thousand fiestas that arouse and excite every villager in Mexico.
Fiestas combine all the folk arts: legend, dance, song, music,
drama, costume, ritual, decoration, sculpture, cuisine, carnival, in
endless variation and recombination. René d'Harnoncourt and
Frances Toor separately picture a fiesta they observed in the ham-
let of Huejotzingo, between Mexico City and Puebla, whose syn-
cretic aspects are at once evident.

This fiesta hinges vaguely on an elaborate legend of a locally
renowned bandit, Agustín Lorenzo, who came from a family of
peons in a small village in the interior of Guerrero. One day as a
youth he saw a little snake cut in two, and bound it together
with palm leaves (Motif E64.18, "Resuscitation by leaf"). A week
later an old man on a black mule offered him a magical white
mare. The mare carried Agustín through the air to escape federal troops pursuing him after he took silver from the government at Iguala. Whenever the federals closed in on him he re-
shod his horse with the shoes on backward, so that they mistook
his path (Motif K534.1, "Escape by reversing horse's shoes"). Always he outwitted the government and the rich *hacendados* and
defended the poor. Once the federals sent a blond beauty in silk to
entrap Agustín. After they had made love in his mountain hut,
he went to sleep. She unlocked the door and left, and the federals
locked it from the outside and set fire to the house. But Agustín
leaped through the flaming roof and dispatched three thousand

[37] Carlos de Sigüenza y Góngora, *Glories of Querétaro* (1680), translated
and quoted in Leonard, pp. 125–29.

federals with his machete before they could tie him up. They took him to Mexico and removed seven quarts of lead from his body, but he jumped from the hospital window onto his horse in the patio below, and still rides the countryside at night. A great crucifix was made from the lead, which Agustín turned to gold; it can be seen today in the church at San Juan de Dios.[38]

Thus the legend, in its magical form. The carnival is supposed to reenact the capture and death of Lorenzo, although the account told by d'Harnoncourt shows little relation to the village tradition or the fiesta action. In the version given him, a Spanish general weds an Indian girl, but a law against intermarriage eventually separates them, and as well their son and daughter. The son becomes a bandit, and falls in love unwittingly with his sister when he spies her in a convent; they ride off together to find a priest and get married. Meanwhile the general has been sent to capture the bandit, and arrives just as the wedding ceremony begins. Their father explains to the lovers who they are, and they embrace as siblings rather than as sweethearts. Here is a sentimental novella, shorn of the supernatural, and suited to the taste of the high-born creole narrator.[39]

In the fiesta the excitement centers on three characters: General, Bandit, and Bride. They parade around the plaza; costumed soldiers, Apaches, and musicians fall in behind them. General and Bride enter the town hall and reappear on the balcony; the Bandit rides beneath and throws a love letter up to his sweetheart, who promptly jumps over the railing and onto a horse. (Bride is a chap named Juan, with a moustache under his veil and a white dress over his clothes.) They ride away together, with the soldiers in merry chase, shooting blank cartridges and shouting lustily. Some hours later the excited crowd gathers around a little hut of branches at one end of the plaza. Inside, Bandit and Bride are married. The soldiers set fire to the hut, Lorenzo is killed, the bride is freed, firecrackers explode, the music screeches, and the drama ends amid hilarity and joyous

[38] Toor, *Mexican Folkways*, pp. 511–12.

[39] René d'Harnoncourt, "The Fiesta as a Work of Art," in *Renascent Mexico*, ed. Hubert Herring and Herbert Weinstock (New York, 1935), pp. 222–24.

dancing. Some changes have been noted over the years. The Mexican soldiers attack the French, who are in possession of the plaza, and drive them out. Bride is the daughter of Maximilian, the Hapsburg emperor placed by France on the throne of Mexico, where he perched uneasily from 1864 to 1867 until facing a firing squad. In this later version, Bride hears of her father's death and changes from a white bridal gown to a black mourning dress.

Brilliant and eccentric costumes give color to the fiesta. A thousand troops formed into battalions represent different European and Mexican soldiery. There are French Zuavos in blue cotton shirts, caps with visors, and white silk kerchiefs floating behind their heads, who carry knapsacks stamped "Viva Francia," with loaves of French bread on top, and wear pink masks and great black moustaches. The fierce Zacapoaxtlas, an Indian tribe that fought valiantly against the French, sport *sombreros* with streamers in the Mexican national colors, plus gold spectacles, masks with black side-whiskers, black tunics over women's panties, and gold sandals.

Individual creations add special touches; one warrior displays across his ceremonial cape a bright red poster advertising condensed milk. A French grenadier faces the foe from behind a long pink apron. So the raiment reflects the pre-Conquest attire of Indian tribesmen and the mid-nineteenth-century uniforms of the forces of Napoleon III, as well as tag ends of Yankee culture, in what has been called "the world's biggest mask dance." [40]

In the attitudes as well as in the garments one sees the blend and mélange of Mexican folklore. The village legend converts the bandit-hero into a Robin Hood defying the creole aristocrats, who wield the power of government to crush the hapless peon. The novella turns the rift and reconciliation of Spaniard and Indian into the affair of Bandit and Bride. Her loyalties divided, Bride sometimes mourns her mestizo lover, sometimes her European father. Updating is seen in the substitution of the French for the Spanish invader. A basic structure holds together the

[40] Ibid., pp. 219–22, 224–26; Toor, *Mexican Folkways*, pp. 194–97; Luis Leal, "The Legend of Agustín Lorenzo," *Western Folklore* 24 (1965): 177–83.

shifting elements of Mexican dance dramas, which from an Aztec base adopted the Spanish pageant of "The Moors and the Christians," and readily replaces Spaniards against Aztecs with French against Mexicans in spectacles retitled "The Conquest of Mexico" and "The Notebook of the Plume Dance." Players and spectators disregard historical inconsistencies, such as Juarés, the Mexican leader, affirming to the French invaders "the sacred patriotism of Maria de Guadalupe, whose sons we are," just before the French attempt to convert him to the religion of the true God.[41] A pre-Hispanic religious symbolism may underlie the whole performance. Luis Leal sees Bandit and Bride representing a boy and girl sacrificed in the burning hut to the god Camaxtli.

The instances of folk syncretism could be indefinitely multiplied. Ernest Gruening provides a long catalog of examples, with the intent of deprecating the Catholic clergy in Mexico, rather than appreciating the cultural forces involved. He notes the common base of Catholic and Aztec rituals in "incense, sacred ointments, holy water, fasting, self-castigation for sins, confession, and charms." Accustomed to a priestly hierarchy, demanding deities, and elaborate ceremonies, the Aztecs absorbed and adopted Catholic externals within their own frame of reference. Saints assume the hues of indigenous gods and goddesses. The Christ of Tlacotepec turned dark during a mass in front of the worshipers, who had been seduced by the devil on the grounds that the Son of God was unlike them in color. "Many are the dark Christs and virgins scattered throughout Mexico and each has its tale." In the village of Amozoc, Indians bring their own personal Christs to the fiesta and boast of the miracles performed by their Christ-images, falling to blows in the heat of the argument and the pulque, even batting each other with the images—hence the saying, "When Christ fights Christ the most worm-eaten loses." [42] In his sensitive studies of Mexican village and town life, Robert Redfield has demonstrated the urban-rural shadings and nuances of Spanish-Indian, Catholic-pagan syncretism on a spectrum that runs from religion to magic, from living ritual to hollow folklore. It is the syncretism that makes the folk what

[41] Gillmor, "The Dance Dramas of Mexican Villages," p. 25.
[42] Gruening, pp. 231, 238, 242.

they are today, and it is the "ways of the folk, largely unwritten and unremarked, that constitute the real Mexico." [43]

Revolutionary Nationalism and Hero Cults

Nations of the New World have, in the process of throwing off the yoke of the Old, created new hero types, and these heroes exhibit a distinctively popular or democratic character. The United States and Latin America rejected the monarchs of Britain, Spain, Portugal, and France for American patriot leaders—George Washington, Simón Bolívar, San Martín, Toussaint l'Ouverture—who inevitably became saviors and father figures. Yet a considerable gulf separates the people's champions of Anglo-America and Ibero-America. The true folk and culture hero south of the border is the *caudillo*, a bold horseman and gunman, a fiery orator, the embodiment of folk passions and prejudices, an emotional foe of the entrenched regime. He is somehow never destined to be, or never is completely comfortable as, an establishment figure himself.

This dramatic personality, so conspicuous throughout Latin American history, most recently in Fidel Castro, does not exist and cannot exist among the Yankees. Alexander Hamilton fancied himself the man on horseback, but he ended up designing the Bank of the United States and a protective tariff. The dashing soldier-heroes of the *gringos* fade away into local eccentrics, like Ethan Allen, or national buffoons, like General Custer. We prefer not to dwell on Ulysses S. Grant as president. The fact is, the States are lean in folk-heroes. A few minor badmen, such as Jesse James, a couple of frontier braggarts like Davy Crockett, some contrived pseudogiants—Paul Bunyan, for example—and the list quickly runs out. Legends have attached to Lincoln, and he comes closest of the national idols to mirroring the thoughts of the common man; but the people do not sing ballads, though they once told stories, about Honest Abe. The forces of patriotism and nationalism, working through the constitutional processes of republican government, have not produced enduring folkloric

[43] Redfield, *Tepoztlán*, p. 1.

figures. Rather they have generated great folk themes, like Manifest Destiny and the Monroe Doctrine.

In Mexico a public does exist, in the preponderant mestizo class, that sings ballads and recounts miraculous tales about heroes. Two phases of Mexican history particularly lend themselves to patriot cults—the struggle for independence from Spain, 1810–21, and the battles of the revolution against the Díaz dictatorship and its immediate legacy, 1910–20. The more colorful and swashbuckling personalities appear in the later period (with the notable exception of Santa Anna), and by this time a new genre of Mexican literature had emerged—the *corrido,* recording the shifts and turns of popular sentiment toward the figures at the stage center of history.

Corridos are brightly tinted sheets with rough illustrations, sold to the singer's audience, and correspond to the seventeenth-century English broadside ballads that presented sensational and startling news in a metrical and musical setting. Although it is a folk ballad, the *corrido* is often printed in this ephemeral form, and becomes a document reflecting the general attitudes of the *pueblo.* Some talented artists, like José Guadalupe Posada, illustrated *corridos* with satirical drawings that subsequently influenced Diego Rivera and other nationalist mural painters. *Corridos* deal with crimes and accidents and revolutions, but in towns like Tepoztlán, as Redfield points out, sensations are rare and the deeds of revolutionary heroes form the staple themes and become, in effect, the local history books.[44] Wherever they are sung —and they are sung all over Mexico—the ballads deal candidly with the strengths and frailties of the famous and infamous.[45]

In his excellent study *The Mexican Corrido as a Source for Interpretive Study of Modern Mexico (1870–1950),* Merle E. Simmons has extracted from the *corrido* literature a mirror of the *pueblo's* (common people's) reactions toward the dominant personalities of the period. All are depicted in the street ballads: dictatorial Díaz, gentle Madero, vicious Huerta, hypocritical Carranza, brave Obregón, anticlerical Calles, colorless Avila Camacho. One thread binds the judgments of the *corridistas* on all

[44] Ibid., p. 186.
[45] Gruening, pp. 647–48.

these successive presidents, save Huerta: their will and ability to carry on the revolution that would restore land, peace, security, and self-respect to the *pueblo*. In this light the two most revered heroes of the people were *caudillos* who never achieved the presidency, Emiliano Zapata and Pancho Villa.

They appear the most frequently of any public figures in the *corridos,* and inspire the highest admiration and awe. Villa, the scourge of the north from the cattle ranch state of Chihuahua, emerges as fury incarnate, "a cyclonic force which ravaged Mexico" [46] in the early years of the revolution. His role is not so much personal as symbolic; in a *corrido* of the battle of Zacatecas, he comes on the scene only once to taunt his enemy and turn the tide, while his lieutenants attend to the military details. Villa's soldiers in turn mock the fleeing Huerta and his army:

> Get ready now, colorados,
> Who have been talking so loud,
> For Villa and his soldiers
> Will soon take off your hides!
>
> To-day has come your tamer,
> The father of Rooster Tamers,
> To run you out of Torreón—
> To the devil with your skins! [47]

A more personal note is sounded in the ballad of "Pancho Villa at Torreón" celebrating the victory of 1914 that swung the revolution in favor of the constitutionalist forces with whom Villa had aligned himself. This *corrido* gives details of the conflict as remembered in 1938 by the ballad singer, himself a *villista*. "General Francisco Villa" is directly quoted, saying, "I don't care about anything, / Let's go, boys, and take Torreón." The soldiers cry "Long live Villa!" as they charge the federals. The *corridista* ends with "Long live Villa forever/ In the hearts of Mexicans! Because your name is brave/ And you conquered the tyrants." And he adds, "Long live the Revolution!" [48]

[46] Simmons, p. 254.
[47] Ibid., p. 549.
[48] Brownie McNeil, "Mexican Border Ballads" in *Mexican Border Ballads and Other Lore,* ed. Mody C. Boatright (Austin, Tex., 1946), pp. 24–26.

Villa was not always the triumphant warrior. Occasionally he is identified with the losing cause of the poor peons against the wealthy *hacendados* in the tradition of nineteenth-century bandit-heroes. After his defeat by Obregón in April 1915, Villa's image tarnishes, and in North American eyes it received a lasting stain folowing his raid on Columbus, New Mexico, in March 1916. Yet the subsequent fruitless pursuit of Villa into Mexico by General John J. Pershing refurbished Villa's luster, by attaching to him the nationalist sentiment against the colossus of the north. Where in fact he killed about seventeen of the townspeople of Columbus, the balladeer credits him with slaying all but seventeen. Villa laughs, and the people gasp, at the sight of *gringos* strung up or earless. (I have heard from Mexican-Americans in northern Indiana the tradition of Villa's enemies—not necessarily *gringos*—seen years later on city streets, without ears.) In his retirement he takes on the soft glow of an ex–freedom fighter tilling the soil. His assassination in July 1923 gives appropriate terminus to the heroic biography and produces a spate of *corridos* that lift Villa toward Valhalla. One singer laments that the Virgin of Guadalupe failed to guard the honorable *caudillo*. A literary *Corrido de Pancho Villa* "presents the popular hero now in full epic panoply. His horse is swift, its rider elusive; when his enemies believe him in Chihuahua, he suddenly appears in Durango. . . ."[49] He mocks his enemies, dynamites trains, shoots prisoners in cold blood, then denounces war. Here is Villa the implacable, unconquerable, tender-hearted.

Many stories swirl around Villa, on both sides of the Mexican-American border. Some are realistic, some are magical, some are coarse. The bandit is celebrated as a deadly and brutal marksman. He shot his own men when they disobeyed orders and fell to carousing; he shot prisoners whom he offered liberty if they could scale a wall ahead of his guns (a deed transferred to him from his lieutenant Rodolfo Fierro); he shot the *hacendado* whom he forced to marry his sister, when he learned the man had used her; and for a grim twist, at the height of the wedding

[49] Simmons, p. 278.

feast he made the bridegroom dig his own grave.[50] At lunch under a tree he ordered captured officers to be shot in front of his party, although one officer begged on his knees for mercy and a lawyer in Villa's group pleaded that he spare them the sight. "You chocolate-drinking politicians want to triumph without remembering the blood-drenched battlefields," sneered Villa.[51]

Daredevil that he was, he made a pact with the Devil at the Hill of the Coffer, north of San Juan del Rio, a habitation for the Evil One and his subordinate sorcerers and witches. Young men went there to sell their souls, and hence that region is known for its lucky gamblers, lovers, horsemen, and merchants. Inside the fiery hill Villa found caves with golden walls lined with rich jewels. The Devil presided, flanked by popes, generals, kings, lovely women, philosophers, and men of all races singing and laughing maniacally. Pancho fought off seven-colored dogs and spotted goats, signed up with Satan, and left his soul crying in a corner. He had to cast off his rosary and saints' relics, renounce all thoughts of God and the Trinity, and replace them with curses and blasphemy. The horse he rode came from, or perhaps was, the Devil, and could scent the enemy and dodge bullets. Villa returned from his visit with invincible strength and cunning.[52]

This legend involves Villa with a deep-rooted complex of traditional beliefs: enchanted caves, demonic inhabitants, bargains with demons, and the worldly success and final doom of the mortal who has ceded his soul. In the village of Tecospa in the Valley of Mexico a number of local legends deal with the demons known as *pingos*. Children born on Tuesdays or Fridays, ill-omened days, cast heavy shadows and see *pingos*, who dwell in hell or, when on earth, in mountain caves. *Pingos* seek out poor people as most liable to temptation. They often appear as well-

[50] Toor, *Mexican Folkways*, pp. 513–14. Fierro's act is reported by Martín Luis Guzmán, *The Eagle and the Serpent*, trans. from the Spanish by Harriet de Onis (New York, 1930), chap. 12 "The Carnival of the Bullets."

[51] Martín Luis Guzmán, *Memoirs of Pancho Villa*, trans. Virginia Taylor (Austin, Tex., 1965), p. 199.

[52] Toor, *Mexican Folkways*, pp. 514–15.

dressed *charros,* but also as black dogs, and can be recognized by their tails that resemble snakes and lizards. The mountains and caves that *pingos* inhabit are known as enchanted places. Rain dwarfs also reside within mountains, raise flower and vegetable gardens there, and keep barrels of thunder and lightning in their cave homes. Mountains themselves are personalized. Popocate-petl, the majestic volcano with snowy peaks visible from Mexico City, was once a fruit vendor, who lost the favor of a noble lady, now the volcano Ixtacihuatl, to a successful pulque vendor, now the little mountain called Teutli. In a jealous fit, the fruit vendor threw a snake at his rival, who decapitated it with a lightning bolt. The snake with its severed head can be seen along the way from San Pablo to Teutli. When the lady died of grief, the fruit vendor built a big mound by her body and sat upon it to smoke a cigarette; hence today he is called "Smoking Mountain" or Po-pocatepetl. Meanwhile the pulque vendor retired within Teutli to enjoy his gains. Indians in the area once dug into the mountain to obtain some of this wealth, but Teutli thundered in wrath and tossed their tools far away.[53]

In Mexican folk belief, mountains and *pingos* enjoy a natural affinity. People in the Milpa Alpa region of the Valley of Mexico tell how Alonso, a thriftless scraper of magueys, let himself be in-veigled by a *pingo* whom he met, dressed as a *charro,* on the road one night. Eventually the *pingo* talked Alonso into the fate-ful bargain. Alonso prospered and sold the best magueys around. But his wife learned about the evil deal, quarreled with him, and disappeared for a week. On her return she recounted the brutali-ties to which the *charro-pingo* had subjected her. In nine months she died giving birth to a monstrous baby with a head like a great cooked *zapote blanco* (a native fruit). Museum officials in Mexico City operated on the child's skull and found it filled with gold but empty of brains. Alonso went mad, and one night his body was found in a ravine, where drunks often fell, with the flesh gnawed off his right leg by dogs. At his funeral the candles flickered and went out, then relighted themselves; his left arm was seen hanging from a nopal stem; the body then dis-

[53] Madsen, pp. 128–31.

appeared, and Alonso's son filled the coffin with stones. Everyone knew the *pingo* had claimed the soul.

Another *pingo* encounter comes still closer to the Villa legend. Tecospans say that a shepherd, Lucas Carnero, fled to the hills after murdering a man. Asleep in the cave, he sensed a presence, drew his knife, and cut off a long ear of the creature, who was a *pingo*. The two concluded a bargain, and Lucas speedily gained fame and riches as the most daring and cruel robber of travelers, stagecoaches, and trains in the region. Others flocked to his mountain fastness, where Lucas kept his plunder safe behind a cávern portal that opened only to "Abrete Selsamo," repeated thrice. Carnero shot one of his men so that his spirit would guard the treasure. A lumberman happened to see the shooting, and learned he could enter the cave on 5 May, when the door swung open for an hour. He took away a bagful of yellow beans that turned into gold dust, which he weighed with a borrowed *cuartello* measure. The neighbor observed gold flecks on his returned measure, ferreted out the secret, and entered the cave. But he forgot to emerge within the hour, and on the following 5 May the lumberman found him, unaware that in his one day in the cave a year had elapsed outside. Both men died soon after, but Lucas Carnero turned *pingo,* and emerged each 5 May for one day.[54]

Here then is the cluster of folk themes that has enveloped Villa, a logical candidate for the legend of the diabolical pact. He was in fact an adroit and successful bandit, outwitting the federals and the *gringos,* attracting followers, leading a charmed life. Some of Zapata's men are also credited with *pingo* relations, but they lacked the stamina to survive. Six *zapatistas* hid in the cave Ostotempa near Milpa Alpa during the revolution. A big stone table stood in the cave's center. Five of the six died shortly after entering, and only one resisted the *pingos* and escaped to tell the tale.[55]

A number of elements familiar in European and Middle Eastern traditional narrative are recognizable here. There comes at once to mind the romance of Ali Baba and the Forty Thieves, in

[54] Ibid., pp. 136–37.
[55] Ibid., p. 133.

which the magic password "Open Sesame" causes the cave door to swing open. Introduced to Europe quite late, in Antoine Galland's French translation of *A Thousand and One Nights* (1704–17), the story rapidly entered the repertoires of folktale narrators, and is now identified as Type 676, *Open Sesame.*[56] Many familiar motifs occur in this legend complex: "Man sells soul to devil" (M211); "Treasure of mountain spirit" (N511.3.1); "Demon as guardian of treasure" (N571), which is close to "Sleeping king in mountain as guardian of treasure" (N573); "Supernatural lapse of time in Fairyland" (F377); "Transformation: objects to gold" (D475.1); "Secret wealth betrayed by money left in borrowed money scales" (N478). The European fiction is a firmly believed event in the Mexican setting.

In an unexpected role Villa, through his spirit, chases away the demons that possess afflicted persons. At the spiritualist centers that have sprung up throughout Mexico in relatively recent times, resident mediums assist troubled clients in communicating with the spirits of powerful and prestigious departed persons. The spiritualist now takes his place alongside the *curandera,* herbalist, and similar Mexican practitioners of folk medicine who cater to unnatural diseases. How the flourishing institution of the *casa de oración* (spiritualist center) got started is still under inquiry, but two likely sources are the cult of a prophet named Roque Rojas, a priest who, after a seizure he experienced in 1866, identified himself with the Prophet Elijah and the Holy Ghost; and a Protestant sect that penetrated into northeast Mexico from Texas in the 1930s. One of the national heroes most frequently requested of the mediums is Pancho Villa, although his "picturesque language" sometimes embarrasses the assembly and in one instance led the operator of a *casa de oración* to request that the group pray for the withdrawal of the foul-tongued spirit.[57]

Be that as it may, Pancho's spirit proves effective, as the following case record reveals:

A young man, ill of a nervous disorder, was taken to a

[56] Stith Thompson, *The Folktale* (New York, 1946), pp. 68–69.
[57] Isabel Kelly, *Folk Practices in North Mexico* (Austin, Tex., 1965), p. 70.

spiritualistic center for treatment. There, the spirit of Pancho Villa presented itself and, using objectionable language, said that the boy was not crazy but that evil spirits had taken possession of him.

We imagined that Pancho Villa drove out the evil spirits by yelling [at them] and by hitting them with a whip. In any case, at every shout the boy let out a cry of pain. Pancho Villa, in not very acceptable language, told the spirits to withdraw and leave the boy free.

He was treated thus for some time until completely cured. After each treatment he was black and blue from blows which he had not administered to himself. This makes us believe that the spirit of Pancho Villa lashed the evil spirits.[58]

In death Villa displayed the same ferocious qualities that had made him so feared a *caudillo* in life. Little wonder that demons quailed before him, as had the *gringos*. Not only as a spirit, but also as a ghost, Pancho Villa still appears to his countrymen, holding his head in his arms. He allows only Mexican peons to see his ghost, never *gringos,* greedy for his loot, and the peons take comfort in his headless presence. A folklore-minded biographer of Villa, Haldeen Braddy, has written, "One of the strongest psychological factors in Mexican politics today is the maimed ghost of the revered liberator." [59]

In 1926, three years after his death, Villa's head was severed from his entombed body in Hidalgo del Parral, Chihuahua. A host of stories spirals about this decapitation. One cycle attributes the deed to a *gringo,* Emil Holmdahl, an adventurer who had once fought with Villa. He defended himself against police charges by gulping down a bottle of alleged embalming fluid found in his car, which he claimed was sterilized water he drank for his fat kidneys. But the suspicions persisted. A ballad, "La decapitación de Pancho Villa," gave explicit details on how the American broke into the crypt and cut off the head, hoping to

[58] Ibid., p. 64.
[59] Haldeen Braddy, "The Head of Pancho Villa," *Western Folklore* 19 (1960): 33 and idem, *Cock of the Walk, Qui-qui-ri-quí! The Legend of Pancho Villa* (Albuquerque, N. Mex., 1955), "Ghost of the Rio Grande," pp. 164–68.

exploit a vein of gold ore. How? One legend attributes to Holmdahl the uncovering of twenty million dollars in gold ingots from Villa's cache in the Sierra Madre, which the *gringo* had located from a map that was tattooed on Villa's shaved head while he was alive; hair grew over the map, but the beheader knew it was there. Another explanation holds that a Chicago institute had offered Holmdahl $5,000 for Villa's skull. Strong evidence points to political enemies of Villa as the ghouls, but the *pueblo* prefer to believe in an American desecrator.[60]

Far to the south in the state of Morelos a black-mustachioed *charro* named Emiliano Zapata was also leading the people of his region against the central government that had betrayed their hopes. More than his northern ally, with whom he was often linked in history and in balladry, Zapata speaks for the peon's aspirations. "Land and liberty" was his cry, echoed in the *corridos.* To these goals were attached the ideals of peace, justice, religion, democracy, and progress, blocked by the *gachupines* and other foreigners whom Díaz favored. Above all, Zapata represents the concrete aims and emotional values of the Indians of Morelos. Balladeers extol his personal bravery, his sentimentality (he wept when one of his generals was killed), his leadership. When in April 1919 he too was assassinated, not yet forty, in a particularly treacherous manner, the *corridos* did not need to alter his image, as in the case of Villa, who required a martyr's death to soften his less attractive aspects. Rather, they enhanced the already sympathetic features of the southern *caudillo.* He is the selfless patriot, the ideal *charro,* relishing cockfights and horsemanship, God-fearing, justly cruel when occasion demands. The most recent *corridos* have emphasized his tenderness for the poor and the wounded.

Predictably he became a subject of legends. Many refused to believe that he was dead, and asserted that they had heard the hoofs of his horse "Lightning" (El Relámpago) clattering at night through village streets and over the mountains and valleys of his native Morelos.[61] During the Second World War people

---

[60] Braddy, "The Head of Pancho Villa," pp. 25–33.
[61] Simmons, p. 310; Toor, *Mexican Folkways,* p. 516; Parkes, p. 364.

said that Zapata lived on and was fighting with Hitler, hence the
success of the German armies.[62]

Villagers in Tepoztlán, a town in Morelos, cherish his name
and feats ahead of all the *veteranos*. (Redfield pairs the *santos* or
patron saints of the *barrios* with the *veteranos* or military heroes
of the revolution as sacred-secular popular figures.) [63] They relate his life history in the form of a folk biography, stressing his
poverty (actually his family was relatively comfortable, and lived
in a stone and adobe house, not a hut),[64] his struggle for the
poor people against the millionaires, his betrayal and murder.
"Zapata was a very great man. The only reason he lost was that
he had no money." Local *corridos* call him "a Napoleon" and
"our defender."

> He charged the forces of the south
> As chief and exalted savior.

When he storms the hacienda of a haughty Spaniard, the earth
trembles.[65] Prose legends as well as rhymed ballads tell of his supernatural powers. No mere mortal could contain or confine him.

> Zapata was miraculously clever at escaping. He was many
> times surrounded but he always got away. One day he was
> penned into a house by the federals. The only entrance was
> by the *zaguán,* where there were federal troops. The wall at
> the back of the house was as high as that shelf [about seven
> feet]. Zapata had a wonderful horse. It was called Relámpago
> ["Lightning"]. When the federal troops were about to close
> in on him, he drove his spurs into Relámpago and leaped the
> wall—he was gone, none knew where.
>
> When he came into a *pueblo* with his forces, they always
> tried to find a house, oh, very clean, for him to sleep in.
> When he was sleeping no one might enter except his orderly.

[62] Oscar Lewis, *Life in a Mexican Village: Tepoztlán Restudied* (Urbana,
Ill., 1963), p. 46.

[63] Redfield, *Tepoztlán,* chap. 11.

[64] John Womack, *Zapata and the Mexican Revolution* (New York,
1969), p. 6.

[65] Redfield, *Tepoztlán,* pp. 198–200. Reminiscences of a *zapatista* are in
Oscar Lewis, *Pedro Martinez* (New York, 1964), chap. 7, "Fighting with
Zapata."

> But many times Zapata would get up in the middle of the
> night and go and sleep under some rock in some secret place.
> None knew how he got there. Thus, though many times
> the federals surrounded the house where he slept, he always
> got away.[66]

How then was he finally trapped by the faithless Jesús Guajardo? The *zapatistas* had their answer. It was not Zapata at all
but a decoy he had sent in his place who was shot. A *veterano* in
Tepostlán declared his belief that Zapata still lived. "Some say he
is in Arabia, and will return when he is needed." The *zapatista*
had seen the body reputed to be his chief, and it did not bear the
scar on the cheek that distinguished Zapata. "He himself is in
hiding, and still lives. He will come back when he is needed." [67]

Others repeated, or varied, this story. They said that Zapata's
body, carefully displayed and photographed in Cuautla to con-
vince the villagers their leader was really dead, lacked a mole, a
birthmark, a missing finger tip. His sorrel horse, turned white,
was seen galloping through the hills toward the Guerrero mountains, riderless, though some saw Zapata astride.[68]

Even if he was dead, his ghost still walked and rode. Some *corridos* speak of Zapata's specter roaming in torment over the countryside in the black night, cursing dreadfully, gnashing his teeth,
jangling his spurs.[69] Sometimes, as in "The Skull of Emiliano
Zapata," this image is linked with a tradition of secret treasure,
and memories of his freebooting days with his false friend Guajardo.

> On the edges of Cuautla
> Floats a horrible flag,
> Clutched by the skull
> Of the veteran Zapata.
>
> Exactly at the stroke of midnight
> He mounts his spirited charger,

[66] Redfield, *Tepoztlán,* pp. 201–2. Note the similarity here with the
legend of Agustín Lorenzo.

[67] Ibid., p. 204.

[68] Womack, p. 330.

[69] Simmons, pp. 310–11.

This indomitable corpse
Rides out with him.

And at a rough trot
He crosses these huge sierras
And goes as far as El Ajusco,
The center of his raids.

And there he parts for the mountain
Where he keeps his treasure,
Which is called El Jilguero,
And there dismounts from his horse.

He folds his black flag,
Sign of angry death,
For in the center is painted
A horrible skull.

And he says: Patiently I wait
To eat this little chicken
With my good friend Guajardo,
And we will do it in *mole* sauce

Stewed with the shin bones
We found by the dozens
On the trains attacked
By my courageous gang.

Happy were those days
When I had such a good time.
How many mountains of skulls
We made of them! [70]

In ballads such as these the spectral figure of Zapata moves closer to the fiendish mask of Villa. Zapata has joined the pantheon of saviors embraced in the Legend of the Returning Hero —Frederick Barbarossa, King Arthur, Siegfried, Prince Marko— who never died but slumber in their mountain fastnesses awaiting the hour of crisis when they will sally forth once again to

[70] Ibid., p. 311. Translated by Jean M. MacLaughlin.

lead their people against the invader.[71] Villa belongs with the
Faustian crew who have obtained their powers from below rather
than above. Yet at points the Returning Hero and the Bandit
Who Sold His Soul to the Devil intersect, as fearless leaders
based in enchanted mountains. Both *caudillos* benefited in legend
from the circumstances of their death. Every bandit-hero of nineteenth-century *corridos* save one died with his boots on, foully betrayed or gloriously fighting[72]—a fate echoed in heroic saga
around the world. A further kinship is evident in the swirl of
buried-treasure legends that keep green the memories of the two
revolutionists. The *corrido* above alludes to Zapata's treasure,
and a whole spate of stories places Villa's caches from Sierra
Madre to Mount Franklin. One of his hiding places is reputedly
in caves deep in the Sierra Madre, along a trail marked by Indians in burro's blood in faint signs that turn scarlet after rainfall.
Diggers still seek the booty.[73] Villa and Zapata alike are in the
truest sense popular heroes, expressing the mood and the dreams
of the people's revolution.

THE UNITED STATES IN MEXICAN FOLKLORE

Mexico plays no part in general American folklore, although she
contributes a major share to the binational traditions that spring
up along the southwestern border. The large Mexican-American
communities in the Southwest and in northern cities possess a
vigorous body of lore and custom, but this is a different matter
from Mexican themes penetrating into the consciousness of the
whole society. But the citizens of New Spain and Mexico have
throughout the past two centuries eyed their northern neighbor
suspiciously, ever since it became a cloud on the horizon following the Louisiana Purchase of 1803. The *gringo* is very much a
folk stereotype in Mexican *corridos,* anecdotes, jokes, and slurs. In
a sense he has replaced the *gachupín* as the target of the *pueblo's*

[71] Edwin Sidney Hartland, *The Science of Fairy Tales* (New York,
1891), pp. 205-21.
[72] Simmons, p. 64.
[73] Haldeen Braddy, "Pancho Villa's Hidden Loot," *Western Folklore* 12
(1953): 77-84.

opprobrium and the menacing symbol of rich and powerful outsiders.

A whole series of episodes inflamed Mexican attitudes toward the giant of the north: the rape of Texas, the military invasion of Mexico in 1846–48 and the annexation of half of Mexico's territory, the capitalistic invasion by the oil companies in the late nineteenth century, the politics of the United States government in supporting or withholding support from Mexican political leaders, Pershing's pursuit of Villa across the border, the treatment of Mexican laborers in the States. In the Tampico incident of 1914, when President Wilson seized Vera Cruz to keep German arms from Huerta, the unpopular Huerta was able to recoup his fortunes by threatening a march on Washington. All these matters find their way into unflattering *corridos* that denounce the *gringos*. (One ballad invokes the Mother of Guadalupe against Yankee intervention.) [74] The *gringo* is seen as cowardly, arrogant, inhumane, and materialistic, in contrast to the valorous Mexican typified in the Nine Heroes of the battle of Chapultepec in 1847, as well as in Villa and less well-known border heroes. Curiously the *gringa* enjoys a more favored status, in her role as a seductive amazonian blonde. One special source of discontent in the *corridos* derives from the pretensions and display of Mexicans who return from the States in a condition of relative affluence.

A group of *corridos* about railroads identifies the iron horse with the bully north of the Rio Grande, who indeed takes physical shape in the snorting machine that bulldozes its way into the calm countryside. The railroad becomes an extension of the *gringo*, symbolizing Yankee capitalist penetration and ruthless uprooting of the old traditional ways.

> The train is a monster
> Of the very worst kind,
> It runs after money
> And eats the cobs as well as the corn.

[74] Simmons, p. 422. An excellent discussion on this whole subject by Simmons is given in his chap. 19, "Mexico's Relations with the United States and North Americans."

Some *corridos* describe train wrecks and the resulting carnage.

> "My God, my leg!" "O, O, my head!"
> "Christ! my arm, I die";
> And others cried, "Where are my parents?"
> "I want to see my children."

There is no doubt who is to blame for this suffering and death, for one *corrido* introduces its subject with "Here come the *gringos*." [75]

The term *gringo* itself calls for a comment, representing as it does a folk epithet of the *Mexicano* against the *Americano*. Originally the word may have derived from the Spanish *griego*, applied to Greek as an unfamiliar tongue. Its modern sense of the aggrandizing Yankee seems to be a late development, according to Américo Paredes, since the *décimas* aimed at the North American invaders in the 1840s and 1850s use *yanqui*, not *gringo*. But by the revolution *gringo* is well established, for instance in the ballad of "The Pursuit of Villa," as a derogatory name for Yankees. Various folk etymologies have sprung up, such as the crediting of *gringo* to American soldiers in the 1846–48 war singing "Green Grow the Lilacs." [76]

A rich body of folk invective employs *gringo* and *yanqui* in colorful combinations. Insults compounded with *gringo* are, in their paler English versions, "wicked big-footed *gringos*" (*patones* has the sense of the clumsy feet of animals); "hell-footed *gringos*"; "ambitious, vile, and opportunistic *gringos*." Compounds with *yanki* include "cunning and cowardly Yankees"; "arrogant, cursed Yankees"; "more than one Yankee felon." Other choice expletives are "despicable foreign traitors" "wretched blond cheats"; "monsters and tyrants"; "fiendish big-feet." [77] The

---

[75] John T. Smith, "Rails below the Rio Grande," in *And Horns on the Toads,* ed. Mody C. Boatright (Dallas, Tex., 1959), pp. 122–35.

[76] Robert H. Fuson, "The Origin of the Word *Gringo,*" and Américo Paredes, "On *Gringo, Greaser,* and Other Neighborly Names," in *Singers and Storytellers,* ed. Mody C. Boatright et al. (Dallas, Tex., 1961), pp. 282–84, 285, 90.

[77] Simmons, pp. 449–50. Translation by Jean M. McLaughlin.

Mexican is never at a loss for words to characterize his neighbor.

During both world wars the sympathies of the Mexican mestizo lay, if anywhere, with Germany, and upon the declaration of war by Mexico against the Axis powers in 1942 some of the *pueblo* hallooed lustily thinking they were in combat against the *yankis*. Chagrin followed when they learned they would be conscripted to fight the Nazis. Now the gods came to the assistance of the distressed villagers. In Tepoztlán the local deity is El Tepozteco, son of the goddess Tonantzin, of Navidad, who maintained a house in town but lived off in the clouds, and looked after his people when they gave him a fine fiesta on 8 September; otherwise he brought sickness through great winds and dried up their water supply. It was El Tepozteco who succored the draftees.

> In those days of worry and confusion, a conscript was walking the streets of Cuernavaca. He was crying because he had been called to the army. Suddenly at the corner he saw a boy, dressed like a peasant. The boy asked the youth why he was crying. "Why shouldn't I cry, for I must be a soldier, and they have ordered me to the war to defend the United States, and I must leave my old parents. If it were to fight for my country it would be bad enough but to fight for the gringos. . . ." Then the boy said, "Go in peace. Your tears are not in vain. Neither you nor other young Mexicans will have to go to fight for a foreign government. You will learn to be a soldier, but you will never leave the country. Go to the village of Tepoztlán and take an offering to my mother, the Virgen de la Natividad." Then the boy disappeared mysteriously.
>
> The soldier was very impressed by what had happened. He told his parents and they decided to go to Tepoztlán with an offering. After that they began to tell the people of that village what had happened, and everyone understood that El Tepozteco had spoken again. El Tepozteco kept his word, for none of the conscripts went to fight for the United States.[78]

[78] Lewis, *Life in a Mexican Village: Topoztlan Restudied,* p. 276.

So the slightly Catholicized Aztec god has used his power for his people against the *gringos*.

A special form of anti-*gringo* folklore developed along the Texas-Mexican border, for here the *braceros* and *vaqueros* came face to face with the Americans. As along the boundary of Scotland and England, a vigorous cycle of border ballads arose in the lower Rio Grande, celebrating the daring acts of underdog heroes against their overweaning neighbors. Perhaps the most famous of these Mexican Rob Roys is Gregorio Cortez (1875–1916), whom three hundred Texas rangers chased all over the county; in the *corrido* that bears his name he laughs them to scorn:

> Then said Gregorio Cortez
> With his pistol in his hand,
> "Ah, so many mounted Rangers
> Just to take one Mexican!" [79]

Another border hero of the *corridos* who mocks the rangers is Jacinto Treviño of Matamoros. He taunts them when they flee his bullets in Baker's saloon, saying

> Come on, you treacherous Rangers:
> Come get a taste of my lead.
> And did you think it was ham
> Between two slices of bread? [80]

The Mexicans not only ridicule the Americans for their fear of a real man but also for their taste for ham sandwiches. These border *corridos* present an inversion of American stereotypes; they deflate the pseudolegends of the rangers' prowess and present instead the Mexican folk view: rangers are hired thugs of the rich ranchers who will shoot unarmed Mexicans in cold blood, then claim self-defense, but who would dare shoot an armed Mexican only from behind.

[79] Américo Paredes, *"With His Pistol in His Hand": A Border Ballad and Its Hero* (Austin, Tex., 1958), p. [3].

[80] Collected by Américo Paredes and printed in Richard M. Dorson, ed., *Buying the Wind* (Chicago, 1964), p. 484.

The outstanding scholar of border folklore is Américo Paredes. His study of Gregorio Cortez as a Mexican hero of border ballad and legend, *"With His Pistol in His Hand"* (1958), is at once an adroit and sensitive portrayal of its immediate subject and an exemplary work in folklore scholarship. It projects the ballad against the cultural setting of the cattle ranch Lower Rio Grande country, severed between Texas and Mexico by the Treaty of Guadalupe Hidalgo; it makes clear the folk psychology of the Mexican borderer, who saw himself vindicated in the manly defiance of Cortez against the hated rangers; it presents both the poetic legend and the reported facts and demonstrates how folklore sources can sometimes contribute to historical knowledge, as in the imputation that Cortez was betrayed to his Yankee captors; it expertly analyzes the poetics of the border *corrido* and considers its relation to the heroic *corrido* of Greater Mexico and the border balladry of other countries. This is sociocultural folklore analysis at its best, explaining the borderer's need for heroics against the *gringo* racist; it is only fitting that President Lincoln's daughter should fall for, and be rebuffed by, Gregorio Cortez.

Paredes has continued to probe into the subtleties of border lore and the Mexican folk stereotype of the *gringo*. In a brilliant paper on "The Anglo-American in Mexican Folklore" he suggests revisions of the traditional attitudes toward the Yankee. Instead of a simple inversion of roles to produce a Mexican Davy Crockett, the tales and songs now offer a gullible American duped by a culturally astute Mexican, and even self-deprecating jests in which Mexicans mock their own inadequacies as viewed by foreigners. The launching pad of this modern lore is no longer the border but Mexico City, where United States popular culture penetrates directly, via the hot line of the mass media.[81]

Born on the border, in Brownsville, Texas, and educated at the University of Texas, where he took three degrees, Paredes is thoroughly bilingual and bicultural. He is the thorough folklorist, equally at home in the field, the library, and the archives, knowl-

[81] Américo Paredes, "The Anglo-American in Mexican Folklore," in *New Voices in American Studies,* ed. Ray B. Browne et al. (Purdue University Studies, 1966), pp. 113–28.

edgeable in Spanish-American and comparative as well as in
Mexican folklore.[82] As a collector he has recorded from Mexican
storytellers two hundred border jests and anecdotal legends. Pro-
fessionally active, Dr. Paredes is editor of the *Journal of American Folklore* and director of the Center for Intercultural Studies
in Folklore and Oral History at the University of Texas. No one
is more uniquely qualified to present the folktales of Mexico.

RICHARD M. DORSON

[82] See his "Concepts about Folklore in Latin America and the United
States," *Journal of the Folklore Institute* 6 (1969), 20–38.

Introduction

The first Mexican folktales may have been current even before the fall of Tenochtitlán. Certainly Bernal Díaz del Castillo, who was present at that event, has left record of some, though the work in which he set them down was not completed until 1568. Of the narratives Díaz del Castillo weaves into his *Historia verdadera de la conquista de la Nueva España,* one of my favorites is the one he tells about Doña Marina or La Malinche, Cortés's interpreter and faithful companion. We hear how she was sold into slavery by her family and rescued by Cortés, and how she later confronted her quaking relatives, forgave them, and loaded them with gifts. There are perhaps a dozen folktale motifs in the complete story, but Díaz—who might have made a good folklorist of the Finnish school—puts his finger right on the main one. "This seems to me," he says, "much like what happened to Joseph in Egypt with his brothers, who came into his power during that matter of the wheat." (Motif N733.3, Joseph and his brethren.") [1]

This little story contains many of the problems faced by the student of the Mexican folktale. It is a European narrative pattern imposed on Mexican Indian materials and presented as historical fact in a semiliterary context. We can only surmise how much of it may have been actual fact, how much was Indian folklore, and how much was the result of the creative remembering of a Spanish imagination excited by a strange new world. There are many other cases in which imaginative explorers in America saw what they expected to see, their expectations being

---

[1] Bernal Díaz del Castillo, *Historia verdadera de la conquista de la Nueva España* (Madrid, 1928), 1:114–16. Motif numbers are from Stith Thompson, *Motif-Index of Folk-Literature,* 6 vols. (Copenhagen & Bloomington, Ind., 1955–58).

dictated by their own folklore and literature. These accounts by
travelers and explorers include much data we now think of as
folklore; Mexico has had many of them, from Bernal Díaz to
Mme. Calderón de la Barca. There are, besides, books such as
Father José de Acosta's *Historia natural y moral de las Indias*
(Seville, 1590), which is full of accounts of customs, legends, miracles, and providences in early Mexico, including stories about
the awful portents preceding the fall of Moctezuma. But there
was another type of ecclesiastic, best exemplified by Fray Bernardino de Sahagún, who compiled the materials for his *Historia
general de las cosas de la Nueva España* in mid-sixteenth century.
Sahagún practiced a kind of applied social science, studying the
Indian cultures in order to change them. He learned the language of his informants and collected in the native tongues. He
made use of bilingual assistants he trained himself and chose his
informants wisely, collecting old traditions from old men, arts
and crafts from artists and craftsmen, divinations from soothsayers, native medicine from local doctors.

After the middle of the seventeenth century, the fervor of ex-
ploration and evangelization passed away, and few works appeared recounting the way things were in New Spain. By the second decade of the nineteenth century, however, Mexico was engaged in a war for independence, and Mexican intellectuals
began to discover their own culture. José Joaquín Fernández de
Lizardi (1776–1827) was the first writer of independent Mexico
to make conscious use of folklore. His *El Periquillo Sarniento*
(1816), Mexico's first novel, is in the *costumbrista* manner, making use of folk customs and folk speech for purposes of local
color. In *Fábulas* (1817) Lizardi published fables after the manner of La Fontaine, but he also tried his hand at a *pastorela* in
imitation of the folk shepherds' plays widely known in Mexico.[2]
Mexican writers have cultivated the *costumbrista* manner from
Lizardi's time to the present, though contemporary local colorists,
like their colleagues in the United States, tend to disguise their
materials as folklore. Luis Inclán (1816–75) deserves notice as

[2] Lizardi's *pastorela* probably was presented in Mexico City in 1815.
See Nicolás Rangel, "El teatro," in *Antología del centenario*, 2:1015–29
(Mexico, 1910).

the author of a precursor to the Wild West novel, *Astucia*
(1865-66), and as the operator of a popular printing press in
Mexico City that was the predecessor of broadside presses of the
late nineteenth and early twentieth centuries, such as those of Va-
negas Arroyo and Guerrero.[3] Inclán appealed to the popular
taste; he never was as highly regarded as Guillermo Prieto
(1818-97), whose most important works from our point of view
are *Musa callejera* (1879), a volume of verse depicting popular
scenes, and *Romancero nacional* (1885), an attempt at a national
epic based on the Spanish folk ballad corpus.

Prieto's books of pseudo-folk poetry mark a change in cultivated tastes from customs and legends toward folksong. The desire to express a nascent nationalism in folk epics and the ten-
dency to seek models in foreign literatures were preliminary steps
to the romantic nationalism of the revolution. But before 1910
genuine Mexican folksong smelled too strongly of the "straw mat
and the pulque shop," as the saying went, to be liked by decent
people. Mexico's first antiquarians did not turn to the folksong,
as did their counterparts in Great Britain, but to the legend,
which had about it a refined odor of the colonial past. Jesús C.
Romero lists *Leyendas históricas y tradicionales* (Guadalajara,
1853) by Pablo J. Villaseñor as the first of a series of collections of
"legends and traditions" that has continued down to the present
time.[4] Every Mexican city of any consequence has contributed or
has been attributed its share of legendary narratives—comic, romantic, and historical. Among the best known of these books
was Juan de Dios Peza's *Leyendas, tradiciones y fantasías de las
calles de México* (Paris, 1870). Peza (1852-1910) was known as
the "household poet." The same type of work finds its way into
English with Thomas A. Janvier's *Legends of the City of Mexico*

---

[3] For a brief treatment in English of Inclán's work see Américo Paredes,
"Luis Inclán: First of the Cowboy Writers," *American Quarterly* 12
(1960): 55-70.

[4] Jesús C. Romero, "El folklore en México," *Boletín de la Sociedad Mexicana de Geografía y Estadística* 63 (1947): 702. Perhaps the same person
as Pablo I. Villaseñor (d. 1855), mentioned by the *Diccionario Porrúa de
historia, biografía y geografía de México,* 2d ed. (Mexico, 1965) as a poet
and playwright from Guadalajara.

(New York, 1910), first published as a series in *Harper's* around 1905.

The actual study of Mexican folklore may be said to begin in 1883 with Daniel G. Brinton's essay, "The Folklore of Yucatan." [5] It includes customs, beliefs, legends summarized, and one narrative text in Maya with English interlinear translation. Brinton's article remained unknown in Mexico for many years.[6] The first time the term "folklore" is recorded in Mexico appears to have been in 1886 in a paper by Joaquín García Icazbalceta (1825–94) called "Provincialismos mexicanos," published in the memoirs of the Mexican Academy.[7] Since García Icazbalceta at the time was director of the academy and engaged in compiling a dictionary of Mexican Spanish, "Provincialismos mexicanos" must have been a progress report. The author mentions folklore as an important source of examples of the spoken language, lamenting that no one had done any true field collecting at that time.[8]

More than a generation passed before the next step was taken toward folklore scholarship in Mexico. The man to take it was Nicolás León (1859–1929), a philologist in the best sense of the word and Mexico's first real folklorist. In 1903 León assumed the chair of ethnology in Mexico's National Museum of Anthropology. Cognizant of the work of British folklorists, he decided to incorporate the new discipline into his lectures. This he did early in 1906, also printing his lecture on folklore in pamphlet form and distributing it to students, friends, and other persons likely to be interested. A copy reached Valentín F. Frías of Querétaro (1862–1926), author of a "legends and traditions" book. Frías responded immediately with a monograph entitled "Foc-lor de los pueblos de San Bartolomé Aguascalientes (Estado de Guana-

[5] Daniel G. Brinton, "The Folk-Lore of Yucatan," *Folk-Lore Journal* 1 (1883): 244–56; reprinted in *Essays of an Americanist* (Philadelphia, 1890), 163–80.

[6] Translated from English into Spanish by Enrique Leal in 1937 and published in pamphlet form; *El folklore de Yucatán,* (Mérida, Yucatán, 1937).

[7] Joaquín García Icazbalceta, "Provincialismos mexicanos," *Memorias de la Academia Mexicana* 3 (1886): 170–90.

[8] García Icazbalceta, p. 189.

juato); Santa María del Pueblito y San Pedro de la Cañada
(Estado de Querétaro), así como de los otomíes del barrio de San
Francisquito de la ciudad de Querétaro y los pueblos ad-
yacentes." Without a doubt this is the first genuine collection of
Mexican folklore to be done by a Mexican. León made Frías's
contribution an appendix to his lecture, added an introduction
calling for the further collecting of folklore by any and all interested persons, and published the whole thing in a series of inserts
in the Mexico City daily, *El Tiempo,* during August 1906.[9] Early
in 1907 the same work, entitled "Foc-Lor mexicano," was published in more permanent form in the memoirs of the "Antonio
Alzate" society.[10] From 1916 to 1925 León was director of the
National Museum, and we also hear from him as an officer in one
of Mexico's numerous folklore societies. Of special interest is his
work on José Vasconcelos, Negro folk poet of mid-eighteenth
century Mexico, a very early treatment of urban lore and a study
of a semilegendary folk artist.[11]

During the time Nicolás León lectured at the National Museum, his classes were attended by Manuel Gamio (1883–1960),
one of the major figures in Mexican anthropology, folklore, and
Indian affairs. Gamio had abandoned a career in engineering to
try his hand at running an *hacienda.* He failed, but acquired a
lasting interest in Mexico's Indian peoples. In 1908 Gamio obtained a scholarship at Columbia with the help of Zelia Nuttal.
At Columbia, Gamio studied under Franz Boas, receiving his
master's degree in 1911. He returned for a doctorate in 1921, and
in 1948 Columbia distinguished him with a Doctor of Letters
Honoris Causa.[12] In 1917 Gamio headed the newly created Direc-
ción de Antropología, a governmental agency charged with coor-
dinating anthropological research in Mexico. Gamio's grand de-
sign was to divide Mexico into culture areas and to carry out in

[9] Romero, p. 711.

[10] Nicolás León, "Foc-Lor Mexicano," *Memorias de la Sociedad Científica "Antonio Alzate"* 24 (1906–7): 339–95.

[11] Nicolás León, *El negrito poeta mexicano y sus populares versos: Contribución para el folklore nacional* (Mexico, 1912).

[12] Juan Comas, "La vida y obra de Manuel Gamio," in *Estudios antropológicos publicados en homenaje al doctor Manuel Gamio* (Mexico, 1956), p. 2.

each an "integral" project of field research that included folklore. He was able to carry out the scheme in only one of the chosen areas, the Valley of Teotihuacán near Mexico City. The results were published in 1922 in a three-volume work, *La población del Valle de Teotihuacán, México,* that included a section on folklore, mostly the work of Eugenio Gómez Maillefert, and another section called "Ethnographic Notes," also containing a good deal of folklore.[13] This was the most impressive collection of folklore materials that had yet appeared. It would be some time before Mexican folklorists would surpass it.

In 1920 Gamio founded the journal *Ethnos* to stimulate anthropological study in Mexico and Central America and appointed Pablo González Casanova folklore editor. González Casanova (1889–1936) was a linguist and a folklorist with special interest in folk narrative. He encouraged folklore collecting by publishing questionnaires and other advice. Gamio went on in the 1930s to become chief of the Demographic Bureau. This was the depression period in the United States, when thousands of Mexican migrants in this country were being summarily deported, while those allowed to stay suffered all kinds of harassments. Gamio undertook a study of Mexican migration to the United States, and one result was a book published in English, *Mexican Immigration to the United States* (Chicago, 1930). The migrant worker's folklore was part of the study; included were several *corridos* (ballads), among them the earliest published text of "El corrido de Gregorio Cortez," epitome of the Texas-Mexican ballad of border conflict.[14] In 1942 Gamio became the first director of the Interamerican Indigenist Institute, a post he held until his death. He did not lose his interest in folklore. In 1945, as editor of *América Indígena,* organ of the institute, he printed three articles on the practical value of folklore, one of them written by him.[15]

[13] [Manuel Gamio, ed.], *La población del Valle de Teotihuacán, México* (Mexico, 1922), 2: 203–417.

[14] For a detailed treatment of Gregorio Cortez, see Américo Paredes, *"With His Pistol in His Hand": A Border Ballad and Its Hero* (Austin, Texas, 1958).

[15] Ralph Steele Boggs, "Valor práctico del folklore," *América Indígena* 5 (1945): 211–15; Manuel Gamio, "El material folklórico y el progreso

Manuel Gamio was without a doubt one of the major figures in Mexican folklore. He and his collaborators did much to encourage serious scholarship in the field. But they were men with many interests, to whom folklore could be no more than a fascinating sideline. The work had to be carried forward by full-time folklorists. By the 1920s such men were at hand, but few had the discipline of the scholar. The first folklorist of this new breed belonged to Gamio's generation. Rubén M. Campos (1876-1945) had something of a folk background. He was, according to Romero, the illegitimate son of Antonio Zúñiga, a regional musician credited with the composition of a number of songs that passed into oral tradition.[16] By the mid-1890s we hear of Campos in Mexico City as a government official and literary man. He published poetry, short stories, and criticism in the magazines of the capital. Then, in 1925, he was appointed to a chair in folklore in the National Museum, the first person to occupy such a chair in Mexico. Nicolás León's lecture on folklore had finally borne fruit, but why Campos was chosen is not clear, except that he was enthusiastic about folklore and willing to devote his time to it.

Just about the time Campos became a folklorist, the Ministry of Education created a system of "cultural missions," groups including social scientists and rural school teachers whose goal was to integrate Mexican Indian subcultures into the nation. The cultural missions were encouraged to collect folklore. This was the kind of situation that led to great folklore archives in Finland and Ireland. The government, however, turned for guidance to its official folklorist, Campos, and instructed him to produce a book to serve as a guide for field workers in folklore. Campos responded with three books: *El folklore y la música mexicana* (1928), *El folklore literario de México* (1929), and *El folklore musical de las ciudades* (1930), all published by the Ministry of Education. These books are excellent repositories of miscellaneous folklore materials, including a goodly collection of jokes

social," *América Indígena* 5 (1945): 207–10; Alfonso Villa Rojas, "Significado y valor práctico del folklore," *América Indígena* 5 (1945): 295–302.
[16] Romero, p. 755.

and other urban lore. But as guides to theory and methods in folklore they did more harm than good. It is easy to condemn Rubén Campos as a literary dilettante who turned back the clock on Mexican folklore studies, and this is precisely what Romero does in "El folklore en México."[17] But even in 1947, when Romero wrote, many of his colleagues were still making folklore studies in the manner of Campos. What happened to Mexican folklore studies in the 1920s was a shift from the occasional scholarship of men like León, Gamio, and González Casanova to the sustained but undisciplined enthusiasm of the romantic nationalists. In this change Campos was more a symptom than a cause.

An interesting feature of this period is the proliferation of folklore societies and the role played in them by the romantic nationalists. At least nine and possibly ten Mexican folklore societies can be identified during 1914 to 1946. The first one on record was founded in 1914 by Severo Amador, a minor poet, musician, and painter, and by Higinio Vázquez Santa Ana, later the author of several collections of song texts. Vázquez Santa Ana, though important as a precursor, was not a scholar. Amador belonged to the local color school, now given new impetus by the revolution's interest in the rough and the earthy. Both were interested chiefly in folksong. There is no evidence that this first society accomplished much aside from serving as an excuse for conviviality and for reciting the verses of Severo Amador. A second society appeared in 1916, encouraged by José de Jesús Nuñez y Domínguez, a poet, journalist, and scholar. The secretary, however, was Manuel M. Ponce, composer of the popular "Estrellita" and one of the major exponents of romantic nationalism in music. Prominent in the organization was Rubén M. Campos. This society also disappeared leaving no great monuments behind it.

A third society is mentioned by Romero as being organized in 1917 with Nicolás León as vice-president.[18] Romero professes to know nothing more about this third society or its activities, though it is somewhat strange that he should know who its vice-president was and yet ignore the name of its president. That

[17] Ibid., pp. 756–58.
[18] Ibid., p. 718.

same year a note appeared in the *Journal of American Folklore* announcing that the "Mexican branch" of the American Folklore Society was being "reorganized . . . at the instance of Mr. Manuel Gamio." [19] No earlier mention is made of the "Mexican branch" in the *Journal*, nor is a membership list or slate of officers ever reported among those of other branch societies except for Gamio, who is listed as president. The "Mexican branch" of the American Folklore Society may have been still another of Mexico's folklore organizations. It is probable, though, that it was the same body mentioned by Romero as the third to appear in Mexico, with Nicolás León as vice-president.

A fourth organization appears in 1928 as a result of the Second National Congress of Music, a congress dominated by poets, artists and musicians strongly influenced by romantic nationalism. This was the Comisión Técnica de Folklore, which in spite of its name was a folksong society. The Second National Congress of Music ended with the rout of Europeanist elements in the National Conservatory and other high musical circles, where Mexican music, Mexican themes, and even the Spanish language had been looked upon with some disdain. From the viewpoint of the history of Mexican culture, the results of the congress were an important advance. The same thing cannot be said from the viewpoint of folklore scholarship. The poets, artists, and musicians involved in the movement were interested in using folklore as raw material. Some important work was done, it is true. Also produced was a quantity of third-rate prose and verse in the *costumbrista* manner, some of which managed to creep into the "field collections" done in subsequent years by friends of the authors. The Comisión lasted about eight months, apparently the average life of most folklore societies in Mexico. Its influence and that of the Second National Congress of Music would last for many years.

A fifth Mexican folklore society appeared in 1930, sponsored by the Ministry of Education. Its members included musicians and intellectuals, as well as actresses and comedians who specialized in folksy roles. During its very short life, Romero reports, its activities were confined to sessions where bad poetry was declaimed

[19] *Journal of American Folklore* 30 (1917): 411.

and to expeditions in search of restaurants serving typical Mexican food.[20] This might well be labeled Mexico's first "folknik" group, except that it was supported by the Mexican government and that the government's official folklorist, Rubén Campos, was named its technical adviser.

The sixth organization was the Sociedad Mexicana de Folklore, created in August 1938 as a branch of the Mexican Society of Anthropology. It came into being in great part through the efforts of a North American, Ralph Steele Boggs, whose special interest throughout his life has been the folklore of Latin America. In 1938 Boggs made a "folklore expedition" into Mexico. He met bibliophiles like Rafael Heliodoro Valle and anthropologists like Alfonso Caso, as well as "a group of musicians collecting folksongs and ballads from all over Mexico, modifying, adapting and mimeographing them for public school use." [21] Whether by intuition or through observation, Boggs correctly judged that folklore in Mexico was being cultivated by two groups that were moving further and further apart: one dominated by artists, poets, musicians, and amateurs, and the other by scholars mostly working in anthropology and related fields. He made an effort to bring the two groups together, using as a base the Mexican Society of Anthropology, founded just one year earlier.

But difficulties soon arose, some theoretical and some matters of pride. The Sociedad Mexicana de Folklore was allowed no president of its own, its highest officers being two secretaries. One of these was Vicente T. Mendoza (1894–1964), who had been involved in the cause of musical nationalism for a good ten years. We first hear of him as a member of the Second National Congress of Music and the Comisión Técnica de Folklore. In 1940 Mendoza led the romantic nationalists out of the Society of Anthropology and established the Sociedad Folklórica de México, with Mendoza himself as president and his wife, Virginia Rodríguez Rivera de Mendoza, as secretary-treasurer, both named in perpetuity. The anthropologists were conspicuous in the new society by their absence.

[20] Romero, pp. 777–78.

[21] Ralph Steele Boggs, "A Folklore Expedition to Mexico," *Southern Folklore Quarterly* 3 (1939): 67.

The society headed by the Mendozas was the eighth in Mexico. A seventh had appeared between the creation of the Sociedad Mexicana de Folklore in 1938 and the falling-out between musicians and anthropologists in 1940. The Instituto Mexicano de Musicología y Folklore, founded in 1939 by Luis Sandi of the Department of Fine Arts, was in a way a continuation of the Comisión Técnica de Folklore, including in its ranks most of the members of the defunct Comisión plus some new ones, among whom were musicians from Republican Spain, refugees from Franco. The instituto was active for about eight months. Romero, one of its members, claims it died of "inanition." [22] The quarrels between the Mexican nationalists and their Spanish colleagues, however, must have contributed to its demise.

The Sociedad Folklórica de México was not the last word in Mexican folklore societies. In 1946, while Mendoza and his wife were in the United States, a splinter group led by José Montes de Oca set up its own society, the Academia Mexicana de Folklore, and received support from the Ministry of Education. At last report the Academia Mexicana de Folklore still was meeting every Friday to hear papers read, though it has never produced any publications.

At present there are other folklore groups in Mexico City, the contemporary folknik or folksong groups influenced by the so-called folksong revival in the United States. Foreign influences are nothing new in Mexican folklore. A complete history of folklore studies in Mexico would have to include the names of Europeans and Latin Americans like Hermann Beyer and Pedro Henríquez Ureña. But most outside influences have come from the United States. Brinton wrote the first essay on Mexican folklore, and scholars from the United States have worked in the field since the days of Franz Boas. Special mention must be made of Ralph Boggs, who exercised great personal influence among Mexican folklorists. Vicente Mendoza and Virginia Rodríguez Rivera looked up to him as their preceptor. Yet it is doubtful whether Boggs's influence was as far-reaching as that of Frances Toor (1890–1956), an enthusiastic lover of Mexico who fitted into the spirit of the times. In her magazine *Mexican Folkways,* popular

[22] Romero, p. 780.

musicians and regional writers rubbed shoulders with linguists, anthropologists, and folklorists. Diego Rivera was the art editor. But the bilingual pages of *Mexican Folkways* betrayed its basic purpose. It was intended for the North American, the potential tourist. With the founding of *Mexican Folkways* in 1925, the wedding of Mexican folklore and the Mexican tourist industry was celebrated, and it has been a most successful marriage. But Mexico is not the only country where folklore has been identified with casual guitar-strumming by public officials and the general public alike. Mexican folklore studies must be judged by the achievements of the Sociedad Folklórica de México and of its leading figures, especially its president, the late Vicente T. Mendoza.

In 1909 Mendoza came to Mexico City from his native state of Puebla to study music. In 1928 he was an active member of the nationalist wing of the Second National Congress of Music and of the Comisión Técnica de Folklore. In 1929 he obtained a teaching post at the National Conservatory, and in 1936 he collaborated with Daniel Castañeda in the publication of *Instrumental Precortesiano de Percusión*. That same year he and Gabriel Saldívar were sent by the National University to collect folk music in the Mezquital Valley as part of a study in depth made of the Otomí Indians. In 1938 he became the University's folklorist in residence, occupying the position of research worker in folklore until his death in 1964. Also in 1938 Mendoza helped found the Sociedad Folklórica Mexicana. The next year he published two important works, *Estudio de la musica otomí del Valle del Mezquital* (Montevideo, 1939) and *El romance español y el corrido mexicano* (Mexico, 1939).

Thus, when Mendoza founded the Sociedad Folklórica de Mexico in 1940 he was already recognized as Mexico's leading folklorist. His production of major works in Mexican folklore continued during his editorship of the society's annuals, among them being *La décima en México* (Buenos Aires, 1947), *Folklore de San Pedro Piedra Gorda* (1952) with Virginia Rodríguez Rivera, *La canción mexicana* (1961), and the posthumous *Lírica narrativa de México: El corrido* (1964). Yet Mendoza's training was only that of a musician. Realizing this, he sought instruction from Ralph Boggs, who came back to Mexico City in 1945 to teach folklore for a year at the National University. In 1946 Mendoza and his wife journeyed to the United States on a Rockefeller grant to study folklore at the universities of Indiana and North Carolina. Under Mendoza's leadership, the Sociedad Folklórica de México was active for eighteen years, publishing twelve volumes of its annual and two supplementary collections of essays. This is without a doubt the most sustained and impressive effort in the history of Mexican folklore studies. At least part of the credit for all of this belongs to Virginia Rodríguez Rivera, during those years Mendoza's wife, secretary, and collaborator. Then they were divorced, and Mendoza and his former wife resigned their offices; and the activities of the society came to a stop.

The Mendozas accomplished much in Mexican folklore, but they did not develop a school of younger folklorists to continue their work. Looking back through the pages of the society's annuals, one is impressed by the fact that Mendoza's most promising students published once or twice and then disappeared from the scene. Theirs was a casual interest in folklore, to be abandoned when they turned to more serious things. The failure of the Sociedad Folklórica de México to hold the interest of younger scholars has been blamed on its alienation of the anthropologists and on the society's adherence to the historic-geographic method.[23] There is no doubt that the withdrawal of the anthropologists from the organized ranks of Mexican folklorists was a serious blow to Mexican folklore studies; but this does not fully explain the lack of consistency and continuity in the work of the Sociedad Folklórica de México. The adherence to the Finnish school is not the answer either, though the historic-geographic method did become the official guide for the Sociedad. As late as 1956, Vicente Mendoza was saying that "the historic-geographic method . . . is the method the Sociedad Folklórica de México has accepted as the best for carrying out its work." [24] But if one looks at the Sociedad's published works, one finds that such ac-

[23] Gabriel Moedano N., "El folklore como disciplina antropólogica: Su desarrollo en México," *Tlatoani* 2, no. 17 (1963): 46–47.

[24] Vicente T. Mendoza, *Nuevas aportaciones a la investigación folklórica de México* (Mexico, 1958), p. 17.

lxx   INTRODUCTION

ceptance was expressed more in thought than in deed. Of all its members, only Virginia Rodríguez Rivera seems to have made a serious attempt to apply historic-geographic principles to her work.[25] The Sociedad Folklórica de México did not suffer any stultifying effects from the Finnish method; on the contrary, there is reason to believe that a rigorous adherence to historic-geographic methodology would have benefited those working under the influence of the Sociedad, by imposing a certain degree of discipline on their work. It is this lack of discipline, unnoticed in the euphoria created by romantic nationalism, that flaws a number of the works published by the Sociedad. Its present inactivity, however, seems to be due to lack of financial support, or rather to a dispersal of such support among too many competing organizations.

Some sucessors to the Mendozas still are active in the field. Among those specializing in folklore studies, the most promising is Gabriel Moedano N., who obtained his basic training in folklore with Virginia Rodríguez Rivera and later studied with Vicente Mendoza. Trained in archeology and ethnology as well, Moedano is with the National Museum of Anthropology, where Nicolás León started it all back in 1906.

Mexican folklorists have emphasized the collection of folksongs, particularly folksong texts. In spite of the Sociedad Folklórica's avowed adherence to the Finnish school, Mexico has produced no specialist in the folktale. As to materials available for study, there is an abundance or almost none at all, depending on the point of view. If the student approaches his materials with nothing but tale types and motifs in mind, he will find a rich field indeed. A wealth of motifs and types may be mined from a variety of publications, ranging from accounts of travelers and explorers to contemporary local color works masquerading as folklore. But if we are interested in reliable folk narrative texts, the field is drastically reduced. After much reading and discarding, the student may end up with a corpus of between eight hundred and fifteen hundred published texts, depending on how he defines "reliable" and "Mexican."

[25] See for example, Virginia Rodríguez Rivera, *Santa Bárbara: Estudio histórico y geográfico de la oración de la Santa* (Mexico, 1967).

Taken as a whole, Mexican folk narrative materials fall into three broad categories. In one we would put translations, summaries, and unadorned retellings of folk narratives. These are good sources for content, and though they tell us little or nothing about style, at least they do not falsify it. Here we would put many of the tales repeated by explorers and missionaries, though we should consider them Mexican (i.e. mestizo) narratives rather than what their writers usually profess them to be, Indian myths or legends. Summaries published by Mexican ethnologists also belong here, as do Mexican tales published in translation by foreign anthropologists.

In a second category would be texts written in a literary or pseudoliterary style. Stylistically these are unreliable, and the authenticity of their content is sometimes hard to determine. We can be sure we are dealing with local color writing masquerading as folklore when we run into a "folktale" beginning something like this: "The dying sun shed its gentle rays upon the fields of ripening corn, as Tiburcio made his way to the *curandero*'s hut." But suppose we are reading a straightforward account of a belief tale as told by a peasant woman. She killed a snake in the morning and hung it on a limb. Returning that evening she reports, "I noticed that despite the many hours elapsed, its vermicular movements had not ceased." Perhaps this is a field-collected text, and the writer has attempted to put it down as he heard it. But he has done the same thing musicians are sometimes said to do when they hear the patterns of art music in the music of the folk. It would be inexact to say that the Mexican intellectual is deaf to the nuances of popular speech. He can use the vernacular in conversation should occasion arise, but he finds it hard to put it down on paper. The romantic nationalists often tried to imitate popular speech, and they came up with grotesque parodies of it reminiscent of the attempts of nineteenth-century writers in the United States to render frontier dialects. It is perhaps in avoiding such parodies that peasant women are made to sound like professors of natural history. Rigorous methods of recording and transcription would prevent this sort of thing, but we must remember that sound recording devices are of recent use, not only in Mexico but everywhere else. It is not only in Mexico that folktale texts have been field-collected more or less in summary form and then recollected in tranquility.

Without departing from the subject we might mention the wealth of materials that have appeared in English translation, mostly in southwestern United States. Again, they are a rich source of material for the tale type hunter. But the creative urge of the local colorist also has been at work. Most Mexican folktales in English fall into two general styles, both adapted from regional writing in the United States. One might be called the Uncle Remus approach, in which the Mexican narrator speaks in a stereotyped form of broken English. The other is the "straight man" approach, with the writer assuming the role of an amused observer watching the antics of his Mexican characters.

In a third category we should put folk narrative texts taken down faithfully as told by informants, either in Spanish or in one of the Indian tongues. A number of them are scattered about in Mexican and foreign journals of various kinds, published singly or in twos or threes. Larger collections with some claim to reliability are few, and most of them have been done by foreigners. Some of the most competent deal not with materials collected within the present borders of Mexico but with Mexican-American texts from southwestern United States.

The first Mexican folktale collected as such appeared in 1883 in Brinton's essay, "The Folk-Lore of Yucutan." [26] It is a belief tale, "Maya Witch Story," in Maya with English interlinear translation. A second folktale text was printed in Albert S. Gatschet's "Popular Rimes from Mexico" which appeared in 1889 in the second volume of the *Journal of American Folklore*.[27] Gatschet collected his materials in Matamoros, Tamaulipas, across the river from Brownsville, Texas, where he was a government employee at the time. No dates or informants are given in Gatschet's collection, but the texts are in the original Spanish and show every sign of being faithful transcriptions. Among Gatschet's "rimes" is a formula tale, a version of Type 2013, *There Was Once a Woman; the Woman Had a Son.*

[26] Brinton, *Essays of an Americanist*, p. 171.

[27] Albert S. Gatschet, "Popular Rimes from Mexico," *Journal of American Folklore* 2 (1889): 48–53.

The first truly scholarly work on Mexican folklore was Aurelio M. Espinosa's "New-Mexican Spanish Folk-Lore," published in 1910 in the *Journal of American Folklore*.[28] It includes eight legends, among them "La Llorona" [The weeping woman]. In 1911 Espinosa published a collection of twelve folktales, all in Spanish, the first real collection of Mexican folk narrative.[29] In 1912 the *Journal of American Folklore* published twelve folktales from Oaxaca, eight of them in Spanish, collected by Franz Boas, as well as two small collections of tales in English translation by J. Alden Mason and William H. Mechling.[30] In 1914 two important works on Mexican folk narrative appeared in the *Journal*, Mason's collection of twenty-two Tepecano folktales and Espinosa's notes on Mexican folk narrative.[31] Other important collections of Mexican folktales appearing in the *Journal of American Folklore* were two by Elsie Clews Parsons, published in 1932, twenty-five tales from Oaxaca and ten from Puebla.[32] A small but remarkable collection was that of John Turner Reid, "Seven Folktales from Mexico," printed in the *Journal* in 1935. Not only are the texts in the original Spanish, but they are accompanied by Aarne-Thompson tale types and references to Espinosa's *Cuentos Españoles*.[33] In 1937 Margaret Redfield published more than fifty narratives from Yucatán, but only five were in Spanish, the rest

[28] Aurelio M. Espinosa, "New-Mexican Spanish Folk-Lore, I & II," *Journal of American Folklore*, 23 (1910): 395–418.

[29] Aurelio M. Espinosa, "New-Mexican Spanish Folk-Lore, III, Folk-Tales," *Journal of American Folklore* 24 (1911): 397–444.

[30] Franz Boas, "Notes on Mexican Folk-Lore," *Journal of American Folklore* 25 (1912): 204–60; J. Alden Mason, "Four Mexican-Spanish Fairy-Tales from Azqueltán, Jalisco," *Journal of American Folklore* 25 (1912): 191–98; William H. Mechling, "Stories from Tuxtepec, Oaxaca," *Journal of American Folklore* 25 (1912): 199–203.

[31] John Alden Mason and Aurelio M. Espinosa, "Folk-Tales of the Tepecanos," *Journal of American Folklore* 27 (1914): 148–210; Aurelio M. Espinosa, "Comparative Notes on New-Mexican and Mexican Spanish Folk-Tales," *Journal of American Folklore* 27 (1914): 211–31.

[32] Elsie Clews Parsons, "Zapoteca and Spanish Tales of Mitla, Oaxaca" and "Folklore from Santa Ana Xalmimilulco, Puebla, Mexico," *Journal of American Folklore* 45 (1932): 277–317 and 318–62.

[33] John Turner Reid, "Seven Folktales from Mexico," *Journal of American Folklore*, 48 (1935): 109–24.

being in English translation.[34] George Foster's collection of
Sierra Popoluca narratives, forty-five texts, is excellent except that
only English translations are given.[35]

Aurelio Espinosa continued his significant work on the folktale. His *Cuentos populares españoles* is a collection of tales from
Spain, but the notes accompanying them are a standard reference
for the folktale in Latin America.[36] In 1937 one of Espinosa's
sons, José Manuel, produced a collection of 114 Mexican folktales
from southwestern United States, *Spanish Folk-Tales from New
Mexico* (New York, 1937), a scholarly and well-documented
work. It was surpassed by one of the father's students, Juan B.
Rael, whose *Cuentos españoles de Colorado y de Nuevo Méjico*
(Stanford, n.d.), with 518 texts, is the best collection of Mexican
folk narrative published to date. The elder Espinosa's collaborators were less successful with folk narratives taken down within
Mexico's present borders. Espinosa and Paul Radin published *El
folklore de Oaxaca* (New York, 1917), 116 tales collected by
Radin, principally from young Indians who wrote them down in
Spanish at his request. There are no notes or collecting data, and
the introduction admits the dubious folk style of many of the
tales. For more than a quarter of a century this was the major
collection of folktales from Mexico in spite of its weak scholarship. Then there appeared Howard T. Wheeler's *Tales from Jalisco, Mexico* (Philadelphia, 1943), compiled with the encourage-
ment of Espinosa, who helped prepare the book for publication.
It is far from a perfect job. No collecting data are given except for
the community in which the tale was found. The English summaries inserted as headnotes often are extremely misleading. A
coon in the Spanish original becomes a rabbit in the English
summary, an old man becomes a boy, major plot elements are left
out or others substituted. The book is plagued with typographical
errors. Only 170 of the 226 texts are annotated, and the accuracy

[34] Margaret Park Redfield, "The Folk Literature of a Yucatecan Town,"
Contributions to American Archaeology 3 (Washington, 1937): 1–50.

[35] George M. Foster, "Sierra Popoluca Folklore and Beliefs," *University
of California Publications in American Archaeology and Ethnology* 42
(1945): 177–250.

[36] Aurelio M. Espinosa, *Cuentos populares españoles, recogidos de la
tradición oral de España,* 3 vols. (Madrid, 1946–47).

of some of the notes is debatable. In spite of these faults, Wheeler's *Tales from Jalisco, Mexico* is still the most reliable of the major published collections of folktales from Mexico, though smaller but better documented collections exist.

Collecting of narratives by Mexican folklorists has not been extensive. In *El folklore literario de México,* Rubén M. Campos gives us thirteen ordinary tales and almost seventy pages of jokes and anecdotes, not all of which come from oral tradition.[37] Campos is frankly impressionistic in his approach to folklore, so we do not expect scholarly apparatus in his works. We are pleasantly surprised, then, when he does give us the place where an item was collected and the informant or collector. Another relatively large collection of narrative is found in *Folklore de San Pedro Piedra Gorda, Zacatecas* (Mexico, 1952) by Vicente T. Mendoza and Virginia Rodríguez Rivera.[38] In a collection of folklore from one Zacatecas town are included sixty-eight narratives, some of them summaries rather than complete tales. There are no comparative notes, but a good deal of data about the informants is supplied. The collections of folk narratives in the annuals of the Sociedad Folklórica de México are fairly consistent in providing collecting data, often giving something of the informant's background as well as his name and the place and date of collection. In spite of this the texts often sound literary, and at times they are frankly local color fiction. There is no attempt at annotation of the texts. *Cuentos y leyendas de México* (Mexico, 1941) by Alfredo Ibarra, Jr., is the only book-length collection of narratives by a member of the society. It was published jointly by the National Academy of History and Geography and the Sociedad Folklórica de México. *Cuentos y leyendas de México,* however, contains no collecting data, no notes, and no bibliography. The texts are rewritten, some put into mouths of characters created by the author, others cast into verse form.

Mexican folklorists of the anthropological school have pub-

[37] Rubén M. Campos, *El folklore literario de México* (Mexico, 1929), pp. 57–67 and 533–601.

[38] Vicente T. Mendoza and Virginia Rodríguez Rivera de Mendoza, *Folklore de San Pedro Piedra Gorda, Zacatecas* (Mexico, 1952), pp. 387–427.

lished some narrative texts, mostly from Indian groups. In 1918 Eugenio Gómez Maillefert published in the *Journal of American Folklore* some of the results of his collaboration in Manuel Gamio's Teotihuacán project, including six belief tales with the authentic ring of oral tradition.[39] Another collaborator at Teotihuacán, Pablo González Casanova, published folktales and articles on the subject in Mexican and foreign journals before his untimely death in 1936. He left a manuscript published posthumously by the National University in 1946 as *Cuentos indígenas* (2d ed., Mexico, 1965). It is a collection of fourteen tales in Náhuatl with Spanish translation, preceded by an introduction showing González Casanova's awareness of international folktale study. Of the three volumes published by the National Indigenist Institute in its Library of Indian Folklore, no. 2 is *Cuentos mixes* (Mexico, 1956) by Walter S. Miller. It contains thirty-five texts in its section on narratives and some others scattered throughout the section on customs and beliefs. There is excellent background material on the cultural context in which the tales are told and on the individual informants as narrators. Although he makes no attempt at a complete annotation of his texts, Miller does give references to the Aarne-Thompson tale type index wherever he can and also cites parallels drawn from collections by other anthropologists.

The work done on Mexican folk narrative is not completely revealed by existing publications. Much significant collecting has not yet seen print. Stanley L. Robe's doctoral dissertation, "A Dialect and Folkloristic Study of Texts Recorded in Los Altos of Jalisco, Mexico" (University of North Carolina, 1949) remains unpublished. It contains twenty-two tales transcribed from phonograph recordings, analysis of motifs and tale types, and full data on informants. By 1947 Robe had collected some two hundred tales in Jalisco; since that time he has done more collecting in other parts of Mexico. At the time this book went to press, he was preparing a collection of Mexican folk narratives for publica-

[39] Eugenio M. Gómez Maillefert, "Supersticiones de la región de San Juan Teotihuacán, Estado de México," *Journal of American Folklore* 31 (1918): 488–95. The same materials were later published in *La población del Valle de Teotihuacán, México*.

tion in Spanish. Virginia Rodríguez Rivera, dean of Mexican folklorists, has also collected much folk narrative material that remains unpublished. Gabriel Moedano is currently engaged in collecting folk narratives but has not yet published in this field.

We must conclude that although some impressive work has been done in the collection of Mexican folksong, relatively little has been done in Mexican folk narrative. In the folktale Mexico has produced no scholarship worthy of the name. There are no comprehensive bibliographies, no type index of Mexican folk tales. Some of the best collections have been done outside the present limits of the Republic of Mexico, in southwestern United States.

As translator for this collection I have sought to achieve the style of each narrator, without making him sound either like a midwestern American or a B movie Mexican. This has not been an easy task, especially if one writes for a monolingual reader who may have his own ideas about how Mexicans should sound. The tales chosen for the collection come from many sources, from different informants and different collectors who may have left their own imprint upon them. Only the texts collected by Gómez, Moedano, Robe, and myself were sound-recorded. I have not used tales that were frankly literary, but the style of those included varies in degree of authenticity. I hope the variations show in translation. Some Indian words found in the original texts and some Spanish words that either are untranslatable or may be translated with more than one meaning have been left unchanged. They are not there for "color"; therefore they are not easily disposed of by putting an equivalent after them in brackets. The reader is referred to the glossary.

With two exceptions (nos. 4 and 25) I worked exclusively with texts available to me in Spanish. Not all translations into English of Mexican folk narrative are poorly or artificially done, but I felt I should work with original texts rather than rely on the translation of others. Again, with the same two exceptions, no texts collected in the Indian languages of Mexico were included: first, because I have no competence in these languages; second, because the translations accompanying Indian-language texts are in my opinion unreliable guides as to the style of the originals. Most often we could do just as well with a tale type summary. This is a problem even with excellent collections of Indian tales such as González Casanova's *Cuentos indígenas*. One has to mistrust a Spanish translation in which we are told that a fox and a dog "gave each other mutual hurts," and that consistently prefers the learned forms of words to the more popular ones. Much the same is true, but for other reasons, of the word-for-word translations by the linguists, who have collected some very good Indian-language texts in Mexico. They give you an excellent idea of the content of the tales and of the structure of the language in which they are told, this being, of course, their main preoccupation. But for the reader interested in style, it is as if he had miraculously acquired the vocabulary of the exotic tongue without learning anything else about it.

In numbers 4 and 25 I was able to work personally with the collectors, Dr. Howard Law and Miss Lila Wistrand, both members of the Summer Institute of Linguistics and both of them friends and former students. I have adapted my English texts from interlinear translations furnished by them and have sought their advice in my adaptations. My changes have been intended to make the reading more natural and colloquial. But it is only proper to emphasize that I have done so without any knowledge of the Indian languages involved. The reader interested in the changes made may compare the text of *Tamácasti* with the English translation published by Law in *Tlalocan*.[40]

This is not to say that these two are our only texts from Mexico's "Indian" groups. There are a number of others collected from similar informants, except that they were given to the collector in Spanish. The stories from Miller and Moedano are good examples. I have used "Indian" in quotation marks advisedly, because it is questionable whether we can talk about such a thing as "Indian" folk narrative in Mexico. Back in 1948 such an authority on the subject as George Foster commented on the difficulty of separating the Indian from the non-Indian elements in Mexican folklore, stating that "the question is begged, since

[40] Howard W. Law, "Tamákasti: A Gulf Nahuat Text," *Tlalocan* 3 (1957): 344–60.

anthropologists have been unable to agree upon a generally acceptable definition of the Mexican Indian." [41] Elsewhere Foster stated that "some groups, at least, are as nearly 16th century Spanish in terms of the content of their cultures as they are Indian." [42] This is not the same as saying that Mexican groups of Indian origin have become completely acculturated, nor does Foster imply it; but there were other anthropologists who were ready to state that Mexican folklore was almost wholly Spanish. Franz Boas was the first to say that as a whole it was largely derived from Spanish sources. [43] Folklorists like Aurelio M. Espinosa concluded that indigenous influence on the Mexican folktale was almost nonexistent. The inference was that native forms and themes either had been eradicated by the "superior" European culture or that, in some instances at least, there had been no native folk narratives to begin with. This extreme position was reached by Ralph Beals, who stated that "except for the Huichol, and possibly the Cora, the folklore of all Indian groups studied is primarily European in type. . . . As an example, the virtual absence of the folktale among the western Mixe Indians of Oaxaca may be cited." [44] Beals's remarks stirred up a controversy that was finally settled with the publication of Walter Miller's *Cuentos mixes*. [45]

There is no doubt that Spanish influence has brought about radical changes in the folklore of the most isolated of Mexican Indian groups. On the other hand, Indian influence has been

[41] George M. Foster, "The Current Status of Mexican Indian Folklore Studies," *Journal of American Folklore* 61 (1948): 368.

[42] George M. Foster, "Mexican and Central American Indian Folklore," *The Funk and Wagnalls Standard Dictionary of Folklore, Mythology, and Legend* (New York, 1950) 2: 711b.

[43] Franz Boas, "Notes on Mexican Folk-Lore," *Journal of American Folklore* 25 (1912): 204–60.

[44] Ralph L. Beals, "Problems of Mexican Indian Folklore," *Journal of American Folklore* 56 (1943): 8, 14.

[45] See for example Paul Radin, "The Nature and Problems of Mexican Indian Mythology," *Journal of American Folklore* 57 (1944): 26–36; George M. Foster, "Some Characteristics of Mexican Indian Folklore," *Journal of American Folklore* 58 (1945): 225–35; George M. Foster, "The Current Status of Mexican Indian Folklore Studies," *Journal of American Folklore* 61 (1948): 368–82.

equally pervasive. The trouble is that identification of Indian and Spanish elements in Mexican folk narrative has been too much the identification of motifs. And there is room for error here. Foster has pointed out that a seemingly European motif may have an Indian basis. The coyote that in Mexican tales is persuaded to take the place of the rabbit or the coon (Motif K842.3) often does so because he expects to marry a beautiful girl, thus corresponding to the coyote's usual character in Indian folklore, that of the lecher.[46] A real evaluation of Indian and Spanish influences in Mexican folk narrative would have to take into consideration such things as diction, style, and the context of narration. Number 48 of this collection, for example, is a somewhat bowdlerized version of a tale Boccaccio might have told, that of the guest who takes advantage of the wife by posing as her husband. It was collected close to the border with the United States, where Náhuatl-speaking Indians never lived and where Indian villages have not existed since Escandón entered the area in 1749 and settled it with colonists of predominantly Spanish stock. But the sponger is called an *achichinque,* from the Aztec *atl-chichin-qui,* literally one who sucks, but used for a sycophant or hanger-on. The Mexicans of Spanish origin who came to the Great Plains called the Comanches *chichimecos,* the Náhuatl word for "barbarian," and referred to the Comanche round shield as the *chimal,* the Aztec word for precisely the same thing. A study of the Spanish and Indian elements in Mexican folk narrative demands a more precise examination of the style and context of folk narrative both in Spain and in Mexico than has been done to date.

I have tried to make this collection as representative as possible, though it is not a faithful mirror of all that is found in print. Part 1, "Legendary Narratives," is the second largest, with twenty-three tales; yet it includes few religious legends and no legends of a historical character. The "legends and traditions" books are full of this kind of material, and there also are a number of translated texts published in southwestern United States. I felt it necessary to exclude publications like these, with the result that some overly familiar legends, such as "La Llorona," have

[46] Foster, "Some Characteristics of Mexican Indian Folklore," pp. 233–34.

been left out. On the other hand, I believe that the "legends and traditions" books reflect an abundance of historical and religious legends in oral tradition, for the most part uncollected or unpublished in a more genuine form. Of the twenty-three texts included under "Legendary Narratives" about half show strong Indian influences, though legends of witchcraft and magic certainly are not unknown in Spain. One-third of the texts in this section are anecdotes about historical characters, usually local ones. The folk hero in a low key, the local "character," is just as popular in Mexico as he is in the United States.

Part 2, "Animal Tales," is the shortest, with only five texts, though if one includes the formula tales, all of which have animal characters, the number could be raised to eleven out of a total of eighty tales. Many of the animal tales in print have a decidedly literary flavor. But animal tales exemplified by number 26 are told and retold by all folk groups in Mexico, Indian and mestizo alike.

Part 3, "Ordinary Folktales," contains eighteen texts, less than one-fourth of the whole collection. Folktales of wonder and adventure still are told in Mexican villages and towns with all the old embellishments. From what some informants have told me, narrating folktales was an art in Mexico not many years ago, with certain families upholding local reputations as expert tellers of the long, elaborate kind of tale that might last the whole night. There is no way of telling how the wonder tale rated with audiences in comparison to historical and religious legendry, and what differences in the storytelling context existed for each. From my own experience as a child in northern Mexico, I would say that the communities where I spent the summers and listened to storytelling cultivated the legend to a much greater degree than they did the wonder tale. These communities may not have been typical of all Mexico. The wonder tale did hold its own throughout colonial times and through the nineteenth century into the twentieth. Whether it will continue to do so is yet to be seen. The preponderance of jokes and anecdotes current in Mexican oral tradition puts the issue in doubt.

Part 4, "Jokes and Anecdotes," is the longest, with thirty-two texts representing twenty-eight different tales. If we take into account the fact that nine of the legendary anecdotes in Part I could also be classified as jests, this gives us a seemingly disproportionate 50 percent of the collection in the category of jokes and anecdotes. The wonder tale and the legend are far from dead in Mexican oral tradition, but the short belief tale, the joke, and the legendary anecdote seem to be predominant. This impression is corroborated by other collectors like Stanley Robe. Religion continues to be a source of humor, as one would expect among a people to whom religion is a part of daily life, but one sees an increase in the jest of the urban type, including the ethnic joke. The United States and the American tourist play a large part in this type of joke. Jokes of this type are not included in the pages that follow, unless one may label number 53 as such, in which the traditional Spanish trickster Pedro de Urdemalas dupes a North American who talks like a Spaniard. The Mexican jokes about North Americans deserve separate treatment.

Finally there are the formula tales in Part 5, six of them in seven variants. They retain their popularity with children, though number 75 was recorded as a song performed by adults for an audience of adults.

Some comment is in order about the apparatus accompanying the texts. Entries in the glossary are cross-referenced with the tale numbers where the item in question appears. The motif and type indexes need no comment. In the notes to the tales, reference usually is made only to the three standard works on the subject: Aarne and Thompson's *The Types of the Folktale,* Thompson's *Motif-Index of Folk-Literature,* and Espinosa's *Cuentos populares españoles.* Occasionally I have noted parallels with Pino Saavedra's *Folktales of Chile* (Chicago and London, 1967), a companion volume in the *Folktales of the World* series, and Hansen's *The Types of the Folktale* (Berkeley and Los Angeles, 1957). I saw no point in repeating non-Mexican references that may be found in standard reference works. Since there is no tale type index for Mexico, I have attempted to supplement Espinosa by citing references to Mexican texts he does not include, either because he does not discuss the tale type or because the text appeared after *Cuentos populares españoles* was published. Texts published in English are also cited. Bibliographical entries referred to in the notes to the tales have been assigned abbreviations, listed alphabetically in the bibliography.

I make grateful acknowledgment to the friends and colleagues who have unselfishly contributed to the making of this book, who have freely allowed me to make translations of unpublished texts collected by them or of printed texts to which they hold copyright. Of the eighty-five texts presented here in translation, only twenty-eight were done from Spanish originals collected by me. Thirty-seven others are translated from the field collections of the following colleagues and students: Virginia Rodríguez Rivera (17), Stanley L. Robe (8), Gabriel Moedano N. (5), Joel Gómez (5), Howard W. Law (1), and Kent A. and Lila C. Wistrand (1). The eight translations from the collection of Stanley Robe were taken from his doctoral dissertation, but they may appear in the original Spanish in Robe's *Mexican Tales and Legends from Los Altos,* now in press, by the time the translations see print. Twenty texts were translated from originals taken from printed sources. I am deeply indebted to the Instituto Nacional de Bellas Artes and its director, Sr. José Luis Martínez, for permission to translate nine texts from *Folklore de San Pedro Piedra Gorda, Zacatecas* by Vicente T. Mendoza and Virginia Rodríguez Rivera de Mendoza; to the Sociedad Folklórica de México and its president, Lic. Fernando Anaya Monroy, for permission to translate seven texts from the annuals of the Sociedad; and to the Instituto Nacional Indigenista and its director, Dr. Alfonso Caso, for permission to translate four texts from Walter Miller's *Cuentos mixes.* To all I owe my sincerest thanks; without their help this book truly would not have been possible. To my own informants I am permanently indebted; they remain anonymous because most of them wish it so. I have profited from long conversations about folk narrative and folklore scholarship in Mexico with my good friends Stanley Robe and Gabriel Moedano. The texts from my own field collecting were recorded with the assistance of a fellowship from the John Simon Guggenheim Foundation and a supplementary grant from the University of Texas.

Américo Paredes

Part I
Legendary Narratives

• ONCE A MAN SAID, "I will go and plow the land." So he began to clear away the brush from the land. When he finished he planted beans, and after he was through with that he went home. Next day, when he went back, he found that the place was all brush again. He thought it was very strange, and he took his machete and cut down the trees once more. But next day he came upon the same thing.

So he says, "Who the devil is doing this to me!"

He did the work once more, but he did not go away. Instead he hid himself in the bushes. There he was, stooped down, watching, when he sees an animal with a little wand tapping on the trees and saying, "Get up! Get up, all of you! Up!" And the trees would get up.

"Ah, so you are the one!" the man said to himself. "Now you'll see!"

The little animal was the rabbit. The man let him get close to where he was, and then he said to him, "Why are you making me lose my time? Why won't you let me work?"

And the rabbit said, "Don't work any more, because the world is coming to an end."

The man did not believe him, and he answered, "If you don't tell me the truth, I'm going to kill you."

And the rabbit said, "I know what I'm saying; you listen to me. Look," he said, "I will go with you. Build a wooden box about the size of a room and put your family in there. And have them make all the tortillas they can. All I can eat is beans and herbs. I'll let you know when it is to happen."

Still the man thought about it for a while. Then he said, "All right; I'll do it."

Once he had finished, the rabbit got inside with him and his family, and they put a padlock on the door. Then it began to rain very hard, and the box went up and up until it reached the sky. All the animals and people were left way down at the bottom. They could see how the weather was, and how high they were, through a little hole in the roof. The box was all closed up, but it had its breathing hole. So they could see that the sky was very close to them, but little by little they came down until they reached the ground, which was dry by now. But it was full of the corpses of animals and men. Then the man opened up and said he was hungry, but the rabbit told him, "You still have some tortillas there, and I can't eat them." So the rabbit went out and found some herbs, which he ate.

The man said to his daughter, "Look, daughter, I'm hungry. Let's cook one of those dead cattle." They dragged it in, they skinned it, and they began to cut it up. They built a fire, and they started cooking it.

Then Our Lord God said to his little angels, "Go see what is happening, who is making all that smoke. But watch out, see that you don't eat anything."

The little angels came straight down and said, "What happened? What are you doing?"

The man answered, "Nothing. I'm eating meat."

The little angels said, "All right."

The man offered some to the rabbit, but he wouldn't eat any. That is why he stayed a rabbit, and the same size he is now. He also said to the little angels, "Don't you want a little piece?"

The little angels took it, and afterward they cleaned themselves well so God would not smell them. But the smell would not go away, no matter how hard they rubbed. They came before God, and he said to them, "What happened? What did you eat?"

And they said, "Nothing."

But you know how it is when you drink liquor or chew gum, or when you have a beer or a peppermint drop, how it smells from a distance. Well, God could smell them just like that. The little angels kept wiping and rubbing, and they would beat their wings. So God said to them, "Well, since you ate of that meat, from now on you will eat nothing but that."

They are the vultures!

And there it ends.

·2· *The Dog That Loved to Hunt Armadillos*

• A MAN HAD a little dog that loved to hunt armadillos. One time he went hunting, and suddenly an armadillo ran out in front of him. The little dog followed it to the hole. The armadillo went into the hole, and the dog followed it, too.

Meanwhile the man kept waiting for his dog, but no matter how long he waited he didn't come out. Since it was already late, he went back home without his dog, thinking he would come back later.

Morning came but the dog didn't come. Then the man took his musket and went out hunting, to see if he could find his dog. He came to the foot of Mactumatzá Mountain and saw where the dog had gone into the ground, but he wasn't there. He kept on walking but he didn't see a single animal. There was no noise at all, not even the sound of a *chachalaca* [a kind of bird]. He sat down on a rock to wait. Just then another man came up and asked him what he was doing.

"I'm resting," he answered.

"Don't you want to come to my house?" he said.

"What's going on there?"

"A fiesta."

"Let's go," he said.

"Good, but close your eyes so I can take you."

The man closed his eyes and before he knew it he was in a great house. He could see animals and treasure on all sides. "I'm in the enchanted place," he said.

"Do you want to speak to the *patrón* [master]?" said the man who had invited him.

"Where's he?"

"Sitting over there."

"No."

"Well then, let me show you what we have here."

He guided him through the huge house, and suddenly he came to a great field where there were deer of all colors: white,

black, sorrel, pinto, and all colors. He looked to another side and
saw cattle, horses, sheep, armadillos, and many other kinds of animals. Suddenly he felt a dog biting playfully at his ankle. He
looked down and saw it was his dog.

"This is my dog," he said. "I'm going to take him with me."

"No."

"Why not?"

"Because he's done a lot of harm to our animals. He chases
them and hurts them. Yesterday he went into an armadillo's hole
and hurt it, that's why we have him here. You're not going to
take him with you because he must pay for what he has done."

They kept on walking and after a while he saw a great number of men loaded down with hay coming toward them. "What
are they going to do with that hay?" he asked.

"It's for the wounded animals. This is what you people do.
You hurt them and then we have to nurse them. Come look."

They took a little stroll and came to a field where the sick animals were: some badly wounded, others with minor cuts, many
of them bleeding. It was a hospital, but an animal hospital under
enchantment.

"That is what happens because of you."

He looked again at the men carrying the hay and didn't see
anyone he knew. But he wasn't satisfied and he looked again,
and this time he saw someone he knew. "But aren't you already
dead?" he said.

"No, I'm alive here, and I carry hay for the badly wounded animals."

The man had died some time before, as was well known, but
since he was under enchantment he was alive here. From that
place he was taken to another where they roasted the buttocks of
men who liked to hunt and gave the roast meat to others to eat.

"Let's go see the *patrón*," his guide said again.

"Let's go. I want to see if he'll give me back my dog."

"Sit there," the *patrón* told him.

"No. All I want is for you to give me back my dog. I want to
take him back with me."

"I won't give him back to you because he's done a lot of
harm."

"Then I want to leave."

"Sit there."

"I won't sit down. I want my dog and for you to let me out of here."

The *patrón* wanted him to sit down to get him in his power. The man kept walking and walking up and down with his rifle on his shoulder, and he kept asking for his dog. "Get him out of here!" he said, very angry.

He says he felt as if he had been picked up and thrown, and then he found himself on the mountain, he didn't know where. He started walking this way and that, and he didn't find a way out. Then he heard a drum.

"My house is over that way," he said. And he began to walk toward the sound of the drum.

After a while he met the people who were looking for him, and they were his family. They were at the rock where he had met the man who took him to the enchanted place. He saw the people, and since he had turned wild he was afraid and was going to shoot at them with his rifle.

They told him not to shoot and little by little he recognized them, and he was talked into going with them. When they got to the town they told him he had been lost three days, but he thought it had only been a little while.

"Didn't you get hungry?" they asked him.

"No."

"And where were you?"

"In the enchanted place."

They relate that to restore him to his former self they had to baptize him again. Then he told them all the things that had happened to him.

· 3 · *Kondoy*

· IN *to'oxykyopk*—the Woman Mountain—there was a cave where people used to store their unshelled corn. That's the place where they found two eggs and took them home.

Two people went there one day, a man and his wife; there is a well there. In that place the woman saw the eggs. She said to her husband, "Give me a stick. I'm going to take the eggs out of there."

So he cut a branch off a tree for her there, and he gave it to her. But she couldn't reach the eggs. She fished and fished for them, but she couldn't get them. They were still there exactly as before.

Then she turned around, and there they were on top of the rock. So she said to her husband, "Go bring them down. They're up there. They're not in the water." And the man went and took them down.

So they took them to their house. Three days later the eggs burst open. When they burst open, out of one came Kondoy, who was people; and from the other one came his brother, who was a great snake.

Kondoy grew fast. In two, three days he was already grown up. His food agreed with him. They brought it to him in baskets, and he finished everything off.

One day he told his mother, "Mother, I'm going to Tehuantepec."

"What will you do there?" his mother asked.

"Oh, I'll see. I want to see the sights there. Don't worry; I'll be back soon."

He left one day and came back the same day, and brought his bundle.

Another day he told his mother, "Mother, I'm going to Oaxaca."

"But what will you do there?"

"Oh, I'll see. My soul is full of emotion. I want to see what there is in the place they call Oaxaca. Don't worry; I'll be back soon."

He left one day and came back the same day. He brought three great jars full of money for his mother. He told her, "Mother, here is this money for you to use. I'm going on my travels now. I want to see everything as it is."

"No, my son. Why must you go wandering about? Stay here."

"No, mother. I'm going now. I'm already grown. I thank you

for taking care of me; you gave me everything. Now I am leaving you this money. You will not lack anything."

Then he set out on his travels through all the region of the Mixe. When he passed through Camotlán, there in *wokkats*—Cliff Gully—he left a pot of money. Since the people were very tall, he put it away just about this high. [Informant raises his hand to the level of his head, or a little higher.]

Then he went into a cave at Trapiche de Chusnabán. There he left a chest of money. But they say the people of Cacalotepec have already gone and taken it all out. They went in a big crowd. That is why Kondoy used to say, "The people of Camotlán are good people. The money I put away when I passed by there still is in its place."

Beyond Santa Cruz, on the road to Trapiche, he had a great battle with one who called himself King Moctezuma. The signs are still there today, the musket balls they shot. Do you remember I showed you that when we were going to Oaxaca? Right there on the road there are many even today. I picked up some of them right there and showed them to you. They are rusty by now, it is true, after so many years, but these are the balls fired by Moctezuma's men when they were fighting against Kondoy.

Kondoy was over here close to Trapiche. But Moctezuma's soldiers were way over there, higher up. Around San Isidro or higher up, that was where he was. He had many men with him, thousands upon thousands. Yes, indeed! Kondoy was all by himself.

Then Moctezuma's soldiers began to fire these musket balls.

All Kondoy did was pick up big rocks; that is what he was going to throw at them; that is what he threw. When the rocks landed way up there, they killed many men. And so they fought for a long time; I think it was more than three days that they fought. Nothing happened to Kondoy; he paid no attention when Moctezuma's bullets came and hit him. Nothing happened to him, the bullets just fell to the ground. And there they still are; those were the ones we picked up. But when Kondoy threw a rock, Moctezuma's men surely died. Those poor men couldn't hold out against him; nobody could hold out against him. All those poor men died there. The rocks are still there. Did you notice how rocky it is around there for more than half a league?

So then Moctezuma left and went back to Mexico once more. That is the way things ended. That is how the old people told it to me.

There in Trapiche, Kondoy sat down to rest after the battle; the signs are still there today. When he got up, he put his hands on the ground and pushed himself up to his feet. The prints of his hands are there. Even the fingers can be seen quite clear.

Then he went on till he came to Mitla. There in Mitla this Kondoy put up his castle, but he set it on solid rock and it was made of nothing but rock. Haven't you seen it? It is still there, they say. The ground is soft in that place. They found out the ground was soft because he was wearing his crown, which weighed more than five *arrobas* [5 × 25 lbs]. His feet began to sink into the ground. This same is true of Tlacolula and Tule; all the ground is soft.

A short distance from Tlacolula, in a place that is now called Caballito Blanco, he wrote upon a rock telling his people where he was going. It cost him no trouble, though he wrote it way up high. He was three meters tall, you see? His machete weighed more than three *arrobas,* and his staff more than five. He stood on top of a big rock at the foot of the boulder, and he wrote just like that, raising his hand a little above his head.

In Tule it was Kondoy who planted that great tree. The ground there is very soft; it isn't firm; there's too much water underneath. Kondoy stuck his staff there, just like this. He stuck it in deep. And then the staff took root and grew, just the way *zompantli* posts take root. So that staff of his became a great tree.

Then he came to Oaxaca, and this was firm ground. He made his capital there. He said, "Even if there is war, and they shoot off cannon, nothing will happen. This is solid ground."

When Kondoy was in Oaxaca, his brother the great snake said, "I am going to Oaxaca. I'm going to see what my brother is doing there."

So he went into the earth there close to Coatlán. He left a trail there; it was a big hole he made when he went in. There under the earth he traveled, the earth trembled where he passed. He was coming into the flat land this side of Mitla when the priest and the bishop went and blessed the place. That was the end of him there.

Kondoy went from there to Mexico and left his crown there. He said, "When someone comes who can wear this, then the government will change."

But nobody has been able to wear it because it weighs a lot. It still is there now, they say. When you go to Mexico, go look for it and send me word whether it is true that it still is there.

Then Kondoy returned. He went in with all his soldiers near a town called Comaltepec. He didn't die. He went into the mountain there, the one called *Ipxyukp* or Twenty Peaks—Zempoaltépetl. He is still there.

·4· *Tamácasti*

I

· THE SHE-DEVIL had a daughter. The maiden was in love. Since the bird talked, he told the maiden he loved her enough to marry her. Her mother said to her, "I don't want any fooling around here."

"So, then, if you do not want to marry me then I'm going." Indeed, since the bird talked, he said it. The bird danced over the maiden. He was a good-for-nothing; he knew what he had done. Afterward, at a later date, he would come again. And afterward, when he came again and found the maiden, he said to her, "Well, we are going to get married anyway."

Her grandmother said to him, "This daughter of mine doesn't want anyone to take up her time. This daughter of mine has a lot of work to do. She doesn't want to be bothered because she is making many *manteles* [napkins]."

He didn't come later because the young man knew the maiden that was in love was pregnant. The she-devil learned of this and afterward she said to her that she saw her daughter was pregnant. She was angry now. She said to her daughter, "As soon as the child is born we are going to grind it and leave it on the leaf-cutter ant hill." Because she didn't want the maiden to have her child.

Indeed, after the child was born they cooked it and the grandmother ground it. She made it into a little ball and went and threw it on the leaf-cutter ant hill. In three days she went to see if the ants had finished eating it. She found it whole. Seeing it was whole, she says, "Why didn't the ants eat it up?"

The child they had ground up was talking. He was saying to the leaf-cutter ants, "Don't eat me because my grandmother is coming." He tells the leaf-cutter ant, "Where you have taken off flesh, stick it back on."

Indeed, in three days his grandmother went to see it again. And the grandmother saw that the leaf-cutter ant had not eaten it. Well, she took it again. She went and threw it in the big river for the minnow to eat. She saw that when she threw it the minnow ate it. She went home. The child talks again with the minnow anyway. He said to him, "Don't eat me. Stick on my flesh again, because my grandmother is coming again to see me." In three days she went to see him again. And she found him again, he was whole. She saw that he was whole. She took him out again.

Her daughter said, "Who knows why neither the minnow nor the ant ate this child?"

His grandmother said, "Then we are going to leave it for the black ant."

Not even the black ant would eat it. He said to him, "Don't eat me. Put my flesh back on again." And when the grandmother went and saw it again, it was whole. Not even the black ant had eaten it. Thus it is that she took it again. She took it home.

She said to her daughter, "Not even the black ant ate it. Thus it is that we are going to leave it in the lake. There let it be eaten by whatever there is that's able to eat it." She threw it in the lake. In three days she went to see it. She found it again. It was floating again on the water like an egg.

When she saw that it was that way, she informed her daughter. She told her mother, "I told you, 'Let's not grind it.' Who knows what my son is up to." She said to her, "Now you see that neither the ant nor the minnow ate him."

"Now," she said, "we are going to catch him with a net." They took two nets. They passed the nets through the water but couldn't catch him. Finally they got tired of trying to catch him. Indeed, his mother cried. She cried and cried. She was not happy about it. She kept on following him anyway. He would move away when she tried to get close to him, don't you see.

When she saw they just couldn't catch him, his grandmother said to her, "Let him stay there now."

His mother said to her, "I won't be happy until I catch him. I am resting for a little while." Afterward she went on following after him as before. And since the child heard, he saw how his poor mother came crying behind him. Finally, then, they caught him there. And then he agreed and they carried him to their house.

They arrived at their house. She said to his grandfather, "Make a trunk for him."

And they put the egg in the trunk. The trunk burst open. When the trunk burst open different kinds of animals were born.

II

All right, so the bird's father went away. His mother didn't know he had gone. In eight days he came and found his grandmother. She was weaving. His mother was not there; she had gone to the river. There was a *nanchin* tree there where she was weaving, and the bird was flying around there. The old lady didn't know it, but she saw she could no longer weave.

She said, "Who is doing this to me, that I no longer know how to weave?" She said, "Why is it happening to me? Maybe it's because of my child that I am no longer able to weave." Since it was the season of the *nanchin* the grandmother shook down a ripe *nanchin* so she could eat it. As soon as she saw that the *nanchin* fell, the grandmother picked it up and she ate.

She said, "How delicious, this big *nanchin*." She said, "Perhaps my child dropped this *nanchin* for me." She no longer paid any attention to her weaving. She said, "My lice are eating me."

So she tore off her scalp. She was taking out the lice. She was completely bald-headed. He saw that his grandmother was completely bald-headed, so he cut a *nanchin* that was green. He threw it at his grandmother on her scalp. That *nanchin* fell. He punished his grandmother. You see, he was angry because she had cooked him and ground him up.

She didn't see the child. He went away again. A week later he came back again. He found his grandmother by herself again. His mother had gone washing. His grandmother was making fried bananas. Then he turned into a cat. He cried because he wanted to eat bananas. He scolded his grandmother because she wouldn't feed him a banana. Anyhow he stole that banana from her. She said, "It must be the cat." But it wasn't the cat. It was her child that had kept on throwing fried banana.

Then the child suddenly laughed because his mother arrived. Since his grandmother was blind in one eye he had kept on throwing pieces of banana at her. His mother was glad because she heard that her child had done it. He said to his mother, "Now I've come back. You cooked me, you ground me up. Now, indeed, I've come back. I came to serve you." He said to his mother, "Let my grandfather make me a netted cradle of spider web." He made it for him.

He told his grandfather, "With your permission, let me go to fetch water at the river." He arrived at the river. A little bird shamed him, also some *tsana* birds. The boy got mad because they were shaming him. He went home. He says to his grandmother, "Let my grandfather make me my bow." His grandfather made it for him.

He told his grandmother, "Now indeed I have my bow. Now, I'm going again to the river to see those who shame me." Arriving at the river, he shot all those who shamed him. All of them he piled up in one place and his grandmother came.

She said to him, "You have really killed all our chickens."

He told his grandmother, "They got me mad because they shamed me." He said that now he would revive all of them again. His grandmother saw they were being eaten by the ants. Those *tsana* birds didn't have any eyes left. He told his grandmother, "All of them I am going to revive again." Right away he cut the seeds of the *cotsisquil* tree for the *tsana* birds' and the *dongolocho* birds' eyes. The ants had really taken out the eyes of all the animals. That's why his grandmother was mad.

She said, "Never are they going to revive." He gathered them up again. He put in the *cotsisiquil* tree seeds. He jumped over them several times and then the animals revived again. Therefore they admired him, because *he* had shamed them. He said to them, "Now you are compliant because you slept." Later he said to them, "Now let whoever is able to catch you, catch you." Tamácasti gave them this advice.

His grandmother saw that her rooster was crowing again. Her daughter said. "Who knows what this son of ours will turn out to be? All of our roosters he has revived again."

Tamácasti went back home. He arrived home. He told his mother, "I really killed all of those foolish ones. Don't you see, they got me mad. That is why I killed them." He told his mother, "Now I revived them again. If they shame me again, I'm going to kill them once for all so they may never shame me again."

"Now," said his mother, "they are revived. Whoever can eat them, let them eat them." His grandmother was provoked because her child was wiser than they, because they weren't able to revive what they had killed.

III

Then the grandfather talked things over with his wife. He said, "This child of ours, I think we are going to eat him now."

But since he was Tamácasti right away he learned that they were going to eat him. Tamácasti got help from a bat so he might kill his grandfather.

Since this Tamácasti slept with his grandfather, the old he-devil said to his wife, he said, "Our son is now big. Now we are going to eat him."

At about eight o'clock his grandmother said to him, "Go fetch water." Tamácasti went to fetch water.

The old he-devil was sound asleep in the bamboo attic. That old she-devil said to him, "Perhaps our son's blood is dripping down." It wasn't her son's blood; it was simply the old man's blood. She opened her mouth. She drank up every bit of the blood. When she was filled up drinking this blood she called her husband. She said, "Drink our son's blood. Ah, how delicious!" She heard that he didn't call her. She climbed up into the attic. She went to see him, and he was already dead. Tamácasti hadn't yet come from the river. Don't you see, his grandmother had forced him to go fetch water.

When he came back she said to him, "My child, likely you killed your grandfather."

He said to her, "How in the world was I able to kill my grandfather, seeing that I was gone to the river?"

She told him, "Your grandfather is dead. I said, 'Perhaps you killed him.'"

He answered, "It wasn't me."

She said, "Well, anyway, now your grandfather is dead. Let him be dead. You go fill two kettles." When he had filled the kettle the grandmother put it on the fire so she could eat her son. She was going to throw him into the kettle. When the grandmother saw that the kettle was already boiling she said to her son, "Ah, my son, fire up the kettle. Fetch a lot of firewood so the kettle will boil."

He said to her, "I'm not going to fetch it. Go ahead, you go fetch firewood." He didn't obey his grandmother. She saw that he didn't obey.

She called him again. She said to him, "Then come here my son. Blow on the kettle."

He told her, "You blow on the kettle." And when the grandmother blew on the kettle, he grabbed her leg and threw her into the kettle. He piled on more wood; it cooked. Only her bones were left. He took out his grandmother's bones again. He piled up lots of wood. He burned them together with his grandfather.

When only the ashes were left, he gathered these ashes of his grandmother and grandfather. Then he looked for someone who might throw it away.

The frog said, "I will throw it away."

He told him, "If you are going to, you should throw it away as far as the other side of the sea, so it won't stay on this side. Go throw it away on the other side of the sea."

The frog said, "I am going to throw it away as far as where you said." He loaded up the frog. The frog carried it to the other side of the sea. It isn't true that he left it on the other side of the sea. He went as far as the edge of the sea. That far only he threw away the trunk. Then when he threw it down, that trunk broke open. Nothing but gnats, mosquitoes, flies, and different animals were born. That's why there are now so many flies, gnats, and mosquitoes.

Tamácasti saw he didn't throw it out where he had told him. There was another one that told him, "I will go put it as far as the other side of the sea." The lizard was the one who deceived him. He didn't fix the trunk right. He met the linnet. He lied that he was going as messenger. The lizard said since he was going he would throw away the ashes of the she-devil and the he-devil. Tamácasti came to his side. He learned he was the messenger.

That lizard didn't take the trunk. The lizard met a skunk. He told him, "You poor thing. Don't carry it because it's heavy." The skunk loaded it on its own back. He went and threw it on the other side of the sea.

The lizard turned back. He arrived. He told Tamácasti, "I myself left it on the other side of the sea." Well, of course, it wasn't true. The lizard deceived him. He went back.

On the third day the skunk arrived at the house of Tamácasti. He said, "I met the lizard. The lizard was struggling. He couldn't carry it because of its heaviness." Then he did him the favor. He carried that trunk for him. He carried it to the other side of the sea.

For this reason Tamácasti disowned the lizard. He split the lizard's tongue. That's the reason even today you see the lizard's split tongue. You see, Tamácasti was angry when he threw away the ashes of his grandfather and grandmother.

IV

Therefore, Tamácasti decided he would go looking for his father. He told his mother, "Now I'm going to see my father because I'm going to get married at home, because the other day my father called me so I would get to know him, because it's

been a long time that he hasn't come. From here the linnet will
go to where my father is so that he will know I'm going there.
At eleven o'clock in the morning I'm going to arrive at my father's house."

That's not how it happened. He got tired in the middle of the
road. He sat down on a stone. He fell asleep. He didn't know
that the stone was swallowing him. When he woke up the stone
hadn't completely swallowed him, and he took out his sword and
cut out its heart so it couldn't revive again. It never grew again.
And then his father waited for him. His son didn't come. He
was the one the stone swallowed. That was the delay. The linnet
went back. Right away he told Tamácasti's father. He sent him a
message, "I was swallowed by a stone but never again will the
stone revive." The lizard was going to his father's house to notify
him.

Tamácasti met the fox. He told him he would be the best
man. He said, "I am going to get married in my country." He
told him, "Go to where my father is because you are my best
man." Since he told him to go, he went to where his father was
in order to let his father know he was his son's best man.

Tamácasti arrived at the father's house with a good band.
That band was made up of wasps. He told his father, "You are
going to ask for a wife for me at the king's house."

His father said, "I myself am going to get a wife for you." So
his father goes. He arrived at the king's palace. He greeted him.
In the middle of the conversation he asked him why he had
come. He said to the king that it was because his son was thinking about the king's palace.

The king said, "If I don't know the young man, I want to get
to know him. Tell him to come here."

So his father learned. He went away thoughtfully since he was
poor; he did not even have clothes that were very good. He was
embarrassed that he had arrived so at the king's palace. Therefore his father told him, "You have to go because that's what the
king told me. Therefore you are going."

He went with his father. They arrived at the king's palace.
They greeted him.

The king said, "Is this the young man that's to marry my daughter?"

He told his father, "There now you see, father, what I told you. The king is going to belittle me." He said to the king, "Well, I'm really much in love with the young girl." So he told him, "Let's see if you'll promise I can marry your daughter."

He told him, "There's a contest for whoever has the ability."

The South Wind likewise had arrived at the king's palace. He also was asking for the hand of the same maiden. There were two of them contending. So he said to them, "Since I'm very poor I won't be able, perhaps, but I'm going to have a try so that perhaps I may marry your daughter."

Since the girl saw that the young man was badly dressed, naturally she said to her father, "I'm not going to marry that young man." She would like to have married the South Wind.

Her father told her, "The one of the two that wins the contest, that is the one you'll marry."

A week later Tamácasti's father returned. He arrived at the king's palace. He asked, "When will the contest be?" Because the contest was to be on Sunday.

He said to him, "There's going to be another one coming here, too."

So that's all Tamácasti's father heard. He went. He returned home. He told his son, "The contest is Sunday. Well then, Sunday you will be there."

Tamácasti told his father, "Father, it will embarrass you when they tease me. The king doesn't fool me."

His father said, "What! Do you already know what the contest's going to be about that day?"

He told him, "I don't know, but perhaps you will see there. First let him try who will be there also." He was going to test himself there against the South Wind.

Therefore he arrived at eight o'clock in the morning, there at the king's house. They arrived. He greeted them. He said, "Good day, my lord majesty Zacarías." And they went into the house. It happened the poor boy was dripping wet with perspiration. So Tamácasti sat down beside his father.

The king said, "Now, since you are all here, I want you to tell me what it is that my daughter has. The one who doesn't know what my daughter has will be shot twenty-five times tomorrow at eight in the morning."

Then Tamácasti answered, "Now I want to know, who was the one who first came asking for her?"

The king said, "It's true you were last to arrive. Well, therefore you will tell me afterward. Therefore let South Wind say first what my daughter has."

So the South Wind says, "I know what your daughter has." And then the South Wind said, "Your daughter has hidden a gold ring."

"But," said he, "in what place does she have it?"

South Wind said, "Your daughter has it hidden on her left leg."

But it wasn't true. Therefore the soldiers grabbed him at once. They took him to the cemetery. He said, "Tomorrow at eight in the morning you will be shot twenty-five times."

So South Wind cried because he was going to die. Then he told Tamácasti, "If you don't know, don't rush in like a fool."

"If I don't know I will say I don't know what the princess has."

So the king said, "I want to know now if you know better what the princess has."

Tamácasti told him, "I know what the princess has." He said, "She has a star of gold on the right side."

The king said, "Well, so you have won the wager, so you both are going to get married right away this next Sunday."

He said, "That's fine, my lord king. Then this Sunday we will get married."

Well, since the South Wind had brothers, they went and told the king, "Why does this young man keep on saying he is so wise? That he can win another guessing test."

Therefore the king knew he was talking that way. Well, therefore he called him right away to present himself again at the king's house. Arriving at the king's house he greeted him. He arrived and sat down. And afterward he said to the king, "I came to find out why you have called for me."

The king said, "Well, young man, you know that you have been going around saying that you can win not only this contest but also more. That you are able to guess even more."

So he said, "I never did go around talking. Who told you?"

He told him, "Well, you don't question me. Therefore tomorrow at eight we are going to make another wager."

He told him, "Well, I will play whatever wager you tell me. So at eight I'll be here with my father."

Therefore he presented himself with his father. When he arrived the king said, "Young man, now for the wager we are going to make. If I lose, I won't be worth anything. I am going to offer you even my palace. Therefore, if I lose, I will leave with only the clothes that I have on." He said, "All right, make out a document."

Tamácasti told him, "Then the one that tattled on us, he is going to leave too."

"Shoot him, then," said the king. "Indeed, for him there is no pardon, because I also am going to leave with just the clothes I have on." Thus they were shot at that point.

Tamácasti said, "Well, the palace is mine if I win the wager."

Then the king said, "The palace is yours. I want you to tell me what it is my daughter has."

Tamácasti said, "Do you know, King, what it is your daughter has? She has planted a sugarcane plant in the middle of the palace and that sugarcane has seven colors. If you want to, let's climb up where your daughter is so she will confirm it."

The king said, "That's right. The wager was legal because I myself said, perhaps you didn't know. Well, my daughter really has it planted in the middle of the house. Well, then if you like, let's go see where my daughter is."

"You didn't know I was such a wise person."

They arrived where his daughter was. They said, "Well then, we came to see what you planted in the center of the house." They arrived there.

Tamácasti says "Do you want to see where that sugarcane of of seven colors is flowering?"

He said, "Well, I want to see where that sugarcane is flowering."

He said, "That sugarcane that you planted is going to flower."
When the lightning flashed, Tamácasti's mother arrived.
When the king looked around, there was a palace of pure gold
much bigger than his palace. They didn't know how that sugarcane flowered. Then the king said, "Now I'm not worth anything. Therefore I'll be leaving for whatever place I can go to."
So he saddled a horse, an old broken-down nag, and then he just
went. Who knows where the horse took him. So the one who tattled on him was shot. He was shot twenty-five times by them. So
the feast began for Tamácasti's marriage. The feast lasted for
eight days for Tamácasti's marriage.

· 5 · *The Pujpatzá*

• ONCE THE SORCERERS of Tecpatán fought with those of Ostuacán, who are also called the *Tzapasnos-quiubay.* The sorcerers
of Ostuacán decided to destroy Tecpatán and all its inhabitants
by flooding it with waters of the Totopac River, which runs
along the edge of the town.

They sent a *pujpatzá,* the alligator that swells up, into the middle of the river. The *pujpatzá* lay down across the river bed and
began to swell and swell and swell until he became as big as a
mountain. Then the waters of the river began to rise and rise
and rise until they came into the town, and the people were in
danger of drowning. And it happened that nobody in the town
knew what was happening, why the water didn't flow as it always did. They didn't know because they were not acquainted
with the *pujpatzá,* the alligator that swells up.

Then the sorcerers of Tecpatán sent all the animals to find a
weak spot in the alligator that swells up. But none of them could
find it. The lizards, the little fish, and the ducks went up to him
and could see nothing. Because they were not acquainted with
the *pujpatzá.*

The crab arrived and went into the water. He went walking
along over the rocks, and the water dragged him up against the
pujpatzá. With his pincers he began to feel the *pujpatzá,* scale by
scale, until he found something soft that was, he said, the weak

spot. He had touched the place where the hands and feet begin, the armpits.

He was satisfied, and he went back and told the sorcerers. So then they said, "Let us make *juguetetoqui,* the fire iguanas, to kill the alligator that swells up."

At this time the people of Ostuacán, who are also called the *Tzapasnos-Quiubay,* had built a huge wall so the people of Ostuacán could not go to Tecpatán and so the people of Tecpatán could not go to Ostuacán. The men of Tecpatán dug some furrows in the rock close to the place known as El Azufre, where sulfurous waters come out of the ground, to hurl the *juguetetoqui* from there. They began to send the *juguetetoqui* from this place to destroy the wall.

They say that when the fire iguanas hit the wall they picked it up as if it was a feather and carried it far away. And the wall remained there, stained with some bloodstains. Another part landed on the farm of Pedro González Valdés, and it can still be seen there.

After that they began to hurl the *juguetetoqui* at the *pujpatzá.* Since they already knew his weak spots, they killed him and the flood ended. The town was saved.

.6. *The Man Who Escaped from the Bathhouse*

• IT'S TRUE THAT the people of Mixistlán used to eat human flesh. They don't do it so much any more, I don't think. Perhaps all that breed is dead; perhaps they don't do it at all any more. But a lo–o–ong time ago, yes!

So the men from over here at Camotlán never went through there when they were alone. When there were three or four of them, they could go through the town. But only in daytime! At night they didn't go through there.

A long time ago a man from Camotlán did go through there. He was called Matewa. He lived over here, but he came from Cotzocón; his son was named Zoriano. Zoriano's son was named

Pedro Celestino. It hasn't been long since this Pedro died, who was the grandson of Matewa.

I don't know what kind of merchandise this Matewa was carrying when he passed through Mixistlán. But he was carrying a load. He carried very heavy loads; I think he could carry six, seven *arrobas* on his back. That was a real man; he could carry a full load. It was almost night when this Matewa got to Mixistlán. So he went and called where he found a house.

"Good evening, senõr."

"Good evening," they answered.

"Will you put me up for the night?"

"Of course! Come in. Put your pack there in the corner. Sit down and rest; this bench is for you."

"Will you lend me some fire to make my coffee?"

"Yes, there it is."

So he made his coffee and ate his tortillas. When he finished his supper he was going to lie down beside his pack. Then the master of the house said, "Senõr, it gets very cold over here; you won't be able to stand it. Why don't we build up the fire in the *temascal* [bathhouse]; you can sleep warm there."

"All right," said Matewa.

That is what the man did. Matewa made his bed inside the bathhouse, and they built a fire inside the door so it would be warm inside. But after a while, when Matewa was asleep, the man threw chile pods into the fire. Then Matewa began to choke; he woke up. But he couldn't get out through the door; the fire was there. And they had closed up the entrance.

Then this Matewa used his strength. He crouched down like this, and he went like this. And he burst through the *temascal* wall just like that, they say. Because this Matewa was really a very strong man. He came out just like that, he ran. He didn't wait for anything; he didn't ask for his pack. He already knew that those people wanted to kill him so they could eat him. And he ran.

But those people came out too. There they came running to catch Matewa; they really were going to kill him. But this Matewa was very clever; he just took off his sash and threw it behind him. Then his sash became a snake, so they say. It was there when those people came up; it almost bit them, since it was poisonous. But those people had their machetes with them. So that gave them an advantage; they killed the snake there.

Matewa was already very far off, but the people chased him again. They were catching up with him. "What will I do now?" thought Matewa.

Then he took his porter's cloth, his shoulder pad. This is what he had used for a pillow; he had put it against his shoulder when he pushed against the *temascal* wall. This is what he threw behind him. It became poisonous animals at once, and when the men came up they stung them plenty. This time they didn't manage so well with their machetes. So it was that Matewa got away. Since it was night he got away; he ran.

He traveled all night, he went through the woods. When dawn came he went and told his story at the municipality of Villa Alta. I believe that's where the soldiers are. So the authorities took action; they sent soldiers.

Then they came to the place where the house of those people was. There was Matewa's pack; there were the signs where he had broken out of the *temascal*. So they killed all those people right there, and they burned their house. So they say. I did see Matewa. He was still living when I was young. He was an old man.

Indeed! This *is* true. Matewa himself was the one who told it. Zoriano his son also knew the story well. But they don't eat many people now. Perhaps it is because all that breed has died out.

· 7 · Horse's Hooves and Chicken Feet

• SILVESTRE GUZMÁN used to tell that when he was a young man he went to a dance one night with some of his friends. They left the dance pretty late, and they heard a faraway music telling of another fiesta going on. So they went toward it.

"Could it be in the Chávez patio?" they said. But it wasn't there. The music could still be heard, though, just a little farther on.

They kept walking until they came to the dance. They went in and chose their partners. But suddenly one of them noticed that the women had chicken feet, and all the men had hooves instead of feet. He signaled to the others and they got out more than fast.

Dawn came while they were still far from San Pedro, and after thinking it over they decided they had walked as far as "La Ti-naja" dam and that they had been at a witches' ball. For a long time afterward they did not go out at night.

·8· The Witch Mother-in-Law

· JULIÁN, Silvestre, and Pioquinto Guzmán used to go to Ojo Caliente at dawn every day to deliver the bread they baked in San Pedro. When they got to Ojo Caliente they had to pass by the house of a friend of theirs. They would greet him and talk with him a while, in order to sell him something. The friend was always worried because of his wife, who suffered from an illness no one had been able to cure.

After some time had passed, the Guzmán brothers heard the following story:

The man became desperate because of the expense which his wife's sickness was causing him, and he began to ask advice of his neighbors. Among his neighbors was one who told him, "Your mother is the one who has done evil to your wife."

The man went to his mother's house; she lived in a place away from the town. And he talked to her in this way. "Mother, I know you have bewitched my wife. I am spending all I have and she doesn't get well. I have no one to help me, and it is important that my wife get well. You can do that for me."

"My son, I have not bewitched your wife nor can I cure her."

"Mother, there is something I will have to do. If you are guilty, you will suffer for it."

On the way back home he bought a load of wood, and when he got home he made a big bonfire. Then he smeared plenty of oil on a black hen and threw it into the fire alive. The animal got out, but he threw it back into the fire until it burned to death.

Next day he went to visit his mother and found her all burned.

She died in a few days, and they say this showed she was the witch. But the sick woman died a short time later after all.

•9• *The Witch Wife*

• They say that in the Náhuatl-speaking district of San Cristóbal Las Casas there lived a man and his wife. The woman was a witch and she was deceiving her husband. It was her custom to say some magic words that made the flesh drop from her bones, leaving nothing but the skeleton. Then she would sprout wings, and the skeleton would go out flying through the air. In this shape she would go out every night and frighten people out at late hours.

When her husband found out she was deceiving him and that her skeleton went out every night, he decided to punish her. One night he lay awake in bed, pretending he was asleep. He heard noises as his wife got out of bed and went out into the street. He got up too and followed her.

Hiding in the shadows he saw how the flesh dropped from his wife's bones and how wings sprouted from her skeleton. Then he saw her fly away, making a noise like bones falling apart. When he got over his fright, he went where the flesh was, and he chopped it up into bits with his machete. Then he sprinkled salt over it so it would die. Then he went back and hid in a corner and waited for the skelton to return.

When this took place the skeleton stood before the flesh and said the words to make it come back in place. But the flesh did not obey because it was dead. The despairing skeleton flew away. Many are the people who see this being flying through the air at night, and they say it announces somebody's death.

•10• *The Pig-Man*

• In mazontic there lived a family of *ladinos* [non-Indians] surrounded by inhabitants who were for the most part Tzotzil-speaking Indians. The *ladino* couple kept their little house in better order than those of their neighbors, and they had a robust child who was the joy of the home. In front of the house was a beautiful tree which threw its shade over the place where the children played. Just a little farther on was the hut of a *compadre* of theirs who was known for his kindness.

They tell that one night the mother had the child in her arms when all of a sudden, as if he had risen out of the shadows, the Indian Manuel Díaz came on the porch and without further explanation told the mother, "I want to hold your son in my arms."

She was astonished and stared at the man, and he insisted once more. In the face of such obstinacy, the woman thought it necessary to run the Indian off, and he left, almost pushed out of the house, muttering, "You'll see what happens to your son."

The mother paid no attention to his words but went and put the child in bed while she continued her chores. Half an hour later the child began to cry. The mother went to see what was the matter and found he had a very high temperature and that he was twisting and thrashing in bed. They tried to do something for him, but no kind of treatment helped. In three-quarters of an hour he was dead.

The poor woman ran out of the house in her despair, to tell her *compadre* across the street what had happened. But when she passed under the tree, she heard two black hogs grunting in the branches. The sound of their grunting struck her dumb with terror, for she had never seen animals like that climbing trees.

She told all this to her *compadre,* who immediately understood what it was all about, because he knew there were many people-eaters in the town. Disregarding the dead child for the moment, the man took his charmed musket, took dead aim at the black shapes that still grunted among the branches, and fired at one of them. At the roar of the weapon, one of them being hit, the two animals fell to the ground and fled toward the river. One of them could hardly move, but it dragged itself into the underbrush and was lost in the shadows of the night. A trickle of blood showed it was wounded.

Next morning, curious people followed the tracks down to the river, where they lost them. They kept on searching, and some meters from the river they found the Indian who the night before had visited the *ladino*'s house wanting to hold the child.

. *11* . *The Phantom Children*

• THIS HAPPENED. My mother used to tell me about it, and I remember some of it myself. Even though we were very little then. It must have been in the days before the revolution, when my brother and I were little children—three or four, both of us. At that time my father used to live on this side of the road, with a big yard at the back toward the *estero* [kind of lake]. The woods were thick over that way, very heavy brush, big, big trees close to the bank. But those were peaceful times. Father would go out on the range, and we would stay all alone, mother and us two. We were the only ones then. There was nothing to fear. Mother would be busy, and we would play—we were children, you know. We would go toward the lake, and we would play there all day.

Well, so mother used to say that once we came home with the story that we had seen some children; we played with them over there by the lake. Well, you know how children are; they imagine all kinds of things. And more when they play. So they paid no attention to us the first time—children's play. But it happened every noontime, when mother would lie down. We would go play with the children over there by the lake. And in the evening we would come and tell mother about it. Well, until she began to believe us, we were at the same thing for so long. And even more, mother used to say, we would tell her what they looked like. The little girl was blonde, dressed in white, and the little boy in a blue shirt-front. Until one day mother says to father, "Listen, do you suppose there are people over there?"

"What's the matter with you! There's nobody. No families for at least a couple of leagues."

"But they tell me exactly what they look like."

"And you believe them!" Father got angry. So she didn't say any more.

But next day she lay down to take the siesta, and she just waited until we were gone. And she followed us. Well, she says she came upon us in a little clearing, and just when she caught sight of us she also saw something white that disappeared behind a bush. Something like a little skirt, she thought. She called us then. "What were you doing? Were you playing with the children?"

"Yes," they say we said. She got frightened. She drove us ahead of her and went straight to an old sheepherder's who lived on our place. So the old man came, and he went all along the path, watching. Up to the little clearing.

And yes, they say he saw them, just as we said. But as soon as he saw them, they ran behind a bush and out of sight. So then the old man grabbed his stick, and he went straight to the spot where they disappeared. There was nothing there. Just a gap in the brush, covered with weeds. He said, "Well, now, *carajos* [lowers voice]. I'm going to see what this is all about." And he went into the gap. And just then he heard a growl. And right there in front of him, in a kind of little cave among the branches. A black dog, huge, growling at him and baring his teeth. And fire was coming out of his eyes.

"Hail-l-l, Holy Mary!" he said. And he crossed himself. That must have been what saved him, because the dog didn't move. He just growled—and kept looking at him with those eyes. He started walking backward, backward, until he got out of there.

Later, a lot of men with guns and machetes went there, but they couldn't find anything. Some said there was money buried there, but father wouldn't let them dig. When the priest came by, they asked him to pray, there at that place. So he prayed. And nobody ever saw anything again.

(COLLECTOR: I wonder what it was.)

They say two children had been killed there—brother and sister. But that happened many years before, not long after the war with the Americans. They were coming from Texas with an uncle of theirs, and they were bringing much money, in gold and silver coins. And when they got about this far the uncle killed them, because of the money. It was them.

(COLLECTOR: And the dog?)

The devil—or the uncle himself, who must be in hell.

· *12* · *Little Saint Michael*

· A MAN WAS GOING along a road toward Bochil. Suddenly he saw a *morral* [woven bag] lying on the ground. He went and picked up the bag to see what was in it and found three bottles of liquor inside. He uncorked one of the bottles and took a drink. Then he left the bag where it was and went on his way.

He hadn't traveled far when he felt like drinking some more, so he came back to the *morral.* He took another drink, but then he decided to take the *morral* with him so he wouldn't have to come back again.

When he got home he hung up the bag with the bottles on a hook. He was pretty drunk by then, so he lay down to sleep. About midnight he began to hear music and singing. He woke his wife up and asked her if she heard music and singing.

"You're crazy and drunk," she told him, and she didn't stir out of bed.

He kept hearing the music, and since it seemed to come from the *morral,* he took it down and hung it in another part of the room. Then he saw that it was from the *morral* that the singing and music came. He lighted the light and searched the *morral,* and he found little Saint Michael inside. It was the saint who was singing and from whom the music came.

This man died some time ago, and he left the image of the saint to his son, who lives in Soyaló. The owner of the image allows people to consult the saint; they take the little box out and take it wherever they wish, and it speaks to them.

· *13* · *Elves*

a

· IT IS SAID that elves are little creatures, and that they play all kinds of tricks. Once they carried off a woman's saltcellar, and they stole a box of chile peppers from another woman. They appear at night, especially in the kitchen, and they play tricks on women who are cooking.

b

• MANY YEARS AGO, in the flour mill at San Pedro Piedra Gorda, elves drowned a little old man in the flour. In those times there were many elves who played really mean tricks on people. One family got so tired of their elf that they decided to move to another house. They did so, and they were leaving their old dwelling when they remembered they hadn't brought the broom along. They were asking each other about it when they heard a little voice saying, "Let's go. I've got it here with me." They saw it was useless to move, and they came back home and made the best of living with their elf.

c

• THEY TELL THAT in San Pedro Piedra Gorda, in the house of Heriberto Rodríguez on a night between seven and eight o'clock, somebody began throwing stones and bricks into the patio, and no one knew where they were coming from. They called the police, who came duly armed and searched the whole house down to the last corner without finding anybody. But the patio was full of stones and bricks as proof of what had happened. Someone pointed out it could have been elves. There are many stories about elves who throw stones on the roofs of houses, and even into the rooms.

•*14*• *Mal de Ojo*

• A LITTLE GIRL went to the country with her parents, and on the road they met a young woman named Sabina who very affectionately picked up the child, kissed her, and played with her. A few minutes later the child, who had been perfectly well, began to have symptoms of fever and melancholy; she started crying until she lay exhausted in her mother's arms.

The mother said to her older daughter, "Go quick and call Doña Alejandra, because the child is suffering from *mal de ojo*. The girl did so, and that afternoon the healer arrived. But earlier, she had already told the girl who went to call her to have the following things ready: rosemary, rue, Saint-John's-wort, lavender, *yerbanís,* laurel, and a brazier with fire.

When she got there she undressed the little girl, made a cross with lime on the floor, set the brazier on it, and threw the herbs into the fire. She passed the child several times through the smoke, making the sign of the cross, and saying,

> "Saint Michael! Saint Raphael!
> Saint Gabriel! Saint Raphael!
> I command you remove the ill
> This child is suffering from."

She would also pass the child over the cross. Then she wiped her from head to foot with an egg. She broke the egg and put it at the head of the sick child's bed, along with a cross made of straws placed over the yolk.

Next day, the herbs used for the fumigation, as well as the egg, were thrown away very far from the house. The person who did so was warned not to look back for any reason toward the spot where these things were left. The child got well.

•*15*• ¡*Qué Veo!*

• QUEVEDO is very well known in some places. A person who was very gross to a certain point, very blunt in his speech. On one occasion he went to France. Over there in France, since he had just got there, he didn't know about places—toilets, bathrooms—places to answer a call of nature.

He had to go. It was a street seldom used by people, very lonely, and he couldn't hold back any longer. So he pulled down his trousers and squatted in a doorway, but facing the other way, not with his back to the wall, but outward.

Just then two old ladies went by. They turn and see that—They see Quevedo's buttocks, and one of them says, "¡Mon Diú! ¡Qué veo!" ["What do I see!"]

He turns around and pulls up his trousers, and he says, "¡*Coño!* They even know me from the rear end!"

· *16* ·   *Quevedo and the King*

· WHILE QUEVEDO was in France, the king received notice of the complaints against him, that he was very obscene in his ways. So he called him and said, "Either you leave my country or I'll have you hanged, because the things you have been doing here are not polite."

"No, Majesty, I will try to behave. Please give me another chance."

He says: "Very well, look. I will give you another chance just to show you I am a conscientious king. I give you license to play a trick on me, any trick that you wish, as long as your apology is grosser than the trick. I give you a period of three days. If within those three days you do not play a trick on me and excuse it with an apology grosser than the trick itself, you must leave the country or hang."

"Very well, Majesty. Give me those three days, and I will be here."

The first day passed, the second, and the third. And he couldn't find a solution for the fix he was in. Finally he has to come to the king's reception hall, and he still hasn't thought of a trick to play on the king and what apology to give, so he could stay longer in France, because he liked it there very much.

He hid behind some curtains. The moment arrived when the king gave audience, to receive all the notables of the town, listen to complaints or give advice or so many things of those times. When the king was passing by the curtains, Quevedo sticks out his hand and grabs him by the private parts.

Then the king says, astonished, "Quevedo! What are you doing?"

Quevedo says, "Pardon, Majesty. I thought it was the queen."

· *17* · *Your Reward Is Up Above*

•THEY SAY THAT Don José D.C. had a sister whose name was Francisca, married to a man of the M———family. One of their daughters died not long ago. One day he comes from the country to visit her. He says [whining voice] "Little sister,"—because that's the way the man talked—"I'm going to stay with you today."

"Yes, *manito.*" They all called each other *manito.* "It's all right."

He went out around there, and he came around here, and he went around over there and over there. Around midnight or thereabouts he comes and knocks at the door. "I'm back, *manita.*"

"Yes, *manito.*"

The man was quite a rascal. The maidservant was sleeping on the floor, and he figured she was there. "Where are you, child? I don't want to step on you."

And his sister says, "Don't speak, child. Don't speak so this scamp of a brother of mine won't know where you are."

"Now, but listen here, sister. Don't give me such a bad name," he says.

So his sister took him to the room where he was to sleep. The beds of those times were high and made of wood. And they had a ceiling on top—could be blue, could be red, could be white—where they hung the mosquito net, and the tops were bordered by pretty fabrics made of fine laces. Well, then, he slept there.

He was a great trickster, a real rogue. At dawn, well, he felt the need to move his bowels and couldn't find where to do it. In those days men used very large handkerchiefs so he got up and did it in the handkerchief. He tied it firmly at the corners and hid it on top of the ceiling of the bed.

In the morning he got up. "I'm going now, *manita.* Many thanks, many thanks for giving me a bed for the night."

"Yes, *manito.*"

"You are a good woman, sister. Your reward is up there above; your reward is up there."

"Yes, *manito*. May God hear your words," the woman said.

It was around the month of May, when the suns are hot. By that afternoon the room was stinking. So, "Girl! What is it that smells so bad in here!"

"I don't know, mistress."

So they looked here, and they looked there, and so they looked over there, and they looked there. Until they saw a moist spot in the ceiling over the bed.

"Just look! It was José! The scoundrel! The rascal! Look what he did there!"

· 18 · Don José and the Water Vendor

· THEY TELL ABOUT this Don José that he had some beautiful horses. He was a fine *vaquero*, a wonderful one; he was a short little man. And he rode some wonderful horses—real horses! They tell that once he came to Matamoros, and that was the time when men went around the streets selling water. They put a couple of traces on the ends of a water barrel and rolled it behind them, pulling and pulling and pulling in the harness.

Around there, a few blocks this way from the plaza—I don't know what the streets were called then, but that is Fourth Street now—Don José came upon a poor man pulling a barrel, tug and tug and tug. He was saying, "Water! Water! Water!" He was selling water. He touched the spurs to his horse, a dark gray—a beautiful animal!

"How much are you asking for your water, boy?"

"Twenty-five cents a barrel, señor." Twenty-five cents was a fortune in those days.

"I'll give you fifty cents—no, I'll give you a whole peso for the barrel. Just follow me."

"Yes, sir. Right away." After all, for a peso. He was paying for four barrels.

"Follow me." So there he goes, on horseback, toward the edge of town. And there comes the poor man, all hot and sweaty, pull-ing the barrel. And there they go.

"Señor!"

"Just a little farther." So there they go again. Until he brought him all the way up here. [Narrator lives on outskirts of town].

He said, "Now listen here!"

"Just up to Arroyo Seco, sonny."

"To Arroyo Seco?"

"Yes, it's just about six leagues more from where we are," he said.

"Ah! You old so-and-so!"

"Shh! Hush, now; hush. Don't say anything about it. You'll see; I said one peso, but here's two." He would do that, even; he'd pay well for his own jokes. "Here. Take two pesos. Now, unplug the barrel there. Unplug it."

"No. Just think, I can sell this water somewhere else. Any-where."

"But I already paid you for it, son. I gave you two pesos for it. Unplug it there."

So he bought the barrel of water, and he paid well for it.

•*19*• *Don José and the Peddler*

• THERE'S ANOTHER STORY they tell about Don José. Arroyo Seco, where he lived, is on top of a hill; the level ground was a long way off. And there was a man who went around with a mule in those parts, selling bread. A big basket on this side, and another big basket over here on the other side. He also carried eggs and chickens and other things to sell on his mule.

COLLECTOR: Was he on foot?

Yes, he walked beside the mule, and all the things he sold were on the mule. Well, he sees him way off in the distance, and he said, "There comes that man." And he thought of playing a trick on him. So he mounted his horse; he always had his horse saddled and ready. He mounted and went off as if he was going to one of his ranches called Rancho Nuevo.

Well, he hadn't gone far when he came to a creek, and it was running full. The river was in flood, and the creek was running full. Now one of those big sea turtles had come up from the river into the creek. Those big ones, like this [holds hands some three feet apart]. The peddler was still far off, very far off.

So Don José dismounted and caught the turtle. It put its head and legs inside the shell, of course. But they have a soft spot on the shell on the side, like a fin, so he took his knife and made a hole there and ran a piece of rope through it. And he picked it up like that.

He said, "Howdy, Trinidad"—I think that was the man's name—"How are you today? Are you going to my place?"

"Yes, sir," he said, "I'm going there."

"How would you like to buy this turtle?"

"No," he said, "what would I do with it? What could I do with a turtle?"

"It's a good turtle, fine eating. But since you won't buy it, will you do me the favor of taking it to my house for me? To that big white house over there."

"Yes, sir, I know the house. I always stop there."

"Yes, that's my house."

"All right, I'll take it for you."

So Don José went and tied it to the pack saddle on the mule, so it would hang down against the mule's flank. He tied it there tight. Well, as soon as the mule went into the water, the turtle put its head and feet out of the shell, and it grabbed the mule right at the groin.

And the mule started bucking and bucking and bucking, right there in the water. And to the devil with all the bread and eggs and chickens and everything else the man was selling! The mule came running out of the creek, and you could see one of the baskets floating here and another there. Then the peddler stepped into a hole and went all the way under. In short, he lost everything he had.

"Eh! You old so-and-so!" And the *pelado* took out a dagger; he was still in the water up to here.

"Now son, now sonny, Don't get mad, don't get mad. What happened? What happened?'

"That turtle! Don't you see what it did to the mule's belly? Look at the mule over there in the flats, bucking and rolling in the dirt!" Of course, the turtle was holding on tight.

He said, "J–j–just a minute. I'll take care of that." He went and cut off the turtle's head and threw it away.

"But look here, you old man! My mule's gone wild on me, and you made me lose everything I had!" Baskets, bread, eggs, and everything was floating down the *bayuco*. The kids were jumping into the water to get what they could. "You'll pay!"

"Of course, sonny. Of course I'll pay for everything. Come along. Don't get mad, now; don't get mad; don't get mad." And he took the peddler home with him.

"Oh, that man!" his wife said.

"Oh, well," he said, "I thought of the trick and I had to play it, even if it cost me a little."

Then he says to the peddler, "Let's see, how much was it?"

"Well, it was the eggs, and the bread, and the. . . ."

"Here. I'll give you fifteen pesos." The whole thing might have been twelve pesos; things were cheap in those days. "Here, take these fifteen pesos."

"But listen, how about that mule. I can't get anywhere near it now."

"I'll trade you for it. Here! Send for the *remuda*." They brought the *remuda*. "Cut out that horse. Look, this is a very good horse."

"Which? *That* one? Now, look!"

"He's very gentle, man! Very gentle, very gentle."

"He's so old he can't see any more. What can I do with him, señor?"

"So much the better, you fool. You don't know anything about horses. You can lead an old horse around, and when you talk to him he'll mind you."

"Well, perhaps what you say is true," the man said. And in truth the horse was not in bad shape. So he put the baskets on the old horse, and Don José paid him.

"The mule. . . ."

"It's still yours. You can come visit it whenever you want."

·20· *Don Bartolo*

• DON BARTOLO was a little old man who loved to tell fantastic tales, which he would innocently say had happened to him. Among them was this one: "Ah, child! One evening just at dark I met a huge wolf. He saw me and came at me to eat me up. But I quickly put my hand in his throat, for he had his mouth opened wide. And I grabbed him by the tail and turned him inside out. That right, Juana?"

"Yes, Bartolo." Juana was his wife, and she vouched for everything he said.

Another time he was riding along when a storm came up. So he put the spurs to his mare and the raindrops just kept sliding off her rump. She kept running faster and faster, and the storm never caught up with them, and they didn't get wet. "That right, Juana?"

"Yes, Bartolo."

Once he was very ill, in bed, waiting for death to come at any moment. Then he remembered that he had a sword under the bed. So he took it out and battled with death for several minutes until he defeated it. "That right, Juana?"

"Yes, Bartolo. I could see you duck."

Another time he was at a rodeo watching some roping. One of the cowboys roped a mare that was a very fast runner, and she was going so fast the rope took off her head. "So there goes the mare, running through the woods without a head," Don Bartolo used to say. "But about a year later I said to myself one day, 'I wonder what happened to that mare that went off into the woods. I'm going to look for her.' And I did find her. Her head was growing back, but it was still a tiny little head. . . ."

·21· *Arnulfo and the Law*

• THIS ARNULFO was a real character. One day he took an ax and hacked away at the church door because he had two maiden sisters who were so very pious they were always at church. He

went home and didn't find them, and since he was drunk he
went at the church door with an ax because his sisters were in
there with the priest.

So to jail he goes! He paid his fine and came out again. And
our *presidencia* [city hall] was just in front of the jail, so he
comes out and begins to yell curses and insults at the mayor and
other municipal officers. Bang! Back in jail he goes.

He pays his fine and they let him out. And again he goes to the
door of the *presidencia* and begins to curse the authorities once
more. So back in jail he goes! This time, before they let him out,
they made him promise he wouldn't go to the *presidencia* and insult the authorities again. He promised, so they let him out.

And in those days, you may remember, the statue of Don Be-
nito Juárez was in the main plaza, facing the *presidencia*. They've
moved it way over there to Sixth Street. Well, there was Juárez,
with his book like this [gesture, holding book] reading the laws
of the Mexican Reform.

Arnulfo goes and kneels before the statue, right there in the
middle of the plaza. "Oh, great Benefactor of the Americas!" he
says. "Please thumb through that little book of laws you have
there, and tell me according to what article was I thrown in jail
by this pack of sons-of-bitches!"

So he's back again!

•22• *Arnulfo Collects a Crowd*

• THIS ARNULFO had a bar, down in the tourist section of town.
But business was very bad. One day a man dropped by the bar
and found him all alone.

"Listen, Don Arnulfo" he said. "What's the matter with the
place?"

"Why?" he said.

"It's dead. There's nobody here. The bar is empty."

"You want a crowd?"

"Well, yes. A man likes to drink where there's a lot of people."

"Just a minute." He reached under the counter and took out a
gun. Bang! Bang! Bang! Bang! He fired it at the ceiling.

A crowd gathered in no time at all. "What happened?"
"What's the matter?" "What's going on?"

"Oh, nothing. This gentleman here wanted a crowd."

•23• *The Mayor of San Fernando*

• THEY TELL A LOT of stories about the people of San Fernando;
they say they're pretty stupid. Well, just think, they won't buy
you a house if there isn't a tree stump in the middle of the yard,
so they can tie the loony to it. Every family has one of its own.
All San Fernando people are one-eyed, because they eat nothing
but jerked beef. It's rubbery, you know, and when they pull on it
with their teeth, it snaps back into their eyes.

They have some interesting customs too. You have to be careful how you knock on a door in San Fernando. If you knock low
down on the door, the woman of the house will yell at you from
the upper story, "Shoosh! Pig! Get away from there!" The streets
are full of them. But if you knock high on the door, she'll come
out with a firebrand in her hand. That's the only time San Fernando people call on each other, when the fire goes out in the
kitchen.

They used to have a mayor in San Fernando who was such a
dolt he couldn't even read or write. He carried his signature
around on a rubber stamp they had made for him, and when he
had to sign something he just stamped it. One morning he gets
to his office and asks the secretary, he says "What's new?"

He says, "Well, among other things here is a letter from the
governor."

"Let's see. Open it so you can read it to me; let's see what it
says."

So the secretary opened it. "Well, it says that he's sending us a
quantity of blanks for us to. . . ."

"Hold it! Call the chief of police and tell him we'll be receiving a shipment of blanks which he'll distribute to the force. Governor's orders. And he's to see to it that they have guns that fit.
Let's see what else he says."

"For us to report to him the vital statistics in town."

"All right, send him a letter. Tell him that we will issue the blanks as soon as we get them. But as for vital statistics, tell him we haven't had any of those for a long time; I run a pretty clean town. Not that we could afford much devilment around this place; we've had a pretty bad year."

Part II
Animal Tales

The Rabbit and the Fox

• So IT HAPPENS THAT there once was a little rabbit who used to go walking along a hill. A fox hunted around there, and the little rabbit fell in love with the fox, you know; and since foxes eat rabbits, the little rabbit was afraid to propose to the fox.

He says, "But look, what a beautiful girl!" The rabbit said, "I'm going to speak to her, and see what she says." He says, "But I'll have to look sharp; I don't want her to eat me."

Little by little he got close to the fox. "Ah, my love!" he says. "How pretty you look! I would like to marry you. I would like for you—for you to say something to me."

"What are you saying? You wicked rabbit!" she says. "Now I'll eat you," she says. And the fox went after him. The rabbit took off running, and he ran and ran. So . . . since the rabbit was so nimble at running, the fox couldn't catch him. The little rabbit went away; he hid. The fox ran one way, and the little rabbit went another. He was badly frightened.

"Tsk! *Carajo!*" he says. "That fox really got mad," he says, "because I proposed to her. Mmmm! But one way or another," he says, "I'm going to have her the first chance I get, whether she wants to or not."

Next morning he got up very early, and he went to the house where the fox lived. The fox had some little ones. And it happened that the mother fox was not at home when he got there. He says, "A very good morning." The little rabbit was looking sharp, you know.

"A very good morning," said the little foxes.

He says, " Is your mother home?"

"No, our mother isn't home."

He says, "Listen," he says. "Would you do me a favor?"

"What favor?"

"To give her a message for me."

"Uhuh. Tell us what it is," he says.

He says, "Well, just say to your mother if she will do what we talked about yesterday."

"Ah, all right," he says.

"And that I'll be seeing her," says the rabbit. And there goes Uncle Rabbit, running, looking sharp just in case he ran into the fox again.

Next morning he went again, you know. The rabbit combed his hair, he slicked his head down. Well, he fixed himself up, you know, so he would look as cute as he could. He says: "Now I'm going again," he says, "to where the fox lives. To see what she says. I hope she doesn't kill me and eat me. Let's see what she will do about me." And there goes the little rabbit. He would hop and look all around, then he would hop again and look all around. Until at last he got to the fox's house. The fox wasn't there; she had gone hunting to get food for her little ones.

He says, "A very good morning."

"A very good morning," said the little foxes.

"Is your mother home?"

"No, she isn't home," he says.

"Mmm, listen," he says. "Would you do me a favor?"

"Let's see; tell us what it is."

"To tell your mother if she will do what we talked about yesterday."

He says, "Why sure. If everything was as easy as that."

He left. He was a sharp one, was Uncle Rabbit, you know. He got to his little house, and he sat down to think. *"Caramba!"* he says, "but this fox is not going to eat me. This is the second time, and the third time is the charm. If she doesn't eat me, I'm going to have her one way or another."

So next morning he combed his hair and fixed himself up, and went out very carefully. He got to the fox's house, keeping a sharp lookout and he says, "Good morning."

"Good morning," he says.

And the little foxes had told the fox what the rabbit said before.

She says, "Now I'm going to show that rabbit. This time I'll have no mercy on him," she says. "I'm going to eat him this time."

So the fox did not go hunting that day but stayed there waiting for the rabbit to come so she could eat him, close to the den where her little ones were. So here comes Uncle Rabbit, looking

sharp, you know. He would hop and look carefully all around, to
make sure the fox would not jump out and eat him. But Rabbit
had already fixed things ahead of time. He was coming well prepared. He had made two holes in his den. At the entrance he
made a big, wide hole, you know, and in the middle he made it
good and narrow, so nobody could go through but him.

He says "When I come," he says, "in case the fox wants to eat
me, when I come to this place I'll get away," he says, "and no
matter what she does she'll fall into the trap," he says. "When
she comes after me," he says, "I'll come running and—whoosh!
—I'll go into my den and come out on the other side. And if she
is angry enough when she chases me, she'll go into the hole after
me for sure, and she'll get stuck there, for sure."

And so he came to the house of the fox, you know. "Good
morning."

"Good morning," the little foxes said.

"Is your mother home?"

"No, she isn't home."

He says, "Did you give her the message," he says, "that I left
with you?"

"Yes," he says, "we gave her the message."

"And what did she say?"

"Ah . . . she didn't tell us anything."

"Ah, *caray*," he says. "Do you mind giving her another message?"

"Let's see; tell us what it is."

"Tell her if she will do what we talked about yesterday."

"Aha!" she says. "You fine . . . rabbit! Scoundrel! I'll get you
this time!"

And the fox went after him. She had been hiding there, you
know, and suddenly she jumped Uncle Rabbit. Uncle Rabbit
shied sideways, and away he goes with the fox after him. Now
she's got him, and now she don't, and Uncle Rabbit runs along,
frisking and jumping. He got to his den and—whoosh!— in he
went and came out through the other hole, you know. And the
fox, since she was eager to eat him and angry besides, she went
into the hole too—whoosh! But since the hole was narrow, she
couldn't get through, and she was stuck there. So the rabbit went

around at once to where the fox was, and he mounted her. And he said to her, "You will! You will! You will!"

He began to have pleasure of her, and the fox would struggle, trying to get her head out of the hole. And the rabbit would slap her playfully. He says, "Ah, my love! How pretty you are!" he says. "I have wanted you so much and I never thought you would make my wishes come true," he says.

And the fox, she was furious, you know. She would struggle, but she was stuck fast, because she had been running so hard. So the little rabbit did what he wanted with her there; he forced her.

He says, "Phtt!" he says. "Now I'll get her out, so she won't die." And he began to scratch on the sides, you know. But he only loosened her up a bit, because if he took her out all the way, well, she was sure to eat the rabbit.

So *carabín carabado,* this tale is ended.

·25· *Good Is Repaid with Evil*

• I AM GOING to tell you a story about a man who went out looking for firewood. He went far away to a mountain with his burro looking for wood. When he got there he was very thirsty, so he went down into a ravine looking for water. He left his burro in the woods and went down to drink some water. Where the water came out, under a large rock, there was a huge snake. The snake says to him, "Take away the rock and free me, for I am dying," he says.

The man said, "But . . . uh . . . no, I won't because you will eat me."

"No, I won't eat you. Take it off because I can't stand it any more. I am dying."

So the man went over and took away the rock, and the snake was free. He came out of there. Then he says, "Now I am very hungry because I was caught under there for such a long time. Now I am going to eat you," says the snake to the man. Then the man says, "No, you shouldn't say that, because I helped you."

So he says, "Don't you know the saying that says, 'Good is repaid with evil'?"

"Ah, no, I do not know that saying," he says.

"Well, then, let's go. Let's go and ask some of those animals in the field over there. And if the animal says he does not know the saying, then I will not eat you. And if he says it is true, then I surely will eat you."

"All right, let us go," says the woodcutter. So they walked and walked far away to the field, where they saw a bony old horse.

They said to him, "Listen, do you know a saying that says, 'Good is repaid with evil'?"

"But why did you come and ask me that?" said the old horse.

"Well, because this has happened. This old man took me out from under a stone, and now I am very hungry and I want to eat him."

So the old horse said, "It's true that good is repaid with evil, because when I was young I served my master well, and he gave me much to eat. Because of me, my master made much money. But now I am old, and I can't work any more. So he brought me here and left me in this field, where I will die all alone. The vultures will eat me," says the old horse.

"What you say is true," says the snake. Then they went down the road again. "Let us go ask a couple more animals in the fields. If they say the same thing, then I really will eat you," the snake said.

They went down the road, walking and walking until they met an old ox, and the snake said again, "I came to ask you if you know the saying that says, 'Good is repaid with evil.'"

"What you say is indeed the truth," says the old ox, "because when I was strong I used to work hard. I plowed the land. That is to say, my master thought much of me because I was a good ox. But he doesn't have any use for me now. He says, 'Now this animal is old. Come on,' he says to those of his house, 'let us go and leave this animal in that field, where he can die all by himself, and the vultures will eat him, because he is of no use to us any more.' That is what my owner said the day he came and left me here. Now I am going to die here all alone, and the vultures will eat me, wretch that I am, because I am old. I can't plow any more. So what the saying says is true."

"All right, now," says the snake to the man. "We have to ask just one more animal, and if the animal says the saying is true, as two animals have said, then I really will eat you," says the snake to the old man.

They went down the road again, walking and walking. The man was very frightened now because the snake wanted to eat him. They came to a place where they met a fox. So the snake says to the fox, "Don't you know . . . I have come to ask you whether you know a saying that says, 'Good is repaid with evil.'"

"What do you mean? Why do you ask me that?" says the fox. He was angry. "No, that is not true," he says. "Where did you hear it said that good is repaid with evil? No, I really do not agree; it's a lie," says the fox.

"Ah! The poor man was happy because now the snake would not eat him.

"No," said the fox, "I cannot believe that; it is not good. Let this poor man go, this woodcutter. Let him go so he can gather his wood. Let him go. Don't believe that saying," says the fox. He gave the snake a good scolding.

So the man was saved, and then he said, "Thank you very much, you have saved me. Now let us do something. I'll go get my wood ready, and I'll go straight home. Then I will wait for you in such-and-such a place. Because I'm going home to see how many chickens I have. I'm going to give you all my chickens in payment for what you did for me," the man says to the fox.

"All right," says the poor fox, since he was very hungry. So the woodcutter went down the road to his house. But they had agreed on the place where they would meet so the fox could get all the chickens in the man's house. The man went to where his firewood was, and then he went home.

He says to his wife "Say, now, a big snake was going to eat me, but I was saved thanks to a fox. So I promised to give the fox all the chickens we have in the house," he says to his wife.

"Oh, you poor thing! What else can we do? Catch all those chickens and take them for the fox to eat. Where did you agree to meet?" she says.

"In such-and-such a place," he says.

Well, then, the day arrived. He took all the chickens and a turkey as well. He tied them all together at his house and put them all in a big sack, and he took them away to the place where he said he would meet the fox. He took the chickens, he was going to give them to the fox, all his chickens. He walked and walked until he passed in front of a *cantina*. Inside were his friends, drinking.

One of them said, "Come, friend, come. Come here and drink a little," he says.

"No, I won't drink, because I'm on an errand," says the man. He had the big sack of chickens on his shoulder and started to walk away.

"Come here, you foolish friend! Come!" he says to him. Well, they talked him into going in. "Come, friend, stay here a short while and have a little drink. Then you can go on," he says. The foolish people in the *cantina* talked him into going inside the house to drink a little. And he left outside there the big sack with the chickens.

He went in and, while he was drinking in there, it is said that a trickster picked up his sack. He felt the chickens inside. "Now, I'm going to look for a dog or two to put in here, and I'll take out the chickens the fox was going to eat." He opened the sack and took out the chickens, and he put a dog inside.

After a time the poor man came out, after he was done drinking. He came out and went down the road, after picking up his big sack of chickens—dogs—to go and give the fox. He thought he was carrying chickens. He arrived at the place where the fox was sitting, waiting to eat the chickens. But a dog was inside. Then he said, "Ready, now. Ready, now, because I'm going to open the big sack. Every time a chicken flies out grab it, each big chicken."

"All right," says the fox. The fox sat there waiting; he was very hungry. He sat there waiting for the sack to be opened so a chicken would fly out for him to catch and eat. When the man opened the sack, a dog jumped out. There really were no chickens in there. The dog chased the poor fox; he chased and chased the fox, on and on, until he ran him into the ravine where the man was almost killed by the snake. Then the fox thought, "So the saying is true that good is repaid with evil."

But it also happened to the man, just a little bit. The trickster found out there were chickens in the sack, and he took the chickens out. Anyway, the fox proved the truth of the saying that good is repaid with evil.

Thus ends the story. I don't know any more.

· 26 · *The Rabbit and the Coyote*

· A MAN AND A WOMAN had an onion patch, and a rabbit would come and tear it up. So the woman said, "You'd better go watch for that rabbit, or he's going to make an end of our onion patch."

The man went to watch for the rabbit, but he fell asleep, and the rabbit came into the patch and ate the onions. So the woman said, "Old man, you're not good for anything. I'll go, and you'll see how I catch him."

So the woman went. She made a doll out of wax and put it right in front of the opening, right in front of the place where the rabbit came in. Then she went off a ways and watched. The rabbit came and said, "Good evening, sir."

Nothing.

"Good evening. Get out of the way and let me pass. If you don't get out of the way, I'll slap your face." So he slapped its face, and his little hand stuck.

So then he said, "Let go of my hand, or I'll slap you with the other one."

And that one stuck, so then he said, "Let go of my two hands, or I'll kick you." He said, "I'm telling you to let go, or I'll kick you." And he kicked, and his foot stuck.

"Let go of my two hands and my foot, or I'll kick you again." And his other foot stuck.

"Let go of my four feet, or I'll bite you."

Nothing.

"I'm telling you to let go of my four feet, or I'll bite you." And he got stuck.

The old woman heard him, and she came out to see. And she said, "Now I got you, you good-for-nothing rabbit. You'll see what's going to happen to you." She picked him up, doll and all, and said to the old man, "You see, husband, I did catch him. Look at him."

"Ah, the good-for-nothing!" said the man. "I'll tie him up right away," he said, "so I can put a tub of water to boil, and then we'll scald him."

Just then a coyote passed by, and he said to the coyote, "Good morning, good coyote. Do you see that tub full of boiling water? They're going to kill a lot of chickens for me, and they want me to eat them all. Why don't you tie yourself up and let me loose," he said. "You're bigger than I am."

"Is that the truth? You're not lying to me?"

"No, I'm not lying to you," he said.

So the coyote said, "Good, tie me up. Let me untie you, and then you tie me up." So he untied the rabbit, and the rabbit tied him up.

And the rabbit said, "All right now. Feet, what are you for!"

"Wife, take a look outside at the rabbit. What if he got away from us."

The woman looked out, and she said, "Husband, husband! He isn't a rabbit anymore; he's a coyote now."

"More reason for scalding him. This is really bad." And no telling what else the man said. So then the man goes out, and the water was boiling. And he began to throw hot water and more hot water on the coyote. Until the coyote couldn't stand it any more; and no telling how he did it, but he managed to break the rope.

He said, "As soon as I find that good-for-nothing rabbit, I'll eat him." He said, "He won't get away from me," he said. Well, he found him way off, eating prickly pears, and he said, "Ah, you good-for-nothing rabbit! You won't get away this time. Just look how I am, all hairless and scalded. And all because of you. You lied to me."

"No, dear little coyote, don't hurt me, and I'll peel some prickly pears for you to eat."

"Is that the truth?"

"Yes, yes, I'll peel them for you," he said. And he got to work peeling prickly pears, and he also put in a few with thorns and all. Then he said, "All right, friend coyote, I think I'll go. I'm leaving you a great many prickly pears." The coyote ate until he got to the ones with thorns, and he stuck himself all over. He was very angry with the rabbit again, and he went after him once more.

After a while he found him very far away, and he said to him, "Now I got you, you good-for-nothing rabbit. You left me a lot of prickly pears with the thorns on, and I got stuck all over." And this and that and the other. . . . And that . . .

The rabbit said, "I'm here holding up this big rock," he said. "They're going to bring me my dinner here, a great big meal."

"No, I just don't believe you any more, rabbit. You're just a big liar."

"No, this is the truth," said the rabbit. "Why don't you take my place," he said, "and you'll see." So the coyote took his place and got stuck there holding up the rock.

After a while a fox went by, and the coyote said, "Dear little fox, help me hold up this rock."

"Who left you there?"

"Why, a rabbit."

"All right. You are there, you stay there." And, "Feet. . . ." The fox ran off and didn't help him.

He managed somehow to get out from under the rock, and he caught up with the rabbit. And the rabbit said, "No, dear little coyote, don't hurt me. Look. See this little stick? I'm a school-master, and these are my pupils. Be sure not to disturb them if I'm not here," he said. "They're going to pay me with a lot of chickens and other food, plenty of it. How can I eat it all? And if I don't eat it, they'll kill me."

"Well, I am hungry indeed," said the coyote.

"All right, why don't you stay here. And after a long while, one or two hours, you whip them. You whip them two or three times and tell them, 'Study, study.'"

The coyote was there for a long time, and nobody brought him chickens or food or anything else, and he said, "It's too quiet in there. I don't hear any sound." He put his ear to the hole and struck three times with his little stick. So out come all the wasps, and you should have seen them go at him. He rolled about in the dirt, and the wasps just. . . . Till he went and jumped into a lake.

He went along, and he went along, and he went along, until

he caught up with the rabbit again. And he said, "No, little rabbit, you've told me just too many lies. I won't believe you for anything."

"No, *hombre,* I swear this is the truth. A policeman just went by and said that anybody who relieves himself in the paths will be thrown in jail or killed."

"Oh, little rabbit! I just relieved myself right in the middle of the path."

"Well, go clean up." So the coyote went back, but no policeman or anybody came.

And then the rabbit got inside a cave, and the coyote came. From a distance he smelled him in the cave, and he went and knocked. But the rabbit kept quiet. Then he said, "Hello there, cave of mine." Nothing. Again, "Hello there, cave of mine. That's strange; when I call, my cave always answers." And he called again. And it answered. So he said, "What the devil! The rabbit's in there." And the coyote ran away.

He went away, and then the rabbit said, "What can I do to get rid of this coyote?" He went into a canebrake, and he cleared a spot very well, burned and cleared it all around, and the coyote found him there. The coyote said, "Now I got you, rabbit. This time you won't get away for anything at all." He said, "I'm going to eat you this time. What are you doing there?" He was always asking questions.

"I'm waiting for a wedding party. There's going to be a lot to eat, meat and plenty of everything. They'll have a lot of things."

"You're not lying to me, rabbit?"

"Of course not. When you hear the popping of the fireworks, you shut your eyes and dance and shout." That's because he meant to set fire to the cane all around, and it would pop.

"All right, but you'd better not be lying to me. I won't let you off again." Well, so the rabbit went off, but to set fire all around. The cane was thick, and it began to burn. And the coyote yelled and yelled and sang and sang, with his eyes shut. Then all of a sudden he felt the heat. Well, like it or not, he had to run through the fire. And he got out of it, anyway.

The rabbit was by the edge of a lake, looking at the moon on the water. The coyote came and said that now he had him and all

that, and just look, it had been a bunch of lies, there was a big
fire, and I don't know what.

"No, dear little coyote; it was the truth. I just don't know
what happened. Some accident, perhaps."

"And now, what are you doing there?" the coyote said.

He said, "You know what I'm doing? I'm looking at that
beautiful cheese in there. But I'm so little. If I go in after it, I'll
drown."

"Is it a cheese?" the coyote said.

"Yes, it is," he said, "of course."

So the coyote jumped in the lake. And the coyote said, "I can't
get to it."

"Dive deeper."

"I can't get to it."

"Dive deeper."

"I can't get to it."

"You'd better come out so I can tie a stone to you. Then, you
can go all the way to the bottom, and you will get to it."

So the coyote died there. The rabbit tied a stone to him, and he
went all the way down to the bottom. But he drowned and never
came out again.

And *colorín* so red, the story is finished.

• 27 • *The Lot of All Asses*

• THERE WAS a young burro, not yet grown, that was just being
trained. And the old man who was his owner gave him a beating. The old man beat him very much, and then he turned him
loose in the corral. And he met an old burro. He said, "What's
the matter, son?"

"Oh," he said, "they just gave me a bad beating." He said,
"How old do you have to be before they stop beating you?"

The old burro told him, "No-o-o, son. For us, in a burro's
life, there is nothing but beatings. From the day you are born
until the day you die."

He said, "But how can that be!"

"Yes," he said, "and just hope you're lucky, that they won't

make a bass drum out of you when you die. For then they'll
keep on beating you on Saturdays and Sundays, even after you
are dead."

·28· *A Rude Retort*

• IN A FIELD there were some animals going out to graze. A little
billy goat moved out ahead. He was walking along, a little billy
goat with a beard. A cow was walking along at a slow pace,
slow, but she caught up with him. And the little billy goat
walked faster so the cow would not pass him. The cow noticed it
and was looking at him out of the corner of her eye.

Finally she turns and says to him, "Mmmmmmm! Such a little
fellow, and he wears a beard!" She began to hurry; she walked
faster and left the little billy goat behind her.

The billy goat stared at her from behind, and he was angry,
because she had insulted him. So then he began to hurry. Faster
and faster. And he managed to catch up with the cow. And once
he was even with her he says, "And you! So big and you never
wipe your ass!"

Part III
Ordinary Folktales

· 29 · *Juan Oso*

• THIS WAS a woman and a man. The woman was named María, and she was very religious. She went to church all the time. Until once the priest lost sight of her, and she never went any more. No sign of her, so he went to see the man, and the woman was lost. He couldn't find her. So the priest said, "It must have been a lion that carried her off. No doubt about it." And so it was. They looked and looked for her, but they could never find her.

After a long time. . . . He would bring her mutton, and whole sheep. And after a long time she had a little boy by the bear. He was very little, and once he grew bigger the woman, when the bear brought her a big sheep, she tanned the hide very well and covered his nakedness with it. The bear went out, and the little boy, he was already about ten years old, he said, "I want to go out, too."

So she said, "Well, go on, but come back soon, before he comes."

So he went out and gathered a lot of mesquite beans and began to chew them. And he said, "I'll take some to mother to see if she likes them."

Well, he did take a lot of them, and the woman said, "Good Lord! What if the bear comes back and finds all this mess here? He's going to say," she said, "that you have been outside."

"And what of it?" he said. "It makes no difference at all. I'm going away anyhow. If you want to stay here, stay. But I'm going where your husband is."

So she said, "All right, if you are going, I'll go too. But I have great fear of the bear."

"He won't hurt you," he said. And then he began to chew the mesquite beans. Afterward he dug a hole and buried all the leavings, so the bear would not see them. He was coming with a little lamb to eat—raw and without any salt, but they ate it anyway.

Next day he went out again. And the little bear said, "Now's our chance. Do we do it, or don't we? Do we go, or do we stay?"

"No," said the woman, "if you go, I'll go, too." Well, so they went out, and the woman says, "All right, God will help us. Let's go." And they went.

They came to the *huisache* tree where she had been washing clothes, and the woman said, "Look, this is the place your father stole me from."

"Yes, he took you from here, but he won't do it again." He was a huge man. From the waist down he was a bear, and from here up he was a human.

So she went where her husband was. Very old-looking, very sad, since he had never heard from her. They had looked for her and never had been able to find her. He said, "Well, how did you come here, wife?"

She said, "I have a son who is half human and half bear."

The man was very frightened. And he said, "Well, where is he? Where did you leave him?"

"Over there where I was washing, I left him there. I came to see if you will take him, so I can bring him with me."

"Yes, I'll take him in, but I won't take care of him. I'm afraid of him. You'll have to take care of him yourself; he's yours. Well, go fetch him if you want to."

She went and fetched him, and you should have seen that man when he caught sight of him! Then the boy went out, and the man said, "You should talk to the teacher to see if he can go to school. To see if he can learn to talk the way people should. He's a little animal, the poor thing."

Well, all right. She went to the schoolmaster, and he said it was all right, that he would take him. And then, next day when he went to school, by that afternoon there were a lot of complaints about the boy. If he laid a hand on another boy he knocked him out. She said, "All right, then, I'll take him out of school."

So she took him out of school. He loved the food they cooked there. That's because he used to eat his meals raw and without any salt or anything. He didn't even know what salt was. So the man said, once when he was not around, "I think you ought to talk to the priest. Remember how much he thought of you. You used to go to church so much, and everything. Perhaps he can keep him over there."

She said, "Say, you're right. I hadn't thought of Father So-and-so." She went over to the church.

He was so happy. "And how are you, María? How did you manage to get back?"

"Well, do you know, I had a son by the bear, and. . . ."

"Is he all bear?"

"No," she said, "he's half bear and half human. But I put him in school and they couldn't stand him there, because he was a bad boy. For any little thing he would lay a hand on a boy, and —good-bye!"

"Bring him to me," he said. "Perhaps I can tame him. It may be that I can." Well, she brought him to the priest. The priest was frightened but, well . . . "I'll put up with him because of María," he said. "She's such a good woman. What else can I do?" So he took him in and gave him odd jobs to do.

He would give him money, and he kept saving it and saving it. Juan Oso [John the Bear] would say, "Give some of the money to my mother."

"All right, sure. I must give her some."

He was ten years old, and he was there with the priest until he was fifteen. So then Juan Oso said he didn't want to be there any more. He wanted to go away; he was tired with it all.

"You must tell your mother you're going. What am I going to say to her?"

"You tell her. I'm not telling her a thing."

"All right, if you want to go away, God bless you. But I wish you wouldn't. Because of your mother. . . ."

"That's all right. Mother will get used to it," he said.

"All right," he said. "I'm going to give you this much money, and this much I'll give to your mother so she can live on it for a while."

"No," he said, "I don't want any money. I want an iron staff weighing fifty pounds."

"Good Lord! What do you want such a thing for?"

"Don't worry, father; it will be useful to me in some way." So the priest had the iron bar made, and he left.

Later he saw the mother, and she asked about him. So the priest told her what had happened. And she said, "Well, it's all right. He was a big boy, after all. There was no way to make him stay here."

So the boy went away. And far, far away he found three companions of his own stripe, who were also leaving home. So they decided to go away together. So they traveled and traveled, day and night. One day they went by a place where there were many animals, even animals like himself. Animals of all kinds. They were quarreling over a dead cow. Some of them wanted this part of it; others wanted that. So Juan Oso said, "Good Lord, look at all the animals there. And we'll have to pass by that place; there's no other way. Well, let's go," he said. "We'll say hello to them and go past. Perhaps they won't harm us." So they came near, greeted each other, and they went by.

They had walked a good bit when the bear said, "Look, let's call that great big boy," he says, "and ask him to divide the cow for us. And whatever he gives us, we'll agree to take it."

They stopped, and Juan Oso said, "Good Lord, I wonder what all those animals want. Good Lord, man!"

"Don't worry, there's four of us. And we are all strong men."

"No, they don't really scare me. With this staff, I'll take on anybody."

Well, so they went back, and the bear said, "Good gentleman, we would like for you to do us a favor."

"I will if I can," he said. "What is the favor?"

"We would like for you to divide this cow among us all, and we'll all be satisfied."

So he began to cut up the meat and to give all of them a share. At last only the head remained, and the little ant kept saying, "How about me! How about me!"

He had not heard or seen her. Now he began to look around till he saw her. "Now, look," he said, "you are the little ant. But I have nothing left to give you except the head. Gnaw on it and get whatever flesh is left on it. And later you can use it for a house."

Then the animals said, "We didn't give the gentleman anything. We must give him something. Look how happy and friendly we are now, and we were getting ready to kill each other. He left us all content." So they called him back again, and he came.

He said, "Good Lord, I wonder what they want." So he came and said, "What is it that you wish?"

"We would like to give you something," they said. Almost all of them gave him a little claw, and the ant gave him one of her little legs. "All you have to do is say, 'God and ant,' and you can go anywhere," she says, "like an ant. And if people see you, they'll say, 'It's an ant.'" So then he put them all in a piece of paper and dropped it in his pocket. All the animals told him the same thing.

So they left and the others told him, "What do you want all that junk for?"

"Hmm. You think all this won't be useful to me? All this will be of help to me." So they left, and Juan said, "We'd better find work somewhere. What are we going to do without a job?" There was a very big farm where they were hiring workers. So Juan went and talked to the big chief there and asked him if he had jobs for him and his three companions.

"Sure," he said, "of course."

So then they said, "One of us will stay to cook and keep house, and the rest of us will go to work." So Pine-Tree-Puller stayed to take care of the house and cook the noon meal. He went around picking up and fixing the house until it was ten o'clock, and then he said, "By the time they come back, I'll have dinner ready." Well, when it was ten-thirty he started making dinner. "This way everything will be ready. Nothing but to heat things up. As soon as they come, they can eat." They were all very scared of Juan. So he did everything he was supposed to.

When it was twelve sharp, a black, black man appeared. It was the Devil. He came and threw all the food about and tore the tortillas to shreds, and he left everything in a mess. So here come the others, and they found nothing to eat.

"Well, what happened to you, Pine-Tree-Puller? Why didn't you cook dinner?" And all sorts of things like that.

"Why, no. A dog came and messed it all up, and I'm just about to do it all over again."

"All right," said Juan. He didn't say anything but "All right." They ate and went back to work. So he said, "Tomorrow the one to stay home will be the Man-with-the-Big-Moustaches."

And the Man-with-the-Big-Moustaches said, "All right, I'll stay. It's better than going to work."

Next day, the Man-with-the-Big-Moustaches stayed home. All morning he went around picking up and fixing the house and everything, and then he started making dinner. And just at twelve sharp, there comes our friend again. So then they came to eat, and there wasn't anything.

Juan said, "What happened to you? Did the same thing happen to you as to the other one? The dogs came and spilled the food? I think there's something wrong here," he said. "Tomorrow I'll stay home, and we'll see what we can find out about the dogs." Well, yes. That was the way it was. "You go on to work and I'll stay," he said.

So he stayed, and he finished his housework, too, and started making dinner. And then he said, "All right, now. Dinner is ready." Just then he saw the. . . .

"Aha! So you are the culprit!" And just as he grabbed the frying pan, Juan hit him with his staff and knocked off one of his ears.

"Give me back my ear."

"No, I won't give it back to you. I won't give it back till you help me out of all my troubles." And he didn't give him anything. He went away dripping blood. He was one of those who lived in the cave where they had the princesses. So the workers came home, and he said, "Come see if dinner is ready. I didn't have any trouble with dogs or cats or anything."

"Well and what about that blood?" said the others.

"Well, now, I don't know what it could be. I don't know, I don't know. Tomorrow one of you stays home, because I'm going out."

So one of them stayed, and he went out and followed the trickle of blood. Followed and followed it, till he saw a cave or something like that. On the way there, when he got tired, he would say, "God and hound, God and tiger, God and bear, God and lion." And when he said "eagle," he would fly. So to get to that place where the trickle of blood went, he said, "God and eagle." And he went and lit on a tree at about eleven-thirty. And at twelve the black man went in there. "There's something strange here," Juan said. "Tomorrow I'm going to a palace. I'll go and look for some woman there, and I'll ask her for a job. And she'll tell me what all this is about."

So he went back and the others said, "Where were you?"

"I don't have to account to anybody for what I do. No matter where I've been. You get to work, and that's all. Tomorrow I'm going out again."

"Whoo! You've taken a liking for going out."

"All right, if you don't like it, here's my staff," he said.

"Oh, no, we're all going to work now," the others said.

At dawn next morning he went to a palace and found . . . . Well, in palaces there are all sorts of places, including poor little houses. He found a woman who had some goats that were tended by a girl. He said to her, "Good morning, granny."

"Good morning, my son."

"What's new around here?"

"Nothing, my son. There's nothing new."

"I'm very hungry," he said. "Would you do me a favor and let me tend your goats, even if it is just for my meals," he said.

The old woman said, "I don't have the means, I'm very poor," the woman said. "We are all alone, me and my daughter."

"No matter," he said. "As long as you have tortillas, coffee, anything you can give me. And I'll take care of your goats."

"All right, you can take care of them," she said, "but please don't take them close to that lake over there." She told him there was plenty of grass and everything, but that nobody went there, because a boar would come out and carry them off.

He said, "All right, granny. Don't you worry. I'll take care of them as much as I can. And if something happens to them, you can do anything you want to me."

The little old woman said to herself, "I wonder what he wants that heavy staff for. Doesn't he get tired carrying it?" Whoo! He carried it as if it was a little toy.

So be began to tend the goats, and the girl became interested in him right away. She kept looking at him and at everything he did. But the first chance he got, he drove the goats right into the. . . . No, he didn't. He drove them right to the edge. And all of a sudden, he saw a boar. He said, "I wouldn't be surprised if this is the animal that eats the goats."

The girl said, "Mother, mother! The man drove the goats right to the lake where the boar is. We won't have a single one left." But no, he brought them back later to where the woman was. The boar never came out to hurt them. It just came near to where they were, around there. But it would look at him and didn't come any closer. It was afraid.

He penned up the goats and went back to the lady, the old woman, and he said, "Well, what's all this about? What is the meaning of that boar?"

"Well, it's a boar," she says, "that carries girls off to a cave. There are three beautiful princesses there. Especially the youngest one; she's very pretty," she said. "But, then, nobody is willing to fight it."

"Well, then, who is in there? What do you call them?"

"One is a bull, one is the Creature-with-Seven-Tongues, and the other is the Soulless Body."

"All right. And that Soulless Body. Why do they call it a Soulless Body?"

"Well, I don't know, child. But if you are brave and want to go to the cave, you can go."

He said, "No, not right now," he said. "I'm not about to go." He was pretending. "How could I ever go, when I'm scared to death of going?" He said, "No, not right now." He was pretending, to see what else he could get out of the old woman.

"Well, yes, child. There's nothing to tell except for that."

"But why do they call the one who is with the youngest princess a Soulless Body?"

"I don't know, my son. You'll have to go to the cave."

"Well, I may go, and I may not go. Who knows? If I feel like it, I'll go."

So the next day he says, "I'm going away now." They gave him some cheeses, and they gave him a kid. [So he went back] with the kid and the cheese and the boys said, "Well, you came back at last."

"Well, yes, I'm back, thank God. But I'm leaving again tomorrow."

"Listen, you don't do anything but go around all the time."

"All right. If you don't like it, why don't you go."

"No," they said, "we wouldn't think of going. We don't know anything about what's going on around here."

So he went off following a trail. Because the black man came again asking for his ear, and he told him he wouldn't give it back. After that he turned into an eagle and followed the man, followed and followed him until he went into the cave again. He said, "This is where the pretty girls are that the old woman talked about." And then he said, "God and hound." He became a hound instead of an eagle. He went this way and that, thinking, "How am I going to get in? Ah, the ant!"

He took the ant's leg and said, "God and ant." And he became an ant and went down and down and down into the cave. He came to where the eldest princess was. Of course, being the eldest, she was no spring chicken. He said, "Are you all alone here?"

"What are you doing here, sir? If my husband sees you, he'll kill you. He'll do this and that and the other."

"Who is your husband?" he said.

"A bull."

"That bull just makes me laugh," he said. "It won't do a thing to me. Are you all alone here?"

"No, we are three sisters. My father is in mourning and all. The city is very sad because they have never heard from us. You must know that there is a lake, and that there is a boar in that lake, and any girl that goes around there. . . . At first we didn't know about it either," she says, "and we went there, all three of us, and all three of us disappeared, and our father never had word from us or we from him," she said.

He thought, "This one is very homely, poor thing. I'm not going to court her." And he said, "Well, and your other sister, where is she?"

"She's somewhere else," she said. "In this same place but somewhere else."

"And who is her husband?"

"The Creature-with-Seven-Tongues."

So he went to her. The lady had a bad fright because at first, as an ant, she didn't see him, but suddenly he said, "God and man." She was very frightened and said that if they saw him they would eat him up, and that they would harm him.

"They won't hurt me," he said. "I'll take care of them before they can do anything to me. And who is your husband?"

"The Creature-with-Seven-Tongues."

He said, "Who else is there?"

"There's another girl, younger than me."

He didn't like the second one, either, so he said, "All right, I'll go see the youngest."

"Her husband is with her. He is called the Soulless Body."

"No matter. I have a body, too, and I also have a soul."

And he went to the youngest one. And the youngest one fell in love with him right away, and he with her. But the girl was terribly frightened when she saw the little ant. "Holy Mother," she said to herself, "there are never any ants here. How did this ant get in here?"

Before she knew it, the boy said, "God and man," and he became a man. Was she surprised when she saw him! She was frightened even more. And the Soulless Body was asleep there. He told her, "Don't be frightened, don't be frightened. I came to get all of you out of here. You'll see that I will get you out of here," he said, "you'll see. As for you, if you love me, you'll have to give me some tokens of your love." She had the crown she wore when she made Holy Communion, a little handkerchief, and a ring. And she gave him all this. He said, "Ask your husband why they call him the Soulless Body," he said. "Tomorrow I'll come back. Let me crawl on your hand so I can hear everything," he says.

"All right," she said. "Do I wait until you come to ask him?"

"Yes," he said, "wait until I come back. When I come back from over there, then you ask him."

So now she did look for the little ant. She saw the ant and put out her hand, and the ant climbed on it. "Make as if you were delousing him, or stroking his hair, and then you ask him, 'Listen, dear, why do they call you the Soulless Body?' And he'll tell you."

And he did. "Well, you are the first woman to ask me that question. I have had plenty of women here. They have died here and all that. But none of them ever asked me anything. And since you have asked me, I'm going to tell you about it." And he said, "Here's my body. My soul is in a boar. Kill the boar, and a hare comes out; kill the hare, and a dove comes out; kill the dove, and an egg comes out. By then I'll be very sick. With me at death's door, if they bring the egg and break it on my head, I'll turn up my toes and die."

So Juan said, "That's it." And out he goes. He said to the girl, "By tomorrow or the day after I'll be here again. I'll come and take all three of you away from here."

"It will be very difficult," said the girl, "for you to get us out of here."

"Yes, we will get you out, all three of you," he said. "I'll get you and your sisters out."

So he went back to the house; he went back to the woman with the goats once more. And this time he did drive them into the canebrake. The girl was very frightened. "Now he's done it, mother. Juan drove the goats into that thicket, and we won't have a single one left." And this and that.

"Just leave him alone, child. He knows what he's doing; I trust him. He said he'd take care of them, so it's all right."

So he sat down to watch the goats. And after a little while the huge animal came out. He just hauled back and hit it over the head with his iron staff. And the girl said, "Mother, mother! Juan has killed the boar." And this and that. Because the girl was in love with Juan.

"What a liar that girl is! Why, there has never been anybody who could stand up to that animal. Nobody has been able to."

"Well, he has killed it. It's down and kicking, and I don't know what."

But it wouldn't die, so he turned into a lion and tore it to pieces. And even then it wouldn't die, so he became a tiger, and then it was that the hare came out, running and running. With the eagle's talons and all, he tore it to pieces. And then a dove came out, so he still said, "God and eagle." He caught it that way. At first he couldn't catch it. So they flew and flew, and at last he caught it. All the while the girl was watching and telling what was happening. So then, when he caught the dove, the egg came out. The egg rolled and rolled. But he caught it without any trouble. Then the boy said—he was so tired he became human again—"I wish I had a *moca* full of corn and a girl's kiss." So the girl went and took him a drink and gave him the kiss.

Then the little old woman went to the boy, and he told her, "It's all right now, lady. You don't have to worry any more. You can put your goats in there any time, where they can eat well, and you can leave them there by themselves. There's no animal to bother them any more."

"Oh, how wonderful! How wonderful! What joy!" The woman patted him on the back, she was so happy he had done away with the animal. Before that they couldn't come near the place, either. If they came close it would grab them.

Juan said, "All right, now, it's time for me to go. I've done a good little job for you. I hope you remember me for many years."

"Of course, of course. Don't forget to come back." And this, that and the other.

So then he went where his friends were, but he didn't tell them anything. "I'm going out," he said.

"All right," they said, "go on. We'll be working."

He went away, and they went back to work. He went into the cave. It was easy for him now; he already knew how to go in and out. He went and hit the ox a blow that took off its horns. He went and killed the Creature-with-Seven-Tongues, and he took out its seven tongues and put them in his pocket. Then he went and killed the Soulless Body, he broke the egg on his head. He didn't take anything from him because there was nothing to take. But he had the girl's handkerchief, and the crown and the ring.

Well, so he went back to the house where the others were, his friends, and he said, "I'll be right back. I'm going to buy a rope, and then I want you to go with me."

"All right," said one of the others, "what do you want the rope for?"

"You'll know later," another one said. "What do you want to know now for? When we get there, we'll know."

He went and bought the rope and came back. He said, "All right, let's go." And they went. He was carrying his staff, he wouldn't let go of it for anything. And he said to the Man-with-the-Big-Moustaches, "Will you go down?"

"Yes," he said, "but if I shake the rope it means I'm afraid," said the Man-with-the-Big-Moustaches.

"All right," said Juan. "Don't worry. As soon as you shake the rope, "I'll pull you out."

He didn't go down this much before he shook the rope, and out he comes. Pine-Tree-Puller was next. He said to him, "Will you go down?"

"Yes, but just as far as I can make it, too. If I get scared, you pull me out." "Sure, just shake the rope, and I'll pull you out," he said.

So Pine-Tree-Puller went down. And soon he shook the rope. He was afraid, so he took him out. Next was the other one, Mountain-Smasher. "Will you go down?"

"Yes, I will. But I don't know how far I can go down before I get frightened. I'm not going all the way to. . . ."

"All right, it doesn't matter," Juan said. "The thing is to see if you want to go down." He was pretending. He knew what was down there better than anybody. So halfway down he shook the rope. And Juan said, "Well, now I'll go down. You put the rope around me, you tie the rope to me. It will be a heavy load because of the staff, but I won't let go of my staff. And the more I shake the rope, the more you let it down and down," said Juan.

"All right," they said. He gave the rope a good, good shake, and he went down and down and still down. And the others on top kept saying how deep it was, how deep it was, and how scary it was in there, and so on. "Juan isn't coming back," they would say. They said, "Well, it's his business. We're safe."

And then he sent up the eldest girl. One of them said, "This one is mine."

Then he sent up the second one and, "This other one is mine."

Then he sent up the youngest one. The third one of them wanted the youngest sister, but she wouldn't have him because she had plans of her own.

Juan said, "These so-and-sos," he says, "they are going to leave

me in the cave." He tied his staff to the rope and stepped aside.
"If it falls on me, it will kill me." Well, that is just what they
did. All they did was take out the last girl, so each had one.
There were three of them, and Juan was left. That was what he
got for all the work he did.

So they went off and took the girls to the king. And—ooh!
Good Lord! Meanwhile Juan was still down there, but then he
remembered. *"Hombre,* I've got my ear with me." He took it out
and bit it, and the black man appeared.

"What does my master desire?"

"For you to take me out of here. Hurry."

"Yes, right away. But you must give me my ear."

"Take me out first, and then I'll give you your ear." He took
him out, but he didn't give him the ear. He said, "This is fine,
thank you."

"Give me my ear, don't be mean."

"No," he said, "I'll give it back when I don't have any troubles.
You'll get it back." And he went to the city, too; he went to the
king's palace. Close by there, not quite at the entrance, there was
a man with a workshop or something like that. His wife saw
Juan coming, and you know how we women are.

The woman began, "Don't you allow that bum in here.
There's a very rough-looking man coming over there, and I
know how you are." Well, so the man got there, and the woman
went and hid. She didn't want to look at him; as soon as she
caught sight of him she disliked him.

"What can I do for you, sir?"

"Nothing," he said. "I've come to ask for a drink of water and
to ask you what's new in the palace."

"Whoo!" he says. "The palace is ready to burst with joy. Just
think, some girls that had been lost for about ten years were rescued by some gentlemen."

"Ha, yes? Some men rescued them. And what happened to the
gentlemen?"

"Why, the gentlemen are going to marry the two older ones,"
he says. "And one of them wants to marry the youngest one."

"And what's the matter with the youngest?" says Juan.

"Well, she says she wants her crown that she took with her

into the cave. They have given up bringing her all kinds of crowns, and none of them is like hers."

"Well," he said, "do you sell nuts?"

"Oh, yes," he said, "we sell a lot of them."

"All right, please sell me five or seven pounds and lend me a hammer."

"Yes sir, take this jar of water, and take the hammer and the nuts. There's a little room over there, where you can stay."

When he left, the wife came out. "What tricks is that dirty bum up to? As soon as I saw him, I disliked him," the woman said.

"Why, no," he said. "He was asking what was new around here, so I told him about the girls that just came back. And he says he'll make a crown for the girls." The truth is that he already had it with him.

"Fine chance that he'll make the crown! Nobody is going to like the crown he makes." And so on.

Well, you could hear the sound of the hammer all night, where he was cracking nuts. And the woman would wake up and say, "You see? He'll never make any crown. There he's been all night with his hammering, keeping people from their sleep, banging and banging away."

So then, early next morning Juan came and greeted the man, who was already up and everything. "Did you make the crown, señor?"

"Yes, of course. I did make it. Here it is. Will you take it to the king for me? I don't want to go."

"Well, no. I don't want to go either. To tell the truth, I never visit him. I'm very poor and all that."

"I'll give you twenty pesos if you'll go take it."

"Ah, well, yes. If you give me some money I'll go. Because I'm really broke."

"All right, I'll give you the twenty pesos."

He gave him the money, and he went. He knocked on the door, and the king came out. "What do you wish, señor?"

"I'm to give you this crown that somebody sent. To see if this is the one that belongs to the youngest girl."

He called the girl, and she came, and so she looked. "This is my crown," she said. "Who gave it to you? Where did you get hold of it?"

"Well, I don't know. It was there in my house. Who knows who might have brought it? I don't know."

"Well, I want to see the man who made it," she said.

He went and told Juan. "How did it go?" he said.

"Very well. The girl said it was her crown, and I don't know what."

"Just think, I made it just like hers. And what did she say?"

"She's calling for the man who made it. She wants to see him."

So Juan went to see the king and the girl. And, ooh! She threw her arms around him right away, and all that. The girl said, "This is the man who saved the lives of all three of us," she said. "I want to marry him. I don't love that other one, because I gave my word to this one."

"How are you going to prove all that?" said the king.

"Just look. One of them was living with an ox, the other with the Creature-with-Seven-Tongues, and the youngest with the Soulless Body."

"And how are you going to prove all that?" he said to Juan.

"Well, look," he said. "I have the proofs right here, from the girl, too. Look at this ring. Do you recognize it?"

"Yes, of course."

"All right," said Juan.

Well, the two who had married the other sisters, they let them be. But they tied the other one to some wild horses, and they tore him to pieces. They killed him.

· 30 · *Blancaflor*

· WELL, THIS is the way my story goes, for your good understanding and my poor telling of it: This was a man who was a magician. And there was another man who was extremely clever at playing cards. So once these two gentlemen met at a casino, and señor Don Juan, who was the magician, won from señor Don Pedro all the riches he had in his pockets. Once Don Pedro's money was gone, he asked señor Don Juan if he would play for a ring of his, and señor Don Juan won it from him. Then he wagered his tie pin, which he also lost, and so on until he had nothing left.

Then señor Don Juan said to him, "We could play for your life; I'll lend you something on your life."

So very well, since he had lost everything, he accepted the offer, and once again he had the misfortune of losing, and he lost his life so he put himself at the orders of señor Don Juan. Señor Don Juan told him he was not in any hurry, that he would have to go where he would tell him and come to his house when he wanted to. That is to say, the house of señor Don Juan. For this purpose he left him a horse and told him that this horse could take him without any other guide. And so they parted.

The magician Don Juan of course expected that the man would keep his promise, because there was no way he could get out of the bargain. And the other man felt as though he was being dragged by a force greater than himself toward the place where he had promised to go. So finally he mounted the horse and went where he had to go, and he left it to the will of the horse to take him wherever he wanted to take him. And quick as thought, between one moment and the next, he was at the house of señor Don Juan.

When he got to the house, señor Don Juan expressed some surprise, declaring that it was strange he should be so punctual in his obligations. Señor Don Juan had a daughter whose name was Blancaflor [White Flower]. So he ordered the girl to prepare Don Pedro's bedchamber, so he could rest after his long journey and so he would be ready, in the best condition to do his first tasks the following day. When the girl Blancaflor saw Don Pedro, who without a doubt was a handsome and agreeable young man, she was sorry for him and she told him what her father's intentions were concerning him, that he intended to kill him in one way or another, in some manner that would not appear to be a crime.

And then Blancaflor said to Don Pedro; "In the first test that my father wants to make, he will try to kill you when I bring you breakfast. It will be extremely hot, but possibly you won't feel the heat until you have eaten it. I'm going to give you this

powder for you to take when breakfast is brought to you. Then
my father is going to ask, 'Are you burning, señor Don Pedro?'
And you will answer, 'No, señor Don Juan. On the contrary, it
isn't hot enough for me.' "

Well, so this was the way it happened. Next morning when
Don Juan and Don Pedro sat down together again, he calls Blancaflor to prepare breakfast, and she brings it. They sit down to
breakfast, and señor Don Juan asks him if he isn't burning. And
he says, "No, sir; on the contrary, it isn't hot enough for me."

"Well, now!" he says. "It seems that you are somewhat clever."
Then he says, "Sir," he says, "the first task I am going to give
you in order for you to regain your liberty and your life is that
my grandparents dropped a ring in a certain part of the sea. And
I am going to give you the task of going and looking for it. And
you must bring it to me."

So then Blancaflor was waiting for him, and she says, "What
did my father order you to do?"

"Let me tell you," he says. "He wants me to get a ring that his
grandparents threw away, which they lost in the sea. 'I'll never
find it!'"

Blancaflor says, "Don't worry; I'll help you. Go on and wait
for me, and I'll turn into a mermaid to look for that ring, if it is
true that they lost it."

So it was that before Don Pedro knew it, the mermaid that
was Blancaflor came out of the waters of the sea with the ring
and brought it to him. When señor Don Pedro came to Don
Juan, it caused him even greater surprise, because two generations had passed, without a doubt—that is to say, that the ring
had been buried that long in the sea. And he repeated the same
words to him, that he was extremely clever. And Don Pedro said
to him that he was only carrying out his orders. Then he ordered
him to go and rest so he would be in the best condition the following day to do the next task.

The girl told him that every morning he would have to pass
the same test, that the chocolate was intended to burn him. So
Don Juan ordered the girl to make the chocolate even hotter that
day, to put more fire into it. But when he saw that Don Pedro
drank his chocolate easily and without a care in the world, Don
Juan asks him, "Are you burning, señor Don Pedro?"

He said, "No, señor Don Juan. On the contrary, it isn't hot
enough for me."

And he again repeated the phrase that he was extremely clever.
Then he says that he wanted him to build a palace in twenty-
four hours, that it should be ready by the next morning so they
could move into it from where they were living. That seemed to
Don Pedro completely impossible; he knew this was asking him
to do the impossible. But Blancaflor, who always waited for him,
says to him, "What did my father order you to do today?"

"Well, let me tell you," he says. "He wants me to construct a
palace for him in twenty-four hours, and if I don't, I must pay
with my life."

"Oh," she says, "don't worry," she says. "I'll help you." She
says, "Take this little wand and strike three times on the spot
where he told you to build the palace, and then some lackeys will
appear, and you can order them to do what my father said: I
want this done by such and such a time!"

So then those lackeys ordered their servants, and you should
have seen them bring up the building materials and open up the
foundations. And so it was that with some carrying and others
building, the palace was finished by dawn, just as señor Don
Juan had wanted. And so he passed that test, and Don Pedro was
quite satisfied with the way he had carried out the orders of Don
Juan. When he went to him and told him that everything was
ready, Don Juan again congratulated him with the same phrase
about his cleverness. He sent him away to rest. He says, "There
is only one task left for you. It will be the only one, the last one
you will do for me so you can return to your country, and it is
the simplest one."

Well, he retired to rest. Next morning he came back, and Don
Juan says, "Blancaflor, bring us breakfast." And he repeats the
same words to señor Don Pedro, if the chocolate did not burn
him.

And Don Pedro says to him again, "No, sir. No, señor Don
Juan; it isn't hot enough for me."

He says, "You are turning out to be cleverer than I am. Well,
as you know," he says, "the only thing I have left for you as a
task before you recover your liberty is a wild stallion that you
must tame for me. Once you leave this charger so that anyone

can mount him, you can have your liberty and return to your country."

So very well, Blancaflor was waiting for him once more and she asks, "What did my father order you to do today?"

"Today?" he says. "What he told me to do is very easy. He says I have to tame a stallion for him, and as soon as I break it then I can go back in complete liberty."

And she says to him, "Well, this is the most difficult thing."

"Why is it more difficult?"

She says, "Because, you'll see, the stallion will be my father. The saddle will be my mother. The saddle strings, skirts, and stirrups will be my sisters. And I am the bridle. What you have to do will be that I will make you a pair of rowels, a pair of spurs. I'm going to give you this whip, but try to use the wrong end of it," she says, "because it is weighted with lead on the other end. And all that I request you to do is that you should hold only to the bridle, and I'll help you. Whenever you can, strike the saddle, strike the skirts and the saddle strings with this quirt, with this metal end. And dig the spurs into the horse as much as you can, so you'll hurt him." Instead of spurs they were more like a pair of awls, something like that—thick, big, and long.

Well, so it was that señor Don Pedro mounted the pony when the hour arrived for him to confront it, and the pony tried to buck him off, but as soon as he put the spurs to it the horse felt, recognized, you know, the strength, the power of his hand which was greater than that of the horse. And the horse tried—it fought to throw him to the ground, to kill him without a doubt, to trample him, but the rider held on tightly to the bridle, you know. He held on to the bridle while he rained blows on the horse's head and on the saddle and, as Blancaflor had told him, on the skirts and saddle strings. In short, the horse was broken; it couldn't even move any more, and it was hurt all over. So then he ended the job and left the horse in the stables.

Then he returned to the palace of señor Don Juan, but señor Don Juan wasn't able to see him. He had left him a message, señor Don Juan, that when señor Don Pedro came back, to give him any horse he wanted out of the stables, and for him to take himself off, that he didn't want to see him. To tell him that he had gone out—that he had been to a bullfight the day before, and the beasts had broken out, the bulls, and that they had bruised him all over so he couldn't say goodbye, but that Don Pedro had kept his part of the bargain, and he could go.

So then Blancaflor says to him, "Look, this is what my father is going to do. My father is very badly hurt, but you should see my mother!" She says, "Her head is one mass of bruises."

He says, "Well, you told me to do it."

She says, "Yes, that was the only way you could master them." She says, "Now my father is going to make you a gift of one of his horses, and they will take you to the stables so you can choose the one you think is the best. There are some beautiful ones," she says, "and there are some bony ones," she says. "But there is one with the bones almost sticking out of his hide," she says. "That's the one you will choose. And the servants, the wranglers, are going to ask you why you are taking that one, because it's so poor it's going to die on you before you leave the house. And you will tell them you are afraid to call too much attention to yourself with one of the fine horses, that you might be held up on the road. But on that nag, well, nobody will pay any attention to you, and no one will harm you."

And it happened just as she said. When they took him to the stables, they took him where all the most beautiful horses were, but he couldn't find the one Blancaflor had told him about. So he kept on insisting that they show him all the stables, until he found that particular horse. So he told them, "This one."

The grooms said, "But sir, this horse isn't any good."

"Well, this is the one I want." So they went and told señor Don Juan that señor Don Pedro wanted the horse Pensamiento [Thought], for this was the horse's name. But since Don Pedro was so upset and hurt, he said to give him the horse and have him get out; he didn't want to see him any more. Well, very well, he agreed to give the horse Pensamiento to him, and señor Don Pedro accepted it because he had been told to select him.

And it happens that Blancaflor now says to him, "What we have to do now is not go to bed all night. We must fill up this glass with our spittle, because I am going away with you." And they tell that they spent the whole night spitting into the glass, until they filled it up with spittle, and in the dead of night they left; they fled.

But Blancaflor's mother, in spite of her pain, leaped out of bed all of a sudden, and she says to señor Don Juan, "*Tú, tú!*" she says. "What if Don Pedro carried off our daughter because you gave him the horse Pensamiento!"

So then señor Don Juan called her, "Blancaflor!"

And he was answered from her bedchamber, "Yes, father. Shall I serve you breakfast now?"

"No, child. Sleep, sleep." He says, "You see now. We shouldn't be disturbing our daughter."

But after a while the mother jumped up again and said to her husband once more, "*Tú, tú!* What if señor Don Pedro carried off our daughter because you gave him the horse Pensamiento!"

He called again, "Blancaflor!"

"Yes, father. Shall I serve you breakfast now?"

"No, child," he says. "Sleep, sleep."

Well, she kept on like that, you know. Frightened, worried because she had a premonition of something. And the spittle was drying up, so the voice was getting weaker and weaker, you know, every time it spoke. But still the wife says to the husband, "*Tú, tú!*" She says, "What if señor Don Pedro carried off our daughter because you gave him the horse Pensamiento!"

He says, "This is just too much! We are disturbing our daughter and keeping her from sleeping. If you bother me once more, I'm likely to beat you." But he called her anyway, "Blancaflor!"

It just barely answered, "Yes, father. Shall I serve you breakfast now?"

He says, "You see? My daughter is sleepy; we haven't let her sleep."

In the end the wife did not desist from her worry, and she braved her husband's anger once more; she brought up the same question, that possibly her daughter had been carried off. So then the husband . . . he beat her.

And he called Blancaflor, but nobody answered this time. Then señor Don Juan says, "It must be because our daughter is extremely sleepy, and she hasn't heard us this time."

Very well then, the matter rested. But as soon as it was dawn, the wife went to Blancaflor's bedchamber, and it was empty. There was nothing but the glass on the table. So she goes and tells him, "You foolish old man! Didn't I tell you that my daughter had gone, that she had been carried off?"

"But she was answering us!"

"That's because they did this," she says. "They left this liquid in this glass, and that is what was answering us. But well," she says, "go overtake them at once and bring my daughter back."

Well, so the husband turned into a bird, and he flew away. And there he goes! Then Blancaflor says to Don Pedro, "*Tú, tú,* she says, "my father is overtaking us. The only thing to do is, the horse Pensamiento and I will turn into a church, and you will be the bell ringer. My father will ask you if you have seen a young man and a girl of such and such a description, and for answer you will say only that this is the last one, that if he doesn't go in, he won't be able to hear mass."

And so, no sooner said than done. The gentleman got there, and Don Pedro was up in the bell tower. And he asked, "Bell ringer, bell ringer, have you seen a young man of such and such a description go by with a girl of such a description?"

And he kept on ringing, ding-dong, ding-dong. "This is the last one, sir. If you don't go in, you won't be able to hear mass today."

"I am asking you something."

"Yes sir, it's the last one. If you don't go in, you won't hear mass today."

He says, "This man is crazy." And he saw it was impossible to catch up with them, so he went back home. When he went back his wife asks him, "What happened? Didn't you catch up with them?"

"No," he says.

"What did you see?"

"Well, I asked about them of a bell ringer that was ringing the bells, and he told me that if I didn't go in, I wouldn't hear mass today."

She says, "It was them, you idiot." She says, "It was them." So then the wife turned into a heron. She says, "Now you'll see how I will catch them." And she went off after them.

After a while Blancaflor says to Don Pedro, "*Tú, tú,*" she says, "my mother is catching up with us. I'm going to throw my hair-brush at her." So then, when she threw the hairbrush down, it turned into mountains, you know, which grew higher the higher the heron flew. But at last the heron passed through the mountains.

Finally she said to him again, *"Tú, tú,* my mother is catching up with us. I have nothing left but my mirror, so I am going to throw the mirror at her," she said. "You and the horse Pensamiento will become a lake, and I will be a little fish."

Well yes, such a lake appeared all of a sudden. The heron arrived and lit on the lake, you know. And the little fish would go about while the heron tried to catch it. Until Blancaflor says, "Mother, you can see me, but you can not take me back."

Then the mother—the heron that was her mother—says, "Very well, daughter. But there is one thing I will tell you. When this man gets back to his homeland, if he allows any of his relatives to embrace him, he must forget you for at least seven years."

Well, so the heron turned back home—the mother. And so then they turned back into their usual shapes, and she says to Don Pedro, "Did you hear what my mother said?"

"No,"

"Well, she says that if you allow yourself to be embraced by any of your relatives the first time you go back home, then you'll forget me for seven years."

So they made up their minds to remember that warning and see that he was not embraced. When they got to the city where he lived, the one Don Pedro was a native of, he says to Blancaflor, "You wait for me here; I'm going to prepare things." He left her in the suburbs of the city because he was going to prepare a reception to greet her. And it is true that when he got home with his family, they tried to embrace him, and he told them not to, but he didn't tell them why. But he was so tired that he fell asleep, and one of his female relatives who had not greeted him as yet came and put her arms around him as he slept.

Meanwhile, they had prepared the festivities, you know, and the music to receive the new visitor, and when he woke up, they told him everything was ready. He says to them, "Everything is ready for what?"

Says, "Didn't you tell us you had brought a girl with you—your wife or companion?"

He says, "But I've never been away from here. How could I bring a wife home?"

"But it so happens that you told us to do this."

"You must have misunderstood me, or you may have imagined it. Because I have not gone out anywhere."

And so it happened as it had been told, for señor Don Pedro completely forgot about the girl. And when he did not return, then she knew exactly what had happened. Since she had infinite magic powers, she built herself a palace at the city's outskirts. And this began to excite the admiration of the people. There was all sorts of gossip as to the meaning of it and who it was, what kind of people resided in that palace. As the days and the months and the years passed, Blancaflor trained a pair of pigeons and taught them to talk. Then she began to tell the two little pigeons the whole story, just as I have been telling it to you. And at the end of the lesson to the two little pigeons, the hen was to say to the cock, "*Tú, tú,* do you remember what my mother told us, that if you let your relatives embrace you when you came home you would forget me for seven years?" Well, in short, she taught them, you know, the narrative about how the story that had occurred had happened.

Well, so a lot of interest was awakened by this enchanted princess, or whatever she was, since they didn't know what kind of personage she might be. So at one of the many times that an event of a social character was being celebrated at Don Pedro's house, they sent out invitations to all those people of the highest lineage. And among them they included that princess or unknown, exotic personage who lived so isolated over there. And she accepted the invitation, but on condition she was not separated from her pigeons, and she was granted permission to bring the pigeons with her. When they were at dessert in the feast, they demanded that someone tell a story, and since the princess Blancaflor had not said a word but had been completely, totally silent, they asked her to say something, because they were curious to know something about her past, what her life had been like.

So then she asked permission for the pigeons to speak in her place and narrate something of her past, of her history, because they really were herself; it was her voice that spoke in them. Then she would tell the little pigeons to tell something of her life since they had met Don Pedro, and they began to narrate it. The little hen began, *"Tú, tú,* do you remember when my father wanted to burn you with the chocolate, and someone told you what to say?"

"I don't remember," the little cock pigeon would say.

And the little hen reminded him of everything. "Do you remember the first task my father gave you, which was to get some rings his grandparents had dropped into the sea?"

"I don't remember," the little cock pigeon would say.

And she kept narrating the whole thing to the end, you know. She says, *"Tú, tú,"* she says, "Do you remember when my mother was catching up with us, that you and the horse Pensamiento became a lake and I a little fish and I told my mother that she could see me but she could not take me away?"

Then the little cock pigeon thought for a while, but he says, "I can't remember."

And the little hen pigeon says once more, *"Tú, tú,"* she says, "do you remember that when my mother said goodbye to me she threatened me that if you let your relatives embrace you when you came home I would be forgotten for seven years?"

Then Don Pedro remembered, you know. The little cock pigeon said, "Now I do remember."

And then Don Pedro jumped up and said, "This is the young lady, this is the girl I told you about a long time ago, that I had forgotten about."

This, then, is the way it happened. And so, once they had recognized each other they reorganized the festival and gave it greater luster. And they served new viands, you know, tasty dishes. And immediately Don Pedro and Blancaflor were installed in a palace, sitting on soft cushions and satisfying their stomachs with delicious tidbits. And while they are being nourished on these rare dishes and sleeping on feather beds, here we are sleeping on straw mats and eating beans and tortillas.

· 31 · *The Little Guava*

• THESE WERE two children, brother and sister, who had no mother; but they did have a stepmother. She was tired of the children, and one day she said to her husband, "See what you can do with your children, because I'm tired of them."

Next day at dawn the father said to the children, "Get ready, children; we are going out to chop wood." And the children got ready and went with their father. When they got to a mountain, he said to them, "Wait for me here, my dear children, and stay together. I'm going to see if I can find some wood around here." And he went away.

The children waited many hours; night came, and since the father did not return, the girl says to the boy, "Little brother, our father has left us here to get lost."

"Why, little sister?"

"Because it is already dark, and he hasn't come."

Then the boy said, "Little sister, let's go back the way he brought us here. I picked a guava and threw the peelings all along the way."

"Well, I put ashes in my coat and scattered them all along the way too."

"Well, let's see if we can find the house," the boy said. "We'll find it, little brother, because our house will be where the ashes and the guava peelings stop."

And they did just that. They walked and walked until they got to their house. Then the girl said, "Now let's climb into the attic so father won't see us."

It was very late at night when the father came back, and he asked for supper. When his wife took it to him, he said just before taking the first bite, "At this hour I used to have supper with my children."

When they heard this, the children answered, "Dear father, here we are."

"Children, how did you find the house?" The children told what they had done, and the father sent them to bed.

The stepmother said, "Well, your children have returned. You must choose between them and me."

The father said, "Tomorrow I'll take them out again."

Next morning he told them, "Children, get ready, because this time we are going for wood. I didn't get any last night." They went, and he took them to the mountain again and said the same words, "Wait here and stay close together."

Night came, and the father did not return. The girl said, "Little brother, now we really are lost."

"Why, little sister?"

"Because father hasn't come back, and it's already dark. Look, little brother, let's find some beehives. You crawl into one and I into another, and we'll spend the night so the wild beasts won't eat us, because there are a lot of them here." The brother, who was the smaller, did what he was told. They found some beehives and spent the night in them.

When it was morning, they took a road and walked a long while on it until they saw a little house, just a little hut. Soon they saw a little old woman who was making pancakes. The girl said, "Look, little brother. You are smaller, so creep up and when you see the little old woman put the pancakes in her little basket, creep up very carefully, take them out, and bring them here."

They did just that, and they divided the little pancakes between them. But the boy did it so many times that the old woman saw him and said, "No wonder I never finish cooking them, if you are eating them."

Then the girl came out and said, "Ma'am, we have been traveling for a long time; we have had no supper or breakfast."

"And why have you traveled for so long without eating?"

"Because our father abandoned us on the mountain," said the girl.

"Very well, come in and I'll give you something to eat." And so she did; she would feed them, sometimes good food and sometimes bad food. One night when the children were in their little room, a lady appeared to them and said, "Tomorrow I will prepare a little rat's tail for you and bring it to you."

The next day she appeared again and gave them the rat's tail, saying, "When someone comes and asks you to show your finger, show them the rat's tail."

Meanwhile the old woman of the house had called some hog buyers and offered them two very fat ones. But they wanted to see them first. They went and told the children to stick a finger through a crack, but they showed the little rat's tail instead. The buyers said, "How can we buy those hogs when they are so lean? Let them get fat, and we'll come back."

The old woman said, "I don't know why those hogs haven't fattened up. I feed them a lot. But anyway, come back in a few days."

So then she gave them a lot more to eat so they would get fat, but one night the lady appeared to them again and told them, "Tomorrow I will bring you a gift."

Next morning she came with a little jackass for the boy and a little jenny for the girl. Since the old woman wasn't up yet, she took them out to the plain and told them, "Each of you mount his donkey, and one of you go left, and the other one go right."

Now my tale is done, and yours has not begun.

• 32 • The Four Sisters

• THESE WERE four sisters, three of them very ugly and envious and another very pretty and good. She was being courted by a prince, so the three bad ones took the two lovers for a ride on a launch. When they came to a very wide place, they turned the boat over. He was drowned, and she reached an enchanted island.

There were many pretty things there, and an idol that was the god of the place. But there were no people. She was afraid and thought, "If I could find my sisters, I would turn them into bitches."

Immediately an angel appeared before her with three chained bitches, and he told her that she must whip each one of them twenty times a day, until the blood ran; or he would leave her there on that island where she would be sacrificed to the god she had already seen. She signed a paper in which she agreed to what the angel had told her, and she saw a launch coming, in which she returned to her country.

She found many treasures aboard, but she was sad because of her sisters. When she got to the palace, she saw three beautiful maidens and sent one of them out to buy what they needed for their dinner. It was a very heavy load, so she found a poor but handsome boy who helped her with it. When they got to the palace, he said he would like very much to go in and see the palace. She told him she would take him in, but he must tell no one about what he saw inside. He promised, and they went in.

He saw such delicious food that he asked for a bite, so they invited him to eat with them. They had a great feast. In the middle of it three very handsome young men arrived, and they also wanted to come in. They were allowed to do so; among them was the prince in disguise. They were very happy until it was twelve midnight. At that hour they brought in the three bitches and began to whip them.

The prince asked why they did that. He was told that it was not possible to give him an explanation, but he said he would be responsible for those three bitches. Then the angel appeared and told the whole story. The son of the king asked mercy for the three guilty ones, and they were told never to do evil things again. The angel said that in spite of everything, a sign must be left on their foreheads so they would be recognized. It was done, and the prince took them away.

• *33* • *The Bad Negress*

• THERE ONCE WAS a prince that married a princess who was very pretty, blonde, blue-eyed, and very good. But one morning she woke up with a whim; he must take her to live in a very leafy tree that grew by the edge of the river. He asks her anxiously how can she abandon her palace where she has everything she needs, but she just said she was tired of luxury, that she didn't want to live in the palace any more. Since he was so fond of her, he found it very hard to deny her that favor she asked of him.

He took her there. They carried her up to her throne, and he sat her there. Every morning he would go visit her to see how she had passed the night. She would say she was doing very well, that the air was very good for her, that the sunshine filtering through the leaves of the tree was good for her organism.

She had a maidservant, an ugly Negress with very kinky hair who was called the Negress Angola. And this Negress had come to hope she would marry the prince. An impossible thing. How could the prince take notice of such a horrible-looking woman?

So one day the Negress went for water. Then she saw the reflection of the princess on the water. And she said to it, "Oh! How pretty I am, and yet I must carry water! I think I'll break the jar and go sit in the drawing room." She thought it was her face that she saw on the water. The princess was watching her. After a while she said again, "How pretty I am, and here I am carrying water! I think I'll break the jar and go sit in the drawing room."

The princess broke out laughing and said to her, "But what is the matter with you, my good Negress?"

"Ah, mistress! So it was you? Well just look, I hadn't seen you." Then she said, "Now, don't you want me to delouse you? I guess that with all this time you have been up there you must have bred a little louse or two."

"No," she said. "I don't itch. I don't think any of those creatures has nested in my head."

The Negress left. She said, "Tomorrow I'll come and delouse you." Then she went away, and after that the sisters-in-law came to see her. They asked her how she had spent the night. She told them very well, quite content, she was as happy as she could be. Then they went to a garden to gather flowers.

The Negress came back for water, and then she said, "It's all right now, mistress. I came prepared this time; I have come to comb your hair. Look how the wind has blown your hair; I'm going to fix it." She went up.

But the Negress was a witch. So she took a poisoned pin and thrust it into the parting of her hair. The princess threw her hair back. She flew away.

When the prince came to greet his wife, imagine his surprise when he found her so frightful. He asked her, "But my love, what is the matter? Why are you so black?"

"Oh, my dear! Why, because of the sun."

"Why is your hair so kinky?"

"Oh, my darling! Because of the dew."

"Why are you so ugly?"

"Oh, my little one! Because of the air."

The prince went away feeling very downhearted, and he said, "Now, just look. I gave her what she wanted, hoping to keep my wife beautiful and happy. But well, I must accept the will of God."

And he went away very sad. When the prince left, his sisters came running up to him and told him, "Have you heard the news from the garden?"

"No. What has happened?"

"There's a little dove that goes about saying:

> The prince with his Negress on the throne.
> And I, poor little turtledove, in the
> fields alone.

"What? What was that?" said the prince.

"What you heard, man. That is what it says."

"What? What does it say?"

> The prince with his Negress on the throne.
> And I, poor little turtledove, in the
> fields alone.

"And why didn't you catch it?"

"No, no," she says. "It won't let us. It goes up very high and flies far away."

Then they sent for birdlime, and they smeared it on a tree. The little turtledove came, and it was caught fast. Then they got it.

Then the prince said, "Let's go show it to the princess."

"Yes, let's go."

They got there, and then they said to the princess, "Look what we found in the garden. A little dove that sings a very strange song. Watch now, let it sing."

Then the little dove said:

> The prince with his Negress on the throne.
> And I, poor little turtledove, in the
> fields alone.

Then the Negress, who knew quite well it was the princess, said to them, "Oh! Poor little dove! Turn it loose so it can fly away. Don't you see it must have a nest with little ones? Ah, how cruel you are? Poor little thing, it was enjoying such great liberty. Oh! You are going to torture it!"

"No, no. Look!" said one of the sisters. "Look! This little ornament is very curious. I'm going to take it off. Poor little thing! It's a thorn."

"Oh!" said the princess. "No, don't pull it out or she'll die."

But the sisters were full of curiosity, since all of us women suffer from that disease, and they took out the pin. Then the princess rose up before them. And then she told them what had happened, how the Negress came for water and said she was so pretty and here she was carrying water, that she would break the jar and go into the drawing room, and how she had laughed at the foolish thing.

Then the prince was so angry he sent for a pair of wild mules. He tied her feet to the tail of one mule and her head to the tail of the other and he let them loose in the fields. The mules ran and ran until the Negress was pulled to pieces, and that is what she got for going around telling lies. The princess was so frightened she went back to her palace and hasn't been out since, not even for a day in the country.

· 34 · *The Greenish Bird*

· THERE WERE three girls who were orphaned, and Luisa did much sewing. The other two said that they didn't like Luisa's kind of life. They would rather go to bars and such things. Well, that kind of women—gay women. So Luisa stayed home. She kept a jar of water on the window sill, and she sewed and sewed and sewed.

So then he came, the Greenish Bird that was an enchanted prince. And of course he liked Luisa a lot, so he would light there on the window sill and say, "Luisa, raise your eyes to mine, and your troubles will be over." But she wouldn't.

On another night he came and said, "Luisa, give me a drink of water from your little jar." But she wouldn't look to see if he was a bird or a man or anything. Except she didn't know whether he drank or not, but then she saw he was a man. She gave him some water. So then he came again and proposed to her, and they fell in love. And the bird would come inside; he would lie in her bed. There on the headboard. And he set up a garden for her, with many fruit trees and other things, and a messenger and a maid; so the girl was living in grand style.

What should happen but that her sisters found out. "Just look at Luisa, how high she has gone overnight. And us," she says, "just look at us the way we are. Let's spy on her and see who it is that goes in there." They went and spied on her and saw it was a bird, so they bought plenty of knives. And they put them on the window sill. When the little bird came out, he was wounded all over.

He said, "Luisa, if you want to follow me, I live in crystal towers on the plains of Merlin. I'm badly wounded," he said.

So she bought a pair of iron shoes, Luisa did, and she took some clothes with her—what she could carry walking—and a guitar she had. And she went off after him. She came to the house where the Sun's mother lived. She was a blonde, blonde old woman. Very ugly. So she got there and knocked on the door and it opened. The old woman said, "What are you doing here? If my son the Sun sees you, he'll devour you," she said.

"I'm searching for the Greenish Bird," she said.

"He was here. Look, he's badly wounded. He left a pool of blood there, and he just left a moment ago."

She said, "All right, then, I'm going."

"No," she said, "hide and let's see if my son can tell you something. He shines on all the world," she said.

So he came in, very angry:

> Whoo! Whoo!
> I smell human flesh. Whoo-whoo!
> If I can't have it, I'll eat you.

He said this to his mother.

"What do you want me to do, son? There's nobody here." Until she calmed him down and gave him food. Then she told him, little by little.

He said, "Where's the girl," he said. "Let her come out so I can see her." So Luisa came out and asked him about the Greenish Bird. He said, "Me, I don't know. I haven't heard of him. I don't know where to find him. I haven't seen anything like that, either. It could be that the Moon's mother, or the Moon herself, would know," he said.

Well then, "All right, I'm going now." Without tasting a bite of food. So then the Sun told her to eat first and then go. And so then they gave her something to eat, and she left.

All right, so she got to the house where the Moon's mother lived. And so, "What are you doing here? If my daughter the Moon sees you, she will devour you." And I don't know how many other things the old woman said to her.

"Well then, I'll go. I just wanted to ask her if she hadn't seen the Greenish Bird pass by here."

"He was here. Look, there's the blood; he's very badly wounded," she said.

All right, so she started to go away, but the Moon said, *"Hombre,* don't go. Come eat first, and then you can go." So they also gave her a bite to eat. As soon as they gave her something, she left. "Why don't you go where the mother of the Wind lives and wait for the Wind to come home? The Wind goes into every nook and cranny; there isn't a place he doesn't visit."

The mother of the Wind said, "All right," so she hid. She said,

"But you'll have to hide, because if my son the Wind sees you, Heaven help us."

"All right," she said.

The Wind came home, all vapory and very angry, and his mother told him to behave, to take a seat, to sit down and have something to eat. So he quieted down. And then the girl told him that she was looking for the Greenish Bird.

But no. "I can't tell you anything about that. I've never seen anything," he said.

Well, so the girl went out again, but they gave her breakfast first and all that. The thing is that by the time she did find out, she had worn out the iron shoes she was wearing. It happened that there was an old hermit way out there, who tended to all the birds. He would call them by blowing on a whistle, and they would all come, and all kinds of animals, too. So she went there, too. And he asked her what she was doing out there, in those lonely wilds, and this and that. So she told the hermit, "I'm in search of the Greenish Bird. Don't you know where he lives?"

"No," he said. "What I do know is that he was here. And he's badly wounded. But let me call my birds, and it may be that they know or have heard where he is, or something."

Well, no. All the birds were called, but the old eagle was missing. The old eagle was right in the middle of it, eating tripe. The prince was to be married, but he had prayed to God that he would get leprosy, something like sores, and he was ill with sores. He was hoping Luisa would get there. But they were getting ready to marry him. The bride was a princess and very rich, but even so he didn't love her. He wanted to wait for his Luisa. Well then, so the old eagle was missing. The old man, the hermit, began blowing and blowing on his whistle until she came.

"What do you want, *hombre?* There I was, peacefully eating tripe, and you have to carry on like that, with all that blowing."

"Wait, don't be mean," he said. "There's a poor girl here looking for the Greenish Bird. She says she's his sweetheart and is going to marry him."

"She's looking for the Greenish Bird? The Greenish Bird is about to get married. The only reason he hasn't married yet is that he's very sick of some sores. Hmm, yes. But the wedding feast is going on, and the bride's mother is there and everything. But, anyway, if she wants to go, it's all right. I just came from there. I was there eating tripe and guts and all that stuff they throw away. If she wants to go, all she has to do is butcher me a cow, and we'll go."

The girl heard, and she was very happy, even if he was getting married and all that. The hermit called her, and she came out, and she saw all kinds of birds. And he said, "The old eagle says that if you butcher a cow, she will take you all the way to the very palace."

All right, she said she would. For she had plenty of money with her. The bird had made her well off from the beginning. He would have married her then and there, if it hadn't been for those bratty sisters of hers. So all right, so they did go. She slaughtered the cow, and the eagle took her and the cow on her back. She would fly high, high, high; and then she would start coming down.

"Give me a leg," she would say. And she would eat the meat. That's why we say a person is "an old eagle" when they ask for meat. She would give her meat. And, "What do you see?"

"Nothing," she would say. "You can't see anything yet. It's a very pretty palace made of nothing but glass. It will shine in the sun," the eagle would say. "I don't see anything yet." And she would keep on going, straight, straight ahead, who knows how far. And then she would fly up, and up, and up.

"What do you see?"

"Well, something like a peak that shines. But it's very far away."

"Yes, it's very far."

So the cow was all eaten up, and still they didn't get there. And she said she wanted more meat. Luisa said, "Here, take the knife." She told the eagle that. "Cut off one of my legs, or I'll cut it off myself," Luisa told the eagle. But she didn't say it whole-heartedly, of course. Not a chance.

Anyway the eagle said, "No, no. I only said it to test you. I'm going to leave you just outside because there are many cops around—or something like that—guarding the doors. You ask permission to go in from one of them. Tell them to let the ladies know you are coming in to cook. Don't ask for anything else," she said. "Get a job as a cook and then, well, we'll see how things go for you."

All right, so she left Luisa just outside the yard. It was a great big yard made of pure gold or God knows what. As beautiful as could be. She asked the guard to let her in. "And what is your reason for going in? What are you going to do?"

She said, "Well, I'm very poor, and I've come from a long way off. And I'm looking for work. Anything I can do to eat, no matter if it is working in the kitchen." And her carrying a golden comb, and all that the Greenish Bird had given her. And the guitar.

"Let me go ask the mistress," he said, "to see if they want to hire some kitchen help." So he went and told her, "A woman is looking for work." And who knows what else.

"What kind of woman is she?"

"Well, she is like this, and this way, and that way."

"All right, tell her to come in, and have her go around that way, so she won't come in through here in the palace," she said. She didn't want her to go through the house.

So she went over there. And everybody was very kind to her. Meanwhile the Greenish Bird was a person now, but he was all leprous and very sick. There was a little old woman who had raised him. She was the one who took care of him. They had her there as a servant. First she had raised the boy, when she worked for his parents. Then she had moved over here, to the bride's house. She was no bride when the old woman first came there, but the girl had fallen in love with him. But he loved his Luisa.

And well, the wedding feast was in full swing, you might say, and he began to feel much better, for he heard a guitar being played, and he asked the old woman why they hadn't told him there were strangers in the house.

And when he heard the guitar, he told the woman who was taking care of him, who came to see him when he was sick, "Who is singing and playing the guitar?"

"Oh, I had forgotten to tell you. A lady came wearing a pair of worn-out iron shoes, and she also has a guitar and a comb."

"Is there anything on the comb?"

"Well, I don't know." She couldn't read any more than I can.

"I don't know what's on it. They look like little wreaths or letters or I don't know what."

"Ask her to lend it to you and bring it here." And once he heard about the guitar, once he heard the guitar playing and all, he began to get well. He got much better. But neither the mother and father of the girl nor anybody else came to see him there.

He was all alone with the woman who took care of him. Because he looked very ugly. But then the woman went and told the princess who was going to be his mother-in-law, "You should see how much better the prince is, the Greenish Bird. He is quite well now."

So they all came to see him. And that made him angrier yet, because they came to see him now that he was well. The girl was very rich and a princess and all that, and Luisa was a poor little thing. But he said, "Go ask her to lend you her comb and bring it to me."

The old woman went and asked for the comb as if she wanted to comb her hair, and she went back where he was. He didn't say anything; he just looked at it.

"What do you say?"

"No, nothing," he said. "Tomorrow, or this afternoon, when they bring me food, have her bring it to me. She's working here, after all," he said.

So when it was time to take him his dinner, she said, "Listen, Luisa, go take the prince his dinner. I'm very tired now. I'm getting old." Luisa didn't want to go; she was putting on. She hung back and she hung back, but at last she went.

Well, they greeted each other and saw each other and everything. And she said, "Well, so you are already engaged and are going to get married," Luisa said. "And one cannot refuse anything to kings and princes."

"But I have an idea, ever since I heard the guitar," said the boy.

"What is it?"

"Everybody is going to make chocolate, and the cup I drink, I'll marry the one who made it."

And she says, "But I don't even know how to make chocolate!"

The old woman said she would make it for her, the woman

who was taking care of him. Because Luisa went and told her about it. "Just imagine what the prince wants. For all of us to come in, cooks and no cooks and absolutely all the women here, princesses and all. And each one of us must make a cup of chocolate, and the cup he drinks, he'll marry the woman who made it." And she said, "I don't know how. . . ."

"Now, now," said the old woman, "don't worry about that. I'll make it for you. And you can take it to him."

Well, the first to come in were all the big shots, as is always the case. First the bride, then the mother-in-law, the father-in-law, sisters-in-law, and everybody. And all he said was, "I don't like it. I don't like it."

The mother-in-law said, "Now, I wonder who he wants to marry?" And, "I wonder who he wants to marry?"

Well . . . nobody. So then the old woman who took care of him came. Neither. Then the other cook went in. And Luisa was the last one. He told them that she was the one he wanted to marry. That she had come searching for him from very far away, and that he would marry her. And he drank all of Luisa's cup of chocolate. Bitter or not, he didn't care. And he married her. And *colorín* so red, the story is finished.

• 35 • The Horse of Seven Colors

• THIS WAS A WOMAN and her husband, and they had three sons, and they also had a fine field of wheat. Every night a horse would go there and do a lot of damage. The man would come home very angry. Until one of the brothers, the eldest, said, "Buy me a rope, father, and I'll go take care of your wheat so that animal won't eat it."

"What makes you think you can do anything about it, as lazy as you are?"

"I will, father; buy it for me."

Well, so the man was talked into it, and he bought him the rope, and the boy went. Next morning the man went out, and the boy still was fast asleep. And the horse had done plenty of damage. All he could eat, he ate, and all he could trample down,

he trampled. Well, the man got tired of waiting, and he went to
see the boy next morning. He was fast asleep. The man was very
angry, and he woke him up and ran him off, told him to go
away.

"All right, I'll go, but first I must go tell mother."

"You can go tell her, but it won't help you a bit. You're getting the devil out of here; I don't want you." The boy went to
the woman, and she cried a lot, but he had to leave anyway.

Next day the man went to see his wheat. He found it all torn
to pieces, in very bad shape. And the second oldest said, "Now
I'll go, father, and I'm sure I'll catch him. We already have the
rope, at least."

"Be quiet. Your big brother couldn't do anything about it, so
how could you."

"You'll see. I'll be the one to catch him." So the second oldest
boy went. He hid and waited for the horse. But he fell asleep,
and the horse came into the field again. And the farmer ran him
off, too. He went to the woman, and she cried a lot, and the man
said why did she cry. That if she loved him so much, she could
go with him. The boy said he would go. If they ran him off, he
would go.

So he went after his other brother, looking for him. After a
few days he found him. "What happened to you? Did father run
you off, too?"

"Yes," he said, "I fell asleep and didn't even know when the
horse came in or when he went out again or anything."

Meanwhile Juan del Dedo [John Finger, i.e. Thumbling] said,
"Buy me a rocking chair, a paper of pins, and a guitar." He was
the best one of the three. He was always good to his father and
his mother, so the man believed him and didn't get angry or anything. He bought him all he asked. He stuck the rocking chair
full of pins, all over, with the sharp ends pointing forward. He
bought him the guitar, and he bought him the rope. He already
had the rope.

So he began to play, any old way. He didn't even know how.
Just to pass the time. And if he moved this way he would get
stuck and if he moved that way he would get stuck, too, and he
would wake up. After a while the horse came into the corn. No,

it didn't come in. It was coming in right close to where he was. And he said, "Ah, you good-for-nothing horse! Because of you both my brothers were run off! But I'm going to catch you."

"Yes, Juan, I'm going to let you catch me. But don't hurt me. I'm going to give you plenty of money for your mother and father, for the wheat. By tomorrow morning, when you leave, you can take a *semita* [kind of bread] made from the wheat to your mother and father. Is it a bargain?"

"Yes," he said, "all right."

The horse gave him a little *morral* full of money, and the wheat bore a harvest, and it turned into bread, which he took to the old people, to the parents. So then the father and the mother loved him very much. But no, he said he was going, too.

The horse told him, "Well? What are you going to do?"

"I'm going after my brothers."

"Your brothers will cause you much harm. But if you ever need anything, just call me. I'll save you from all the troubles your brothers will cause you."

Time went by. It took him almost a month to find them. But before that, the horse had given him some money, a magic towel, and a wand.

The oldest brother said, because he had been looking about on all sides, "Look, there comes that other one. I bet you he's been chased out, too. As soon as he gets here, I'm going to make him go for some water out of that well. I'm very thirsty."

The second brother said, *"Hombre,* how can you ask him to go down for water in that well? He can't do it; he'll drown."

"No matter." In those days they wore pieces of cloth tied around their waists. "We'll make a rope out of these cloths we're wearing."

"And what will he get the water in?"

"He can use his hat," he said. And as soon as he got there, he told him, "What happened to you? Did they run you off?"

"Yes," he said. He didn't tell them anything. "Yes, they did run me off the place just like you."

"All right, but we are very thirsty. Go down into the well and get us some water."

"But how can you ask me to go down in there? I can't do that. How will I go down?"

"We'll make a rope of the sashes we're wearing." So they made a rope and let him down. He did a good job of getting them the water, and he kept going up and down. And after they drank all the water they wanted, they cut the rope.

But the horse was close by. "I don't know whether to call the horse or not. God knows." Well, he struggled for a while, and then he said, "Little horse of seven colors, if I could see you, I would call you."

And the horse came at once. "What happened to you?" he said.

"Well, you see. The rope broke when I was getting water, and I fell in."

"Oh, no," he said, "don't lie to me. It was your brothers that cut the rope. I tell you that your brothers are not going to give you any peace. But all right," he said. He let down his tail and said, "Grab hold of my tail and close your eyes."

So he grabbed hold of the tail, and he got out. Then the horse said, "Where are you going?"

"I'm going after my brothers."

"How stubborn you are! Look, they're going to make you go to some houses far away to get them something to eat. And on top of that, they're going to build a fire, and they'll throw you in it. But it's all right," he said. "I'll save you from everything. Just so you won't believe I'm telling you lies. And you are going after your brothers?"

"Yes, I am."

"All right, go ahead."

After many days, they looked back, and he said, "Look, there he comes. I'm beginning to think he knows a few tricks," said the oldest.

"He wouldn't know anything like that," the other one said. "God knows how the poor fellow managed to get out of that hole you put him in. Poor thing. He wants to travel with us, and you do evil things to him."

"Just wait and see. I just noticed some houses very, very far away. And some thick woods," he said. "As soon as he gets here, I'm going to make him go ask for food at those houses."

"That's terrible. It's a long way off."

"Well, then, you go," he said. "If you don't want him to go, you go." They were afraid of the oldest. So the other one didn't say anything else.

Juan came closer and closer, and as soon as he was there his brother said, "Look, you see those houses? Go there and bring me some food."

He went a short distance, at a slow walk, and then he went into the woods. He stayed there for a good while. Until he figured he had taken enough time to get there.

Then he took out his wand and said, "Magic wand, by the power you have and by the power God gave you, get me plenty of food." Rice, beans, and all that; coffee and tortillas. All those things to eat. But he stayed there a while longer and worked up a sweat and everything, so they would think he had gone all the way. He didn't tell them about the wand or the towel. It was the towel that had magic powers. The wand was for something else.

He got there all covered with sweat. "Look," he said. "Poor Juan. See how he is, all wet with sweat," said the second brother.

"Yes, I see. What do I care? I'm hungry. Perhaps you don't like eating." All three of them sat down and ate. When they finished, they put everything away.

Then the oldest said, "Now go and gather plenty of firewood."

"What do you want firewood for?" said the second brother.

"You shut up and get me the wood," he said. They gathered plenty of wood, and he set fire to it. And when he saw the fire was going well, he took Juan and threw him in.

So there comes the little horse, before Juan could call for him. He came and took him out. "See what I tell you? Your brothers wish you evil. Now, what are you going to do?"

"I'm going after them."

"You just won't listen. You're very stubborn. See what has happened to you," he said.

Well, so after many days, he caught up with them again. He said, "Look, there he comes. I tell you he knows some tricks."

"How would he know anything like that?" he said.

"All right, let's go to the house of some king, and find one of the poorest villagers there. We'll ask for lodging there for a few days."

"All right," he said. So all three of them went there.

They came to an old woman's house. "How are you, granny?"

"Very well, my children. Where are you from?"

"From a long ways off. Will you give us lodging here?"

"Yes, of course," she said.

"And we're going to give you this boy." His age was that of a big boy, but he was as big as a finger. He said, "We're going to give you this boy. Don't you want him?"

"Yes, of course. I can use him to carry water for me, and wood, and. . . ."

"What's new around here, granny? Are there any jobs?"

"The only one who could give you work is the king. As for news, there's a platform with a princess on it, and whoever can hit her on the breast with a golden apple, or one of those for eating, can marry her."

"No matter who he is, granny?"

"Yes," she said, "no matter who he is. A prince, a poor man, a rich man. The one who hits her on the breast marries her."

Well, so it got dark, and the two of them went. "You stay here," said the oldest boy to Juan del Dedo. So he stayed with the old woman, the lady.

They came back that night about ten or eleven. "How did you make out, my children?"

"Not very well," he said. "We just went to look. There were many men throwing shiny apples at her, but they couldn't hit her. Such beautiful horses!"

During the day the boy carried a lot of water and wood. And that night the two older boys went to see the princess again. Just to look at her. They couldn't do much on foot. It got dark, and the boy said, "Will you let me go, granny, where the boys went?"

"You know what they told me, child, not to let you go out. What if they see you?"

"I won't let anybody see me, granny. I'll stay out of sight at the edge of the crowd."

"All right, go then. But come home early, before they get back," she said. So he went, and he saw his brothers there, but they didn't see him because he kept out of sight.

So he went. And the horse appeared. "Listen, Juan, what do you think? Would you like to hit the princess on the breast?"

"Yes, I would like that, but how can I do it?" he said. Because there were many policemen all around to keep anybody who hit her from leaving.

The horse said, "No, we'll go tonight, and they won't stop you. Just lean over and turn a little peg I have close to my ear," he said, "and we'll fly over policemen and everything."

"All right," he said.

Afterward, just before he went home, he asked the magic towel for things to take the old woman . . . fruits and little junk like that. The woman was startled and said, "Listen, child, where did you get all this? Who gave it to you?"

"Ooh, granny! You should have seen how many friends I made," he says. "They all gave me things, and I couldn't eat any more, so I said, 'I'm going to take granny some.'"

"Well, how nice, child. Now go to bed before your brothers come."

He went to bed, and the brothers came. And they said to the old woman, "Just think, the most beautiful horse came in there . . . Jesus!"

Oh, no. He didn't go to bed. He stayed there, and the brothers came. He was there with the woman when the brothers came. She said, "How did things go, child?"

"Very well, granny. Just imagine, a boy came in there on a very strange horse, with many colors. He had three shiny apples with him. He hit the princess with all three. And neither the police nor anybody else knew how the horse disappeared after that."

Then Juan said, "Could it have been me?" And bang! They slapped his face. So he went to his room crying, and he went to sleep.

Next morning the woman told him not to be a fool, not to go around saying things like that. Why did he say such things? And he said, "All right."

That day the brothers stayed at the old woman's house all day.

As soon as it got dark, they went over there again. And after a while, Juan went. And the horse appeared. "What do you say, Juan? Will you let them catch you this time?"

"Hombre, she's a very pretty girl," he says. "And she will marry anyone," he says. Well, so he asked the wand again for a very showy suit, and a tie. Well, many things. And the golden apples. And a saddle all silvered over with gold. All the fittings on it were pure gold. And a hat and everything. His brothers didn't recognize him. He went in. And he went in, and he hit her. With the help of the pinto pony, of course. And this time the horse did let them catch him.

The horse said, "They can catch me, but don't let them put me in a stall or anything like that. Tell them you will go later to take care of me because your horse will not let anybody touch him but you. And I'll go away by myself." And he said, "Don't think I'm going far. I'll be watching after you," he said. So the horse went away by himself, and he stayed.

The brothers came back and thought Juan was in bed. They didn't look for him because they didn't think much of him. "How did things go with you, child?"

"Go on, granny, this time the boy let them catch him," he said. "He's so pleasant and handsome." They didn't know who he was. "And the apples, they were so pretty."

"That's because they are made of gold, child," the woman said.

So next day there was no Juan. The old woman began to sniffle; she had got to like him. But the brothers didn't care. They couldn't find Juan, and they couldn't find him. They went to the palace to look, but there was no sign of him. Much later, after some days, almost a month, the princess and the boy came out on the balcony.

The oldest said, "Look where Juan is," he said. "We'll have to do him some harm. Tomorrow we'll go to the king, and we'll tell him this and that."

"What for? Leave him alone," the second oldest said.

"No," he said, "because then I'll take it out on you." So the second oldest kept quiet.

Next day they both went, but it was the oldest who did the talking. He knocked on the door of the king's house, and the king came out and said, "What does my master command?"

"*Sacarreal majestá*, I've come to tell you that your son-in-law has been saying he can bring you the puppets you used to play with when you were little."

"All right, let my son-in-law come here." So he sent for him.

And he says, "I didn't say any such thing."

"All right," he said, "I give you three days. If you don't do it in three days, you forfeit your life."

Well, so there he was. Very worried. And the princess going this way and that. And Juan didn't know what to do, for three days was such a short time. And he thought the horse was tired of doing things for him. He didn't want to bother him any more. But no, he did go toward the stables, and the horse came. "What's the matter, Juan? Why are you so sad?" the horse knew but pretended he didn't. "What happened to you?"

"Well, just think, my brothers said this and this."

"I tell you, but you won't listen," he says. "But come on. Don't worry," he said. "Let's go to the seashore, and you take a guitar and a loaf of bread. You sit away from the water's edge. A whale is going to come out, and in the whale is the box with the puppets the king used to play with when he was little."

So they went there, him and the horse; the horse hid. The whale came out, and Juan began to play and play. He sang and sang and threw bits of bread and more bits of bread. The whale came closer, but it was afraid. The horse said, "If I come out, I'll scare the animal off."

But no, luckily the whale decided to come all the way out. Then the horse told the boy to cut its belly open, and later he could fill it full of sand and sew it up and throw it in the sea. So he caught it and slit its belly open, and he took out the box with the puppets.

"All right, let's go so you can take them to the king. But you're not through," the horse said. "You troubles are not over."

Well, so he went, and the king was extremely happy. Once when he was little, they had taken him to the seashore, and he was carrying that little box. Then the whale came and. . . . The king was very happy. For the little animals in the box were something really fine.

Well, so they gave him about a month. Because they didn't sit out on the balcony or anything. After a month or two the princess asked him to sit out on the balcony. And those two were out walking. Just looking. And they saw him. So again. They went to do him harm. They went and told the king, "*Sacarreal majestá,* your son-in-law has been saying he can go and bring you the greenish bird that is by the sea."

So there goes Juan again. And again, "I didn't say any such thing. I didn't say any such thing."

But, "No matter. You have three days."

So there comes the horse. And he told the horse what had happened. "I know all about it," the horse said. "That's why I came to see you. Don't worry. Come along," he said.

When they came to the edge of the sea, the horse said, "Over there by the shore there's a Negro and a giant. When the Negro's eyes are closed, he is asleep. And when the giant's eyes are open, he is asleep." That is because giants sleep with their eyes open, they say. "And there are many cages, of all colors and kinds. But you must bring back the raggedest bird there is. And the oldest cage."

There were some cages made of pure gold. Good heavens! They were so beautiful! But then he said, 'I'd better take the one the horse told me to take because. . . ."

"Because if you take another one, the other birds will make noise, and you'll be lucky if you're not killed." Well, so he took the shabby one.

"Which one did you bring?" said the horse.

"The oldest one. There were some that were so beautiful!"

"I was afraid you might take one of those," the prince said to Juan. The horse was a prince.

So then the horse said to Juan, "No, Juan. If you can't bring yourself to do evil to your brothers, at least you must go complain to the king and tell him what they have said," he said.

"Well, I'd rather not."

"You'll have to. Because this was the last thing I'm doing for you. Now I'm going to be disenchanted. I'm going to turn into a man like you. I won't be able to do any more," said the horse.

Well, he made up his mind. And he said, "What do I have to tell the king?"

"Tell him your brothers have been saying they can put out a burning house full of gunpowder just shouting and waving their hats."

He went and told the king. And the king called them. They said they hadn't said any such thing. They hadn't said any such thing. But the king said, "Yes, you said it, and I'm giving you three days." Then he said, "No, I won't even wait three days. Shut them up in a house full of gunpowder."

Afterward Juan was very sad. He looked as if he was going to cry and all that. And after all the fire from the gunpowder was out, he asked the king if he could please gather up all his brothers' little bones. The king told him why he had never said they were his brothers. He would have given them some other kind of punishment instead of killing them.

The gentleman who had been a horse and had turned into a prince was quite satisfied. He told the boy to go see his father and his mother. Over where they were. They went armed, and they took plenty of food. Because it was very far. And they took a lot of money, of course. The princess and Juan and the other prince that used to be a horse all went. And they found them still alive but very old. They kept asking about their other sons, but all they said was, "No, I don't know what happened to them." The prince had told him not to tell them what had happened to his brothers. Or to the prince. He said he had taken one road and they another, and he didn't know what became of them.

They tried to take the old people with them, but they wouldn't come. So they built them a new house that was almost a palace. The old people wanted them to stay. "No," says Juan, "I can't stay because the princess has her parents over there."

And that's all there is.

· 36 ·   The Poor Woodcutter

· HERE IS ANOTHER TALE. Anacia Ventura was the boy's name. He was an orphan. He went into the forest to chop wood.

One day he heard the cry of an animal. It was crying and crying out there in the forest. He thought, "What could be wrong with that animal? I'm going to see what's the matter with it."

And he went. When he got there, he saw that a serpent had caught a deer. It was the deer that kept crying out. So then he came close. He saw the serpent had seven heads. It was trying to bite the deer, but it could not manage to kill the deer, because its mouths were too small.

Then Anacia said: "Poor little animal! How can you get anything to eat like that? I'm going to help you."

So then he killed the deer and cut it up in nice little pieces. Piece by little piece, he fed it into each little mouth, until the deer was all gone. Nothing was left but a pile of bones and the head.

Then the serpent said: "Thank you very much for feeding me. Now come with me. I'm going to take you to my father's house."

So they went. She took him where her father was. But she changed shape. She no longer was a serpent but a very beautiful woman. When they got to the house, she said to her father, "Father, I've brought a boy here with me. He helped me very much. I wanted to eat a deer very much. I caught it, but I couldn't kill it. He killed it for me and fed it to me very nicely. I'm full now."

"How good, daughter. Now, what are we going to do with him? Let's give him livestock."

"No, father."

"Then we'll give him money."

"No, father."

"Then, what are we going to give him?"

"Father, give him what you have in your pocket."

"No, daughter. What would I do then?"

"That is what you are going to give him, father. You can get another one for yourself."

So he took a little round mirror from his pocket. And he said, "This is going to be useful to you. Just handle it like this. Move it around like this. [Informant gestures: right to left and left to right at shoulder height and very close to the body.] Then you command, 'Bring me money, bring me food,' or anything else. 'Do this.' That is what you will say."

"Very well, señor." And Anacia went home. He stopped working. All he had to do was move the mirror like this and command. "Bring me food, bring me money."

One day he said to his mother, "Mother, I want to marry the king's daughter."

"You do, my son?"

"Yes, mother. I want you to go to the king with a marriage offer."

"Very well, my son." And she went to where the king was.

"Lord king, here I am. My son wants to marry your daughter."

"He does?"

"Yes, lord king."

"Well, all right. I have heard he's very clever. Let's see. Let him come and work for a while. Then he can marry my daughter."

Then the woman went home and told her son. So Anacia went to work at the king's house. The first task the king gave him, he gave him full sacks, all mixed up, of beans, corn, and pumpkin seeds. Three, four sacks he gave him, and he said, "You are going to put all of this, each in its own sack. You will work one night. Tomorrow you must have for me each of these sacks, beans and corn and pumpkin seeds." And he gave him plenty of candles, so he could work all night.

So then, when the king was gone, Anacia took out his mirror. He commanded, "Sort all of this out, pile by pile." The ants were the ones who helped him. They made separate piles of beans, corn, and pumpkin seeds. The work took only an hour. Then he lay down to sleep.

Next day, the king came. "Wake up! Get up! Have you done your work?"

"Yes, there it is, sack by sack."

"Well, you are really clever. Today you are going out to clear some ground for planting. You will work for three days. I want to plant three, four hundred pounds of grain. Let's see how much grain I will plant."

He worked just one day. The king planted four hundred pounds of grain.

Then the king said, "Now we'll see whether you really are clever. You are going to sleep with my daughter. And by about midnight, she must bear a child."

"All right," said Anacia, and the king went away.

Then Anacia thought, "Who can help me now!" He took out his mirror, and he called the *tsox,* that bird that brings the babies. About four in the morning, the *tsox* brought the babies. There they were, crying, and the king woke up. And there you have the king, taking care of the babies and changing their diapers.

Next day he said, "Truly you are very clever! You are going to marry my daughter right now!"

· 37 · The Louse Skin

• It so happens that there was a woman who had a husband, and this man spent his time cutting wood to make a living. With the coming and going of time, the man got tired of the work he did, and he said to his wife, "Look, wife, I'm going out to seek my fortune, because I'm tired of the kind of work I do. It's a very dull job, and I don't want to do it any more. I want you to fix me some provisions so I can eat on the road."

So the boy went away. On the road he met a little mouse, and the little mouse said to him, "Good friend, where are you going?"

"Friend," he says, "I'm going to seek my fortune."

"Look," he says, "don't you want to take me with you?"

"No, little mouse," says, "because you are very mischievous."

"No, good man," he says, "I promise to behave."

"All right, if that's the case," he says, "I'll travel with you. I'll take you with me." The man picked up the little mouse and took him along. He put him away in his pocket. Farther on he met a dungbeetle. The dungbeetle was going along, rolling his little ball of dung.

And he said, "Good man," he says, "where are you going?"

"I'm going to seek my fortune, good dungbeetle, because at home," he says, "I got tired of working. I'm going out to see what fate has in store for me."

The dungbeetle says, "I'll go with you," he says, "if you will take me."

"No–o, good dungbeetle," he says, "because you are very filthy."

"Look," he says, "if you take me with you I'll be very clean while I'm with you. I'll go," he says, "and take a bath somewhere and I'll go with you nice and clean."

"All right, if that's the case, let's go." He picked the dungbeetle up and wrapped him in a piece of cloth and took him along. Farther on he found a little puddle. He bathed his beetle, and they all went to a kingdom where there was a king who riddled— who had a riddle. There was a sign that said, "Whoever guesses what kind of skin my daughter's shoes are made of, he will be master of my kingdom and my daughter," it says; "he will be married to my daughter."

So the man said, "Look," he says to his mouse, "look what's there. They have a riddle. Do we go?" he says.

"Let's go," says the little mouse.

The good man says, "Now, it's been a long time," he says, "since I have eaten well in my house. And there they will give you three, four days of feasting. Even if it is just for those four days," he says, "of good eating," he says, "I'll be content to die if I have to, because since I don't know how to riddle, I'm going in there without knowing if I can guess anything or not."

So the man went until he got to the kingdom. He wished them good-day, and he said, "Good king, I have come," he says, "in answer to the sign you put up about the riddling."

"Is that right," he says, "good boy?" he says.

"Yes, good king," he says.

He says, "But you know," he says, "that the man who does not guess right forfeits his life," he said, "and the man who guesses right will be master of my kingdom. He'll be the boss here," he says.

The boy was determined to do it. He gave his word, no matter what. It was almost certain they would kill him. He didn't know how to riddle. After a while a prince arrived, to riddle. So there were two of them. The next night they went and called him to supper, and they went to eat supper, and the little mouse said, "Look," he says, "you're going to eat supper," he says, "but don't be a poor friend," he says. "Bring me a little bit, because I'm hungry, too."

"Of course," he says, "if I can get some, I'll bring it to you." So he went, and he ate well. When he was leaving, he took a piece of bread for his little mouse and his dungbeetle.

So then, his master gave the mouse some bread, but he wasn't satisfied. He says to his master, "Look, friend," he says, "I'm not full. Let me go see what I can find around there, so I can finish up."

The good man says to him, "No, little mouse," he says, "because there's a cat around there," he says, "and he might eat you," he says.

"Look, let me go, and I'll be careful." So the mouse went, you know.

Just then the wife of the king was picking up the table, because they were going to bed. And the king says, "Listen, wife," he says. "Do you think," he says, "that those riddlers will guess," he says, "what kind of skin our daughter's shoes are made of?"

"No," says the queen, "no. Oh," she says, "they'll never know, they'll never imagine," she says, "that our daughter's shoes are made from a louse. And how will they ever know what the louse was fed on," she says, "that we found it on our daughter and put it in a can, and we would pour blood in there so the louse would grow. And afterward we took it out of the can and put it in a big pot, so the louse would have more room to grow, where it drank as much as five or six liters of blood a day."

The little mouse was listening to the talk of the riddle makers, you know, so he could pass it on to his master. And then the king's wife began to sweep. The king's wife began to clear off the table, and as she was clearing off the table, the little mouse quickly jumped to get a piece of bread. But since the cat was watching, he jumped at the mouse to catch him, and the little mouse barely got away from between the cat's paws, and he ran away; he really went.

He really got there. "Oh! Oh! Oh! Good master," he says, "if you don't, if you don't doctor me up, we'll both be dead," he says.

"Why, little mouse?" he says.

"Because I'm badly wounded," he says. "The cat got me."

"The cat got you? But I told you not to go," he says.

"Yes," he says, "but take care of me," he says, "or I'll die," he says. "And you will be lost," he says. "I bring good news."

So the man, for the sake of finding out what news the mouse had brought, began to nurse him. He made as if he was doctoring him, and the mouse was not really badly hurt. It was more of a fuss he was making. So then the mouse said, "We're going to win," he says.

"We're going to win?" said the man.

"Yes," he says.

"How?" he says.

"It's that just," he says, "just when I came close to the table out there," he says, "hiding," he says, "I found the king and the queen," he says, "talking," he says, "about the riddling. And then I found out what they are made of, what kind of skin the daughter's shoes are made of," he says.

He says, "What kind of skin?" he says.

"Well just think," he says, "they're made of louse skin."

"Louse skin?" he says.

"Yes, louse skin," he said. "And they said they had found it on their daughter, and they put it in a can, in a can where the louse could eat, and they let it grow. And when it was too big for the can, they put it in a big pot where it would have more room to grow, and where it drank five or six liters of blood a day."

So then, since there were two guessers, the other one, the prince, heard what the little mouse said, you know, that the girl's shoes were made of louse skin. Well, so it was their bad luck that they called on the prince first.

"The hour for the riddling has come. I want you to tell me what kind of skin my daughter's shoes are made of," says the king.

"Well, lord king," he says, "they are made of louse skin."

"All right, so let's send for the other one," he says, "because there are two of you." They sent for him. He came looking sort of absent-minded.

"Listen," he says, "what kind of skin are my daughter's shoes made of?"

He says, "Louse skin, lord king," he says.

"Louse skin," he says. "And how do you know that my daughter's shoes are made of louse skin? Since a louse is so small."

"Yes," he says, "the louse was very small," he says, "but you made it grow. You found it on the young lady, and you put it in a can," he says. "You put it in a can, where you raised it on blood," he says. "And after it was too big for that can, you put it in a big pot where the louse used to drink five or six liters of blood a day."

"All right," says the king, "at last," he says, "the two of you guessed it," he says. "Now," he says, "now my daughter will see which of you she likes better for a husband."

Well, since the prince looked very elegant—he was dressed in better clothes—the first night she slept facing the prince. Except that the king had told them they had to respect her, they must not do anything bad to the girl, because then, too, they would lose their lives. Then the girl slept facing the boy.

But then the beetle says, the mouse says, "Well, now we have lost for sure," he says. This was when he saw that the girl pushed the boy aside and turned toward the prince. "Now we have lost for sure, my good master," he says.

Then the dungbeetle says, "No, no. We haven't lost, because they haven't heard from me yet."

"But what can you do?" said the good man, he says.

"You leave that to me," he says. "I'll see what I can do," he says. "I must change the girl's mind whatever way I can," he says. Once it was late in the night, he said, "Listen," he says, "it's time," he says, "for you to turn me loose," says the little dungbeetle.

His master turned him loose. He says, "All right now," he says. "You're loose. Go on!"

So then the little dungbeetle flew off . . . Buzz, buzz, buzz, buzz! Whoosh! He went right at his—he got into his—in that part of the body, you know. And he began to take the dung out of that man and smeared it all over the sheets and the bed.

Finally, about dawn the girl says, "Phew! He soiled himself without a doubt!" she says. "How filthy he is! So big and so dirty!"

All right, so that night went by, and the next night the same thing happened. The little dungbeetle did his job, you know, when the time came, when they were all asleep. The dungbeetle got up, and he flew off. And he went into the interior part of that man's body. And he took out more of his dung and smeared it on the sheets and everything. He was just doing his usual work as a dungbeetle, you know. And next day the girl says, "Phew! He soiled himself again. What a filthy, indecent man!"

The man was embarrassed, because this had never happened to him, to soil himself in bed. But it was the doing of the little dungbeetle; that's what was taking place. "Well," he says he's very much ashamed. And he said, "What can I do," he says, "so this won't happen to me again? I think I'll look for a carpenter," he says, "so he'll do a little job for me."

So then he went where there was a carpenter, and he said, "Listen, friend," he says, "will you do me a favor?" he says.

"Of course," he says. "What is it?"

"It's a little job I need done," he says.

"Let's see. Tell me what kind of a job it is."

He says, "Well, just think," he says, "I have a bet with the king," he says, "and things are going pretty bad for me. Just think," he says. "Every night I soil myself in bed. It has happened to me the past two nights, and it had never happened to me before," he says.

"Hmm. And now, what is it that you want?" says the carpenter. "What is it that you want?"

"Well, I want you to make me," he says, "a kind of plug, so it won't happen to me again."

"Hmm," he says, "if only everything was as easy as that. In just a moment," he says, "I can make it for you."

So he made himself comfortable, and then the carpenter began to work. He made him a plug just the right size, and he put it in for him. So he went back with his plug, feeling pretty safe. This was the night to win or lose.

Then the dungbeetle said to his master, he says, "Listen," he says, "It's time," he says.

"No–o," he says, the man said, "later; wait a while longer."

"Hombre, it's time," he says.

Then he turned him loose, and the little dungbeetle flew off. Buzz, buzz, buzz, and whoosh! He went straight at the—the prince again. But the prince was well protected, and the little dungbeetle banged his head on the plug and plop! He fell to the ground.

The man says, "What happened? That fellow killed my dungbeetle." "Pfft! The rascal!" he says. Well. He was still for a while, to see if he heard from the dungbeetle. Then he lit a match and began to look around, and he saw his little dungbeetle lying over there. He got off the bed and went and got him. And he said, "What happened to you? What happened to you?"

The little dungbeetle didn't answer.

He says, "He did kill him."

But after a while the dungbeetle says, "Oh, oh! My head hurts," says the little dungbeetle.

"What happened to you?"

"Hmm, just think," he says, "that the prince, would you believe it? He has a plug in there," he says. "And I banged my head against it, you can't imagine how hard. It almost killed me," he says. "Pfft!"

Then the little rat says, "What was that?"

He says, "He's got a plug, and I almost got myself killed."

"Hmm," he says, "just leave it to me," he says. "I'll get it out."

So there goes the rat, running to where that boy was asleep. The rat went up and found himself a good place, and he put his tail in the prince's nose and made him sneeze. And at the sneeze, the plug came out, so there goes the little rat, running, and he says, he says, "I took care of him for you," he says. "The plug is out," he says.

"Are you sure?"

"I'm sure," he says. "Go ahead," he says.

The dungbeetle flew off in a rage. He took aim and. . . . Whoosh! He went farther than ever into that man. So then he took out all the dung he had, and he smeared it on him and on the girl. Well, he made a filthy mess of the bed. And then the girl gets up, furious.

"Ugh! You filthy thing, look what you've done to me!" Well, she scolded him, and then she went off to where the king was. She says, "Father! Father!"

"What is it child? What do you wish?"

"I don't want to marry this boy."

"Why?" he says.

"Just look at me," she says. "He got me all dirty; he soils himself every night. I'd rather sleep with this other one," she says. "Yes, I want to marry him."

"Are you sure?" he says.

"Yes," says the girl.

Well, so then the girl had him bathed, that poor little tramp. She saw to it that he was shaved and dressed up. And he looked even handsomer than the prince, if that is possible.

And the wedding feast must still be going on right now. And so *carabín carabado,* this tale is ended.

· 38 · The Priest Who Had One Small Glimpse of Glory

· IN A CHURCH there was a priest who was very good, and one day, when he was already in his vestments and about to go say mass, he said, "Oh, my Lord! Allow me just one small glimpse of your glory!"

When he went out to the altar, he heard a little bird sing, but in such a marvelous way that he stopped, and raised his eyes looking for the bird. When he came to, he hurried toward the altar to say mass, but he saw that the church was in ruins. There was no altar or anything any more.

So he asked some people who were going by, "What happened to the church?"

"But father, don't you know that a long, long time ago there was a priest who was going to say mass, and as he left the sac-

risty he heard a little bird sing, and none of his parishioners ever
saw him again? No priest had ever asked us that question; you
must be that priest without a doubt."

Then he, as well as the villagers, understood what had happened. And if because of one little glimpse of glory, he was in ec-
stasy for so many years, what would it be like if he saw God's
glory in all its splendor?

· 39 ·   Christ Is the Better Smith

· THEY TELL A STORY about Saint Peter and Christ, that they
were passing by a blacksmith shop, and they saw a sign there,
put up by the blacksmith, and it said, "There is no smith as good
as me."

So Christ and Saint Peter were passing by, and Christ says,
"Listen, Peter, what does it say there?"

"Well, it says there's no smith as good as me."

He says, "Well, let's go see this blacksmith. Let's see, Mister
Blacksmith, will you lend us the tools you work with?" And he
said, "Saint Peter, go straight down that road and bring me the
first person you meet."

And who should he meet but an old man, and he brings him
to Christ. When he got there, they took him and threw him in
the fire. And he began to burn very nicely until he got red-hot.
They took him out and hammered away at him, and then they
put him back in the fire after he had been worked into shape—
like a piece of iron, let us say—and then they took him out again.

And Christ says to Saint Peter, "We made him all over again."
[Informant makes gesture with finger indicating height of a
person.] And when they had made him, Christ blessed him, and
he became a boy. So they asked the blacksmith how much they
owed him for using his tools. He said they didn't owe him anything. So Saint Peter thanked him, and they left.

Now there was an old man who was the blacksmith's father,
and the blacksmith did the same thing. He brings him and
throws him into the fire to make him all over again. But he
turned black instead of red-hot, so they sent the servant to look

for Saint Peter and Christ. And he told them, "My boss says, will you please come."

He says, "What for?"

He says, "I just don't know."

Christ says, "Listen, Peter, you didn't steal anything?"

Saint Peter says, "Of course not, Jesus!"

He says, "Let's go see." They got there, and he says, "What was it that you wanted?"

The blacksmith said he had tried to do the same thing Christ had done, but his father's body did not get red-hot; on the contrary, it turned black.

He says, "Oh, is that all?" He says, "We'll fix it right now." He says, "Come on, Peter; help me." So they took him out and hammered away at him, and they put him back again. And this time he turned red-hot. After he got red-hot, they took him out again.

Christ says, "Listen, Peter, work on the gentleman." They worked on him. He asks the blacksmith, "How did you want your father? Do you want him young or old as he was?"

The blacksmith says, "Just make him the way he was."

And Christ says, "Here you have him; here's your father."

The blacksmith wanted to know how much he owed. And Christ says he didn't owe anything, just to take down the sign he had put up, because he was no blacksmith at all. Christ is the better smith. That's where it ends.

· 40 · *The Hard-Hearted Son*

· THERE WAS an old couple who had a married son. They were very poor, and one day they went to visit their son to see if he would give them some corn and ask them to dinner. His corn bins were full, and his table was laid out with many good things. For dessert there was candy in a large dish made of crystal.

When he saw his parents coming, he told his wife, "There come those old people! Put the cover on the candy dish and hide the food, so we won't have to ask them to dinner."

The wife did so, and when his parents came in and saw it all, they asked their son for a few handfuls of corn. But he told them he didn't have anything, that he hadn't harvested his crop yet. "It's all right," his parents said. "God bless you and give you more." And they left.

When they sat down to dinner, they found the food had spoiled. The man went to his corn bins and found it all eaten by weevils. He came back, and when he was going to eat the candy, a serpent came out and wound itself about his neck and strangled him.

It was his parents' curse; rather, a punishment for his greed and hard-heartedness.

·41· *The Flower of Lily-Lo*

• ONCE THERE WAS a family consisting of the parents and three sons. The youngest was loved the most by the parents and by the whole town as well, but the two older ones were very envious of him. One day the mother fell sick, and no physician could cure her. They didn't know what was wrong with her until a witch told them they must look in the forest for a flower called "The Flower of Lily-Lo." And she would be cured with it.

The father sent his three sons to look for the flower. The two big ones hid among the trees. The smallest, when he saw he was lost, began to run this way and that and to cry out. He walked a long way, and he finally found the flowers; he took several and came back. The others came to where he was, and when they saw the flowers, they fell into a fury, and they beat him. They dragged him to a hole in the ground, and they threw rocks over him until the hole was covered up.

Then they went home with the flowers. When they got there, the father took the flowers, made a potion out of them, and gave it to the mother, and she was cured instantly. But since the smallest one did not return, he asked what had happened. They said he must have lost his way. The parents got many people together to go look for him, but two or three weeks passed, and the little one was not found, so they gave him up for dead. He must have been eaten up by wild beasts, they thought.

Meanwhile, a boy was going through the woods, coming back to his native town, and on the way he came to a tree covered with flowers. He was curious enough to pluck one and blow on it, and it made a little song that said,

> Oh, little boy, don't blow on me;
> Don't blow again, no, no.
> My brothers they have killed me
> For the Flower of Lily-lo.

At first the boy was frightened, but then he blew again and the flower sang the little song again. So he decided to fill his pockets with the flowers and sell them in town. He did so, and fate willed it that the boy should come and stand close to the house where the parents of the lost child lived. He began to blow and to offer the flowers for sale, and people crowded around him out of curiosity. The parents of the lost child recognized the voice of their son, and they came out on the street to see where the voice was coming from. So they called the boy and asked him for a flower. The father blew on it, and the flower sang,

> Oh, father dear, don't blow on me;
> Don't blow again, no, no.
> My brothers they have killed me
> For the Flower of Lily-lo.

The father was frightened, and he gave the flower to his wife. She blew on it and heard the flower say,

> Oh, mother dear, don't blow on me;
> Don't blow again, no, no.
> My brothers they have killed me
> For the Flower of Lily-lo.

They called the brothers at once and made them blow. The flower said,

> Oh, brothers mine, don't blow on me;
> Don't blow again, no, no.
> My brothers, you have killed me
> For the Flower of Lily-lo.

The parents were furious, so they took the wicked boys and shut them up in a room. They lighted a fire inside and threw a lot of chile peppers on the flames so they would choke to death. They also asked the boy to take them where he had found the flowers. They went with him, followed by many people from the town. When they came to the place, they took away the rocks and found the little boy asleep under the tree trunk. They took him out, and he woke up at once, and this made everybody happy, and there was much merrymaking. And *colorín* so red, my story is said, and yours is still to tell.

•42• *The Three Shining Stones*

• THIS IS THE WAY my story goes, for your good understanding and my poor telling of it, for this was a king who had an extremely beautiful daughter. She was besieged by many personages of high lineage—courtiers, counts, marquises, dukes, and I don't know what. But she disdained them all, perhaps because they weren't the type of men she longed for in her dreams or her imagination, and she always lived in despair, because she did not know what she wanted. Aside from this, it is told that the princess was gifted with second sight. Whenever suitors would arrive to see her, she would tell them what they were going to say before they could tell her what they thought or what messages they carried.

Her father lived in anguish because of his daughter's restlessness, because she was not happy, and he had the idea once of proclaiming an edict in which he sought some knight who would make a favorable impression on his daughter. And as a condition, he stated that they must bring three riddles. The king in his edict proclaimed, that is to say, that he was looking for a suitor who would favorably impress his daughter. No matter his rank, either nobleman or plebeian, if the aspirant to the hand of the princess came with three riddles, and she guessed them, he would be punished. But if she did not have the wit to guess the riddles, he would be the chosen one, the future husband of the princess, but first he must make the princess say, "That cannot be!"

Well then, way out in the country a *ranchero* got ready, a poor devil. He wanted to go, too, and see if it was his fortune to become the princess's husband. So he said to his mother, "Mother," he says, "make me some tortillas, because I'm going on a journey."

"Now, where are you going, son?" the little old woman asked him.

He says, "Don't you know the king has passed a law asking for suitors to make matrimony with the princess?" He says, "I'm going to see if I can marry the princess."

Knowing how poor they were, the mother of the *ranchero* told him he would only be going to get himself executed, you know. Cut his neck off, decapitate him. But he kept on asking her to prepare him some provisions for the journey. He saddled his little burro, mounted it, and left.

He traveled, and he traveled, and he traveled, until he began to feel hungry. It was late in the afternoon, and then it began to get dark. Then he saw a light way off in the distance. He says, "When I get to that bonfire, I'll get off my burro and warm over my tortillas." So the closer he got to the fire, the brighter was the light that came from it, more and more brilliant. But no sir, it was not a fire but a precious stone that was shining there.

Hmm! He didn't know just what it was, but he picked it up and put it in his *morral*. He kept on going, he kept on going, and farther on he saw another light in the distance. He says, "This time I will be able to stop and have my supper at that fire, because I am very tired and very hungry." It turned out to be the same thing; it was another stone, but more beautiful than the first. He picked it up and put it in his *morral* and kept on going, looking for a place where he could warm over his tortillas.

What happened was that later he saw another light, farther away. He says, "This is the right one. It is much brighter, so it must be a real fire." But the same thing happened; when he got there, it was another stone, even bigger and more beautiful. In short, the day dawned on him, and he had not found a fire, so he kept on going. With the first light, he saw something in the fields; it was an ox. It happened that the ox had got into a wheat field. He says, "I don't think it is right for that animal to eat the wheat. I'm going to drive it out." He says, *"Caray!* This is where I make up a riddle for my princess. Yes. I'll say to her, 'I drove the good out of the better.' Hmm!"

He went on. Later he ran out of water; he had used up all the water in the gourd he carried, the way *rancheros* do, you know, and he was very thirsty. The little burro was sweating and sweating from the fatigue of the journey. And in his torment he went and put his lips against the little burro, to wet them. He says: *"Caray!* This is where I make another riddle for the princess. I will tell her, 'I drank water not rained from the skies or gushed out of the earth.' Let's see if she can riddle that." In the end he may have quenched his thirst or he may have not, but he made up his riddle.

Toward the end of the journey, he ran out of provisions and didn't have anything to eat. And as always happens, you get hungrier than ever when there's nothing to eat. He passed by a place where a sow was giving birth to some piglets, but the piglets could not get born. So he stared at the sow and he says, "I'm going to help that sow have those creatures." And he cut the piglets out of the sow. *"Caray!"* he says. "I must roast one of these, let me see how I'm going to do it. It may be very young, very tender, but my hunger is great."

But he couldn't find firewood or anything; all he found was a lot of paper, leaves from a book perhaps, or newspapers. He made his fire with them and roasted his meat. "Ah," he says, "here is where I make up another riddle for the princess. This will be the third," he says. "I'm going to say to her, 'I ate meat that was never born, roasted on words.' Hmm, *caray!"*

He finally came to the imperial city. He came to the door of the royal palace, and the sentinels asked him what he wanted. Why, it just happened that the royal edict had echoed to the very limits of the kingdom, where he lived, and he also was a suitor for the princess's hand. Well, those fellows didn't turn him away, because it was the law, you know, an imperial or royal order. They went and told the king that there was a beggar out there who wanted to take part in the contest too, among those chosen to talk to the princess. The king ordered them to let him in. So he came in, and the servants laughed, all those charged with taking care of the guests, for the most select nobility was there, the richest of the rich, you know, hoping to be favored by fortune. So they ordered this beggar to be put in the stables, over among the chicken coops. And it was ordered that they take him what was left from the banquets they were celebrating, and a tallow candle. He was content to be over there in the chicken coops, but that night he didn't use the tallow candle they gave him. They say he took out the first stone he found.

When the stone was uncovered, it shed such a brilliant ray of light that it awoke a certain curiosity in the palace, to the point that the princess sent to find out what was the reason for that shining light. So her maids of honor came, and they told her the beggar had something never seen before. Something large and marvelous. So then the princess says, "Go tell that beggar to sell it to me, cost what it may. But he must not say no."

So the maids of honor, or the servants, of the princess went and told the beggar that the princess said he must sell her that stone or that light, cost what it might. But he must not say no. So then he says, "Tell the princess I will not sell it to her; I am giving it to her as a gift. But she must let me sleep by the door of her bedroom."

So they went and told the princess the condition set by the beggar, for that was what they called him. The princess was alarmed, you know; she was full of scruples. She said, "No. Not that."

But her ladies-in-waiting said, "Young mistress, what does it matter, princess?" Or your highness. "You will be inside, and he outside. What harm is there in that?"

"Well. Tell him it is all right, to give me the stone."

The next night he did the same thing. By this time, they were treating him better, you know. They gave him better lodging, better treatment, more courtesy. The next night he took out the next stone. The same thing happened; it alarmed the palace people because of the strong light, the brilliant light it gave off. Again the princess inquires through her servants, and they tell her it is another stone, even more precious, that the beggar has. She sends them to tell him to sell it to her, and he must not say no. So when he is told what the princess says, he tells them once more he will not sell it; he will give it to her as a gift if she will let him sleep at the foot of her bed.

And they come and tell her, and she is alarmed, so the ladies say to her, "But what does it matter, highness? The beggar can go no farther than he is allowed, and he will be content with that. Furthermore," they say, "we will be close by."

"Very well." She accepted then.

The third night the same thing was repeated, you know, with the prettiest and biggest stone, the most valuable. The princess herself considered the stone was worth more than all of the palace where she lived. She sent word to him in the same manner, that she wanted the stone, but he must not say no. So he told them, "Go tell the princess I will give it to her as a gift. But she must say no to everything I say to her."

So the ladies went and told the princess what the beggar said. "Oh, no," she said, "not that."

"But what does it matter?" they said. "If he says anything to you, all you have to do is say no. Suppose he tries to go too far, all you have to do is say no."

"Oh, well. Tell him it's all right."

Now the beggar already had the privilege of sleeping at the door and of sleeping at the foot of her bed. So once he was there, he says, "Princess, you won't be offended if I sit on the edge of your bed?"

"Well, no."

"Princess, you won't be offended if I take this stone?"

"Well, no." Because she had agreed to say no to everything he said and not a word more. So he took the smallest stone and put it in his *morral*.

"Princess, you won't be offended if I take this other stone?"

"Well, no." So he put the middle-sized stone into his *morral*.

"Princess, you won't be offended if I take the other stone?"

"No, no." So he put the biggest stone into his *morral*.

"Princess, you won't be angry if I ask you for your night-gown?"

"Well, no." So he took her nightgown and put it in his *morral*.

"Princess, you won't be angry if I get in bed with you?"

"No." And that was the way the thing ended.

Next morning he left with all those things in his *morral,* you know. And this was the day he was to be judged on his riddles. But the princess was provoked because of all the things he had done, so during the night she lulled him to sleep and asked him the answers to his riddles. And he told her. So he appeared before the king's audience that day, and he was no longer the ragged beggar but was dressed in a fine suit and couldn't be told from the rest of the courtiers who were there as suitors. So he went in and said his riddles to the princess before the king. And the princess answered all three of them. So then the king told his lackeys to punish the beggar by giving him fifty blows with a stick. It would kill him, more or less.

So then the beggar says, "Your majesty, give me a boon."

The king allows it. "What do you wish?"

"Permission to go out in the hall and sell these fifty blows they are going to give me."

"Sell them! How?"

"Well," he says, "I'll take care of that."

So the king said yes. When he went out of the audience chamber, all the rest of them were there—marquises, counts, and I don't know what—full of curiosity and laughing at the man, you know, because they didn't take him seriously. He was the funniest thing they had ever seen in all their lives. They asked him what had come of his audience with the king. Would he marry the princess?

"No," he says, "but the king has made me a gift. Fifty of them."

"Fifty what?"

"The finest wood that grows in the realm. But I don't want them. I can't take them away with me; they're no use to me."

The nobles thought it was fifty acres of woodland, so they said, "We'll buy them. How much do you want for them?"

"Oh, fifty pesos. A peso apiece."

So one of them bought them, and the beggar goes back to the king and says, "Majesty, I have sold the blows you were going to give me, at a peso apiece."

"You don't say! Who bought them?"

"I'll bring you the buyer right now."

So the king says to the buyer, "Is it true that you bought what I promised to give this gentleman?"

"Yes, Majesty. All fifty of them."

Then the king ordered the blows given to the buyer, and the princess said, "Father, that cannot be!"

And the beggar says, "The prize is mine."

So then the king says, "How can you be so daring as to aspire to reach a star?" Because he was nothing down here below, and who can reach the stars?

But then he says, "Well, look, Majesty. All things are easy if you know how to do them. And the hand of the princess belongs to me for reasons I will explain. But first let me tell you a little story. On the way to your palace a hare ran suddenly in front of me, and I barely had time to pick up this stone and throw it at her. I almost hit her."

"Ah!" says the king. "What a beautiful stone! It's a treasure, a great treasure!"

"Well then," he says, "I resumed my journey, and a little farther on the same hare ran across the road again. I tried to catch her," he says, "so I bent down and picked up this other stone and threw it at her. And I hit her in the hind legs," he says. "She almost stopped," he says. And he put down the second stone before the king.

"Good Heavens!" says the king. "This is an even greater treasure!"

"So I resumed my journey," he says, "and the same hare crossed my path again, so I picked up this other stone and threw it at her. And this time I did get her." And he put down the third stone before the king.

He says, "Look. As proof of what I said, I brought along her hide." And then he took out the princess's nightgown.

Well then, with those proofs, you know, the king had to consider that, well, he had already gone pretty far. And so it is that after having lived in complete wretchedness, and having slept in a chicken-coop, he is now sleeping in the richest and most comfortable beds, covered with silken coverlets, and with one of the most desirable of women. And us over here, living this sad life of ours.

•43•   The Five Counsels

• THIS WAS AN OLD MAN who lived in a little village, and he had a bit of property and some farming land. But since this old man was dying—he had only one son—he says to him, "My son, I am going to leave you all my fields, so you can get along in life."

The old man died. So then the son thought—he remembered the old saw that you should throw a horn in the air and go away in the direction it points to. And he did so. He took the path that led away from those surroundings, and when he got halfway up the hill, there was a tree with a large branch leaning out toward the road. And the thought came to him that it would perhaps be in the way of people traveling the road, so he climbed up and began to cut the tree—the trunk—the branch.

And when he was up there among the branches, another traveler passed by and told him, "But man, what are you doing? Don't you see that if said branch falls, you will fall with it too?"

He said, "A soothsayer had already told me that." And he made fun of the man. He kept on cutting. He cuts off the branch, and he falls down with it. And then he says, "That man foretold it." And he followed him and told him, "Friend, you are a soothsayer."

He said, "No, I'm not a soothsayer. But, didn't you stop to think that if the branch fell, it would fall with you, too?"

"Very well."

The fellow went away. But as he came to the top of the hill he arrived at an *hacienda* which was there, and he says, "*Patrón,* I would like to work." To the owner of the *hacienda.* He gave him work.

"How much do you want to make?" the *patrón* told him.

He said, "A *real* a year." Which is twelve cents a year.

He worked for five years. He would work day and night, tickled to death with the job. Then it happened that at the end of five years he says to him, "*Patrón,* I would like for you to please give me my wages."

He said, "Well, how long did you work?"

"Well, five years."

"I will give you five *reales*." Which is sixty-two cents. "But, man! It should be more."

He says, "No, sir. You give me what I earned, and it can't be more than that."

Well, that was a good bargain he struck; he gave him nothing but the sixty-two cents. He said good-bye and left. He took a road, however, and came to a place. He caught up with a fan-maker who was going along the road making fans, walking and working at the same time.

And he says to him, "Señor, do you know any tales? Tell me a tale."

"Well, give me twelve cents."

"Here it is." He gave them to him.

Immediately he says, "Don't leave the main road for a side road."

A little farther on he says, "Señor, tell me another tale."

"Give me another twelve cents."

"Here."

The fan-maker says to him, "Don't ask questions about what doesn't concern you."

Farther on he says, "Señor, tell me another tale."

"Well, give me another twelve cents."

"Here they are."

He says, "Wherever you go, do as others do."

Farther on he says, "Tell me another tale."

"Well, give me another twelve cents."

So he gave them to him.

And he says, "Mmm. A married man should keep his eyes open."

And then, farther on he says, "Señor, tell me another tale."

"Well, give me another twelve cents."

"Here they are. I don't have any left."

And he gave them to him.

Then he said, "The old saw says, 'The more the rich man has, the more he wants.'" And he said good-bye; he went away.

But he began to make use of the tales. He saw he was going

toward a certain town, and he could see that the road was very straight—the main road and a path that went out in a very straight line. He thought of following the path, but he remembered the first tale, and he said, "The tale says, 'Don't leave the main road for a side road.'" Tale number one. So he elected to follow the main road.

Going by the road, he came to the house of some bandits without knowing it. He asks for lodging, and lodging is given to him. He passes the night there, and he sees many signs there of corpses and of bloody handprints, many signs showing that those robbers slaughtered many victims there.

So then when morning comes, the chief of the robbers says to him, he says: "Friend, I am going to give you a gift because you did not ask questions about what didn't concern you. Look. Do you know that path that goes along over there? If you had taken it, you would already have been a victim here. But since you didn't ask any questions while you were here, nothing is going to happen to you." He says, "We are going to give you a hundred pesos and the road, so you can leave. It is time for you to be traveling."

They put him out on the road, and he left. And he came to a town. In that town some soldiers were out marching. So without knowing why, he turned the handle of the ax like this, and he went along, on and on and on, marching behind the soldiers. So then the soldiers go—some of their leaders—and say to the king, "Señor, *sacarreal majestad*. An unknown man is marching behind us. I don't know for what purpose he does it."

So then the king says, "Call the young man here."

The young man came, and the king says to him, "Young man, why are you marching behind the troops?"

"Señor, I don't know why. The tale says—the third tale—it says like this, 'Wherever you go, do as others do.' I see everybody marching, and I am marching too. I don't know what it is all about. Please tell me what it is all about, and then I will do it or not do it."

The king says, "Well, look. You must know that year after year there is a lottery here. A huge serpent comes down from the mountains and eats a girl who is chosen by lot, and this year the lot has fallen on my daughter. And because I want the soldiers to defend her from that event, I have ordered them to march so they can exercise, so they can battle that huge serpent."

He said, "Well, señor. If you wish—I am not a soldier nor a great warrior—but if you wish, such a thing is suitable to me. I will defend your daughter. What will you give for her?"

The king said, "Her hand. The man who defends her will marry her."

"Well, have a double-edged sword made for me, a meter in length, and I will watch over that girl."

There was nothing else to do, except to trust he would protect her. Good. The king had everything done for him. There on top of a scaffold they placed the girl. There she was, blindfolded, awaiting the will of God while he walked up and down there at midnight without going to sleep.

He would say, "A married man should keep his eyes open." The fourth tale. He kept on walking and watching the girl, when it arrived. The noise began, and he went out to meet it, and he began to struggle with said serpent many city blocks away from the scaffold. And he cut off heads and more heads. And the king had told him that he should bring the tongues as proof that he had killed the huge serpent, the seven tongues that belonged to the seven heads. And when the young man finished killing them, when he finished cutting off the heads, he took out the seven tongues. He put them away, and he went to dally with the girl, very happily.

Just at this time a charcoal burner went by, who was going to town, and when he sees the dead serpent, he begins to take out eyes, and more eyes, and more eyes. He took out the eyes from the seven heads. He puts them away wrapped in a paper.

Well, the king still isn't up when the charcoal burner is knocking there already, saying, "Señor, señor. I have killed the seven-headed serpent."

"Is it true?" says the king.

"Yes, sir."

"What do you bring me as proof?"

He said, "The eyes."

"Didn't the heads have any tongues?"

He said, "Well, I didn't notice, señor. Let me go see."

He said, "No, wait around there. We shall see in due time."

After a while the boy gets there, around dawn, with his wife on his elbow. He says, "Señor, here I am to serve you. Here is your little girl, safe and sound. And here are the signs you told me to bring you."

"Let's see. What are they? Really?"

He takes out the tongues and gives them to him. Then he says, "Well, to tell the truth, you really did kill it. But this gentleman will have to be executed. Kill him." And he died.

And later the king made him a palace. He married the boy to her. He made him a palace. He put him in there to live. But next morning the boy remembered the fifth tale, which said, "The more the rich man has, the more he wants."

The owner of an *hacienda* lived just over there, downhill. That man didn't know that the prince had married the princess. So then the prince says to the girl, "Listen, wife; tell me. The fifth tale says that the more the rich man has, the more he wants. Whose is that elegant *hacienda* down there below?"

She says, "Well, it belongs to Mr. So-and-so. Mr. X."

"Well, I'm going to get hold of that *hacienda* if you will help me, and if father and mother help me. Let's see, let's go see. Hold on to my elbow. Let's go over there."

They get there. "Father, father. I have business with you, with you and my mother. I want to get hold of an *hacienda* that I saw down there in the distance, which is said to belong to a Mr. So-and-so, Mr. X. I think I'll get hold of that *hacienda* because the fifth tale says, 'The more the rich man has, the more he wants.' I already find myself in the position of wanting more." He says, "If you help me win that *hacienda,* you and my mother, I'll get hold of it."

"How do you want us to help you?" the king said to him.

He said, "Very well. Go there tomorrow at noon, no later than that, to take me my dinner; but you must not fail, because I am going to gamble my life against that man's *hacienda,* under written contract if you will do me that favor. If I can count on it, I'll do it; if I cannot, I won't do it."

"You can count on it," he said.

"On your word of honor, sir?"

"On my word of honor. Go now and don't lose any time."

He went home. He said, "Wife I want you to please have them make for me a big, fat tortilla that will take an *almud* of corn—four liters—to make. I don't care whether the dough is finely ground or not."

He made a hole in said tortilla, put a loop of rope through it, and hung it around his neck. He took on a mean appearance, putting on the clothes he was wearing before; he dirtied his hands, his feet and eveything, and he went to ask for work over there from that farmer, from the *patrón* who owned that *hacienda*.

And he says, "Señor, do you have a job? I want a job."

"Do you know how to work, *hombre?*"

"Yes, sir. I know how."

"Let's see. Give this man a yoke of oxen and let him draw a furrow here in this unplowed land. After I see him do that I'll know whether he knows how to work or not."

"Yes, sir."

He took the yoke. He drew a very straight and very good furrow that convinced the *patrón* he knew how to work.

"And how much do you expect to make?"

"Señor, you are the one to say what I'll make. What all the others get."

"Very well. Get to work, then."

He hung his tortilla from a tree there, and the *patrón* asked him what did he want that torilla for, since he had just eaten. Very well. Good.

Then, the lunches for his comrades began to arrive, and they would say to him, "Friend, come over here and sit with us."

He said, "No, I won't eat until the king and the queen come and bring me my lunch."

"But won't that be a very long wait?" And they began to mock him, to laugh at him and make fun of him; in short, to say things about him. All of them, they began to pick on him.

Suddenly the *patrón* comes and notices. He says, "What is the matter with this man? Why are you making fun of him?"

He says, "Well, he says he isn't going to eat, to please not offer

him anything, that they go ahead and eat, but he isn't doing anything until the king and the queen bring him something to eat."

"Whoo! The man is mad!" And then he broke out laughing.
He also made fun of him.

And then he says to him, "Señor, why don't we do something?
Let's make a bet. I wager my life against your *hacienda*. I bet
they will bring me something to eat, and you bet they won't,
isn't that right? Draw up the papers."

He said, "Yes, but you must die by hanging."

"Any way you like. I bet my life against your *hacienda*. Good.
Draw up the papers."

And he drew up the papers. He kept one for himself and gave
the other to the *patrón*. And then he began to jerk up his head.
He would say, he said, "When will the king and the queen get
here?"

"They must be held up somewhere," the others would say.
And they would make fun of him.

But after a while they began to get there; it was still about ten
o'clock. The first wagon arrived with the tables and the chairs.
Then the *patrón*'s face fell. And then the menservants and the
maidservants began to arrive, with the tables and the different
foods and all. And then the troops of soldiers began to arrive,
and with the last body of soldiers came the king and the queen
and the princess, bringing the clothes of the prince who was
plowing there. They kept coming, and coming—Well!

And then, after that they began to lay the tablecloths and to
dress him, and then she says, "Look, So-and-so. I brought you
your clothes. Come."

Then he threw away his rags and went to get dressed. And all
of them were shamed and began to pay him homage and to say
to him, "Señor, what are we going to do?"

"You may keep on working here if you want to work."

So then he dressed himself like a prince and took charge of everything, and then he says to the king, "Father, let's go see the
patrón and invite him to eat with us."

They went. "Señor, you may come eat with us."

"No, thank you, gentleman. I cannot go over there."

"What is this all about?"

He says, "This *hacienda* is mine, father." The prince told the king, he said, "Lord father, this *hacienda* is mine. I made a bet with this gentleman who is owner of it. Who was the owner. Now it is mine. I present you this paper. Here it is."

The king read the paper and said, "Well, yes. It is yours in truth."

And then he says to the *patrón,* "Señor, will you come eat with us?"

"A thousand thanks, señor. I can't eat anything. I am extremely sad. It doesn't matter, you go ahead. I'll stay over here." He took his family and left.

So a *ranchero* band started playing and livened things up. All of them began to eat, and then he says to the help, "You know that now I am the *patrón.* Don't be afraid because you did your best to make fun of me. I am your friend at all times. I am your *patrón.* Come and eat with us. This is your house."

They all ate together there, and they were very happy with their *patrón.* And the king and the queen and the princess and the prince went home.

So, each to his house.

> And I go into the spout
> And then I come out,
> I come out through the other;
> May a stallion kick you
> If you don't tell another.

·44· *The Three Questions*

• THERE ONCE WAS a priest whose brother was a bum and a drunkard. He would drink wherever he could get it, and he would borrow money, and the bills would go to the priest. Once he went and put up a placard on the door of their house: "The man who has money rules the roost, and he can do what he pleases."

The king passed by. He said, "Well." He said, "Why does he say that the man with money rules?" He says, "Go bring the priest before me, immediately, so I can ask him why he put that placard there. Am I not the one who rules here? Is he the ruler perhaps? Go. Let him come at once."

The priest went, and the king says to him, "Why did you put that placard on the door of your house?"

He says, "No, señor, I didn't do it. I have not put it there. I don't know anything about that placard."

The king says, "Yes. It says that you can do whatever you want, that the man with money can do what he pleases. No. That is not true. I am the ruler here."

"Very well," the priest says. "I didn't do it. But if you say I did. . . ."

He says, "So you have to answer these three questions I am going to ask you, and if you do not answer them in three days' time, I will have you hanged at once."

So the priest went home very sad. When he was already home, a card came with the three questions he must answer. "How much am I worth?" "What am I thinking?" and "What is the extent of my power?" Very well.

He says, "Well. Me, how am I going to answer these questions? I don't know the answers." He tried this way and that, but he could not answer them. A day went by, and he was very sad, waiting. "What am I going to do?" he says. "There are only two days left." Another day went by, and the third day came. The third day was almost over, when his brother came by, in the afternoon, and he says, "Say, brother, why are you so sad?"

He says, "Umm." He says, "How can I help being sad. Just think; the king has ordered me—he called and told me I had to answer these three questions. I have to tell him how much he is worth, what is the extent of his power, and what he is thinking." He says, "I won't be able to find the solution to them."

The brother says, "Umm." He says, "Let me do it. Let me have your cassock, your shoes, your hat," he says. "Your staff. I will go before the king."

The priest says, "But what are you going to do? I have studied more than you, and I can't answer them, so how can you?"

The brother says, "Let me do it, and you'll see." He went off.

He plucked a very pretty flower, and he went to see the king. And the king says, "Come in, please. Have you come to answer the questions?"

He says, "Yes, sir. Here I am."

The king says, "Let's see." He says, "How much am I worth?"

He says, "Umm." He says, "You want to be worth something." He says, "Our Lord Jesus Christ, who was Our Lord Jesus Christ, was sold for thirty coins." He says, "So you can't be worth more than one, and you'll be doing pretty well at that."

"Good. Very well. That question is answered. Now for the second. What is the extent of my power?"

"Well, I don't think you have any power at all." He says, "If you did—Let's see; make me a flower like this one."

The king says, "Well, no. I can't make it."

"Well, I've come out ahead of you for the second time."

"Now for the third one. What am I thinking?"

He says, "You're thinking you're talking to the priest, but you're talking to his crazy brother."

The king says, "Is that the truth? Then, you aren't the priest?"

"No sir. I'm that crazy brother of his, the drunkard," he says, "who went and put the placard on the house," he says, "and they blamed the priest," he says, "but it wasn't him. I was the one who put up the placard."

"It's all right," the king says. "Let's see." He says, "You have answered the questions very well. Now you can ask me anything you want."

He says, "Umm." The little old drunkard thought it over. He says, "If I ask him for money, lots of money, a time will come when it will all be gone. What do I want to ask for?" He says, "No, look." After thinking it over for a long time he says to the king, "Look, your majesty. You know what I want you to give me? A little burro."

"And that is all you ask of me?" he says.

"Yes," he says, "with a placard between its ears," he says. " 'A king never goes back on his word.' And with your signature."

The king says, "Very well." He says, "It is done." And he signed the placard, and they put it on the little burro, and he went away. He would go into the saloons and ask for drinks, not only for himself, but for all his friends as well. And he would also ask for a lot of money and everything.

"Pay me!"

"Of course you'll get paid. The king never goes back on his word."

In short, I think he still is around there drinking in all the saloons with his little placard. *Colorín* so red, the story is said.

· 45 · Ixte' que (The Thief)

• THERE WAS A WOMAN who had four sons, and she looked for a place to work and got a job with a *patrón* who had a lot of money. So one day her *patrón* asked her if she had four sons, and the woman said yes, she did. And what did the four of them do for a living? Well, the four of them—one of them was a shoemaker, the other was a tailor, and the other one was a carpenter. There were four of them, but the woman did not want to say, because this other one was a thief. She didn't want to answer him, because he was a thief, until she did answer, "The other boy is a thief."

The *patrón* said, "Now, if it is true that you have a son who is a thief, I'm going to send out four loaded mules to see how good a thief he is."

And the woman said, "I'm going to tell my son the thief to see what he says." When she got to the place where her son was, she told him, "My *patrón* says that if you don't steal this money from him, if you don't rob these four mules on the road, you will be killed."

And the thief said he would. "Don't worry, mother; I'll get that money away from him."

When the time came, he told his brother the shoemaker, "Do me the favor of making me a pair of shoes, like boots."

And the shoemaker said, "What do you want them for?"

The thief said, "Well, now. I know."

When he got the shoes, the thief went and waited by the road where they would come. He threw one shoe in the road, and then he hid. Well, I don't know just where. Where they wouldn't find him. And there come the soldiers and a captain, with four mules loaded with money, wherever they were taking it. That was why the shoe was in the road.

The captain said, "This is a good shoe. Let's see if it fits me." He said, "This one does fit me, but I wonder where the other one may be." He said to the soldiers, "Look for it around there. Look for the shoe around there so we can go ahead and take the money."

So when the captain had put on both boots, they looked for the mules loaded with money, but they couldn't find them. So then they went back. They looked for them everywhere and could not find them. They came before the *patrón,* and he asked them, "Did you go take the money where I told you?"

The soldiers and the captain answered, "The thief took the money away from us."

And the *patrón* said, "Weren't you carrying rifles so you could have killed the thief instead?"

The soldiers said, "Well, no. We never knew how he took the money away from us."

So the *patrón* sent those soldiers to the Devil, because he thought that perhaps they were not telling the truth, and he got himself the bravest soldiers. "Well, he's taken that money from me, but I'm going to do it again. Now that I have these real son-of-a-bitching soldiers. I'm going to send another load of money."

So then the mother went to see her robber son. "Let's see if you can rob him again, as you did the other day with the other soldiers."

And the thief said to his mother, "Yes, I'll find a way to do it." And the thief went to his brother the tailor. The thief said to his brother, "Make me some suits of clothes for priests and one for a sexton. Do it as fast as you can, because I need them right now."

So the tailor made the suits of clothes for priests, and one for a sexton. And the day they had agreed on, the thief came for the clothes for the priests and the sexton. His brother dressed as the sexton and carried a book and holy water. Except that the holy water was not really holy water but liquor, so strong that one glass was enough to get drunk on. So then, here come the soldiers and the captain with the money. And the priest came down the road they were taking and met them. The captain asked, "Where are you going, little father?"

"I'm going to say mass to a town farther down the road."

The captain said, "Will you do me the favor of praying for us, little father? Because we are going to meet the thief very soon." The captain did not know the priest was the thief.

He said, "No, because I have to go say a mass."

And the captain begged him, "Please do it, because the thief is coming, and he will steal the mules and the money from us."

At last the priest said, "All right, I will pray for all of you." He took hold of his book and began to pray, and the sexton was there; that was the way they had made their plans. So the sexton told them it wasn't holy water, but liquor, and while the priest was praying, the sexton had a drink.

The captain was close by, and he said, "Won't you offer me some of that?"

The sexton answered, "This isn't holy water, but wine for saying mass."

The captain said, "Give me a drink." The sexton said no, but he was just pretending. After a while he gave the captain a drink, and he offered all the soldiers some. Meanwhile the animals loaded with money were standing against some trees. When they began to drink the priest's liquor, they got drunk with just one drink, and they didn't know what they were doing. All the soldiers got drunk and fell asleep, because of the drink the sexton gave them. The priest kept on praying until he saw that all the soldiers were drunk. They were all gone! Well. So they dressed the soldiers like priests, and they didn't wake up. They didn't even know where they were. They were not thinking about the mules any more, or where they were. So then the thief took the mules away, and they didn't know about it.

When the soldiers woke up, they were dressed in priests' uniforms. When one of them woke up, he said, "Why am I like this?" He didn't recognize his uniform and he didn't know he was dressed like a priest. So all the soldiers woke that were there. When they woke up, the money was gone, and they were dressed like priests, so they left right away. They passed through a little town, and the people saw them coming dressed like priests. They weren't priests, but soldiers. They said in the little town, "Here come the missionaries."

They climbed the tower and began to ring the bells. The soldiers said, "We aren't missionaries; we are soldiers." That is what they said when they went through that little town.

They came to the *patrón* and reported, and the *patrón* said, "Why did you come here like that?"

"Because the thief changed our clothes." The *patrón* couldn't believe it. "Well, now I want you to stay right there. I'm going over there. He's likely to steal everything I own." And he set the soldiers to guard his house.

The woman came, and he told her, "Your son robbed me again, but he must steal from me one more time. This is the last time; but if he can't do it, I'll have him shot, and you, too."

She went and told her son the thief, "This is the last time you have to steal from my *patrón*. If you can't steal from him, they'll kill me, too. The *patrón* says you must steal a new poncho that is over there in his house, where he sleeps. See if you can steal it."

The thief said, "Yes!" He went at once to his brother the carpenter. He told him, "Make me a wooden dummy, one that will move."

He made the dummy. So the thief carried it to the house he was going to rob. The *patrón* slept on the second floor. So then the thief went up and found out where the *patrón* slept, and he put the dummy up to the window. The *patrón* thought it was the thief. He took out his pistol and fired several shots at the dummy.

Then the *patrón* said to his wife, "Wake up; I killed the thief." But his wife didn't wake up. The *patrón* hurried down to see if the thief was there, to see if he was dead. The thief saw the *patrón* come down, and he went up to his bedroom. And since the *patrón*'s wife was still asleep, the thief began to say, "Wake up, wife, for I have killed the thief. Give me the poncho the thief was going to steal from us, because I have already killed him. And let me give you a kiss," said the thief. And there's no telling what other things he said to the *patrón*'s wife.

Meanwhile the *patrón* was looking everywhere, trying to find where the thief had gone. He couldn't find him anywhere. So the thief went away with his poncho and left the *patrón*'s wife his kisses, and no telling what other things he did to her. The *patrón* was so angry he died.

•46• *The Tailor Who Sold His Soul to the Devil*

• THERE LIVED in a certain place a tailor who one day asked a favor of the Devil. The Devil offered to do what the tailor asked, it he could have his soul. The tailor agreed, provided the Devil beat him in a sewing contest.

The Devil joyfully accepted, but he threaded his needle with an extremely long thread. He got all tangled up with it and had to stop many times to untangle it and pick it up from the floor. The tailor, on the other hand, took a very short thread, and he sewed away so fast that the Devil was astounded. In the end the tailor finished his sewing first, and the Devil did not get his soul.

That is why mothers in Piedra Gorda say to their daughters, when they thread their needles with a long thread, "Child, that is the Devil's thread."

Part IV
Jokes and Anecdotes

·47· The Drovers Who Lost Their Feet

• THIS IS HOW the people from Lagos are. There were five drovers traveling together. They were tired. They sat down against a tree, and all of them stretched out their legs. They said, "What are we going to do? We won't be able to get up any more. We are no longer able to tell which of those feet belong to which. What are we going to do? We'll just have to stay here."

Whoo! There they were, pretty hungry and thirsty there, and they couldn't get up.

A man passed by, and he says, "What are you doing there?"

"Well, here we are. We can't get up."

"Why?"

"Because we don't know which feet belong to which."

"For goodness' sake! How much will you give me if I tell you?"

"Well, we'll give you something, as long as you tell us which of those feet belong to which."

He took a big pack needle and began to stick them with it. He stuck one of them.

"Ouch!"

"That's yours. Pull it in."

He stuck another one of them.

"Ouch!"

"That's yours. That one. Pull it in."

And he stuck all of them the same way until he had the very last one on his feet.

·48· El Achichinque

• THIS WAS a couple, and the husband had a friend who came to visit him often. And the wife didn't like it; she didn't want him to come. So once the friend came, and the man of the house took his horse, unsaddled it, and took it away, while the friend stayed in the house.

Then the wife said, thinking it was her husband who was

there, "You! Never happy unless you're bringing *achichinques* [spongers] to the house."

"You be quiet! Go kill a chicken for his supper!"

So the wife went and got a chicken and killed it and called them to supper. They made a bed for the friend, some distance away, over there in another room. And later the husband says, "Now, what's going on? Why did you kill a chicken now that my friend came, when you wouldn't kill a chicken for me?"

"You told me to do it."

"I never said such a thing."

"When the *achichinque* went to take away his horse, you told me."

"It was him," he said. "He stayed there."

So then the friend left before dawn because he was embarrassed.

·49· *The Man Who Was Full of Truth*

• THIS WAS A MAN who was a great liar, the biggest liar in the whole town. Never in his life did anyone know him to tell the truth. So in the end he died, as all of us must. And so they came to bury him.

And the widow, when the coffin was going out the door, began to weep and yell, "You are leaving us; oh, little carcass so full of truth! You are leaving us; oh, little carcass so full of truth!"

Finally one of her *comadres,* who was her best friend, asks her, "Listen, *comadre,* why do you keep calling it a little carcass full of truth? Wasn't my *compadre* just a bit on the lying side?"

"Plenty," she said. "That's why he's leaving us so full of all kinds of truths. He never let one out."

·50· *The Miraculous Mesquite*

• THIS WAS A MAN who was very bad to his wife, somewhere in the back country. He beat her every day, terrible beatings that left her all black and blue. Life was hell for the poor thing. And sometimes she said, "Oh, I wish he would die, so I could have some rest."

So one day he had a fit and fell down like dead. They put him in the coffin, held a wake, prayed over him. And early next day they took him out to bury him, on the shoulders of four *rancheros* from the village. The coffin was just a poor box, and they wouldn't put the lid on it until they got to the cemetery.

As the body left the house, the widow began to tear her hair and scream, for this was what she was supposed to do, no matter how happy she was to see him dead now. Just then, as they were passing with the box under a mesquite, the man woke up from the fit he had. So he sat up in the box and grabbed hold of a branch of the mesquite, a branch that was hanging low.

At this they put the box on the ground and took him out; they cared for him, and he ended up hale and hearty. So he went on as before, drinking and beating his wife. And so on for a few months, until he had another fit that was the real thing. Well, this time the wake lasted three days, until the body began to smell. But no. This time he was good and dead.

Well, so they take him out on their shoulders once more, and the widow began to cry and yell the same as the first time. But she was watching where they carried the body through the yard, and now and then she would stop crying and yell at them [weepy voice], "Don't take him under the mesquite! Don't take him under the mesquite!"

·51a· *The Mourning Fee*

• THIS WAS A WIFE whose husband was very sick. And she didn't know how to cry. But she had a *comadre* who could cry very loud. So then she asked her if she would do her the favor of crying for her when her husband died. And she said all right, if she would give her a bushel of corn.

So when he died, she began to cry. And then the wife would say, "Cry me a good cry, *comadre,* and your bushel shall be filled to the brim."

·*51b*·   *The Widow's Cat*

• THIS WAS A WOMAN whose husband died. So her *comadre* came to offer her condolences. But the woman was making *tamales* when the *comadre* arrived, so she put the lid on the pot. But she didn't cover the pot well enough, and she left it there. So the *comadre* came, and she covered her head and began crying, "Oh, my dear *comadre!* Oh, my dear *comadre!*"

Now she had a cat named Lot, and when she peeked out from under her shawl, she saw the cat was taking a *tamal* out of the pot and eating it. Then it took another. And then another. But since the *comadre* was there with her condolences, she couldn't chase the cat away.

So the widow began to say, "Oh, cursed Lot! To lose them, one by one!"

And the *comadre* said, "What are we going to do, *comadrita.* If God wills it so."

And she kept saying every time the cat took a *tamal,* "Oh, cursed Lot! To lose them, one by one!"

"*Comadrita,* we must be resigned to our fate."

So at last she broke out and said, "No, *comadre!* It's that wicked cat that is carrying off all my *tamales!*"

·*52*·   *Who Spittled?*

• THERE WAS a Negro woman who was deceiving her husband. One day she was with her lover when they saw the husband coming. The woman hid the other man behind the door, but in his fright he spit on the floor before he hid. The husband comes in and sees the spittle on the floor.

"Who spittled?" he says.

"I spittled!" says the other man, coming out from behind the door.

"Well spittled!" says the husband, when he saw the other man was bigger and fiercer than he was.

·53a· *Pedro de Urdemalas and the Gringo*

• ONCE PEDRO DE URDEMALAS was going along the main road, driving along the little burro he had with him. It still was a long way to the place where he was going, his money was almost gone, and soon he would be left with nothing at all. So then he thought of selling his little burro, the only wealth he had left. But naturally he wanted to get the most profit possible out of the sale. So he made the burro eat the last of the coins he had left.

Next day, while they were traveling, the little burro felt like shitting, and it cast out the coins it had eaten the night before, along with the manure. Pedro got down at once and began to pick out the coins that were mixed into the dung. He was very busy picking them out when a *gringo* came up, well mounted and driving a pair of mules loaded with small bundles.

When he came close to Pedro he said, "Oh, *coño!* What doing there, you?"

"I'm gathering up the coins my little burro just shit."

"How's that, *coño!* Your little burro shit money instead of dung?"

"Sure, *coño,* he does it five or six times a day, and I gather a handful of coins each time, like this one you see here."

"*Coño!* Then you being rich from so much gathering money."

"Not very rich, but I have enough to live on without working."

"Why not you selling me your little burro, *coño?*"

"Oh, no!" says Pedro, crossing himself, "this little burro has a power in his stomach which sees to it that all he eats is turned into money. There isn't another like him in the world."

"Me giving you these two mules loaded with money for him."

"Not if you give me four, *coño.* What do I want with two mules loaded with silver, when my little burro can give me enough in a few days to load a whole herd of mules?"

"Oh, *coño!* Me giving you my horse, too, so you can ride on him."

"But what do I gain by riding your horse, when I am more

content riding my burro? Besides giving me an easier ride, I also have the pleasure of getting down now and then to gather coins. I might sell him to you if you gave me the two mules loaded with silver, your horse, and that suit with the gold buttons you're wearing now."

"Oh, yes, *coño!* Me give you all you ask! But little burro must be mine."

"Of course," says Pedro. "So get off the horse and take off your clothes, quick because I'm in a hurry."

Pedro put on the *gringo*'s clothes, mounted the horse, and drove off the mules. "Good-bye, *coño,*" said Pedro, transformed into a fine gentleman. "Give plenty of feed to the burro so he'll do a good job shitting on your hand."

Each of them went his own way, and no one has heard of them to date.

· *53b* · *Pedro de Urdemalas and the Gringo*

· PEDRO WAS GOING along the main road, to some nearby town on some very urgent business. But he was walking so fast that when noon came, he was already very tired. Just then he came to a *huijul* tree loaded with foliage, and he stopped to make a little burro out of wood on which he thought to continue his journey. When he finished it, he mounted it and acted as if he was riding. Just then a *gringo* came by mounted on a good horse.

When he saw Pedro on the wooden burro, the *gringo* said, "Say, *coño,* your little burro be very pretty. You selling her to me? I giving you much money for her."

No, *coño,*" Pedro says, "I won't sell her for any kind of money. She's so good there isn't a horse to equal her. If I sell her to you, how can I finish my journey?"

"Oh, *coño!* You selling her to me for any kind of money."

"I can't sell her to you, I tell you," Pedro says again, "because I would miss her a lot. I couldn't find another one like her in the world. This is an enchanted little burro, that's why she is the way you see her now. But when she starts traveling, her hoofs scarcely touch the ground, and you don't even feel she's moving. The only way I would let her go is by trading her for your horse, but only if you give me your clothes besides."

"Oh, *coño!* It's a deal. You taking my clothes and my horse, and me keeping your little burro."

The *gringo* thinking that the little wooden burro would be a great novelty among his countrymen, did not hesitate in giving him what he asked. And once Pedro was ready to go, he told the *gringo,* "Well, *coño,* you stay here with my little burro, and I'll move along with your horse. Try to be very patient and very calm, because it will cause you some trouble at first to get her moving. I hope you have a lot of fun with her. So long. Ah, *coño!*" says Pedro. "I had forgotten to tell you that you mustn't mount right away, because if you do she will disappear right from under you, and you won't ever see her again. Wait till I'm beyond the mountain pass, and when I have crossed it, you can mount."

After he said this, Pedro spurred the horse and went on his way. When the *gringo* figured Pedro had reached the spot, he mounted the little burro and tried to make her go. At first he talked to her lovingly, "Let's go, dear little burro! Let's go; move!"

When he saw she wouldn't move no matter how much he urged her, he began to lose patience and said, "Let's go, burro! Let's go, burro; move!"

Since the burro didn't move, his impatience grew so much that he took a stick and beat her to pieces. The *gringo* was very angry because of the trick, and he began to insult Pedro and to slash at the air with his knife, saying, "These are for you, *coño.* May they catch up with you and pierce your soul."

Pedro, on his part, had a good deal of foresight, and as he rode along, he kept saying to himself, "That for your mother, you red-faced *gringo,* just in case you are remembering mine."

·54a· Pedro de Urdemalas and the House with Strange Names

• A VERY IMPRUDENT BOY went to a house and kept asking about the names of things. The mistress of the house didn't want to tell him, so she answered with other names. Like for example, there was a hog's head, and she told him it was the Eternal Father. A round cheese she called the moon, sausages were angels, and a pretty girl living there was the cool breeze.

Next morning he left while it was still dark, and he went and told the mistress of the house: "I will enjoy the cool breeze as I walk along with the moon. May the angels accompany me, while the Eternal Father is with you."

That is, he was taking the girl with him, as well as the cheese and the sausages. Since the hog's head was too heavy to carry, he was leaving it to the owners of the house.

·54b· Pedro de Urdemalas and the House with Strange Names

• THIS SAME BOY went to another house and also asked questions. And he was told that the mistress of the house was named Haste; the master, Powers of the Air; the cat, Saint Petercatkins; water, patience; the bed, easy chair; and the fire, illumination.

On hearing a noise that night, the boy looked and saw the eyes of the cat shining in the dark, so he cried out:

> Arise, arise and come with Haste,
> O Powers of the Air;
> Here comes Saint Petercatkins
> Full of illumination;
> Put it out with patience
> Or he'll burn your easy chair.

·55· *Pedro de Urdemalas and the Priest*

• THERE ONCE WAS a very quick-witted boy. His head had been shaved, and he was roaming about the streets when he met a priest. The priest said, "Where do you come from, hairless?"

"From where they shaved my head."

"Where does this road go?"

"Nowhere; it stays in the same place."

The priest thought, "This boy is very clever; I'll give him an education."

"Will you go live with me?"

"Sure, why not." And they went to the priest's house.

"What's your name?"

"Thus."

Well, all right. He served the priest for some time, and one day the priest told him, "Go get me what is half I and half not I."

The boy cut a leaf from a maguey plant and peeled it on one side. He handed it to the priest, thorny side first, and he got stuck and said, "¡Ay! [Ouch!]"

"That's the ¡ay! half," said Thus. "The other half isn't ¡ay!"

The priest didn't like this, but he didn't send the boy away. Just about this time somebody gave the priest some cheeses, and he put them away up high in his cupboard. A few days later he saw that the boy had eaten the cheeses, and he asked him how he had managed to reach them.

"I made use of your library," said the boy.

The priest thought the boy had been reading his books, so he began to go through them himself to find what the boy had learned. But no, what the boy had done was to pile up the priest's books so he could reach the cheeses.

The next day the priest asked for a chicken, done nice and brown in the oven. The housekeeper prepared it, but the boy ate a whole leg of it on his way from the kitchen to the table.

"What's going on? Why does it have only one leg?"

"Father, haven't you seen them in the barnyard? They have only one leg."

"Let's go see."

So they went and looked, and the chickens did have only one leg. They were sleeping with a leg drawn up. But when they were called, they lowered the other leg. "You see, father?" he said. "Just like yours. You should have said, 'Chick! Chick!' before you ate it."

Finally, one day Thus took all the priest's money and disappeared. While the priest slept, the boy had smeared soot all over the priest's face. Next day the priest went out asking people, "Has anybody seen me Thus?"

Everyone would look at him in astonishment, and they would say, "No, father. We have never seen you look like this before."

And they say he's still looking for the little rascal.

• 56 • *Pedro de Urdemalas, Schoolmaster*

• ONE DAY PEDRO said to his wife, "I'm going to set up a school."

"But how can that be? You can't even read or write."

"That's none of your business. Don't meddle in things you know nothing about."

All the villagers sent their children to Pedro's school, and all they were taught was to say, "You can't, and I can't either."

After some time had passed, the parents asked their children, "Let's see. What have you learned in school? What does that writing say?"

"Well, it says, 'You can't, and I can't either.' "

Another one told his father, "It says, 'But you can't, and neither can I.' "

"But it couldn't say that."

"Yes, father, that's what the teacher said."

So they understood what it meant, "You can't read, and I can't either." All the villagers got together, and they went to see the famous teacher. But he had disappeared in a cloud of dust along with his wife. And so they were tricked.

·57· *The Sham Wise Man*

• THERE WAS A KING who had a very good horse that he loved very much. One day some bandits stole it. No matter how much they looked for it, they couldn't find it. Then the king called together many wise men and soothsayers. Among them was a very poor man who was in such great need that he pretended to be a soothsayer, just to see if he could find the horse by accident.

He was, on top of everything, a great drunkard, and he was in this state when he decided to take the chance and said, "I'll go see what I can say, and perhaps I'll make some money."

But once there, cold sober and surrounded by wise men, he began to feel very frightened. None of the wise men could tell where the horse was or who had stolen it. It came the drunkard's turn, and the king stared at him and thought, "This one is no soothsayer." Finally he said, "You have three days to find out where my horse is. Do you dare? What will you offer as security?"

"My head," said the drunkard, and he went away feeling very sad.

They shut him up in a room with some windows. Next day a man came and talked to him through the window. "What's the matter? Why do you look so worried? Is it true that you said you would find the king's horse?"

"That's right. And one of them is here already." He meant one of the three days the king had allowed him.

The robber was frightened, and he went and saw the other two and told them what the soothsayer had said. "And he said, 'Here's one of them already.'"

The next day the second robber went to see the drunk through the window and started a conversation like the first. The soothsayer said, "That's right. And now here is the second." He meant the second day.

The robber was greatly frightened, and he went away. The next day the third robber came and asked him questions the way the others had done. The soothsayer said, "That's right. And here is the third and last one."

The bandit was convinced, and he thought to win him over to their side, so he said, "Yes, we stole the horse. But if you say nothing about it, we'll give you part of the money we're going to get for it."

"No, you'd better bring it back so I can get out of here."

That same day, just as they were going to behead him, the robbers appeared with the horse, and they were the ones who were executed. But the king still didn't believe in the man, so he said, "I'm going to find out if he really is a soothsayer."

He had a pot filled with excrement and commanded the soothsayer to tell what was in it. The poor little drunk kept walking round and round the pot, greatly distressed, and he finally said, "Oh, what a crock of shit!"

Since that was what the pot contained, they gave him another riddle to solve. They buried a sow and took him to see if he could guess what was buried there. This time he was completely disheartened and knew that all was lost, so he said, "Oh, my God! This is where the sow turned up her tail and died!"

And since that's what was buried there, they were fully convinced he was a soothsayer, among the best of them, so they gave him some bags full of money.

· 58 · *Laziness Rewarded*

• Do you already know the tale about, "When God wishes to give, he will bring it to my house?" Well, then, I'll tell it to you.

There were two *compadres*. One was a very hard worker. Every day he went to the fields. He worked his piece of land, brought home his load of wood. You never found him just sitting around. The lazy one never wanted to work. He never went to the fields; he didn't sow his cornfield; he brought home no wood. Nothing but lying in his hammock.

Every day his wife would say, "Go on, lazy! Get up! Go on to the fields like your *compadre!* Clear your field and plant your corn! Bring some wood! Don't be so lazy! Get up!"

But the lazy one always answered, "Hush, woman! I'm staying here. When God wishes to give, he will bring it to my house."

But the poor woman was tired of seeing this lazy man just lying there, and she had to bring in all the wood, all the water. She was the one who worked hard to support the lazy man. Finally, she said one day, "This is too much. I can't stand you any more. Go on! Get up! This time you are going to work with your *compadre*. He's going to clear some land over there. Come here and get your machete. Here's your lunch. Now, go!" And she pushed him out of the house.

"Ah, what a woman," he answered. "Haven't I told you, 'When God wishes to give, he will bring it to my house'? It's no use for me to go to the woods and clear a piece of land. Work doesn't agree with me."

But he had to go anyway because his wife was very angry. Because of that he went with his *compadre*. But once they got to the place where they were going to clear the land, the lazy one made a little house—just a little shed, for shade—and he hung up his hammock. He spent the day lying there.

Next day he brought an old pot with him. He put it in a corner there. This was going to be his toilet; he was that lazy. His *compadre* worked every day, but the lazy man didn't clear even a tiny bit of land.

His *compadre* would tell him, "Come on, *compadre,* get up and work. Don't you see time is passing! It's almost time for planting. If you don't clear and burn the land soon, you won't be able to plant your cornfield."

But he only answered, "Leave off, *compadre*. I'm not going to do any clearing. When God wishes to give, he will bring it to my house." And he would stay there, sitting under his little shed.

Some days later, when the *compadre* planted his cornfield, the lazy one no longer went. Then the hardworking one came and told him, "*Compadre,* I found a pot of money where I was working. Do you want to go get it?"

"When God wishes to give, he will bring it to my house," the lazy one answered.

The hardworking one got very angry at his *compadre*'s laziness. He was thinking of the pot he had seen the lazy one use as a toilet. So then he went and brought it back very carefully. The lazy *compadre* and his wife were already asleep, so he went and put it right on the door of the house, so when somebody went and opened the door, the pot would fall into the house and spill all the filth inside.

"Now," he thought, "let's see if he says, 'When God wishes to give, he will bring it to my house.' "

Early next morning the lazy man had an urgent need, and he rushed outside. When he pulled at the door, the pot fell inside the house and broke. All that was inside the pot spilled over the floor of the house. When the lazy man came back, he took a pine knot to see what had fallen when he went out. Well, there was a pile of gold coins there.

He woke his wife at once. "Look here! Haven't I told you a thousand times? And you scolding me every day. You see? Just as I told you, there it is. When God wishes to give, he will bring it to my house. This must be the pot that my *compadre* told me about. He must have been the one who brought it to me. Go take a big gourdful of gold to my *compadre* and thank him for me."

So the woman went. It was barely light when she called the *compadre*. "*Compadre, compadre*. Your *compadre* sends you this gourd. Thank you for bringing us the pot full of gold."

"Gold, indeed!" the *compadre* thought.

He got up and opened the door. There was his *comadre* with a great big gourd full of gold coins. So he went to see for himself at his *compadre*'s house. There was the old pot. Just as he had thought, it fell inside and broke up completely. But instead of filth scattered about, there was nothing but gold.

"You see, *compadre*? You also were always scolding me and pestering me to go work. Didn't I tell you that when God wishes to give, he will bring it to my house?"

· 59 · *The Two Psychiatrists*

· Two MEXICAN PSYCHIATRISTS decided to analyze each other. And one of them says, "I had a very strange dream; I don't know how to interpret it according to the doctrine of Freud. That after Kennedy was here I got a phone call, 'Kennedy speaking. Come on over, because I want to see you.' So I went to the airport, and there was a jet waiting for me from the United States, courtesy of JFK. So to Washington, where they gave me a dinner, a great banquet. And then on another plane across the continent to Seattle and the World's Fair. Nothing to do but enjoy myself for three months."

"Now," says the other, "my dream was even stranger. Just think, I dreamed I was living in an apartment house, an extremely elegant one. And I was just about to go to bed when somebody knocked on the door. I opened. And who do you think it was? Marilyn Monroe. I asked her in, and we had a highball. And then, we were sitting there drinking, when she began to take off her clothes until she was completely naked.

"But just think, before anything could happen, somebody knocked on the door again. I opened. And who do you think it was? Kim Novak. I asked her in, and she had a highball. And then she began to take off her clothes until she was naked. And there I was, with these two beautiful naked dames, one on each side of me, and I couldn't do anything."

"God damn!" he says. "Why didn't you call me?"

"I did," he says. "But they told me you were in Seattle."

.60. All's for the Best

• THIS WAS A MAN who went to ask for work. To a town. And he came to a place and asked for work, and they told him, "Do you want work as a street-sweeper?"

"Yes, of course." The poor man didn't know how to do any kind of work.

They said, "Let's see. What's your name?"

"Well, so-and-so."

"Sign your name here."

"Well, I don't know how to write."

"If you can't write your name, we can't hire you. Not even as a street-sweeper."

"I can make an X."

"No, it isn't enough. You must know how to read and write."

The man went away very sad, and since he had to make some kind of a living, he began to sell a few little tomatoes on the street. And he did very well. He bought himself a flivver and kept on selling vegetables. And he kept doing well. And after that he opened a little stand and went up in the world with his tomatoes, those little tomatoes that he sold. And with the passing of the years he got to be rich.

One day he went to the bank, and he was carrying a lot of money. He went and put it in the bank. When they made him the slip—"Sign here, if you please"—he made an *X*.

He said, "Listen, señor. Please put down your name."

"I don't know how to write."

He said, "Just think, señor. You don't know how to write, and you are so rich. Imagine how rich you would be if you knew how to write."

"If I knew how to write, I would be sweeping the streets out there."

.*61a* . *The Rider in the Brambles*

• IN A VILLAGE whose name is no longer remembered, a man was traveling on horseback. He had to pass through a forest that was haunted, it was said. When he entered the place, he felt all of a sudden that somebody was holding on to his waist, so tight he couldn't get away.

Half dead with fright, he spent the rest of the night there, scarcely daring to breathe. With the first light of dawn, he saw he was being held fast by some brambles.

.*61b* . *The Stake in the Graveyard*

• WELL, MY GRANDFATHER used to tell us this one. He was a physician, and he went to visit a patient one night, and it was raining and there was a high wind. There was a lot of lightning and thunder and I don't know what. And on the way back, he stopped at a little *cantina* for one last drink before going to bed.

He went inside and sat down at a table somewhat apart, by himself. And then he saw two or three men arguing over at the bar. They were a bit drunk already. And one of them bet another he wouldn't go to the very center of the graveyard that night. It was a little town, and they were agreed more or less as to which grave represented the center of the graveyard. So the other two bet he wouldn't go to the very center and drive a stake into the grave, exactly at midnight.

Grandfather used to say it was about eleven-thirty. So they kept on drinking for a while, until it was twelve. And then this man went off by himself, with a stake and a hatchet. Not a hammer, a hatchet. And he said, "I'll be back in a little while and take all of you to see where I drove the stake. Just to show you I'm not afraid, because I've got them."[Gesture, signifying big, heavy testicles, symbol of courage.]

So the man left all by himself, and they stayed there in the *cantina* drinking. The graveyard was close by, some three, four blocks. They could see him until he went in the gate, every time the lightning flashed. It was still raining hard, and the wind was blowing hard, too.

So the man went off and didn't come back, and grandfather decided to stay just to see what would happen. Well, it got to be 12:15, and then 12:20, and finally half-past twelve. And the man didn't come back.

Well, so they organized a party, with lamps and lanterns and this and that, and they all went to the graveyard in a group, all those who had been at the *cantina*. And grandfather in the bunch. They went, and they found him there, with the stake driven right into the center of the grave. But they found him good and dead, stiff. As if he had tried to run and died like that, all stiff like that.

What happened was that when he squatted down to drive in the stake, the wind blew his cloak, and he drove the stake over the cloak. And when he tried to leave, he felt that something pulled at him, and he died of fright.

Grandfather used to say that his eyes were opened wide, great big.

[From audience (In English): *"By the way, did he have brown eyes?"* Laughter.]

.62. *The Fool and His Brother*

• THIS WAS A WOMAN and two boys. One of them was a fool, and the other one was bright. One day the bright one was out working while the fool stayed home taking care of their mother. When the bright one came home to eat at noon, the other one said, "Listen, mother is very sick."

"As soon as I eat, I'll go get the doctor. Heat some water so we can bathe her." So the bright one went to get the doctor, and the fool stayed home heating the water. He got the water boiling hot, and then he grabbed her and ducked her in it. Then he sat her down in the doorway so she would scare away the chickens, with a stick in her hand. She was grinning with all her teeth, good and dead.

The bright one came back, "How is mother?"

"Whoo! She's fine; just look at her. There she is smiling happily and shooing the chickens."

"Ah, you stupid fool! What have you done? Just look! You killed our mother," he said. Well, so they began to call the neighbors and all that. People got together, and they fixed her up and laid her out and buried her.

Then the bright one said, "I'm not staying here. I'm going away."

"If you go away, I'm going too."

"I don't want you with me. You stay here. I don't want anybody to go with me. I want to go by myself."

"No," he said, "I'm going with you."

They were a ways off when he remembered they had a boar pig tied up in the yard. So the bright one said to the fool, "Go untie the boar, poor little thing. Let him wander off to the village. Let him go where he likes. What is he going to do tied there?"

Well, no. . . .

After a while he hears hammering. "Oh, what could that fool be doing? Good Lord! He's got me so I. . . ." Well, so there he came at last with the door on his back. "Man, I didn't tell you to bring the door. I told you to untie the boar."

"Oh," he said, "this was going to be my share of the house, so this is what I'm taking."

"All right, carry it then, as long as you want. But don't think I'm going to help you," he said.

They traveled along, and so they went until they found a park belonging to twenty-five robbers. It was a very pretty place, with some tables very nicely set and plenty of food. And a lot of horses and money. They had all sorts of things, being robbers. So the bright one said, "This is a robbers' park," he said. "We must listen to see if they are coming."

"I won't listen or anything. I'm going to eat." And he begins to eat. Then they heard the clatter of horses.

"Listen, horses are coming," says the boy who was not a fool. He said, "Let's climb up the tree. Leave that door there."

"No, I'm taking the door with me. I won't leave it." And he carried it up.

So the robbers got there, and the leader ordered them to put plenty of food on the table. And they began to eat. And the fool was up there. He had just eaten. He said, "Brother, brother, I want to shit."

"But you can't shit, man. They'll know there's people up here, and they'll kill us."

"I'm going to do it anyway." And he pulled his pants down.

The captain said, "Throw that food away and bring some more! Just look at what those filthy birds did! They crapped all over everything." So they threw it all away and cleaned up very well. And they began again.

And after a while, "Brother, brother, I want to piss."

"Man, don't be a fool. They'll kill us. They didn't catch on the first time, but they will this time."

"I'm going to do it anyway." So he pulled out . . . . He began to piss.

"Why, just look, man, at those birds. We'll have to kill them one of these days. We can't let them stay there, because they keep getting our food dirty. Throw that away and bring some more."

They set the table again, nice and clean. And the fool said, "Brother, brother, I want to let go of the boar."

"Man, if they haven't found us out yet, they will this time."

"I'm going to do it anyway," he said. "I'm going to let go." And down comes the door, making a terrible racket on the tree-tops, breaking branches and everything.

So the captain said, "Good Lord! This is God's punishment. Let's go," he said. "Because God wants to punish us for the things we are doing." And they left just as the bright brother was about to lose all hope.

So they came down from the tree. And the bright one said, "There's no time to lose. Let's pick out a few horses and load all the money we can."

"You load up on money, and I'll load up on food." And he leaned on the table like this, looking after the men who had run away. One of them, who was a bit braver than the rest, had stopped just at the edge of the woods. The fool saw him and called him over. So he came. And he said, "What's your name? How are you? We're friends, aren't we? I'm a robber too."

"Yes," the man said, "sure."

"But you look very skinny and pale. Why? Let's see. Stick out your tongue," he said. When the robber stuck out his tongue, he grabbed it and cut it off.

He ran off saying, "Blub! Blub! Blub!" And the others ran all the faster.

"That's what you get for going back," they said to him. So they kept running and went away. When the robbers were very far away, the bright one made the fool come back. He loaded up on jerked beef and cooked meats, but the other one did not.

He said, "Now we'll go visit our aunt. But be very careful. She has some very pretty daughters."

"Go on. You're always talking about her pretty daughters. You're always in love. What do I care whether the daughters are pretty or not?" said the fool.

"All right, but I want you to be very careful. Look," he said, "when they invite us to dinner and I step on your foot, you stop eating."

Well, so they walked and walked for many days, until they got to the aunt's house. The aunt cried a lot because of her sister and all that. Then she called the girls to cook for them, and they had supper. So suppertime came, and the fool began to eat, and the bright one too. They were just starting to eat when a dog went by and stepped on the fool's foot. He didn't know it was the dog, and he still wanted to. . . .

So the aunt said to him, "Eat, my boy. Why don't you eat? Don't be embarrassed. I'm your aunt by blood; your mother was my sister," she said.

He didn't say anything. Silent. Then the bright one said, since the aunt was begging him so much, the bright one said, "Come on. Eat."

"Yes, go on and eat. After you told me yourself that when you thought I'd had enough you'd step on my feet. Well, you stepped on them already. And I stopped eating."

"Oh, I didn't say any such thing." And so on. The boy was terribly embarrassed and all that. So he got up from the table and didn't eat either.

The aunt told them, "Those rooms over there, one is for you, and the other is for the other boy, my other nephew."

Well, so it came time for them to go to bed. They all went to lie down, each in his own place. Then, at midnight, the fool got very hungry, so he got up. Before that, he looked very carefully where the beans had been put away, where all the food was put away. So he got up and went there, and he ate until he was full. Then he said (they called him the fool, and he did the same to others) he said, "I'm going to take some to that fool brother of mine. He never eats well because he's always silly and in love."

So he went and stumbled on the old woman. She was all uncovered, and he smeared plenty of beans on her. Then she broke wind. And he says, "Don't blow on them. They're cold."

Then the old man turned over and felt that she was wet. And he said, "Wife, wife, wife!"

"What, dear?"

"Dear nothing! You shit! You dirty old woman, go wash at the well."

She rubbed herself and smelled, and she says, "It's beans, dear."

"Of course. That's what you ate, wasn't it? Go wash."

Meanwhile the fool had caught his hand in the pot. Then he saw a light, when the old woman went out, and the fool went out too. And he goes and hits her over the head with the pot.

The old woman cried out, "Oh, my dear! Don't beat me. It's beans."

"I'm over here, as quiet as can be. Don't make such a fuss. I'm not hurting you," said the old man.

So the bright brother said, "All this is the doing of that nuisance of a fool," he says. "I'm tired of him; I don't know what to do with him." So the bright one got up at that hour. But he didn't go out where the old woman was. He went out the back way and got the horses ready, and then he called the fool, and they went away.

All along the way he scolded and scolded, and the fool said, "Well, it's your fault. Why do you tell me to do things?"

So they traveled until they came to a palace. And the bright one said, "Let's look for a poor woman, one of those living down here, so we can ask for a place to stay, because, what are we going to do? We don't know anyone."

So they came to a place, and the woman said, "Come in, my children. Tell me what I can do for you."

"We are looking for a job, granny."

"Well, the one who has lots of jobs is the king."

"Yes, but I don't want to go to the king."

"What's the matter with him? Is he your brother? What's wrong with him?"

"He's a bit stupid. I can't stand him any more," said the bright one. "I'd like to get him a job and let it end at that with us, because I'm just so. . . . He has done a lot of harm, even killed our mother. He has done a lot of damage."

The old woman said, "You don't have to worry about that. Look, go to that house over there, and they'll give you plenty of money. But you won't be alive the next day. They are all dead by morning. Because a ghost haunts the place, and they tell all sorts of things about it," she said. "Just now they already have a man who's going to watch there tonight. We can go tomorrow very early. But you'll have to ask your brother if he wants to go. Because if he doesn't want to, what can you do?"

Well, so they had supper there that night at the old woman's house, and they went to bed. The next day dawned, and the two of them came out. "Listen," he said, "do you see that house?"

"Yes."

"Would you like to go there and look after it? You'd be surprised how much they pay."

"Uh, sure, why not? Don't anybody else want to do it?"

"They don't," the bright one said. "They don't want to because anybody that goes there doesn't last the night. He dies. They say you can hear groans and that you see ghosts. They say all sorts of things."

"I don't mind the ghosts or anything," he said. "Just buy me plenty of bread and *piloncillo* [brown sugar loaf], and a candle. I'll go watch the place," he said.

So they went and saw the judge, and the judge said it was all right. That night the brother bought him everything he wanted and took him there. And he started eating right then and there. Plenty of bread, because the brother knew how the fool loved to stuff himself. So he was eating and eating when he heard a voice, "Do I come down, or don't I come down?"

"Wait a while. I'm eating."

So the ghost said to itself, "This is the one who will get the treasure. At least he spoke to me. All the others have just keeled over." But it kept on saying, "Do I come down, or don't I come down?"

"I'm telling you not to. Don't you understand what I say? Let me finish my supper, and then you can come down."

And it kept on saying, "Do I come down, or don't I come down?"

"Well, come on down, confound it! You just won't listen, will you? I've been telling you not to come down, and I'm tired of saying it. So come on down, and let's see what you look like," he said.

Well then, a pile of bones fell down, and he just kept on eating and eating and eating. In a sack. And then it became a ghost, nothing but the skeleton. So he looks it up and down and says "All right now, and what are you doing here?"

"Oh, nothing. I haunt this house."

"And why do you haunt it? Let's see you tell me that."

It said why. There was a room bigger than this one we're in, with a dirt floor, and all of it was full of money, jewels, gold, silver, and everything. And it said, "You know why I haunt this place? Because I have a lot of money here. All these lands and everything are mine, everything that's here, lands and all. But I made a vow I didn't keep, so the man who can stay alive in this place must fulfill the vow for me, and after that everything in here is yours."

Well, so he went. He said, "And how am I going to prove that all this is mine?"

"Finish your supper and let's go to that wardrobe. Get that bunch of keys over there." He opened the wardrobe, and the ghost gave him the deeds to the lands. It gave him everything, all he needed to be the owner.

So it was nothing but dig and dig all the blessed night. He dug all night. He pulled out one pot after another. He didn't lie down to sleep until about four in the morning. And by five o'clock, there comes the priest and his acolytes, and the fool's brother. They knocked and banged, but he was sleeping like a stone. After they called him five or six times and banged a lot on the door, the judge said, "It's no use. We'll have to break down the door with an ax. Men that spend the night here never see the dawn."

"What's that? Are you going to use an ax on the door? Why, here I am, safe and sound. As lively as you please," he said.

"Well, open the door," said the brother, all confused.

He opened the door. And, "Well, what are all these men in petticoats doing here? What did you bring them for? All these monkeys with red hats? Tell them to go, all of them! All this is mine."

The judge said, "What do you have as proof that all this is yours?"

"Look," said the fool. And he showed him everything. "Now all of you can go. And you come here," he said to the bright brother.

And he showed him everything. He told him to get married, that it was all for him because he had no use for all that. So the bright brother did pretty well, and *colorín* so red, the story is said.

.63. *Thank God It Wasn't a Peso*

• THIS WAS a little bum who got drunk every night, and he woke up every morning with a horrible hangover. And he would always pass by the church very early in the morning. Outside the church, almost in the street, there was an image in a niche; and every morning the drunk would say, "Give me a peso, O Sacred Heart, because I've got it really bad."

The sexton had pity on him after hearing him so many times, so one day he took a half-peso piece and wrapped it up in paper. And to give it weight, he also put a stone in with the coin. When the bum came to beg of the Sacred Heart, he threw the little bundle from a window, and it went and hit him right on the forehead. It raised a great big bump.

The drunk picks up the package and finds the coin. And he says, "O Sacred Heart! If you had given me a peso instead of just a half, you would have killed me!"

.64. *The Stupid Drover*

• THERE WAS a little old man and a little old woman who took care of an orchard. One night he fell sick, and the wife went out to the edge of the road, to see if she could find somebody to come help her pray over him so he could die a Christian death. She found a drover and asked him to help her, but the man didn't want to because he said he didn't know what to do.

He says, "What will I say?"

"Things about the church."

"Altars, vestments, monstrances, candlesticks?"

"No, no! Things that are sweet to the soul."

"Taffy, candied citron, glazed pumpkin?"

"No, no! tender things."

"Green squash, string beans, tomatoes?"

"No, no! Things that will move the soul."

"Ah, things that remove the soul. Cutlasses, daggers, knives?"

And in the meantime the little old man died.

·65· *The Rosary of Amozoc*

• THEY TELL THAT in Amozoc there used to live a woman who was very gay. She loved to drink and carouse, and she was called "La Culata." She could always be found in saloons and pulque shops with men. Then some missionaries came to town, and when they heard about the life this woman led and about other excesses among the townspeople, they organized a series of meetings.

They called on everyone to abandon their vices and become decent people. They made remarks about "those bad women you sometimes see, who drink and scandalize the town, who fight and do other improper things." And then they began to sing a litany.

The people in church heard them say, *"Mater Immaculata."*

They began to whisper to each other, "You heard. They say to kill La Culata" [Matar La Culata].

Some said yes and others said no, and pretty soon the dispute became a riot, and this gave rise to the saying, "To end up like the Rosary of Amozoc."

·66· *God Gives a Hundred for One*

• THIS WAS a little Indian who owned a cow. The priest of the village took a fancy to the animal; he wanted to breed it to his bulls. So one day he said to his parishioners during the sermon, "We must give alms to the church and help our neighbors, for God gives a hundredfold for one."

A few days later he asked the Indian for his cow, but the Indian said he couldn't give it to the church, because that was the only one he had. But the priest insisted. Then the Indian's wife said, "All right, let him have her."

But before giving up the cow, she bathed it in salt water and dusted it with powdered salt. Then she said to her husband, "The little cow is ready. Let them take her away."

The Indian did so, and he left his cow at the priest's. But the other animals smelled all the salt on it, and they crowded around and began to lick it. The cow was used to its own corral, so it jumped the fence that night and went off. And all the bulls followed it.

Next day the priest sent some men for his livestock. But the Indian told them, "No, this livestock is mine. God has given me a hundred for one. So I'm going to count the cattle, and if there aren't a hundred of them, the priest will have to make up the difference."

After this lesson the priest never again asked for tithes.

.67. All Priests Go to Hell

• A LITTLE OLD INDIAN was on his deathbed, and his wife went to see their father confessor. But the housekeeper said, "I'm not going to wake him up."

"But my poor husband is dying."

They kept arguing until the priest got up to see what it was all about. Finally, after a good deal of argument, he agreed to go see the sick man and give him confession. But when they got there the man was already dead.

So then the priest was very angry, and he said to the Indian woman, "Why didn't you call me in time?"

"But, little father, when I went and called you, there was still time."

Then the dead man sat up and said, "God gives me permission to come back to life only to say to you:

> That most Indian women are saved,
> And some Indian men as well,
> But all you priests go to hell."

.68. I Can't Hear a Thing

• IN A CHURCH there was a sexton who took care of the place. Once the priest tells him, "Listen, my son, it's time you came to confession. You have not confessed for a long time."

"It's all right, father." So he came up to the confessional. But he says to the priest, "I want to confess on the side where you can't see my face."

"It's all right," he says. "Of course."

He went over to the side where women confess, where neither the face of the priest nor the person confessing can be seen. So then, when he was there, the priest says, "Let's see now, my son, tell me all your sins."

So the sexton began to tell all his sins. The priest knew that the sexton had been robbing the poor box. So he says, "Now let's see, my son. Have you by any chance taken something that does not belong to you?"

He says, "Father, I can't hear you. Speak louder."

"I asked if you haven't taken something that does not belong to you. Something, let's say, like money from the poor box."

"*Hombre,* father! I can't hear a thing!"

The priest says, "How strange!"

He says, "Look, father. Why don't you come over on this side of the screen, and I'll go over there, and you'll see that you can't hear a thing."

So the sexton takes the priest's place and the priest goes where the sexton was. And he says, "Now, little father, can you tell me who has been sleeping with my wife?"

And the priest says, "You are right, my son. I can't hear a thing."

·69·   *The Big Christ and the Little Christ*

· THERE WAS A SPANIARD. He had a son he loved very much, and he fell sick one time. Doctors and more doctors came, but he got no better. There was somebody, a friend, who told him, "*Hombre,* why don't you go to church and ask the miracle-working Christ there if he will do a miracle and cure your son?"

"*Hombre,* you may be right! I have no faith in the saints, but I will go ask him. If he works this miracle for me, then I will end up believing that everything you say is true."

And he went to the church, and he asked the Christ. He told

him that his son was very sick and would he cure him, and if he cured him he promised an offering and, well—some money, you know, for that miracle. And then he said besides, that if he came back later—he said it in anger then—that if he went back home and his son was no better, he would come back and break his head.

So he goes back home and finds his son is already dead. And he said, "Well. There's only one thing to do. I promised the Christ I would break his head. Surely he did not do right by me. He didn't do as he should have; he didn't cure my son that I love so much. I'm going to keep my part of the bargain."

In the meantime, the sexton, who had been listening, you know, went and told the priest: "Well, sir. There came a Spaniard named So-and-so to ask for a miracle, that his son was very sick and that if he didn't do the miracle of curing him that then he would break his head."

And the priest tells him, he says, "Look, so it won't cost me too much, you know, go take away the big image of Christ and put a smaller one in its place. It won't cost me so much that way. It doesn't matter if he breaks its head."

Well. So the sexton went and took away the big Christ and put a little one in his place.

When the Spaniard gets there, he looks all around. He just stares. He looks for the big Christ and doesn't see him. All he sees is the little one. Then he says, "Look here, boy. Go tell your father to come here; I don't have any quarrel with you."

·70· *On Holy Week*

• IN SOUTHERN MEXICO they also have the custom, on the day the body of Our Lord Jesus Christ is taken down from the cross, to hire a man to dress in the clothing of Our Lord Jesus Christ, with his crown and all, and they lay him out in the coffin. And they pray around the coffin with candles, all of them there in chorus, and they sing psalms and what have you.

And one time they couldn't find anybody, and they kept looking around. So some friends told a fellow who had got up with

a terrible hangover that morning and didn't have any money
for a drink, "Go on, man; the priest will give you five pesos for
the job. All you have to do is play the part of Our Lord Jesus
Christ, and you have enough for a drink. And you can buy us
one, too."

"So what do I have to do?"

"Nothing. Just lie there in the coffin for about half an hour,
while all of us pray around you."

"All right."

So they laid him out, and they all began to walk around the
coffin, praying and singing psalms. But suddenly he began to
break wind—phew! A drunkard's farts, you know—terrible
stink!

And these guys, friends of his, would go by the coffin and say,

> Here lies the body of Christ,
> What an odor comes from it!
> What can we do but surmise
> That our Redeemer has shit.

·71· *The Miracle of San Pedro Piedra Gorda*

· A RANCHERO WENT to ask a miracle of San Pedro, the patron
saint of the village, and he said, "Look, if you will do this miracle for me, I'll bring you a bull."

The miracle was granted him, and then he thought giving a
bull was really too much. So he came to the church door with
the bull and shouted to San Pedro, "Here's your bull! Where do
you want it?"

The image of the saint did not answer, so the man kept asking until he got tired, and then he said, "All right, I'll just tie it
to your waist." He did so, and as soon as he moved away, the
bull jerked at the rope and dragged the image out of the church
and into the fields.

The man watched it until he could see nothing but the red of
the saint's chasuble. And he yelled, "Hold 'im, redshirt!"

·72·   The Sermon on the Arrest of Jesus

• IT WAS MAUNDY THURSDAY, and the priest was saying the Sermon on the Arrest of Jesus.

The steward of the religious brotherhood that organized the ceremony had to pay for the sermon, and to do this he had to collect from a man who had bought some cowhides from him and had not paid up yet.

Since he couldn't find the man, the steward thought he might be in church listening to the sermon, so he went in and started looking for him. He looked among the congregation and kept going from one end of the church to the other, looking for the buyer of the hides.

Meanwhile the priest was giving his sermon, and he said just then, "Whom seek ye?" (Words that Jesus said when he was apprehended.) But the steward was so preoccupied that he answered quickly, "The man who bought the hides, father."

The priest didn't notice and kept on with his sermon. A short while later he said again, "Whom seek ye?"

The steward was still looking around, and he shouted impatiently, "The man who bought the hides, father. He owes me the money to pay you for the sermon."

·73·   The Famous Sermon

• THERE WAS A PRIEST who loved to preach with great vehemence in the village church about the Seven Last Words of Christ. For this he had the help of the sexton, who would make the image of Christ crucified bow its head in death at the proper moment in the sermon.

Well then, on this occasion the priest said in a voice full of emotion, "Look, my brothers, how Our Savior dies on the cross." He turned to look at the image, but the head did not move.

He began the sermon again and stopped at the same place, but nothing happened. At last he got impatient and shouted, "Why don't you die, oh Jesus mine?"

"Because there's no grease on the thong!" the sexton shouted back.

·74·   *A Current Story*

• THERE'S A LOW DIVE around here in Matamoros that's known as "El Bastantito" [diminutive of *bastante*—plenty, enough]. Because they'll give you plenty to drink for just a few coins. They gather the leftovers from other saloons and sell them of a morning to all the hung-over bums who are good and broke by then. They gather in front of the place very early in the morning, waiting for it to open.

But some of them are so broke they can't scrape up enough for a single drink. So you know what they do? Six or seven of them get together and collect enough for one good drink of mezcal, real rotgut stuff. And then they draw lots to see who is going to drink it.

And then they all stand in line in front of the door of the saloon, and when they serve the mezcal to the first man in line, they all hold hands in the form of a chain. The first man downs the mezcal and begins to quiver and twitch, and then the man next to him begins to do the same, and so on down the line until the shock has passed down to the last one.

Part V
Formula Tales

La Chiva (The Nanny Goat)

·75· *The Nanny Goat*

• I HAVE MY *real* and a half; with a *real* and a half I bought a nanny goat. The nanny had a kid. I have the nanny, I have the kid. And my *real* and a half still is not spent.

I have my *real* and a half; with a *real* and a half I bought a she-ass. The she-ass had a colt. I have the she-ass, I have the colt. I have the nanny, I have the kid. And my *real* and a half still is not spent.

With a *real* and a half that I used to have I bought a turkey hen. The turkey hen had a chick. I have the turkey hen, I have the chick. I have the she-ass, I have the colt. I have the nanny, I have the kid. And my *real* and a half still is not spent.

With a *real* and a half that I used to have I bought a bitch. The bitch had a little puppy. I have the bitch, I have the puppy. I have the turkey hen, I have the chick. I have the she-ass, I have the colt. I have the nanny, I have the kid. And my *real* and a half still is not spent.

I have a *real* and a half; with a *real* and a half I bought a

Negro woman. The Negro woman had a little Negro. I have the Negro woman, I have the little Negro. I have the bitch, I have the puppy. I have the turkey hen, I have the chick. I have the she-ass, I have the colt. I have the nanny, I have the kid. And my *real* and a half still is not spent.

With a *real* and a half that I used to have I bought a *gringo* woman. The *gringo* woman had a little *gringo*. I have the *gringo* woman, I have the little *gringo*. I have the Negro woman, I have the little Negro. I have the bitch, I have the puppy. I have the turkey hen, I have the chick. I have the she-ass, I have the colt. I have the nanny, I have the kid. And my *real* and a half still is not spent.

With a *real* and a half that I used to have I bought a Chinese woman. The Chinese woman had a little Chinaman. I have the Chinese woman, I have the little Chinaman. I have the *gringo* woman, I have the little *gringo*. I have the Negro woman, I have the little Negro. I have the bitch, I have the puppy. I have the turkey hen, I have the chick. I have the she-ass, I have the colt. I have the nanny, I have the kid. And my *real* and a half still is not spent.

·76· *The Ram in the Chile Patch*

• THIS WAS A LITTLE BOY who had a little patch of chile peppers. He tended it with the greatest care. That was what gave him his livelihood. And then one day a little ram got into it.

So the boy began, "Little ram, little ram, get out of that chile patch."

"You unmannerly boy, what are you about? Get out of here or I'll kick you out."

"Little ram, little ram, get out of that chile patch."

"You unmannerly boy, what are you about? Get out of here or I'll kick you out."

Finally he did try to get the little ram out, and the little ram, instead of leaving, gives him a kick and knocks the boy down. He struggles to his feet, and he goes away crying.

He meets a cow, and she says, "What's the matter, little boy?"

"*¡Ay, ay, ay!*" he says. "The little ram knocked me down."

"And why?"

"Because he's in my little chile patch."

"Just wait. I'll go get him out."

The cow comes up, "Moo, moo, moo! Little ram, little ram, get out of that chile patch."

"You big-horned cow, what are you about? Get out of here or I'll kick you out."

"Little ram, little ram, get out of that chile patch."

"You big-horned cow, what are you about? Get out of here or I'll kick you out."

Finally she did try. She tried to hook him with her horns, but the little ram turned around and kicked the cow out.

Then comes the dog, and he says, "I can get him out for sure." And he begins to bark. "Bow-wow-wow-wow! Little ram, little ram, get out of that chile patch."

"You shameless dog, what are you about? Get out of here or I'll kick you out."

"Little ram, little ram, get out of that chile patch."

"You shameless dog, what are you about? Get out of here or I'll kick you out."

The dog kept insisting and he got closer and closer, so the little ram gores him and leaves him the same as the cow.

Then comes the cock. He begins to crow, and he says, "Little ram, little ram, get out of that chile patch."

"You big-eared cock, what are you about? Get out of here or I'll kick you out."

Finally the ram gores the cock and leaves him there with his legs in the air, and he goes away.

He kept on eating up the little chile patch, and the boy was very sad because his chile patch was being eaten up. The burro comes, and he says, "Don't worry, little boy, I'll go get the ram out."

The burro begins, "Little ram, little ram, get out of that chile patch."

"You long-eared burro, what are you about? Get out of here or I'll kick you out."

"Little ram, little ram, get out of that chile patch."

"You long-eared burro, what are you about? Get out of here or I'll kick you out."

At last the ram comes up close. He gores the burro and throws him out. And the boy sees that his little chile patch is almost gone, when a little ant comes, and then he says, "Little ant, little ant, if you would get the little ram out of my little chile patch for me, I would give you a lot of corn."

"How much will you give me?"

"I'll give you a bushel."

"That's too much."

"I'll give you half a bushel."

"That's too much."

"I'll give you a *kilo*."

"That's too much."

"I'll give you a handful."

"All right, then."

So the boy went, while the little ant got the ram out, he went and started grinding the corn so the little ant could carry it away without much trouble.

The ant went little by little, little by little, and climbed up one of his little legs. She started to climb, and climb and climb until she got to his little ass.

She stings him and the ram jumps, it leaps and then begins to say, "Oh, my soul, oh, my soul! She has stung me in the hole! Oh, my soul, oh, my soul! She has stung me in the hole!"

And that is how they were able to get the little ram out.

•77a• *Pérez the Mouse*

• THERE WAS A LITTLE ANT who was very busy sweeping, and she found a penny. And then she said, "What will I buy? If I buy bread, it will soon be gone. If I buy sweets, they will soon be gone."

So she bought a ribbon. She put it on. She sat down in the doorway.

An ox went by, and he said to her, "Little ant, how beautiful you look! Will you marry me?"

She said, "Let's see. How do you talk?"

"I talk, 'Mooo!' "

"No. You have a dreadful voice."

Then a dog went by. He said, "Little ant, how pretty you look! Will you marry me?"

"Let's see. How do you talk?"

"Bow-wow!"

"No. You have a dreadful voice. You frighten me."

Then a lion passed by. He said, "Little ant, how pretty you look! Will you marry me?"

"Let's see. How do you talk?"

He talked in a dreadful voice.

Then a little mouse went by, "Little ant, how pretty you look! Will you marry me?"

"Let's see. How do you talk?"

"Eee! eee! eee! eee! eee!"

"Yes, yes. You have a pretty voice."

So then they were married and they lived quite content. One day the little ant said, "I'm going to mass, so you mind the fire for me."

She went to mass. The little mouse stayed home and minded the fire, and she told him, "Use a big spoon, because if you don't you'll fall in."

The little mouse fell in the pot when he tried to eat the onions. The little ant came back from mass and began to shout, "Little mouse, come here and eat! Little mouse, come here and eat!" But the little mouse didn't come. And since she was very hungry, she began to eat. She took out a plateful, then another, and in the third the little mouse came out of the pot.

Then she was very sad, and she dyed the ribbon black. And she sat down in the doorway, and she cried and cried, "Pérez the Mouse, he fell in the pot, trying to eat the onions! Pérez the Mouse, he ate the pot, trying to eat the onions!"

Colorín so red, the story is said.

·77b· *Pérez the Mouse*

• THIS WAS A WOMAN who had no husband, and she had a servant girl. And every day she would miss the onions. Then one day the woman told the servant girl that if the onions were missing again, she would answer for it with her life. And when she told her, then the girl she sat down and cried and cried, sitting there on a stone.

Then a little ant showed up, and the little ant said to her, "My good girl, why are you crying?"

And she said, "Mmmm. You think not? Pérez the Mouse fell in the pot, trying to eat the onions. And the woman told me that if the onions are missing again, I will answer for it with my life."

And then the little ant said, "In that case I will climb the tree."

And she climbed the tree. And then the tree said, the tree said to her, "Little ant, why do you climb?"

And she said: "Mmm. You think not? Pérez the Mouse fell in the pot trying to eat the onions. And the woman told the servant girl that if the onions are missing again, she will answer for it with her life. And I, I climbed up here."

And then the tree said, it said, "Well then, I will shed my leaves."

And it shed its leaves. After a while some little birds came to nest, and they said to the tree, "Tree, why are you so leafless?"

It said, "Mmm. You think not? Pérez the Mouse fell in the pot trying to eat the onions, and the woman told the servant girl that if the onions are missing again, she will answer for it with her life, and the little ant climbed up on me, and I shed my leaves."

Then the little birds said, "Well, then, we will shed our feathers."

And they shed their feathers. Then, afterward, the little birds went and lighted on some oxen, and the oxen said to them, "Little birds, why are you so featherless?"

They said, "Mmm. You think not? Pérez the Mouse fell in the pot trying to eat the onions, and the woman told the girl that if the onions are missing again, she will answer for it with her life, and the little ant was climbing the tree, and the tree shed its leaves, and we shed our feathers."

Then the oxen said, "Well then, we will dehorn ourselves."

And they dehorned themselves. Then they went to drink water from a pond, and the pond said to them, "Oxen, why are you so hornless?"

Then they said, "Mmm. You think not? Pérez the Mouse fell in the pot trying to eat the onions, and the woman told the girl that if the onions are missing again, she will answer for it with her life, and the little ant was climbing the tree, and the tree shed its leaves, and the birds shed their feathers, and we de-horned ourselves."

Then the pond said, it said, "Well then, I will dry up."

And it dried up. Then some girls went for water, carrying big pitchers and little pitchers, and then they said, "Pond, why are you so dry?"

Then it said to them, "Mmm. You think not? Pérez the Mouse fell in the pot trying to eat the onions, and the woman told the servant girl that if the onions are missing again, she will answer for it with her life. Then the little ant was climbing the tree, and the tree shed its leaves, and the birds shed their feathers, and the oxen dehorned themselves, and I dried up."

And then the girls said, "Well then, we will break the big pitchers and the little pitchers too."

And they broke them. And they went to their father, who then said to them, "Where is the water?"

"Didn't they tell you about it?"

"Why did you break the big pitchers and the little pitchers, too?"

Then they said, "Mmm. You think not? Pérez the Mouse fell in the pot trying to eat the onions, and the woman told the girl that if the onions are missing again, she will answer for it with her life. The little ant was climbing the tree, and the tree shed its leaves, and the birds shed their feathers, and the oxen dehorned themselves, and the pond dried up, and we broke the big pitchers and the little pitchers too."

Then the king said, "Well then, I will put on yellow clothes."

And he put on yellow clothes. Then he went to the queen, his wife. Then his wife said to him, "Why are you wearing yellow clothes?"

Then he said, "Mmm. You think not? Pérez the Mouse fell in the pot trying to eat the onions, and the woman told the girl that if the onions are missing again, she will answer for it with her life, and the little ant was climbing the tree, and the tree shed its leaves, and the birds shed their feathers, and the oxen dehorned themselves, and the pond dried up, and the girls broke the big pitchers and the little pitchers too, and I put on yellow clothes."

Then the queen said, "Well then, I'll cut myself open."

And she cut herself open. That's the end.

·78· *The Little Ant*

· ONCE THERE WAS a little ant who went out on the street one day; but it had snowed a lot, and as she was walking along, all of a sudden she broke her leg in the snow.

Then she went to see the judge and said, "I come to bring suit against the snow for breaking my leg."

The judge sent for the snow and said, "Come here before me, snow. You think yourself so high and mighty because you broke this leg."

"Well, the sun is mightier, because he melts me."

"Come here before me, sun. You think yourself so high and mighty because you melt the snow that broke this leg."

"Well, the cloud is mightier, because she hides me."

"Come here before me, cloud, that hides the sun that melts the snow that broke this leg."

"Well, the wind is mightier, because he pushes me."

"Come here before me, wind, that pushes the cloud that hides the sun that melts the snow that broke this leg."

"Well, the wall is mightier, because she stops me."

"Come here before me, wall, that stops the wind that pushes the cloud that hides the sun that melts the snow that broke this leg."

"Well, the mouse is mightier, because he gnaws me."

"Come here before me, mouse, who think yourself so high and mighty because you gnaw the wall that stops the wind that pushes the cloud that hides the sun that melts the snow that broke this leg."

"Well, the cat is mightier, because he eats me."

"Come here before me, cat, who think yourself so high and mighty because you eat the mouse that gnaws the wall that stops the wind that pushes the cloud that hides the sun that melts the snow that broke this leg."

"Well, the dog is mightier, because he chases me."

"Come here before me, dog, who think yourself so high and mighty because you chase the cat that eats the mouse that gnaws the wall that stops the wind that pushes the cloud that hides the sun that melts the snow that broke this leg."

"Well, the stick is mightier, because he beats me."

"Come here before me, stick, who think yourself so high and mighty because you beat the dog that chases the cat that eats the mouse that gnaws the wall that stops the wind that pushes the cloud that hides the sun that melts the snow that broke this leg."

"Well, the fire is mightier, because she burns me."

"Come here before me, fire, who think yourself so high and mighty because you burn the stick that beats the dog that chases the cat that eats the mouse that gnaws the wall that stops the wind that pushes the cloud that hides the sun that melts the snow that broke this leg."

"Well, the water is mightier, because she puts me out."

"Come here before me, water, who think yourself so high and mighty because you put out the fire that burns the stick that beats the dog that chases the cat that eats the mouse that gnaws the wall that stops the wind that pushes the cloud that hides the sun that melts the snow that broke this leg."

"Well, the cow is mightier, because she drinks me."

"Come here before me, cow, who think yourself so high and mighty because you drink the water that puts out the fire that burns the stick that beats the dog that chases the cat that eats the mouse that gnaws the wall that stops the wind that pushes the cloud that hides the sun that melts the snow that broke this leg."

Well, the knife is mightier, because he kills me."

"Come here before me, knife, who think yourself so high and mighty because you kill the cow that drinks the water that puts out the fire that burns the stick that beats the dog that chases the cat that eats the mouse that gnaws the wall that stops the wind that pushes the cloud that hides the sun that melts the snow that broke this leg."

"Well, the blacksmith is mightier, because he forged me."

"Come here before me, blacksmith, who think yourself so high and mighty because you forged the knife that kills the cow that drinks the water that puts out the fire that burns the stick that beats the dog that chases the cat that eats the mouse that gnaws the wall that stops the wind that pushes the cloud that hides the sun that melts the snow that broke this leg."

"Well, God is mightier, because he made me."

And the judge had to stop there, because he could not question God.

•79• *Talking Animals*

• MORE ABOUT THOSE little animals that used to speak in ancient times. They tell a story, a legend—so many things—that when Christ was born the cock crowed and said, "¡*Cristo nació!*" ["Christ is born!"]

Then somebody asked, "Where?" And the little bearded billy goat says, "*En Beléeeeeen.*" ["In Bethlehem."]

And then the billy goat began to jump for joy and before he knew it he fell into a well. On hearing his desperate cries and all the commotion that was made, the dove looks down into the well. And she stares down and sees the little billy goat swimming desperately to keep from drowning, and she says in her cooing way, "*Por pendejo se cayó. Por pendejo se cayó.*" ["He fell in because he's a damned fool."]

Since the commotion made by all the little animals did not stop, the turkey comes out all puffed up, and he says, "*Cien dólares al que lo saque. Cien dólares al que lo saque.*" ["A hundred dollars to the man who gets him out."]

•80• *Round*

Este era un gato
con patas de trapo
y los ojos al revés . . .
¿Quieres que te lo cuente otra vez?

Once there was a cat
With its paws made of cloth
And its eyes turned back. . . .
Do you want me to tell it again?

Notes
to the Tales

PART I

LEGENDARY NARRATIVES

· 1 · *The World*

Deluge myth. Collected by Gabriel Moedano N. in the Otomí *barrio* of Tlaxco, Puebla, 30 October 1963. Told in Spanish by Manuel Vidal Valderrama, thirty-eight, bilingual Otomí Indian. Informant says he learned the tale from the "old people." Though he is an Otomí speaker, his grandparents spoke Náhuatl. In Tlaxco, according to the collector, Otomís, Totonacs, Nahuas, and Tepehuas live side by side.

Principal motifs: A522.1.2, "Rabbit as culture hero"; A1021, "Deluge: escape in boat (ark)"; A1711, "Animals from transformations after deluge or world calamity"; A1730, "Creation of animals as punishment"; A1931, "Creation of vulture"; A2435.4.5.1, "Carrion as food of vultures"; B437.4, "Helpful rabbit"; C221, "Tabu: eating meat"; D551.3, "Transformation by eating flesh"; V236, "Fallen angels."

An essentially indigenous narrative with European accretions such as the Christian God, the angels, and possibly Noah's ark.

· 2 · *The Dog That Loved to Hunt Armadillos*

Collected by Jacob Pimentel S. in Tuxtla Gutiérrez, Chiapas, 8 April 1956. Told by Constancio Cnamé, a seventy-seven-year-old Zoque Indian who traveled for many years throughout the state as an oxcart driver. Pimentel, "Miscelánea," p. 221.

Principal motifs: C92.1, "Tabu: killing sacred animals"; D2121.2, "Magic journey with closed eyes"; E480.1, "Abode of animal souls"; F419.3*, "Spirit as protector of animals"; H1270, "Quest to lower world"; Q563, "Punishments in hell fitted to crimes."

Retribution against the hunter is explicit in this text. The motif of the animal guardian or animal master (F419.3, "Special spirit for each species of animal to act as its protector") is generalized; the *patrón* or master of the underworld visited by the hero is guardian of all wild animals rather than just one species. Cf. Foster "Sierra Popoluca Folklore," no. 8, "Why Copal Is Burned for the Chanekos," in which a man closes his eyes and is taken to an enchanted place, where he sees the deer he has wounded. Some important points in our text are elucidated by what Foster has to say about the beliefs in *chanekos* among the Veracruz Popoluca, a people linguistically related to the Zoques:

> Hunting and fishing must be accompanied by proper and precise ritual. In all mountains live the *chanekos*. . . . They are the "masters" of all fish and game, particularly deer. . . . They become angry at men, sometimes for no apparent cause, but more often if one is greedy and kills too many deer, or is careless in hunting and wounds deer. In such cases they punish the man by kidnaping his soul and keeping it in their *encantos* [enchanted places] under the mountains; unless they relent and return the man's soul he will eventually die [Foster, "Sierra Popoluca Folklore," p. 181].

Foster goes on to say that agouti, wild boar, rabbit, and armadillo are hunted with dogs and that their hunting also demands ritual observances. For one thing, "it enables the souls of the animals to return to the *encantos* of the *chanekos"*; for another, it makes it possible for the dog's soul to find its way to the hereafter once it dies (Foster, "Sierra Popoluca Folklore," p. 186, n. 26).

The armadillo has some reputation as a chthonic being in Mexican belief. For example, much the same beliefs reported in Miller (p. 208) from southern Mexico are familiar to me in northern Tamaulipas and south Texas: as an eater of poisonous snakes the armadillo may be fatal to one who eats its flesh unless proper precautions are taken. Clumsy and weak away from its hole, the armadillo is possessed of supernatural strength in hind feet and tail if its head is inside its hole.

For the animal master among Mexican mestizos see Jacob Pimentel S., "El dueño de los venados."

· 3 · *Kondoy*

Collected by Walter S. Miller in San Lucas Camotlán, Oaxaca. Told in Spanish by José Trinidad, sixty-two, who also gave the collector a Mixe version. Miller considered this informant one of the best narrators in the community. The informant, however, tended to simplify his Spanish versions, adapting his style to the collector's writing speed. Miller, no. 6.

Hero legend with resemblances to Type 650A, *Strong John*. Principal motifs: A511.1.9, "Culture hero born from egg"; A526.7,

"Culture hero performs remarkable feats of strength and skill"; A571, "Culture hero asleep in mountain"; A901, "Topographical features caused by experiences of primitive hero"; A1145.1, "Earthquakes from movements of subterranean monster"; B877.1.2*, "Giant serpent exorcised by clergy."

Miller gives other variants for parts of this narrative, showing its currency among the Mixes. Another informant, for example, stated that the eggs from which Kondoy and his brother were born were "laid by the earth" (p. 108). As to Kondoy's serpent brother, the Mixes explain earthquakes as caused by a supernatural being in the form of a snake (pp. 205–6). According to Miller, Kondoy was still very much alive as a lengendary hero at the time of collection (p. 203).

·4· Tamácasti

Collected by Howard W. Law in Mecayapan, Veracruz. Told in Nahuat by Victor Cruz, about thirty-two. Text presented here is an edited version of an English translation obtained in manuscript through courtesy of the collector, Dr. Law. The Nahuat text and a free English translation were published in Howard W. Law, "Tamákasti: A Gulf Nahuat Text."

Hero legend largely of indigenous origins; fourth episode is a version of Type 850, The Birthmarks of the Princess, combined with other Old World motifs. Principal motifs: A511.1.9, "Culture hero born from egg"; A511.2.1.1, "Abandoned culture hero captured by use of net"; A1422, "Assignment of edible animals"; D641.1, "Lover as bird visits mistress"; G11.15, "Cannibal demon"; H511, "Princess offered to correct guesser"; H525, "Test: guessing princess's birthmarks."

In a note to the editor the collector says, "The story may be viewed as containing three episodes that are predominantly native. The final section constitutes a fourth episode and is predominantly European." This is borne out by the presence of motifs like H511 and H525 and in certain peculiarities of diction found in the fourth episode. Although the original narrative is in Nahuat, when Tamácasti addresses the king he uses an apparently meaningless phrase in Spanish, "Mi señor Zacarías majestad" ("My lord Zacharias majesty"). The phrase becomes intelligible if compared to similar ones used in mestizo texts such as nos. 35 and 43 in this collection, "sacarreal" or "sacarrial majestá": a corruption of sacra y real majestad, "sacred and royal majesty."

The first three episodes are made up of indigenous elements shared with other Mesoamerican groups. A similar narrative from a neighboring but linguistically unrelated people may be found in Ben Elson, "The Homshuk: A Sierra Popoluca Text." Law, in comparing Elson's text to his, notes twenty motifs held in common, all of them occurring in the first three episodes of "Tamácasti." (Private communication to the editor.) Foster, "Sierra Popoluca Folklore" also is quite similar to the first three episodes of our text; its hero also is called Homshuk. Foster notes that Homshuk is the god of maize and is "pictured as a being three feet tall with hair of corn silk" (p. 180). Foster's Homshuk, like Miller's Kondoy and Law's Tamácasti, is born from an egg. Miller, nos. 1–4 contain similarities to "Tamácasti," especially the girl unknowingly made pregnant by a bird, the killing of the grandfather, and the unwitting act of cannibalism.

·5· The Pujpatzá

Collected by Jacob Pimentel S. in Tectapán, Mezcalapa, Chiapas, in 1954. Told by Pedro González Valdez, seventy-eight, who learned it as a child from his parents. According to collector, the story dates from the 1860s. Pimentel, "Miscelánea," p. 216.

Legend of witchcraft and magic with possible elements of earlier myth. Principal motifs: A977, "Origin of particular groups of stones"; B91.6, "Serpent (alligator) causes flood"; B268.4, "Sorcerer's army of magic animals"; D1719.1, "Contest in magic"; Z311.4, "Man (monster) can be injured only in armpits."

Narratives built around D1719.1 are frequent in Mexican folklore, especially in "Indian" Mexico. See for example, Foster, "Sierra Popoluca Folklore," no. 13 and Beals, "Zapotec Tales," no. 1, in both of which there is conflict between wizards of two different towns. In the Beals text, an English summary only, one wizard has Lightning for his familiar, the other Water Snake. Tales of this sort may be a narrative expression of rivalries between towns or *barrios,* often noted by students of these areas. In a more Christianized context they take the form of legendary, half-joking accounts about fights between the patron saint of one *barrio* and the saint or virgin of another.

·6· The Man Who Escaped from the Bathhouse

Collected by Walter S. Miller in San Lucas Camotlán, Oaxaca. Told in Spanish by José Trinidad, the informant for no. 3, "Kondoy." Miller, no. 23.

Local legend, *blason populaire;* resembles Type 327, *The Children and the Ogre,* but with strong man as hero instead of Thumbling or lost children. Principal motifs: D672, "Obstacle flight"; F610, "Remarkably strong man"; G11.18, "Cannibal tribe (village)"; G422, "Ogre imprisons victim."

Miller notes that the Mixe, unlike the Popoluca, do not attribute cannibalism to demons, ogres, or foreign peoples. But cannibalism is attributed to the people of Malacatepec and Mixistlán, both Mixe towns. Miller cites a case of cannibalism reported in Mixistlán in the 1870s. He also calls attention to the fact that in this story cannibalism is practiced secretly and only by certain families rather than by the whole town. At all events, the legend is basis for actual behavior: the people of Camotlán will not go through Mixistlán except in groups of three or more, and then only during the day (pp. 204–5).

Miller's comments raise the question whether the narrative is a folklorized account of fairly recent historical events or a reworking of indigenous narratives influenced by Old World stories about ogres. Our text's resemblances to Type 327 have been remarked upon; one must also keep in mind, however, that D672, "Obstacle flight," is an oft-reported motif in North and South American Indian narratives. See also Parsons, "Mitla," no. 1, both A and B variants. Here there is also cannibalism, though unintentional, in the attempt to kill the heroes (two orphans) in the *temascal,* followed by the obstacle flight. The orphans, brother and sister, become the sun and the moon. The use of chile peppers thrown into the fire to suffocate a victim is an especially Mexican touch, also found in no. 41 of this collection.

·7· *Horse's Hooves and Chicken Feet*

Collected by Vicente T. Mendoza and Virginia Rodríguez Rivera de Mendoza in Zacatecas, Zacatecas, on 14 September 1948. Told by Aureliano Guzmán, thirty-six, who learned it from his father in San Pedro Piedra Gorda, Zacatecas. Mendoza, *Piedra Gorda,* p. 469.

Told as a *caso* or belief tale, but widespread in Spanish America. Compare for example Rael, *Cuentos españoles,* no. 500. Principal motifs: G216.1, "Witch with goose (chicken) feet"; G247, "Witches dance"; G303.4.5.3.1, "Devil detected by his hoofs"; Q386, "Dancing punished."

A moralistic attitude toward dancing, especially public ballroom dancing, is more prevalent in Spain and Spanish America than is realized by North Americans who think all Puritans come from New England. In prose narrative the theme is developed in tales such as this one, or if the protagonist is a girl she is carried away by the demon she is dancing with. In the Mexican *corrido* the same moralistic attitude is expressed in more realistic terms: the girl goes to a dance in spite of her mother's prohibition and is shot by a jealous lover.

·8· *The Witch Mother-in-Law*

Collected by Vicente T. Mendoza and Virginia Rodríguez Rivera de Mendoza in Mexico, D. F., on 28 June 1948. Told by Petra Guzmán Barrón, sixty-nine, who learned it in San Pedro Piedra Gorda, Zacatecas. Mendoza, *Piedra Gorda,* p. 467.

Caso or belief tale. Principal motifs: G211.3.1, "Witch in form of hen"; G275.3.1, "Witch burned by burning bewitched animal"; S51.1, "Cruel mother-in-law plans death of daughter-in-law."

In very much the same form this tale is told as a localized legend in many parts of Greater Mexico. Of interest to the psychologist is the frequency with which neighbors, friends, and even close relatives may be accused of witchcraft.

·9· *The Witch Wife*

Collected by Jacob Pimentel S. in San Cristóbal Las Casas, Chiapas, on 24 September 1954. Told by Efraín A. Paniagua, thirty-five, a schoolteacher, who learned it in Colonia de Yuquín, Simojovel, Chiapas. Pimentel, "Creencias," p. 159.

Localized legend. Principal motifs: E574, "Appearance of ghost as death omen"; G229.1.1, "Witch who is out of skin is prevented from reentering it when person salts or peppers skin"; G250.1, "Man discovers his wife is a witch."

Another story of witchcraft widespread in the Greater Mexican area. Compare J. M. Espinosa, no. 83 and Foster, "Sierra Popoluca Folklore," no. 14. In the Foster text the witch is the husband instead of the wife. He is turned over to the authorities and is burned alive. See also Brinton, *Essays,* p. 171.

·10· *The Pig-Man*

Collected by Jacob Pimentel S. in San Cristóbal Las Casas, Chiapas, 24 September 1954. Told by Efraín A. Paniagua, thirty-five, a schoolteacher, who learned it in Mazontic, Simojovel, Chiapas. Pimentel, "Creencias," p. 161.

Legend of witchcraft. Principal motifs: D1096.1, "Magic gun"; G211.1.6, "Witch in form of hog"; G269.10, "Witch punishes person who incurs his ill will"; G275.12, "Witch in form of animal is killed as result of injury to the animal."

The basis for this narrative is in Mexican Indian beliefs about the *nagual*. For a discussion in English see George Foster, "Nagualism in Mexico and Guatemala." European ideas of werewolves are also present, as well as the European stereotype of the Indian as a witch. The pig is European, of course, as is the very Spanish ambivalence toward the animal. Its flesh is prized as food, yet it is considered unclean and a familiar of devils and witches. This attitude is an old one in Spanish tradition, as may be seen from such euphemisms for *puerco* (pig) as *sancho/chancho* (*sanctus*, holy one) and *el de la vista baja* (he of the downcast eyes).

Compare Miller, nos. 18 and 19 and Foster, "Sierra Popoluca Folklore," no. 12. In these the *nagual* takes the form of snakes or of lightning. In northern Mexico and southwestern United States the witch is more likely to turn into an owl. See Rael, *Cuentos españoles,* no. 511, J. M. Espinosa, no. 86, and Barker, p. 64.

· *11* · *The Phantom Children*

Collected by Américo Paredes in the *municipio* of Matamoros, Tamaulipas, 14 September 1962. Told by G. T. G., unmarried mestizo female in her late fifties, of rural background.

A good example of the *caso,* a belief tale about a personal experience. Principal motifs: B15.4.2.1, "Dog with fire in eyes"; E225, "Ghost of murdered child"; E334.2.1, "Ghost of murdered person haunts burial spot"; E577, "Dead persons play games"; G303.3.3.1.1, "Devil in form of dog"; S71, "Cruel uncle"; V254.4, "Devil exorcised by 'Ave.'"

· *12* · *Little Saint Michael*

Collected by Jacob Pimentel S. in San Cristóbal Las Casas, Chiapas, 24 September 1954. Told by Efraín A. Paniagua, informant for nos. 9 and 10, who learned it in Colonia de Yuquín, Simojovel, Chiapas. Pimentel, "Miscelánea," p. 163.

Saint's legend. Principal motifs: D812.1, "Magic object received from saint"; D1040.1, "Drink supplied by magic"; D1193, "Magic bag"; D1275.1, "Magic music."

Though this is a saint's legend, it is very much like a *caso,* since it relates what supposedly was an actual experience. Miraculous objects are common enough in Mexico and the Southwest; many are consulted by hundreds of believers. The *morral* is a carryall in Chiapas and other parts of Mexico (see Glossary) and often is used for carrying bottles of liquor. But the miraculous appearance of a *morral* full of liquor bottles, supplied by a saint at that, is an original twist.

·13· Elves

Three very short belief tales collected by Vicente T. Mendoza and Virginia Rodríguez Rivera de Mendoza and printed together to read like a complete narrative. Text *a* was collected in Mexico, D.F., 23 November 1947, from Petra Guzmán Barrón, sixty-eight; *b,* also in Mexico, D.F., 1 September 1948, from Francisco Quintero, sixty-eight; *c,* in Zacatecas, Zacatecas, from Aureliano Guzmán, thirty-six, on 12 September 1948. All are said to be originally from San Pedro Piedra Gorda, Zacatecas. Mendoza, *Piedra Gorda,* p. 387.

Casos or belief tales. Principal motifs: F482.3.1.1, "Farmer bothered by brownie decides to move; brownie goes along too; farmer returns home"; F482.5.5, "Malicious or troublesome actions of brownies."

These seem to be direct transplants from European tradition, especially F482.3.1.1, but they are no less a genuine part of Mexican folklore because of that. I have encountered the brick-throwing episode along the Texas-Mexican border. At a Matamoros *cantina* with a patio, I walked in one night in 1953 to find the patio full of bricks. I asked the waiter about it, and he said "somebody" had thrown them. Who? He shrugged. "No one knows; the police couldn't find anyone." A neighbor? No. Enemies of the owner? No. A passing drunk? No. Nobody like that. Like Frost's apple farmer, I could have said "elves" to him but preferred he say it for himself. But he was a waiter at a bar in a border town, cynical and wise. He would not say it, contenting himself with, "It could not have been people."

·14· Mal de Ojo

Collected by Vicente T. Mendoza and Virginia Rodríguez Rivera de Mendoza. Mendoza, *Piedra Gorda,* p. 470.

Caso. Principal motifs: D1273.0.2, "Magic spells mixed with Christian prayers"; D2064.4, "Magic sickness because of evil eye"; D2161.4.2, "Disease transferred to objects."

One of the most common types of belief tales in Mexico. We may identify two main forms of the narrative: one in which the patient recovers, as in our text; another in which the patient dies. The majority of those I have heard in Texas and northern Mexico are of the latter variety, and are usually told about strangers. Tales in which the patient recovers are more likely to be told as happening to friends or relatives.

Many North American writers, even those with enough Spanish to know better, ignore the linguistic implications of the name by which this folk illness is known throughout Mexico. It is called *mal de ojo,* not *mal ojo:* "sickness caused by the eye" rather than "evil eye." In spite of this, most folklorists and anthropologists call it the "evil eye" and base their conclusions about Mexican attitudes accordingly. In the Southwest and in northern Mexico, at least, the sickness is believed to be given involuntarily rather than intentionally as in Europe. Persons are endowed by birth with "strong" eyes and can do nothing about their effects, except to protect possible victims by countermagic, such as touching them. People capable of "giving the eye" to others may be young and attractive as in our text. See Isabel Kelly, *Folk Practices in North Mexico,* especially pp. 41–44.

·15· ¡Qué Veo!

Collected by Américo Paredes in Ajusco, Mexico, 20 November 1962. Told by J. F., mestizo male in his fifties; informant is a native of Ajusco and a printer by trade.

Legendary anecdote. Principal motif: J1805.1, "Similar sounding words mistaken for each other."

The Quevedo involved is Don Francisco de Quevedo y Villegas (1580–1645), Spanish poet and satirist who has become a legend as a trickster both in folk and sophisticated literature. There is a whole cycle of Quevedo stories, known wherever Spanish is spoken. They bear comparison with the anecdotes woven about another literary figure, Virgil, during the Middle Ages. In one Quevedo story the hero is left suspended in a basket from a woman's window. (See K1211, "Virgil in the basket.") Like our text, the basket story depends on a play made on Quevedo's name. The night watch goes by and demands that he identify himself. Quevedo, swinging in the basket, replies, "¡Quevedo! *¡Que no sube ni baja pero no se está quedo!"* ("Who goes neither up nor down but cannot stay still").

Our "¡Qué veo!" story is one of the best known of the Quevedo anecdotes. I first remember hearing it told by a Spaniard in Brownsville, Texas, about 1930. Hansen lists it as Type **1709C in his index, somewhat unaccountably under "Other Stories about Stupid Man," reporting it from Cuba.

16. Quevedo and the King

Collected by Américo Paredes from same informant who told no. 15 in this collection.

Principal motifs: H1050, "Paradoxical tasks"; J1160, "Clever pleading"; J1485, "Mistaken identity: 'I did not know it was you'"; J1675, "Clever dealing with a king."

·17· Your Reward Is up Above

Collected by Américo Paredes in Matamoros, Tamaulipas, 14 September 1962. Told by C. T. G., mestizo male in his late seventies; informant was a farmer and rancher during his active life and belongs to one of the old families in the area.

Anecdote about local character. Bears comparison with Types 1355C, *The Lord above Will Provide,* and 1528, *Holding down the Hat.* Principal motifs: K1252, "Holding down the hat"; K1271.5, "The Lord above will provide"; K2310, "Deception by equivocation."

In the original Spanish the story involves a play on the word *cielo* ("ceiling," "sky," "heaven," and also the word for the canopy over the bed). The trickster's exact words are, *"Del cielo te caerá la recompensa."* He means, "Your reward is up there in the canopy." His sister understands, "Your reward is up in heaven." In the region where the tale is told the saying, *"Del cielo te caerá la recompensa"* is used as a proverbial expression meaning, more or less, "Thanks for nothing."

The name of the protagonist in this and the two tales following is not given in full because he is the revered ancestor of a number of people well known in the Brownsville-Matamoros area. Oral tradition has made him a trickster character much like Quevedo, except that his fame is strictly local. The informant claimed that as a boy he knew "twenty or thirty" stories about Don José.

·18· Don José and the Water Vendor

Collected by Américo Paredes from same informant who told no. 17. Principal motif: K1200, "Deception into humiliating position."

·19· *Don José and the Peddler*

Collected by Américo Paredes from same informant who told nos. 17 and 18. Principal motif: K1200, "Deception into humiliating position."

·20· *Don Bartolo*

Collected by Vicente T. Mendoza and Virginia Rodríguez Rivera de Mendoza in Mexico, D. F., 18 October 1948. Told by Petra Guzmán Barrón, sixty-nine, who said Don Bartolo was her grandfather's contemporary in San Pedro Piedra Gorda, Zacatecas. Mendoza, *Piedra Gorda,* p. 394.

Anecdote about local character; tall tales, including Type 1889B, *Hunter Turns Animal Inside Out.* Principal motifs: K134.2, "The horse swifter than the rain"; R185, "Mortal fights with Death"; X1124.2, "Hunter turns animal inside out"; X1720, "Absurd disregard of anatomy." Also X1796.3.1*(b) (Baughman), "Horse runs so fast that only tail of man's raincoat and the rear end of the horse get wet."

See Rael, *Cuentos españoles,* nos. 513, 514, and 516. Also Whatley, p. 42.

We have here another local character, like Don José of nos. 17–19, reputedly a recent ancestor of local people in the region. Don Bartolo, however, is a gifted liar rather than a trickster like Don José. His tall tales are more universal than Don José's tricks.

·21· *Arnulfo and the Law*

Collected by Américo Paredes in Matamoros, Tamaulipas, 14 September 1962. Told by I. V., mestizo male in his sixties; informant was born in Guanajuato and operates a gasoline station on the border.

Anecdote about local character. Principal motifs: J552, "Intemperate pugnacity"; J1289, "Repartee with ruler, judge, etc."; X800, "Humor based on drunkenness."

In this and the following text we have the contemporary character who has become legendary in his lifetime. Arnulfo's exploits are set in the recent past; the statue of Juárez, for example, was moved from Matamoros's main plaza about twenty years ago. He was said to be alive and in town at the time these texts were collected. His name, of course, is not Arnulfo. These two are not the only stories told about him, by the way.

It is worthwhile to compare Don José of nos. 17–19 with Arnulfo, as two types of comic folk characters developed in the same locality but during different historical periods. Don José, a character from the Díaz period, is a sly trickster who more often than not uses his social inferiors as his victims. Arnulfo is the post-revolutionary he-man, the *macho* ready to take on the church, the state, and the American tourist.

· 22 · *Arnulfo Collects a Crowd*

Collected by Américo Paredes from same informant who told no. 21.

Cf. Type 1693, *The Literal Fool,* except that Arnulfo acts not from ignorance but from pure cussedness. Principal motifs: J552, "Intemperate pugnacity"; J2460, "Literal obedience."

· 23 · *The Mayor of San Fernando*

Collected by Américo Paredes from same informant who told nos. 21 and 22.

Localized jest used as *blason populaire.* Cf. Type 1698G, *Misunderstood Words Lead to Comic Results.* Principal motifs: J1703, "Town of fools"; J1765, "Person thought to be animal"; J1803, "Learned words misunderstood by uneducated"; X680, "Jokes concerning various cities."

The towns along the lower Texas-Mexican border that have become legendary victims of the *blason populaire* are Cerralvo and Cadereyta in Nuevo León and San Fernando in Tamaulipas. Cerralvo perhaps owes its distinction as a town of dolts to linguistic accident. In the language of the *albur* (word play), *"Es muy cerrado"* ("He's very stupid," lit. "closed") becomes, *"Es de Cerralvo"* ("He's from Cerralvo").

Cadereyta and San Fernando are old provincial towns that have sent many of their sons to seek their fortunes in the capitals of their respective states, and perhaps for this reason they have become symbols of the backwoods, from which eager hicks come to the city to make good. Cadereyta Jiménez (its full name) is a town of 8,000, some twenty miles from Monterrey, the capital of Nuevo León. It was founded in the seventeenth century, not long after Monterrey itself. San Fernando contains less than 4,000 souls and is deep in the interior of Tamaulipas, far from the capital and from the border with the United States as well. All this notwithstanding, the men of San Fernando have made their mark as far as the national capital itself.

The introductory parts of our text include a number of peculiarities attributed both to San Fernando and to Cadereyta, though the one about the jerky eaters who all lose one eye is more commonly told about San Fernando. The introduction is used to point up the ignorance of the mayor of San Fernando, displayed in Motif J1803, "Learned words misunderstood by uneducated." This motif, in much the same form given to it here, is quite popular on the Texas-Mexican border, usually being attributed to a public official or some other prominent person. See for example "La Flora y la Fauna" in Dorson, *Buying the Wind,* p. 454, where the dolt is a Mexican official at the Brownsville-Matamoros bridge. In but slightly different form, the motif is used in a jest concerning Mrs. John F. Kennedy.

PART II

ANIMAL TALES

· 24 · *The Rabbit and the Fox*

Collected by Gabriel Moedano N. at a fishing camp in Peña Blanca, Oaxaca, 10 January 1967. Told in Spanish by Miguel Cruz Ayuzo, twenty-six, born in Juquila, Oaxaca, and now living in Río Grande, Oaxaca. Collector remarks that though the informant is an Indian he participates in the Negro culture of the area.

Type 36, *The Fox in Disguise Violates the She-Bear.* Principal motifs: J1117, "Animal as trickster"; K730.3, "Leopard (rabbit) traps lion (fox) by having two doors to cave, one large, one small; attack from rear"; K1384, "Female overpowered when caught in tree cleft (hole in hedge)."

No references are given for Spain or Spanish America by either Aurelio M. Espinosa or Terrence L. Hansen. Espinosa mentions the type in *Cuentos,* 3:260–63, as a subtype of his no. 205, but knows no Hispanic versions. Hansen lists the type without any Spanish American references; his **74D contains only the rabbit's disguise by painting, Motif K521.3, often found in the type but not a part of our text. Yolando Pino Saavedra in *Cuentos Folklóricos de Chile,* vol. 3, prints two examples of Type 36, nos. 230 and 231. Both are very short anecdotes in which a fox is enamored of a lioness that chases the fox

into his cave and gets stuck. In Pino's no. 230 the violation of the
lioness by the fox is implied, though the action is euphemized into
a beating given the lioness by the fox. In Pino's no. 231, told by a
child, all sexual implications disappear and the emphasis is on the
beating given the lioness.

·25· *Good Is Repaid with Evil*

Collected by Kent A. Wistrand in Xayacatlán de Bravo, Puebla, in
1964. Told in Mixteco by Guadalupe García Pérez, twenty-eight, a
bilingual schoolteacher of Mixteco descent.

Type 155, *The Ungrateful Serpent Returned to Captivity*. Principal
motifs: J1172.3.2, "Animals render unjust decision against man since
man has always been unjust to them"; K235.1, "Fox is promised
chickens: is driven off by dogs"; K332, "Theft by making owner
drunk"; W154.2.1, "Rescued animal threatens rescuer."

See A. M. Espinosa, *Cuentos*, 3:420–31. Other Mexican variants not
in Espinosa: Aiken, "Pack Load," p. 4; Boas and Haeberlin, no. 10;
A. M. Espinosa, "New-Mexican Spanish Folk-Lore, VII," no. 19;
Foster, "Sierra Popoluca Folklore," no. 34; González Casanova,
Cuentos indígenas, no. 1; Guerra, p. 191; Parsons, "Santa Ana," no.
1; Robe, no. 2; Storm, p. 24.

Espinosa calls this "one of the most popular tales in European
and Oriental tradition." He cites 310 variants, among them sixteen
Spanish American variants of his subtype IV A, in which the woman
and not the man is responsible for tricking the helpful animal. In
Wheeler, no. 195, the husband is so remorseful over his wife's duplic-
ity that he gives her a good beating.

The English version of the Mixteco text presented here is based on
an interlinear translation into English done by the collector and his
sister, Lila C. Wistrand, through whose kindness the text appears in
this collection. In the original the key phrase "Good is repaid with
evil" always appears in Spanish: *Un bien con un mal se paga*. This
is a well-known proverbial expression in Spanish and the most common title for the tale. Many other Spanish words are scattered
throughout the Mixteco text. Some, like *burro, toro,* and *cantina*
obviously are loan words for concepts that did not exist in the indigenous culture before Spanish times. But the informant also uses
Spanish words for such common concepts as friend, fool, strong,
turkey, field, and place. At one point the woodcutter's wife says,
"Pobrecito! Ndahvun!" which may be translated as "You poor thing!"
repeated in Spanish and Mixteco. Some of this may be a peculiarity

of the informant, though the collectors state that the whole town is pretty well acculturated in this respect.

One of the interesting things about this text is its moral tone. The fox does not trick the ungrateful serpent into returning to captivity (Motif J1172.3). It scolds the serpent into repentance. Both the woodcutter and his wife are more than happy to part with their chickens; they even add a turkey for good measure. It is drink, bad companions, and a trickster that combine to produce the discomfiture of the fox. "But it also happened to the man." He suffers remorse. All this may be due to the fact that the informant is a recent convert, though we must take into consideration as well the remorseful husband in Wheeler, no. 195.

· 26 · *The Rabbit and the Coyote*

Collected by Joel Gómez in La Encantada, Texas, April 1968. Told by Mrs. P. E., seventy-four, a lifelong resident of the area. La Encantada, formerly El Ranchito, is a village some eleven miles upriver from Brownsville, Texas, and Matamoros, Tamaulipas. The informant belongs to regional folk groups that have inhabited the area on both sides of the Rio Grande for some two centuries. She learned folktales from her mother and still tells them to younger members of the family. Her stock of folktales also is a source of proverbial expressions used within the family.

Types 175, *The Tarbaby and the Rabbit*, 1530, *Holding up the Rock*, 49A, *The Wasp's Nest as King's Drum*, 66A, *"Hello, House!"* and 34, *The Wolf Dives into the Water for Reflected Cheese*. Principal motifs: J1791.3, "Diving for cheese"; K607.1, "The cave call"; K751, "Capture by tarbaby"; K842.3, "Tied animal persuades another to take his place"; K844, "Dupe persuaded to play for wedding party"; K1023.5, "Dupe induced to strike at bee's (wasp's) nest"; K1035, "Stone (hard fruit) thrown into greedy dupe's mouth"; K1055, "Dupe persuaded to get into grass in order to learn new dance; grass set on fire"; K1251, "Holding up the rock."

See A. M. Espinosa, *Cuentos*, 2:163–227, for discussion of Type 175, and ibid. 3:264–72, for other types. Other Mexican variants not in Espinosa: Aiken, "Six tales," p. 49; Boas and Haeberlin, no. 4; J. M. Espinosa, *Cuentos*, no. 106; Foster, "Sierra Popoluca Folktales," nos. 32, 33; González Casanova, *Cuentos indígenas*, no. 7; Johnson, p. 215; Mechling, "Stories and Songs," nos. 1, 2; Mendoza, *Piedra Gorda*, pp. 409, 410; Miller, no. 29, Parsons, "Santa Ana," no. 1; Reid, no. 7; Robe, nos. 1, 11. See also *Folktales of Chile*, no. 2.

This is a very popular tale in Mexican tradition, combining a number of short types in Aarne and Thompson and usually ending with Type 34. Type 175 is the usual beginning but is not essential. It is the tricks played on the coyote after the escape from the tarbaby that are enjoyed the most. Sometimes the whole complex may begin with Type 100, *The Wolf as the Dog's Guest Sings.*

·27· *The Lot of All Asses*

Collected by Américo Paredes in Matamoros, Tamaulipas, 14 September 1962. Told by G. T. G., unmarried mestizo female in her late fifties, of rural background.

Principal motifs: B211.1.3.1, "Speaking ass"; N255.2, "Ass gets progressively worse masters: finally farmer beats him living and will not spare his hide when he is dead."

·28· *A Rude Retort*

Collected by Américo Paredes in Ajusco, Mexico, 20 November 1962, from same informant who told nos. 15 and 16.

Principal motif: J1369, "Rude retorts."

PART III

ORDINARY FOLKTALES

·29· *Juan Oso*

Collected by Joel Gómez in La Encantada, Texas, April 1968. Told by Mrs. P. E., seventy-four, the informant for no. 26 in this collection.

This is a combination of Types 301, *The Three Stolen Princesses,* better known in Hispanic tradition as *John the Bear,* and 302, *The Ogre's Heart in the Egg.* Principal motifs B392, "Hero divides spoils of animals"; B601.1.1, "Bear steals woman and makes her his wife"; B635.1, "The Bear's Son"; D532, "Transformation by putting on claw, feather, etc., of helpful animal"; E711.1, "Soul in egg"; E713, "Soul hidden in a series of coverings"; F96, "Rope to lower world"; F601.3, "Extraordinary companions betray hero"; F612.2, "Strong hero overcomes playmates: sent from home"; F612.3.1, "Giant cane for strong man"; G475.1, "Ogre (devil) attacks intruders in house in woods"; H80, "Identification by tokens"; K677, "Hero tests rope on which he is to be pulled to upper world"; L113.1.5, "Goatherd as hero"; L161, "Lowly hero marries princess"; R11.1, "Princess abducted by ogre"; R111.1, "Princess rescued from captor"; T68, "Princess offered as prize."

For Type 301 see A. M. Espinosa, *Cuentos*, 2:498–504. Other Mexican variants not in Espinosa: Boas, no. III-1; Foster, "Sierra Popoluca," no. 38, Goodwyn, p. 143. See also *Folktales of Chile*, no. 3. For Type 302 see A. M. Espinosa, *Cuentos*, 3:33–43. Other Mexican variants: Aiken, "Pack Load," p. 79; Aiken, "Fifteen Mexican Tales," p. 44; Boas and Arreola, no. 5; Rael, *Cuentos españoles*, no. 251, Robe, no. 13, Wheeler, no. 112. See also *Folktales of Chile*, no. 4.

· 30 · *Blancaflor*

Collected by Américo Paredes in East Chicago, Indiana, 2 May 1963. Told by J. A., mestizo male in his sixties, who learned the tale in Guanajuato, Mexico, from his paternal grandfather. Informant used to narrate the tale in Guanajuato but does not tell it in East Chicago, where he is now employed in a steel mill.

Type 313, *The Girl as Helper in the Hero's Flight*. Principal motifs: D671, "Transformation flight"; D672, "Obstacle flight"; D1611.5, "Magic spittle impersonates fugitive"; D2006.1.3, "Forgotten fiancée reawakens husband's memory by having magic doves converse"; G465, "Ogre sets impossible tasks"; H335.0.1, "Bride helps suitor perform his tasks"; S221.2, "Youth sells himself to an ogre in settlement of a gambling debt."

See A. M. Espinosa, *Cuentos*, 2:470–82. Other Mexican variants not in Espinosa: Aiken, "Pack Load," p. 61; González Casanova, "Cuento en mexicano," p. 25; Mendoza, *Piedra Gorda*, p. 416; Parsons, "Mitla," nos. 17, 18. According to A. M. Espinosa (*Cuentos*, 2:473) the hero who is a gambler and thus gets involved with the Devil is a typically Spanish motif.

For examples of Type 313 in other volumes in the Folktales of the World series, see *Folktales of China*, no. 27; *Folktales of France*, nos. 6, 12; *Folktales of Hungary*, no. 3; *Folktales of Norway*, no. 78.

· 31 · *The Little Guava*

Collected by Virginia Rodríguez Rivera in Tlaxcala, Tlaxcala, 11 April 1947. Told by Antonia García, sixty-five, who learned it from her father at Villahermosa, Tabasco, in the 1880s. From unpublished manuscript by courtesy of collector.

Type 327, *The Children and the Ogre*. Principal motifs: G82.1.1, "Captive sticks out bone instead of finger when cannibal tries to test his fatness"; G401, "Children wander into ogre's house"; R131.11.4, "Deity (Virgin) rescues abandoned children"; R135, "Abandoned children find way back by clue"; S143, "Abandonment in forest."

Other Mexican variants: J. M. Espinosa, no. 8; Foster, "Sierra Popoluca Folklore," no. 37; Parsons, "Santa Ana," no. 10; Rael, *Cuentos españoles*, no. 495.

A version of Type 327 is in *Folktales of France*, no. 50.

· 32 · The Four Sisters

Collected by Virginia Rodríguez Rivera in Tecamachalco, Puebla. Told by María Silva, twenty-five, who learned it from her grandfather. From unpublished manuscript by courtesy of collector.

Principal motifs: D141.1, "Transformation: woman to bitch"; D683.8, "Transformation by angel"; D691*, "Daily beating of woman transformed to bitch: as punishment"; D936, "Magic island"; K2212, "Treacherous sister"; Q556.2, "Mark of Cain"; S142, "Person thrown into the water and abandoned."

Bears resemblances to Hansen 403**D and to *Folktales of Chile*, no. 15. But this tale has its ultimate origins in literary versions of Type 910B, *The Servant's Good Counsels*. The counsel, "Do not ask questions about extraordinary things" is put to test when the hero is invited to the house of a lady, who has two bitches brought in and soundly whipped during the festivities. The animals are her envious sisters. They regain their human shape, and the wronged sister marries the hero. The drowned prince, the island, and the helpful supernatural also are part of the story. See the discussion of Type 910B, especially the versions in the *Thousand and One Nights* and their relation to Spanish oral tradition, in A. M. Espinosa, *Cuentos*, 2:281–82.

· 33 · The Bad Negress

Collected by Stanley L. Robe in Valle de Guadalupe, Jalisco, in 1947. Told by Concepción Ramírez de Ojeda, thirty-two, female, primary school teacher with six years of primary school education. Informant has lived all her life in Jalisco and has learned her stories from her grandmother. She is described by the collector as an excellent informant. Robe, no. 21.

Type 408, *The Three Oranges*. Principal motifs: D154.1, "Transformation: woman to dove"; D582, "Transformation by sticking magic pin into head"; J1791.6.1, "Ugly woman sees beautiful woman reflected in water and thinks it is herself"; K1911.1.3, "False bride takes true bride's place at fountain"; K1911.3.1.1, "Substitution of false bride revealed by true bride in her animal form"; K2252, "Treacherous maidservant"; K2261, "Treacherous Negro."

See A. M. Espinosa, *Cuentos*, 3:460–69. Other Mexican variants not in Espinosa: Mendoza, *Piedra Gorda*, p. 413; Rael, *Cuentos españoles*, nos. 115, 179–82.

Our text lacks the opening episode of the princess in the orange, making her presence in the tree the result of a feminine whim. The narrator takes advantage of this to give his ending a special turn, yet following a traditional pattern, that of relating the events told to his own time and place.

A version of Type 408 appears in *Folktales of Germany*, no. 30.

· 34 · *The Greenish Bird*

Collected by Joel Gómez in La Encantada, Texas, April 1968. Told by Mrs. P. E., seventy-four, the informant for nos. 26 and 29 in this collection.

Types 432, *The Prince as Bird*, and 425, *The Search for the Lost Husband*, IV. Principal motifs: A711.2, "Sun as a cannibal"; B322.1, "Hero feeds own flesh to helpful animal"; D641.1, "Lover as bird visits mistress"; D1234, "Magic guitar"; D1500.1.24, "Magic healing song"; G84, "Fee-fi-fo-fum"; H383.4, "Bride test: cooking"; H1232, "Directions on quest given by sun, moon, wind and stars"; H1385.5, "Quest for vanished lover"; K2212, "Treacherous sister"; N825.3, "Old woman helper"; N843, "Hermit as helper"; Q502.2., "Punishment: wandering till iron shoes are worn out"; S181, "Wounding by trapping with sharp knives."

See A. M. Espinosa, *Cuentos*, 483–97, for discussion of Type 425, with Type 432 discussed as a special subtype of 425. Other Mexican variants not in Espinosa: J. M. Espinosa, no. 13; Rael, *Cuentos españoles*, nos. 112–15; Robe, no. 7. For type 432 see also *Folktales of Chile*, no. 17.

The collector reports that his informant learned her folktale reper-

216 FOLKTALES OF *Mexico*

tory from her mother, who not only was well known locally as a
narrator, but also was celebrated for her singing and playing on the
guitar. This may have some bearing on the fact that the heroine in
this text sings and plays the guitar, carrying the instrument with
her wherever she goes.

Variants of Type 425 in other Folktales of the World volumes can
be found in *Folktales of France,* nos. 9, 40; *Folktales of Ireland,* no.
19; *Folktales of Israel,* no. 58; *Folktales of Japan,* no. 27.

· 35 · *The Horse of Seven Colors*

Collected by Joel Gómez in La Encantada, Texas, April 1968. Told
by Mrs. P. E., seventy-four, the informant for nos. 26, 29, and 34
in this collection.

Types 550, *Search for the Golden Bird,* and 531, *Ferdinand the
True and Ferdinand the False.* Principal motifs: B313, "Helpful animal an enchanted person"; B401, "Helpful horse"; D700, "Person
disenchanted"; D1234, "Magic guitar"; D 1440, "Magic object gives
power over animals"; F535.1, "Thumbling"; F813.1.1, "Golden
apple"; G634, "Genie sleeps with eyes open"; H316, "Suitor test:
apple thrown indicates princess's choice"; H331.16, "Suitor contest:
throwing ball (apple) to princess"; H912, "Tasks assigned at sug-
gestion of jealous brothers"; H1132.1, "Task: recovering lost object
from the sea"; H1154.8, "Task: capturing magic horse"; H1331.1,
"Quest for marvelous bird"; H1471, "Watch for devastating monster
(horse)"; K2211.0.1, "Treacherous elder brothers"; L10, "Victorious
youngest son"; L161, "Lowly hero marries princess."

See A. M. Espinosa, *Cuentos,* 3:26–33, for discussion of both types.
In the form presented here, the tale is widely known throughout
Spanish America, usually under the title "El caballito de siete col-
ores." As in no. 34 of this collection, the informant introduces the
guitar as an important element in the action. See note for no. 34,
above.

The combinaion of Types 550 and 531 is found in *Folktales of
Hungary,* no. 5, and Type 550 alone is in *Folktales of Israel,* no.
56.

· 36 · *The Poor Woodcutter*

Collected by Walter S. Miller in San Lucas Camotlán, Oaxaca. Told
in Spanish by José Trinidad, the informant for nos. 3 and 6 in this
collection. Miller, no. 33.

Type 560, *The Magic Ring*. Principal motifs: B391, "Animal grateful for food"; B491.1, "Helpful serpent"; D391, "Transformation: serpent to person"; D630, "Transformation at will"; D812, "Magic object received from supernatural being"; D1470.1.38, "Magic wishing mirror"; D1501, "Magic object assists woman in childbearing"; D1581, "Tasks performed by use of magic object"; H335, "Tasks assigned suitor"; H1020, "Tasks contrary to the laws of nature"; H1091.1, "Task: sorting grains: performed by helpful ants"; H1103.1.1, "Task: making garden in three days"; L161, "Lowly hero marries princess"; T589.6.1, "Children brought by the stork."

See A. M. Espinosa, *Cuentos,* 3:67–70. Other Mexican variants not in Espinosa: Foster, "Sierra Popoluca Folktales," no. 23, Wheeler, no. 146. See also *Folktales of Chile,* no. 24.

Espinosa found relatively few variants of this tale in Spanish oral tradition, and most of them are fragmentary forms of Type 560. Some Mexican "fragments" are consistent enough, even when found in widely separated geographic regions, to suggest a Mexican subtype. J. M. Espinosa, no. 29, collected at the other extreme of the Mexican culture area from that of our Mixe text, still is surprisingly similar to it. The hero also is an Indian who helps an enchanted prince and receives a magic mirror as his reward. As in our text, the theft of the mirror and its recovery by helpful animals are missing. The main difference is that in the New Mexican variant the Indian feeds and helps the deer, instead of feeding the deer to the serpent as in our text. Rael, *Cuentos españoles,* nos. 158 and 159, also follow the same general pattern. In Foster, "Sierra Popoluca Folktales," no. 23, the Indian hero receives a magic ring from a serpent, but merely as a gift, having done nothing to deserve it. Besides, he is married already.

Miller comments on the *tsox,* saying that this is the first and only reference he found to a bird bringing children. When questioned the informant said, "We don't have that kind of bird here." Is it the stork? Miller asks (p. 181). He does not say whether *tsox* is a Mixe word or resembles one. It certainly is not of Spanish derivation.

A version of Type 560 is given in *Folktales of China,* no. 62.

· 37 · *The Louse Skin*

Collected by Gabriel Moedano N. in Peña Blanca, Oaxaca, 10 January 1967. Told in Spanish by Miguel Cruz Ayuzo, twenty-six, the informant for no. 24 in this collection.

Types 621, *The Louse Skin,* and 559, *Dungbeetle,* III. Principal motifs: B437.2, "Helpful mouse"; B482.2, "Helpful dungbeetle"; B873.1, "Giant louse"; F983.2, "Louse fattened"; H315, "Suitor test: to whom the princess turns"; H511, "Princess offered to correct guesser"; H522.1.1, "Test: guessing nature of certain skin—louse-skin"; K431*, "Mouse's tail in nose of sleeper causes him to sneeze"; L161, "Lowly hero marries princess"; T171*, "Suitor driven from bridal chamber."

See A. M. Espinosa, *Cuentos* 2: 89–98, for discussion of Type 621. Espinosa labels the incident of the dungbeetle and the soiling of the bed by the prince as Element G and lists only three variants of Type 621 with this "extraordinary element"— his own no. 9, a Puerto Rican text collected by Boggs (*JAF* 42: 164–66), and Rael, *Cuentos españoles,* no. 32. He notes that the same element is found in the *Pentamerone* 3: 5 though this last is not a louse-skin story.

Both Types 559 and 621 are found in *Folktales of France,* separately, in nos. 14 and 30.

· 38 · The Priest Who Had One Small Glimpse of Glory

Collected by Virginia Rodríguez Rivera in Mexico, D. F., 19 July 1948. Told by Petra Guzmán Barrón, sixty-nine, who learned it in San Pedro Piedra Gorda, Zacatecas. Our text is from a Spanish manuscript version obtained by courtesy of the collector. A similar text was published in Mendoza Piedra Gorda p. 419.

Type 471A, *The Monk and the Bird;* also cf. Type 775A*, *A Living Man Wants to See God.* Principal motifs: B172.2, "Magic bird's song brings joy and oblivion for many years"; D2011.1, "Years seem moments while man listens to song of bird"; J2072, "Short-sighted wish."

· 39 · Christ Is the Better Smith

Collected by Gabriel Moedano N. at San Juan Tianguismanalco, Puebla, 29 January 1965. Told by Antonio Cruz, thirty-six.

Type 753, *Christ and the Smith.* Principal motifs: D1886, "Rejuvenation by burning"; E15, "Resuscitation by burning"; E121.2, "Resuscitation by Christ"; F663.0.1, "Skillful smith calls self master of all masters"; J2411.1, "Imitation of magic rejuvenation unsuccessful"; K1811, "Gods (saints) in disguise visit mortals."

See A. M. Espinosa, *Cuentos,* 3:140–50. Espinosa cites twenty-four Hispanic texts, a third of them from Mexican tradition.
An example of Type 753 is in *Folktales of England,* no. 36.

·40· The Hard-Hearted Son

Collected by Virginia Rodríguez Rivera in Mexico, D. F., 9 March 1947. Told by Catalina Villagrán Ramírez de Espinosa, thirty, who learned it in Monterrey, Nuevo León. From unpublished manuscript by courtesy of the collector.

Type 779C*, *Hard-Hearted Children Punished.* Principal motifs: D444.2, "Transformation: food to toad (serpent) as punishment for ungrateful son"; D472.1, "Transformation of food to muck as punishment"; Q281.1, "Ungrateful children punished"; Q557.2, "Serpent chokes undutiful son."

Tales of this sort are much more common in Mexican oral tradition than published reports indicate. On the other hand, *corridos* about disobedient children and their unhappy ends have received due notice in published collections.

·41· The Flower of Lily-Lo

Collected by Virginia Rodríguez Rivera in Mexico, D. F., 20 April 1952. Told by Jorge Carlos González Avila, twenty-four, who learned it from his grandmother. The grandmother, Ana Urrutia de Avila, seventy-three, had learned it in Acanché, Yucatán, around 1900. From unpublished manuscript by courtesy of the collector.

Type 780, *The Singing Bone.* Principal motifs: D1318, "Magic object reveals guilt"; D1500.1.4, "Magic healing plant"; D1610.4, "Speaking flower"; E631.1, "Flower from grave"; E632, "Reincarnation as musical instrument"; K2211.0.1, "Treacherous elder brothers"; N271, "Murder will out"; Q211, "Murder punished."

See A. M. Espinosa, *Cuentos,* 3:89–93. Other Mexican variants not in Espinosa: Jiménez, p. 161, Mendoza, *Piedra Gorda,* p. 412, Rael, *Cuentos españoles,* nos. 91, 92.

·42· The Three Shining Stones

Collected by Américo Paredes in East Chicago, Indiana, 2 May 1963. Told by J. A., mestizo male in his sixties from Guanajuato, Mexico, who was also the informant for no. 30 in this collection.

Types 851, *The Princess Who Cannot Solve the Riddle,* and 853A, *"No."* Principal motifs: D1645.1, "Incandescent jewel"; H81, "Clandestine lover recognized by tokens"; H151.1.1, "Attention drawn by playing with remarkable jewel"; H342.1, "Suitor test: forcing princess to say, 'That is a lie' "; H551, "Princess offered to man who can outriddle her"; H565, "Riddle propounded from chance experience"; H573.3, "Riddle solved by listening to the propounder talk in his sleep"; H790, "Riddles based on unusual circumstances"; K187, "Strokes shared"; K1331, "Princess seduced by getting her to answer 'No!' to all questions"; K1361, "Beggar buys, with jewel, the right to sleep before the girl's door, at foot of her bed, in the bed"; K1581, "The lover's gift regained"; L161, "Lowly hero marries princess."

See A. M. Espinosa, *Cuentos,* 2:79–88, for discussion of Type 851. Other Mexican variants not in Espinosa: Rael, *Cuentos españoles,* no. 216, Wagner, no. III-5.

·43· The Five Counsels

Collected by Stanley L. Robe in Tepatitlán, Jalisco, in 1947. Told by Serapio Cornejo, sixty-eight, male, tinsmith. Informant could read and write but had spent very little time in primary school; he had lived in the Jalisco area all his life, having traveled only as far as Guadalajara, the capital, a short distance away. Collector describes him as representative of the poorer class of city dwellers. Robe, no. 16.

Types 910B, *The Servant's Good Counsels,* and 300, *The Dragon-Slayer.* Principal motifs: B15.1.2.6.1, "Seven-headed serpent"; H105.1, "Dragon-tongue proof"; J21.5, "Counsels proved wise by experience: Do not leave the highway"; J21.6, "Counsels proved wise by experience: Do not ask questions about extraordinary things"; J163.4, "Good counsels bought"; K100, "Deceptive bargain"; K1932, "Impostor claims prize won by hero"; K2262, "Treacherous charcoal burner"; L161, "Lowly hero marries princess"; N2.2, "Life wagered"; S262, "Periodic sacrifices to a monster"; S262.3, "Sacrificial victim chosen by lot"; T68, "Princess offered as prize."

See A. M. Espinosa, *Cuentos,* 2:271–86, for Type 910B; and 3:9–26, for Type 300. Espinosa studies forty-three Hispanic variants of Type 910B, one with two counsels, two with four, and the rest with three counsels. Robe also notes that the counsels usually are three, rarely four. In all respects ours is a remarkable text; at first glance one is likely to consider it a confused assortment of motifs, the result of the informant's individual deficiencies as a narrator. The number of counsels aside, there is the matter of their being called "tales" (*cuentos*) instead of counsels. This is strange enough, but the addition of Type 300 after Type 910B seems very much like a case of garbling by the narrator. The wager with the *hacienda* owner again seems like a very local, if not individual, touch of the narrator.

It is quite a surprise, then, to find three separate variants in J. M. Espinosa, collected from three different informants in three different sections of New Mexico and representing "the second and third generations since the United States began to rule in New Mexico" (p. xvi), all of which closely follow our text from Jalisco. These are J. M. Espinosa, nos. 25, 26, and 69. In all of them the young hero buys his counsels, and in nos. 25 and 26 they are called "tales" (*cuentos*). In all three, Type 300 follows after Type 910B, and in nos. 25 and 26 the serpent has seven heads. Again, in all three the boy marries the princess and then wagers his life against the property of a prince (nos. 25 and 26) or a rich man (no. 69) that royalty will bring him his lunch while he works in the fields as a laborer. Obviously, what we have here is a well-established type rather than a case of bungled telling by a narrator.

Whether this is a "Mexican" type is another matter. Hansen reports no similar texts from South America or the Carribean, though he does list a combination of Types 910B and 302, *The Ogre's Heart in the Egg,* from the Dominican Republic. Nor does A. M. Espinosa mention any combinations of 910B and 300 in his discussion of these two types. Espinosa makes some interesting comments about the hero's wagering his life against the rich man's property that a princess will bring him his lunch to the fields where he works as a laborer. Espinosa has noted the motif in some variants of Types 570 and 571; he says of these that they end "in a very different manner, with the details of the wager the victorious aspirant makes with his master or some other person, that the princess, whom he has already married, will bring him his dinner to the fields where he is working." (*Cuentos,* 3:187. My translation from Espinosa's Spanish.) Espinosa gives three Hispanic examples that end in this fashion, all of them Mexican: J. M. Espinosa, nos. 68, 69 and Wheeler, no. 166. Some other Mexican texts besides those mentioned that end with the same motif are: with Type 300 alone, Rael, *Cuentos españoles,* nos. 317, 318, 319; Wheeler, nos. 92, 106; and with Type 910B, Wagner, no. III-7. Foster, "Sierra Popoluca Folklore," no. 39 has as its basic motif the wager, after the Ash-Lad type of unpromising hero has tricked a princess into marrying him.

For Type 300, *The Dragon-Slayer* see also *Folktales of France*, no. 8; *Folktales of Germany*, no. 29; *Folktales of Hungary*, no. 8; *Folktales of Japan*, no. 15.

·44· *The Three Questions*

Collected by Stanley L. Robe in Tepatitlán, Jalisco, Told by Agustina Gómez, twenty-four, female, housewife. Informant has primary school education and can read and write, has lived in the region all her life; she learned her stories from older women in the town. Robe, no. 17.

Type 922, *The Shepherd Substituting for the Priest Answers the King's Questions*. Principal motifs: H524.1, "What am I thinking?"; H541.1, "Riddle propounded on pain of death"; H561.2, "King and abbot"; H631.2, "What is the strongest? God"; H711, "Riddle: How much am I (the king) worth?"; K170, "Deception through pseudo-simple bargain"; K1961.1, "Sham priest"; M203, "King's promise irrevocable"; Q115, "Reward: any boon that may be asked."

See A. M. Espinosa, *Cuentos*, 2:101–11. Other Mexican variants not in Espinosa: Aiken, "Six Tales," p. 78.

Versions of Type 922 appear in *Folktales of England*, no. 63; *Folktales of Israel*, no. 38.

·45· *Ixte'que* (*The Thief*)

Collected by Gabriel Moedano N. at San Miguel Canoa, Puebla, 30 January 1964. Told in Spanish by Tomás Luna Cóyotl, thirty-five, bilingual, whose other language is Náhuatl.

Type 1525, *The Master Thief*. Principal motifs: F660.1, "Brothers acquire extraordinary skill"; H1151, "Theft as task"; H1151.3, "Task: stealing sheet from bed on which person is sleeping"; K301, "Master thief"; K301.1, "Youth learns robbery as a trade"; K332, "Theft by making owner (guards) drunk"; K341.6, "Shoes dropped to distract owner's attention"; K362.2, "Thief holds a corpse up to a lord's window; lord shoots the corpse and leaves to bury it"; K362.4, "Theft by posing as master of the house; wife deceived in the dark."

See A. M. Espinosa, *Cuentos*, 3:229–33. Other Mexican variants not in Espinosa: J. M. Espinosa, nos. 56, 58, 59, Rael, *Cuentos españoles*, nos. 351, 352, 353. See also *Folktales of Chile*, no. 39. Espinosa remarks that the combination of Types 1525 and 950 occurs frequently in Hispanic tradition (p. 229). Type 950 is not present in our text, but some motifs are common to it, such as K332.

·46· *The Tailor Who Sold His Soul to the Devil*

Collected by Vicente T. Mendoza and Virginia Rodríguez Rivera de Mendoza in Mexico, D. F., 20 January 1948. Told by Petra Guzmán Barrón, informant for nos. 8, 20, and 38 in this collection. Mendoza, *Piedra Gorda,* p. 419.

Type 1096, *The Tailor and the Ogre in a Sewing Contest.* Principal motifs: K47.1, "Sewing contest won by deception: the long thread"; K210, "Devil cheated of his promised soul."

See Wheeler, no. 180.

PART IV

JOKES AND ANECDOTES

·47· *The Drovers Who Lost Their Feet*

Collected by Stanley L. Robe in Tepatitlán, Jalisco. Told by María de Jesús Navarro, forty-five, female, housewife and shopkeeper. Informant has no formal education and can neither read nor write. She has lived in the area all her life, though she has visited Guadalajara and Mexico City. Collector comments that her speech is markedly rural. Robe, no. 20.

Type 1288, *Numbskulls Cannot Find Their Own Legs.* Principal motifs: J1703, "Town of fools"; J2021, "Numbskulls cannot find their own legs."

Here Type 1288 becomes a *blason populaire* directed at the residents of the town of Lagos de Moreno, Jalisco, who have the reputation of being numskulls. Robe says, "One of the more common [stories] is that the *laguenses* saw a prickly pear cactus growing on the roof of the parish church and built a platform so that an ox could climb there to eat it." (p. 359) This sounds very much like current North American jokes about how many Poles, Italians, or Texas Aggies it takes to change a lightbulb. Cf. also no. 23 in this collection.

·48· *El Achichinque*

Collected by Américo Paredes in Matamoros, Tamaulipas, 14 September 1962, from the same informant who told no. 27 in this collection.

Type 1526A, *Supper Won by a Trick*. Principal motifs: K455.1, "Supper won by trick"; K1832, "Disguise by changing voice."

·49· *The Man Who Was Full of Truth*

Collected by Américo Paredes in Matamoros, Tamaulipas, from same informant who contributed nos. 27 and 48.

Principal motifs: J261, "Loudest mourners not greatest sorrowers"; K2052.4, "The hypocritical widow"; X111.7, "Misunderstood words lead to comic results"; X909.1, "The incorrigible liar."

This jest is well known along the Lower Rio Grande border, and the woman's cry, "*¡Te vas, cuerpecito lleno de verdad!*" is often used as a proverbial expression. Cf. one of the tasks given the hero in Hispanic versions of Type 570, *The Rabbit-Herd*, to fill a sack full of truths, H1045.

·50· *The Miraculous Mesquite*

Collected by Américo Paredes from the same informant who contributed nos. 27, 48, and 49.

Principal motifs: E1, "Person comes to life"; E90, "Tree of life: resuscitation by touching its branches"; J261, "Loudest mourners not greatest sorrowers"; J2450, "Literal fool"; K2052.4, "The hypocritical widow"; N694*, "Apparently dead person revives as he is being prepared for burial."

·51· *The Mourning Fee* and *The Widow's Cat*

Both 51a and 51b were collected by Américo Paredes from the same informant who contributed nos. 27, 48, 49, and 50.

Principal motifs: (51a) J261, "Loudest mourners not greatest sorrowers"; K2052.4, "The hypocritical widow." (51b) J261, "Loudest mourners not greatest sorrowers"; J2493, "Names of dogs (cat) literally interpreted"; K2052.4, "The hypocritical widow"; X111.7, "Misunderstood words lead to comic results."

A feature of continuing interest to folktale scholars is the influence of the individual narrator's personality on his repertory. This particular informant has contributed eight texts to the collection, nos. 27, 48, 49, 50, 51a, 51b, 60, and 80. Four of them—49, 50, 51a, and 51b—are based on two motifs: J261, "Loudest mourners not greatest sorrowers" and K2052.4, "The hypocritical widow." As stated previously, the informant is in her late fifties and unmarried.

· 52 · *Who Spittled?*

Collected by Virginia Rodríguez Rivera in Mexico, D. F., 5 March 1941. Told by Vicente M. Mendoza, eighty-one, who learned it in Tlacotalpan, Veracruz, in 1890. From unpublished manuscript by courtesy of the collector. A variant, collected elsewhere, is printed in Mendoza, *Piedra Gorda,* p. 422.

Cf. Type 1419F, *Husband Frightened by Wife's Paramour in Hog Pen.* Principal motif: J2626.1, "Cornered paramour threatens the husband."

Cf. also J. M. Espinosa, no. 78, which is a variant of another "Negro" story published in Mendoza, *Piedra Gorda,* p. 422. In J. M. Espinosa the characters are called "Mano Fashicos," in Mendoza "Fracicos." Both are forms of the given name Francisco and represent a comic Negro type perhaps dating from colonial times.

· 53 · *Pedro de Urdemalas and the Gringo* (*a & b*)

Both 53a and 53b were collected by Celedonio Serrano Martínez in the state of Guerrero. No. 53a was told by Guillermo Serrano Martínez, thirty-three in Puerta de Arriba, Tlalchapa, 4 March 1949. No. 53b was collected from Ireneo Serrano Soto, twenty-four, in Tanganguato, Pungarabato, 25 March 1949. Serrano Martínez, p. 426.

Type 1539, *Cleverness and Gullibility.* Principal motifs: (53a) K111.1, "Alleged gold-dropping animal sold"; K330.1, "Man gulled into giving up his clothes"; X600, "Humor concerning races or nations." (53b) K135, "Pseudo-magic animals sold"; K330.1, "Man gulled into giving up his clothes"; X600, "Humor concerning races or nations."

Type 1539 covers a series of episodes that often appear as independent stories, in Spanish tradition usually with the trickster Pedro de Urdemalas as the protagonist. See A. M. Espinosa, *Cuentos,* 3: 151–62, where twenty-seven Hispanic variants are considered. An especially interesting feature of our texts is the gulling of the foreigner (in this case a North American) by the trickster, who takes not only his horse but his clothes. This seems to be a favorite situation with American Indian narrators in both Mexico and the United States. See for example Mason, "Utes," no. 8, in which Coyote dupes the white man by magically changing a stick horse and a rabbit into swift race horses. See also McAllister, no. 26, from the Kiowa-Apache, in which Coyote tricks the white man of his clothes and his horse (K341.8.1,

"Trickster pretends to ride home for tools to perform tricks").

Another noteworthy thing about these texts is the stereotype of the foreigner who serves as the trickster's victim. He is clearly identified as "a redfaced *gringo*," a North American; yet, his favorite expression is the obscenity *¡Coño!* This is an identifying characteristic of the peninsular Spaniard stereotype. In fact, the peninsular Spaniard in Mexican folklore is often called a *coño*. (See *coño* and *gringo* in the Glossary.) Both jests and ethnic names in Mexican tradition suggest that many stories and epithets once applied by Mexicans to Spaniards, Frenchmen, and other ethnic groups have been transferred to the man from the United States.

For a general discussion on Pedro de Urdemalas, see A. M. Espinosa, *Cuentos,* 3: 127–29. Pedro seems to have been the prototype of the Spanish *pícaro* in oral tradition by the sixteenth century. Cervantes, among others, used the name of Pedro de Urdemalas for a picaresque character. Oral tradition has made numberless variations on the name. Espinosa considers the Pedro de Urdemalas tales as narratives of social protest. See, by the way, Foster, "Sierra Popoluca Folktales," no. 38, a variant of Type 301, "John the Bear," in which the hero is a soldier called Pedro de Mal.

An example of Type 1539, also told on Pedro de Urdemalas, is in *Folktales of Chile,* no. 44.

·54· Pedro de Urdemalas and the House with Strange Names (*a & b*)

Both 54*a* and 54*b* were collected by Virginia Rodríguez Rivera at Chavinda, Michoacán, 16 December 1939. Told by Esperanza Espinosa Villanueva, twenty-five; collector adds note that they date from 1910 and are Pedro de Urdemalas stories. From unpublished manuscript by courtesy of the collector.

Both these tales are based on the literal interpretation of metaphorical language, specifically the strange names given to objects by the owner of the house visited by the trickster. They have separate numbers in Aarne-Thompson, however; no. 54a is Type 1545, *The Boy with Many Names*. Principal motifs: J2470, "Metaphors literally interpreted"; K331, "Goods stolen while owner sleeps"; K359.2, "Thief beguiles guardian of goods by assuming equivocal name"; K475, "Cheating through equivocation." No. 54b is Type 1562A, *The Barn Is Burning*. Principal motifs: J1269.12, "Youth announces fire in imitation of priest's metaphorical language"; J2470, "Metaphors literally interpreted."

See A. M. Espinosa, *Cuentos,* 2: 260–64. His no. 57 includes the elements of both our 54a and our 54b. Espinosa mentions but one Mexican text, Rael, *Cuentos españoles,* no. 288, which resembles our no. 54b.

· 55 · *Pedro de Urdemalas and the Priest*

Collected by Virginia Rodríguez Rivera in Mexico, D. F., 30 July 1950. Told by Manuel Guevara, forty-eight, who learned it in Cerritos, San Miguel de Allende, Guanajuato. Collector adds that story dates from 1890 and belongs to the Pedro de Urdemalas cycle. From unpublished manuscript by courtesy of the collector.

Types 1545, *The Boy with Many Names,* 921, *The King and the Peasant's Son,* and 1138, *Gilding the Beard.* Principal motifs: H561.4, "The king (priest) and the clever youth"; H1377.3, "Quest for hazelnuts of ay, ay, ay"; J1252, Quibbling answers"; K402.1, "The goose without a leg"; K602, "Noman: escape by assuming equivocal name"; K1013.1, "Making the beard golden: such a one."

For discussion of Type 921 in Spanish tradition, see A. M. Espinosa, *Cuentos,* 2: 143–48. Other Mexican variants: Aiken, "Pack Load," p. 47, Parsons, "Mitla," no. 20, Rael, *Cuentos españoles,* no. 461, Wheeler, no. 19. See also *Folktales of Hungary,* no. 17.

· 56 · *Pedro de Urdemalas, Schoolmaster*

Collected by Virginia Rodríguez Rivera in Mexico, D. F., 10 October 1949. Told by Concepción Mangold de Curtis, eighty, who learned it in Puebla, Puebla, around 1880. From unpublished manuscript by courtesy of the collector.

Resembles Type 1628*, *So They Speak Latin.* Principal motifs: K150, "Sale of worthless services"; K1958, "Sham teacher."

· 57 · *The Sham Wise Man*

Collected by Virginia Rodríguez Rivera in Mexico, D. F., 11 February 1951. Told by Manuel Guevara, fifty, who learned the tale in San Miguel Allende, Guanajuato, around 1925. From unpublished manuscript by courtesy of the collector.

Type 1641, *Doctor Know-All.* Principal motifs: K1956, "Sham wise man"; N611.1, "Criminal accidentally detected: That is the first"; N688, "What is in the dish: Poor Crab."

Other Mexican variants: A. M. Espinosa, "New-Mexican Spanish

Folk-Lore, III," no. 6; Hudson, "King," p. 179; Miller, no. 31; Rael, *Cuentos españoles,* nos. 13, 14, 15; Rael, "Cuentos españoles," no. 12; Robe, no. 22; Zunser, nos. 5, 6.

Versions of Type 1641 are in *Folktales of China,* no. 11; *Folktales of Germany,* no. 54.

· 58 · *Laziness Rewarded*

Collected by Walter S. Miller in San Lucas Camotlán, Oaxaca. Told in Spanish by Pedro Molino, thirty-nine, son of a Zapotecan resident in Camotlán and a Mixe woman of the village. Pedro Molino is a nephew of José Trinidad, considered by Miller his best informant. Miller describes Pedro Molino as one of the few young persons in Camotlán who showed aptitude as narrators. Miller, no. 35.

Type 1645B*, *God Will Care for All.* Cf. also Type 986, *The Lazy Husband.* Principal motifs: L114.1, "Lazy hero"; L140, "The unpromising surpasses the promising"; N142, "Destiny better than work, show, or speculation"; N170, "The capriciousness of luck."

See Hudson, "To Whom God Wishes to Give," p. 128, for a text from Jalisco.

· 59 · *The Two Psychiatrists*

Collected by Américo Paredes in Matamoros, Tamaulipas, 15 September 1962. Told by R. G., mestizo male in his forties, who at the time was an official of the Mexican federal government.

Type 1626, *Dream Bread.* Principal motif: K444, "Dream bread: the most wonderful dream."

In its "straight" form (the bread or other food, the dream contest to see who eats the bread, the fantastic dreams told by two of the three characters, and the announcement by the third character that he ate the bread while the other two were in Heaven, in fairyland, etc.) this tale is widespread in Mexican oral tradition, at least in northern Mexico and southwestern United States. It is strange that it is not often reported in print; see, however, Rael, *Cuentos españoles,* no. 87. Obscene or slightly off-color versions such as this one also are common. See Abrahams, pp. 255 ff., for a discussion of versions in American Negro and in Mexican traditions.

A variant of Type 1626 is in *Folktales of Israel,* no. 45.

·60· All's for the Best

Collected by Américo Paredes in Matamoros, Tamaulipas, from the same informant who contributed nos. 27, 48, 49, 50, 51a and 51b; informant is an unmarried female in her late fifties, of rural background, primary school education.

Principal motifs: L144, "Ignorant surpasses learned man"; N170, "The capriciousness of luck"; W26, "Patience."

·61· The Rider in the Brambles and The Stake in the Graveyard

The Rider in the Brambles (61a) was collected by Vicente T. Mendoza and Virginia Rodríguez Rivera de Mendoza in Zacatecas, Zacatecas, 8 September 1946. Told by Aureliano Guzmán, who learned it in San Pedro Piedra Gorda, Zacatecas. Same informant told no. 7 in this collection. Mendoza, *Piedra Gorda*, p. 389.

The Stake in the Graveyard (61b) was collected by Américo Paredes in Brownsville, Texas, 10 September 1962. Told by Q. H. G., mestizo male in his late thirties, bilingual but with strong roots in Mexican tradition. Informant learned the tale from his grandfather in Tamaulipas.

Type 1676B, *Clothing Caught in Graveyard*. Principal motifs: (61a) J2625, "Coward is frightened when clothing catches on thistle"; (61b), H1400, "Fear test"; N384.2, "Death in the graveyard; person's clothing is caught."

Although collected in Texas from a Texas-Mexican, 61b is a longer version of 61a and closer to the type. In much the same form, it is well known in Tamaulipas, where the informant learned it. It is told not as a joke but as a legend, and it is as a legend that the informant tells 61b. Some forty years before I collected this on tape, I heard the same story from my mother, as told to her by *her* grandfather, who supposedly witnessed the events narrated. In my mother's variant, as I remember it, there was no fatal ending; the student merely gets a good scare. He drives a nail into the wooden cross at the head of a grave and nails down his cloak. Our 61b was told during a bilingual joke-telling session, being in effect an interpolation into a different context. This is clear from the remark made by one of the audience, in English, "Did he [the dead man] have brown eyes?" This is in reference to a bilingual joke told immediately before our text. A drunkard is told that women with brown eyes are always unfaithful. He goes home and finds his wife apparently asleep. He lifts her eyelids and sees her eyes are brown. "Brown!" he cries. And Brown comes out from under the bed where he has been hiding. Obviously, the audience does not accept 61b as a legend, as intended by the narrator, turning it into a joke instead.

The "Brown" joke interpolated by the member of the audience is a merry version of Type 1641, *Doctor Know-All,* specifically N688, "What is in the dish: Poor Crab." A number of these versions exist in both North American and Mexican oral traditions. Both 61a and 61b, however, are standard variants of Type 1676B in Spanish-American tradition. Hansen's Type **1677, reported from Puerto Rico, is 61b; his *1710 is our 61a.

·62· *The Fool and His Brother*

Collected by Joel Gómez in La Encantada, Texas, April 1968. Told by Mrs. P. E., seventy-four, the informant for nos. 26, 29, 34, and 35 in this collection.

Types 1681B, *Fool as Custodian of Home and Animals,* and 1653B, *The Brothers in the Tree.* Principal motifs: E373.1, "Money received from ghost as reward for bravery: 'Let it fall' "; H1411.1, "Fear test: staying in haunted house: 'Shall we fall?' "; J1805.1, "Similar sounding words mistaken for each other"; J2450, "Literal fool"; J2541, "Don't eat too greedily"; K335.1.1.1, "Door falls on robbers from tree"; K825, "Victim persuaded to hold out his tongue: cut off"; K1413, "Guarding the door"; K1462, "Washing the grandmother, in boiling water"; N696, "Fugitive in tree urinates on robbers"; X431, "The hungry parson and the porridge pot."

See A. M. Espinosa, *Cuentos,* 3: 191–98 and 212–22. The combination of Types 1681B and 1653B in the same tale is common in Hispanic tradition. Other Mexican variants: A. M. Espinosa, "New-Mexican Spanish Folk-Lore, VII," nos. 13, 14; Parsons, Mitla, no. 14; Rael, *Cuentos españoles,* no. 273.

·63· *Thank God It Wasn't a Peso*

Collected by Américo Paredes in Ajusco, Mexico, 20 November 1962. Told by J. F., mestizo male in his fifties, also the informant for nos. 15, 16, and 28 in this collection.

Type 1689, *Thank God They Weren't Peaches.* Cf. also Type 1543,

Not One Penny Less, in which an eavesdropping sexton gives a suppliant money, but under different circumstances. Principal motifs: J2563, "Thank God they weren't peaches"; K464, "Eavesdropping sexton duped into giving suppliant money."

·64· The Stupid Drover

Collected by Virginia Rodríguez Rivera in Chavinda, Michoacán, 13 December 1939. Told by Trinidad Espinosa, sixty-five, spinster, who learned it in Chavinda about 1900. From unpublished manuscript by courtesy of the collector.

Types 1437, *A Sweet Word,* and 1696B*, *Say Only Round (Good) Words.* Principal motifs: J1541.1, "The good words"; J2470, "Metaphors literally interpreted"; J2497, "Honey is sweet."

·65· The Rosary of Amozoc

Collected by Virginia Rodríguez Rivera in Tepeaca, Puebla, 25 May 1951. Told by Manuel Centeno, fifty-two who learned it in Amozoc, Puebla, early in the century. From unpublished manuscript by courtesy of the collector.

Type 1699, *Misunderstanding because of Ignorance of a Foreign Language.* Principal motifs: J1803, "Learned words misunderstood by uneducated"; Z62, "Proverbial simile."

"To end up like the Rosary of Medina" (or of some town in Spain or Spanish America) is a proverbial expression known throughout the Spanish-speaking world. In Mexico the town most commonly referred to is Amozoc.

·66· God Gives a Hundred for One

Collected by Virginia Rodríguez Rivera in Mexico, D. F., 30 July 1950. Told by Manuel Guevara, forty-nine, who learned it from a sixty-year-old narrator in Cerritos, San Miguel Allende, Guanajuato. From unpublished manuscript by courtesy of the collector.

Type 1735, *Who Gives His Own Goods Shall Receive It Back Tenfold.* Principal motif: K366.1.1, "Cow makes a hundredfold return."

See Rael, *Cuentos españoles,* no. 463, very similar to our text. Again the protagonist is an Indian, but he is naive about the matter. He is, however, a "wild" Indian, and he threatens the priest with bow and arrow.

·67· All Priests Go to Hell

Collected by Virginia Rodríguez Rivera in Mexico, D. F., 25 May 1950. Told by Manuel Guevara, the informant for no. 66 in this collection, who learned the tale in Cerritos, San Miguel Allende, Guanajuato. From unpublished manuscript by courtesy of the collector.

Type 1738, *The Dream: All Parsons in Hell.* Principal motif: X438, "The dream: all parsons in hell."

·68· I Can't Hear a Thing

Collected by Américo Paredes in Ajusco, Mexico, 20 November 1962. Told by the same informant who contributed nos. 15, 16, 28, and 63 in this collection.

Type 1777A*, *I Can't Hear You.* Principal motif: X441.1, "I can't hear you."

This tale, with the slightest variations, is universal throughout the Greater Mexican area. Just as widespread is the proverbial expression, *No se oye nada* (I can't hear a thing), to mean, "Nothing doing."

·69· The Big Christ and the Little Christ

Collected by Stanley L. Robe in Tepatitlán, Jalisco. Told by Pedro González, twenty-six, male, a mechanic with three years of primary school who has lived most of his life in his native town of Acatic. His mother also is a narrator of folktales and was one of Robe's informants. Robe, no. 3.

Type 1347*, *The Statue's Father.* Cf. also Types 1479**, *Statue Avenged,* and 1832N*, *Lamb of God Becomes Sheep of God.* Principal motifs: J1823.1.2, "Image of Christ said to be son of the one that broke man's arm"; J2212, "Effects of age and size absurdly applied"; K1840, "Deception by substitution"; V123.1, "God under compulsion: suppliant threatens to mutilate holy image if his wish is not fulfilled."

This tale belongs to Type 1347*, except that in the Aarne-Thompson type the fool has come to thank the "father" statue rather than revenge himself upon it. Robe, the collector, cites an analogue from the *Libro de los Enxemplos,* no. 393, in which a suppliant blames the image of Saint Nicholas for his misfortunes, but that tale is of a miraculous type. Cf. Rael, *Cuentos españoles,* no. 476, in which

a group of village Indians complain to the image of Saint Anthony
about the hail damage done by his "son," the image of the Child
Jesus in Saint Anthony's arms. See also Wheeler, no. 21: Some villagers take an image of the Virgin in procession through their
parched fields and a torrential downpour follows, so they want to
borrow an image of the Child Jesus to show him the damage done
by his mother.

All these tales belong to a class of European jests satirizing the
naive interpretation of Catholic ritual. In Europe the principals in the
stories usually are peasants. In Mexico, where Catholicism has taken
on pre-Conquest accretions, the characters most often are Indians.
In jests I have collected along the Texas-Mexican border, the characters are likely to be Americanized migrant workers or Anglo-
Americans. In Europe the point of the jests is the ignorance of the
peasants, a socially inferior class. In Mexican tales with Indian characters, there is both social snobbery and ethnic bias, since the Indians
are peasants and also people with strange customs and a special way
of speaking Spanish. In the border Mexican jests, the butt of the joke
is the Anglo-American and his strange, Protestant culture, which the
Mexican migrant worker sometimes apes. Our no. 69 is remarkable
in that the main character is a Spaniard—a character one would
expect to be the epitome of correctness in such things as Catholic
ritual and pronunciation of Spanish. But the Mexican stereotype of
the Spaniard or *gachupín* has always shown him as a crude foreigner
who speaks a Spanish much like that spoken by the stage Moor in
Spanish golden age drama. This, to my mind, relates the pre-1890
Mexican stereotype of the Spaniard to the present-day stereotype of
the North American or *gringo*. See also the notes for no. 53 as well
as *coño* and *gringo* in the Glossary.

·70· *On Holy Week*

Collected by Américo Paredes in Matamoros, Tamaulipas, 14 September 1962. Told by I. V., mestizo male in his sixties, born in Guanajuato. Informant comes from a devoutly Catholic background, as do
most narrators of tales of this type. The same informant contributed
nos. 21, 22, and 23 in this collection.

Principal motif: J2495.3*, "Religious exercises given absurd or obscene turn: Christ in the Passion Play."

Cf. Types 1678*, *In Passion Play the Christ Says, "I Am Thirsty"*
and 1829, *Living Person Acts as Image of Saint.* See also Wheeler,

no. 16, in which a drunk accidentally substitutes a pig for the image
of Christ during a festival.

·71· *The Miracle of San Pedro Piedra Gorda*

Collected by Virginia Rodríguez Rivera in Mexico, D. F., 21 June
1948. Told by Petra Guzmán Barrón, sixty-nine, who learned it in
San Pedro Piedra Gorda, Zacatecas. From manuscript by courtesy of
the collector. A very similar text, from the same informant, appears
in Mendoza, *Piedra Gorda,* p. 426.

Type 1840A, *The Parson's Ox.* Principal motifs: J1851.3, "Gift
made to object"; K231.3, "Refusal to make sacrifice after need is
past."

Cf. also Type 1849*, *The Priest on the Cow's Tail,* and Hansen
**1644A, in which the devotee takes a heifer to a saint and lets it
run loose in the church.

·72· *The Sermon on the Arrest of Jesus*

Collected by Vicente T. Mendoza and Virginia Rodríguez Rivera de
Mendoza in Mexico, D. F., 22 June 1948. Told by Petra Guzmán
Barrón, the informant for nos. 8, 20, 38, 46, and 71 in this collection,
who learned it in San Pedro Piedra Gorda, Zacatecas. Mendoza,
Piedra Gorda, p. 425.

Type 1833, *Application of the Sermon.* Principal motif: X435,
"Boy (man) applies the sermon."

The context of this story is closely related to customs well known
to all Mexicans, the organization of religious festivals by *cofradías* or
brotherhoods, as well as the custom requiring rich or prominent men
of the village to bear the cost of masses and secular festivities. See
Hansen 1833**E for a similar tale from Cuba: the priest asks the
same question as a captain's adjutant enters church looking for the
captain and his wife to give them an umbrella.

An instance of Type 1833A appears in *Folktales of England,* no.
61.

·73· *The Famous Sermon*

Collected by Virginia Rodríguez Rivera in Jerez, Zacatecas, 15
September 1948. Told by Jesús Romero Flores, fifty-two, who learned
it in Piedad de las Cavadas, Michoacán. From unpublished manuscript by courtesy of the collector.

Type 1831, *The Parson and the Sexton at Mass*. Cf. also Type 1839*, *Making Thunder*. Principal motif: X441, "Parson and sexton at mass."

See also A. M. Espinosa, *Cuentos*, no. 43.

·74· *A Current Story*

Collected by Américo Paredes in Matamoros, Tamaulipas, from the same informant who told nos. 21, 22, 23, and 70 in this collection.

Principal motifs: X800, "Humor based on drunkenness"; X1740, "Lies: absurd disregard of natural laws."

An example of the Mexican tall tale, with a somewhat modern twist.

PART V

FORMULA TALES

·75· *The Nanny Goat*

Collected by Américo Paredes in Matamoros, Tamaulipas, 24 August 1954. Sung to guitar accompaniment by Juan Guajardo, sixty-three, who at time of collection was well known as a singer of *corridos, décimas, coplas* and other Mexican folk songs.

Principal motifs: Z22, "Ehod mi yodea"; Z23, "How the rich man paid his servant." Cf. Type 2010, *Ehod mi yodea*, and also 2010 I, *How the Rich Man Paid His Servant*.

Although sung, this text has the structure of a cumulative tale rather than that of folk poetry. It is made up of two unrhymed and loosely constructed parts, the second one growing with each cumulative repetition. The tune is based on an eight-bar pattern with additional bars being added after the fourth, two bars at a time. The first time this second part is sung to ten bars, the second to twelve, etc.

This is neither a children's cumulative tale nor a ritual song like the "Song of the Kid" in the Jewish Passover ritual, but it bears comparison with both. For discussion of the "Song of the Kid" from a folkloric viewpoint see W. W. Newell, "The Passover Song of the Kid" and Leah R. C. Yoffie, "Present-Day Survivals of Ancient Jewish Custom."

·76· The Ram in the Chile Patch

The Ram in the Chile Patch was collected by Stanley L. Robe in Tepatitlán, Jalisco. Told by María del Refugio González, female, forty-five, primary school education, working as a clerk in a store. She has lived in Tepatitlán all her life but has visited as far as Mexico City; described by collector as an active informant who tells stories to her younger brothers and sisters. Robe, no. 18.

Type 2015, *The Goat Who Would Not Go Home*. Principal motif: Z39.1, "The goat who would not go home."

See Rael *Cuentos españoles,* nos. 403 and 404; in the Rael texts, however, the goat gets into a wheat field and an orchard. There is a specially Mexican touch here in that the field invaded is a chile patch.

Variants of Type 2015 are in *Folktales of France,* no. 39 and *Folktales of Germany,* no. 9.

·77· Pérez the Mouse (a & b)

Both 77a and 77b were collected by Stanley L. Robe in the state of Jalisco. No. 77a was told by María Soledad Orozco, fifteen, female, at Capilla de Guadalupe. Informant has primary school education but no longer was in school at time of collection. No. 77b was told by Clemente Martín, eleven, male, schoolboy with four years primary school, at Pegueros, where informant has lived all his life. He learned his stories from his father. Robe, nos. 4 and 10 respectively.

Type 2023, *Little Ant Finds a Penny*. Principal motif: Z32.3, "Little ant finds a penny, buys new clothes with it, and sits in her doorway." Coincidentally, 77a and 77b together make up the complete tale type. In 77a the ant finds the penny, is courted by different animals, marries the mouse, and loses her husband when he drowns in the stew; 77b completes the story with the chain of events following the death of the mouse.

See A. M. Espinosa, *Cuentos,* 3: 445–50. Espinosa's nos. 271 and 272 are most like our 77a, even in the lack of the series of mourners; Espinosa's no. 274 is like 77b, with its emphasis on the chain of events following the death of the mouse. That is to say, in Spain, too, the story may exist as two independent episodes. Other Mexican variants not mentioned in Espinosa: Hiester, p. 233; Pérez, p. 81; Wagner, no. II–25.

·78· *The Little Ant*

Collected by Vicente T. Mendoza and Virginia Rodríguez Rivera de Mendoza in Mexico, D. F., 20 January 1948. Told by Petra Guzmán Barrón, informant for nos. 71 and 72 in this collection.

Type 2031, *Stronger and Strongest*. Principal motif: Z42, "Stronger and strongest."

See A. M. Espinosa, *Cuentos,* 3: 450–58. See also *Folktales of Chile,* no. 50.

·79· *Talking Animals*

Collected by Américo Paredes in Ajusco, Mexico, 20 November 1962. Told by same informant who contributed nos. 15, 16, 28, 63, and 68 in this collection.

Type 2075, *Tales in Which Animals Talk.* Principal motifs: B210, "Speaking animals"; B251.1.2, "Animals speak to one another at Christmas."

A tale popular among people of Mexican culture. A version I used to hear as a child has the cock cry, "Christ is born!" The sheep says, "In Bethlehem." And the turkey gobbler says, *"Gordo, gordo, gordo, gordo"* (Fat baby). See Miller, p. 207 for a Mixe text seriously told among people who according to Miller believe animals could talk before the birth of Christ.

·80· *Round*

Collected by Américo Paredes in *municipio* of Matamoros, Tamaulipas, 14 September 1962. Told by G. T. G., mestizo female in her fifties, of rural background.

Types 2013, *There Was Once a Woman,* and 2320, *Round.* Principal motifs: Z17, "Rounds"; Z49.4, "There was once a woman; the woman had a son; the son had red breeches, etc. Shall I tell it again?"

This is a very popular formula tale in Mexican tradition. A variant of it was collected by Albert S. Gatschet some eighty years ago in the same area from which our text was obtained. It is no. 27 in Gatschet's collection of folklore from Matamoros entitled "Popular Rimes from Mexico." Gatschet did not recognize his text as a formula tale, listing it as a counting-out rhyme, probably because the Spanish verb *contar* means both "to count" and "to narrate."

See A. M. Espinosa, "New-Mexican Spanish Folk-lore, VII," no. 50 and Parsons, "Santa Ana," no. 4 for other Mexican variants. The Parsons text is especially interesting because it is used as a conventional opening for a much longer, unrelated narrative.

Glossary

achichinque From Aztec *atl*, water, and *chichinqui*, sucker; see Santamaría, *Mejicanismos*, who also gives variants *achichincle, achichintle*, and *achichintli*. Originally a worker who bailed out water from the mines; familiarly a sycophant or hanger-on. (No. 48.)

albur Chance, hazard, game of cards. More specifically, word-play between men involving insults couched in a kind of Joycean, distorted language with double or triple meanings. (Note to no. 23.)

almud Spanish dry measure, roughly equivalent to the bushel but with varying equivalents, not only in different parts of Latin America, but in different regions of Mexico as well. In Mexico the measure varies from three to twenty liters, depending on the area (see Santamaría, *Mejicanismos*.) In Jalisco it is equivalent to four liters, not only according to linguists like Santamaría but according to Robe's informant. (No. 43.)

arroba Old Spanish weight, antedating the metric system and equivalent to twenty-five pounds; still in use by farmers and ranchers in many parts of Mexico. (Nos. 3, 6.)

bayuco Cf. North American "bayou," said to derive from Choctaw *bayuk*. In northern Tamaulipas, applied to creek-like outlets formed by rivers in flood. Santamaría, *Mejicanismos*, is perhaps in error in defining it as a mudhole in the road. (No. 19.)

cantina "Saloon" in the old sense of the term, any tavern, bar, beer joint, etc., for men only. *Bar* is more often used for places where couples are served. (Nos. 25, 61b.)

caramba, caray, carajo(s) *Caramba* and *caray* are two of the many euphemisms for *carajo*, the penis. A common exclamation of displeasure or surprise among all people who speak Spanish. Among some groups *carajo* itself has lost its original meaning, existing merely as one of many forms of the same exclamation, often used adjectivally. (Nos. 11, 24, 42.)

chachalaca   Gallinaceous game bird whose name, according to Santamaría, *Mejicanismos,* comes from a Náhuatl word meaning "garrulous"; more often heard than seen in the brush, it will continue to cackle when the rest of the woods are silent. When the *chachalaca* is not heard, the woods are silent indeed. (No. 2.)

colorín   Shiny red seeds of several related plants, notably *Erythrina coralloides;* according to Santamaría, *Mejicanismos,* the seeds were used by water carriers in Mexico to count the number of trips they made with water to a particular house, leaving a seed with the housewife for each trip. Use of the seed as counters may be the reason for the presence of the *colorín* as part of the formal close of a story. The informant for nos. 24 and 37 has changed *colorín colorado* (red *colorín*) to *carabín carabado.* (Nos. 24, 26, 34, 37, 41, 44, 62, 77a.)

compadre   Also *comadre* (fem.), *comadrita* (dimin. fem.), *compadrazgo* (state of being a *compadre* to another person). Speaking from a strictly ecclesiastical point of view, the state of *compadrazgo* exists between the parents of a child and the couple who sponsored him as godparents at the child's baptism. *Compadre,* therefore, should not be translated as "godfather," as some folklorists have done. It is a relationship existing between members of the same generation. *Compadrazgo,* however, is given a variety of meanings, depending on the area of Latin America involved, and may be summed up somewhat loosely under the term "ritual brotherhood." Men and women may participate in any number of rituals which will result in their becoming *compadres* or *comadres.* *Comadre* may mean "neighbor" or "gossip"; *comadrear* means to go around the neighborhood gossiping, and when little girls play house they are said to play at being *comadritas.* Boys or men who are pals or buddies may be said to be *compadres.* When Anglo-Americans and Indians met on the Great Plains, there was talk of "white brothers" and "red brothers"; when Spaniard and Mexican met the same Indians, the term employed was *compadre*. The fraternal character of *compadrazgo* was already present in medieval Europe, since the church forbade as incest the marriage of couples who had stood as sponsors at a baptism. Apparently *compadrazgo* has supplanted a number of native ritual relationships in Spanish America. (Nos. 10, 49, 51a, 51b, 58.)

coño The common "four-letter" Spanish word for the vulva, much used by some peninsular Spaniards as an obscene exclamation; less common among Spanish Americans, who therefore call Spaniards *coños* because of their alleged overuse of the term. In some places, as in northern Tamaulipas, the original meaning of the word has been lost, the term standing simply for Spaniard, a state of affairs conducive to some embarrassing situations. Santamaría, *Mejicanismos,* notes *coño* as a name for Spaniard in Chile but fails to register the term for Mexico. (Nos. 15, 53a, 53b.)

corrido The Mexican ballad form, usually in octosyllabic, rhymed quatrains; a late development from the Spanish *romance* found in Spain and other parts of Spanish America but evolving in Mexico in a characteristically Mexican way. (Notes to Nos. 7, 40.)

costumbrismo, costumbrista From *costumbre,* custom; strictly speaking the use of folk customs, folk speech, etc., for the purpose of local color in fiction, though some critics would include as *costumbrista* writers golden age dramatists such as Lope de Vega, who also made use of folklore in their works. *Costumbrismo,* though, is related to antiquarianism and appears in Spain around the 1830s. One of its more successful cultivators was Fernán Caballero (1796–1877).

estero Dictionary meanings for *estero* include "estuary" or a salt-water lake or tidewater creek. In the area where the text was collected, *estero* invariably means a freshwater lake occupying an old river bed. (No. 11.)

fiesta A difficult word to translate in some contexts, since it may mean anything from a neighborhood birthday party to a religious festival. (No. 2.)

gringo From *griego,* Greek; in the past applied to any non-

Spanish speaking foreigner, and still used this way in Argentina and other places in South America. *Gringo* to mean specifically North American apparently began in southwestern United States and northern Mexico, spreading south after the end of the war between Mexico and the United States. (Nos. 53a, 53b, 75.)

hacienda Robe (p. 336) says that in Los Altos this means "a large agricultural enterprise, as distinguished from the much smaller and individually owned *rancho.*" In some contexts may refer to the pre-Revolutionary landed estate. (No. 43.)

hombre Literally "man" and so translated when it applies; but may also mean "Well!" "Now!" or "Hey!" (Nos. 26, 29, 34, 35, 37, 68, 69.)

huijul May be the same as the *juijuy,* listed by Santamaría, *Mejicanismos,* as a rosaceous plant belonging to the genus *Licania.* (No. 53b.)

huisache From the Aztec *huixachi,* thorny. Various species of a thorny bush of the *Acacia* family, growing to tree size in well-watered country. Grows throughout Mexico and Texas. (No. 29.)

juguetetoqui The collector defines this as *garrobos de fuego,* that is "fire iguanas." Pimentel, "Miscelánea," p. 217. (No. 5.)

kilo Always for "kilogram." (No. 76.)

ladino In Chiapas, according to Santamaría, *Mejicanismos,* refers to the non-Indian; a European or mestizo. Also applied to an acculturated Indian, who no longer speaks his own language, being therefore "Latinized"; variation of *latino,* Latin. In more general usage means sly or cunning; in northern Mexico term is applied to maverick cattle wise to the ways of man and therefore difficult to cope with. (No. 10.)

macho Literally the male animal. *Machismo,* the exaggerated cult of the male, has caused Mexican sociologists and psychologists much concern, though much the same phenomenon is found in the United States in Theodore Roosevelt and Ernest Hemingway. (Note to no. 21.)

manito(a) Shortened form of *hermanito* and *hermanita,* affectionate diminutives of "brother" and "sister"; common among rural people throughout Mexico, though in the literature of social science in the United States, the terms have been taken as belonging peculiarly to Mexican-Americans from New Mexico. (No. 17.)

moca   An indefinite unit of dry measure common to Mexicans of the regional groups along the lower Rio Grande border. It is most commonly used in reference to shelled corn and is variously and vaguely defined by informants, usually by pointing to the nearest container available: "A *moca* would be about what you could put into that tin can over there." It seems to be equivalent to "a few handfuls." One borrows a *moca* of shelled corn, for example. A small amount, therefore, a little bit; and by extension, in the expression *cualquier moca* (any old *moca*), something of no account. In some border country folk verses about horseracing, a horseman says of his mount, "Don't go thinking he's *cualquier moca;* he's a riverbank horse." Santamaría does not register the term in his *Mejicanismos*. He does include it in his earlier work, *Diccionario general de americanismos* (Mexico, 1942), noting that in Ecuador *moca* means a mudhole, in Honduras a boys' game, and in Puerto Rico a kind of tree. Santamaría adds, "The Spanish Academy's definition for Mexico as 'a glass of wine' seems in error, since the word is unknown there." I have never heard *moca* defined as a glass of wine, but it is interesting that in a text in our collection the strong hero, after killing a magic boar, asks for a girl's kiss and a *moca* of corn. A *moca* of wine would go better with a kiss. (No. 29.)

morral   The Mexican bag, usually made of woven ixtle, called a feed bag or nose bag in southwestern United States. Border Mexicans do use the *morral* as a feed bag and only secondarily as a receptacle for groceries and other goods. In southern Mexico the *morral* is used almost exclusively as a carryall. (Nos. 12, 35, 42.)

nanchin   Perhaps the same fruit tree variously listed by Santamaría, *Mejicanismos,* as *nance, nancen, nache, nancis, nanche,* and *nanchi;* a tree with a yellow fruit shaped something like a cherry, common in Veracruz, Tabasco, and other Gulf Coast areas. (No. 4.)

patrón Depending on the context, may mean master or boss; used for a saint or other supernatural, it is closer to patron. (Nos. 2, 43, 45.)

pelado Literally skinned or plucked; as an adjective it may mean "flat broke"; as a noun it is the Mexican equivalent of the Spanish *pícaro,* the shiftless, impoverished, but ingenious low-class character. By extension it can mean "fellow" or "guy." (No. 19.)

pendejo Literally pubic hair; used both in masculine and feminine as a strong term meaning stupid or foolish; perhaps "stupid bastard" would be a close equivalent. Sometimes may also mean cowardly. (No. 79.)

piloncillo Brown sugar loaf in form of a truncated cone. Formerly it was the only source of sugar in many parts of rural Mexico, as well as among Mexican groups in southwestern United States. It was used to sweeten coffee, for baking, and as candy. It is not uncommon to eat it with bread. (No. 62.)

presidencia In a Mexican town, the building where the municipal offices are located, especially the office of the mayor or *presidente municipal.* (No. 21.)

ranchero Inhabitant of a *rancho* and by extension a rustic, clodhopper, hillbilly. By further extension and amelioration, especially since the revolution, it has become indicative of rural virtues. (Nos. 42, 43, 50, 71.)

real As unit of monetary value, ⅛ of a peso, or of a dollar; still in current use in Mexico and southwestern United States. More common than "bit" in English, but given the same usage: twenty-five cents is two *reales,* seventy-five cents is six *reales,* etc., whether Mexican or American money is meant. (Nos. 43, 75.)

remuda String of horses used as remounts, as in southwestern United States. (No. 19.)

sacarreal majestad Also *sacarreal* and *sacarrial majestá.* Corruption of *sacra y real majestad,* your sacred and royal majesty. (Nos. 4, 35, 43.)

semita Spanish *cemita* and *acemita,* a bread made from *acemite* or wheat flour mixed with bran. In south Texas and northern Mexico, the *semita* is a finer kind of bread, made from wheat flour, eggs, and such spices as anise seed. (No. 35.)

señor Has a wide range of meanings and for that reason not translated in some contexts. Most common meaning is "sir," but it may also mean "lord" or "sire," depending on the context. (Nos. 6, 18, 19, 29, 36, 43, 44, 60.)

tamal Singular of *tamales,* rather than "tamale" as in English. (No. 51b.)

temascal Native Mexican steam bath, something like the Finnish sauna. (No. 6.)

tsana (birds) Same as Santamaría's *zanate*(?), from Aztec *zanatl,* a kind of black bird known as a pest in the corn fields. (No. 4.)

¡tu! ¡tu! Literally, "You! You!" but with completely different connotations, especially as used by women in rural Mexico. It has familiar, affectionate associations that approximate those of a very shy "dear." In our variant of *Blancaflor* the cooing sound of *¡tu! ¡tu!* is utilized by having both the girl and her doves use the words. Another phrase typical of the rural Mexican woman is (or was) *¡ay, tu!* equivalent to "Oh, dear!" or "Oh, my!" (No. 30.)

vaquero Usually a cowhand but may also mean "horseman" in phrases like "he is a good vaquero." (No. 18.)

zompantli Santamaría also gives *zompantle* and *zompancle.* Same plant as the *colorín.* (No. 3.)

List of Abbreviations

ASFM = *Anuario de la Sociedad Folklórica de México*
JAF   = *Journal of American Folklore*
TFSP = *Texas Folklore Society Publications*

Bibliography

AARNE, ANTTI, and THOMPSON, STITH. *The Types of the Folktale: A Classification and Bibliography*. Helsinki, 1961.

ABRAHAMS, ROGER D. *Deep down in the Jungle: Negro Narrative Folklore from the Streets of Philadelphia*. Hatboro, Pennsylvania, 1964.

ACOSTA, FR. JOSÉ DE. *Historia natural y moral de las Indias*. Sevilla, 1590.

AIKEN, RILEY. "Fifteen Mexican Tales." *TFSP* 32 (1964): 3–56.

———. "A Pack Load of Mexican Tales." *TFSP* 12 (1935): 1–87.

———. "Six Tales from Mexico." *TFSP* 27 (1957): 78–95.

BARKER, RUTH LAUGHLIN. "New Mexico Witch Tales." *TFSP* 10 (1932): 62–70.

BAUGHMAN, ERNEST W. *A Type and Motif-Index of the Folktales of England and North America*. The Hague & Bloomington, Ind., 1965.

BEALS, RALPH L. "Problems of Mexican Indian Folklore." *JAF* 56 (1943): 8–16.

———. "Two Mountain Zapotec Tales from Oaxaca, Mexico." *JAF* 48 (1935): 189–90.

BOAS, FRANZ. "Notes on Mexican Folklore." *JAF* 25 (1912): 204–60.

BOAS, FRANZ, and ARREOLA, JOSÉ MARÍA. "Cuentos en mexicano de Milpa Alta, D.F., recogidos por Franz Boas, traducidos al español por el profesor José María Arreola." *JAF* 33 (1920): 1–24.

BOAS, FRANZ, and HAEBERLIN, HERMAN K. "Ten Folktales in Modern Náhuatl." *JAF* 37 (1924): 345–70.

Boggs, Ralph Steele. *Bibliografía del folklore mexicano.* Mexico, 1939.

———. "A Folklore Expedition to Mexico." *Southern Folklore Quarterly* 3 (1939): 65–73.

———. *Index of Spanish Folktales.* Helsinki, 1930.

———. "Valor práctico del folklore." *América Indígena* 5 (1945): 211–15.

Brinton, Daniel G. "The Folk-Lore of Yucatan." In *Essays of an Americanist.* Philadelphia, 1890, pp. 163–80; reprinted from the *Folk-Lore Journal* 1 (1883): 244–56.

———. *El folklore del Yucatán,* trans. Enrique Leal. Mérida, Yucatán, 1937.

Campos, Rubén M. *El folklore literario de México.* Mexico, 1929.

Comas, Juan. "La vida y obra de Manuel Gamio." In *Estudios antropológicos publicados en homenaje al doctor Manuel Gamio,* pp. 1–26. Mexico, 1956.

Díaz del Castillo, Bernal. *Historia verdadera de la conquista de la Nueva España.* 2 vols. Madrid, 1928.

Diccionario Porrúa de historia, biografía y geografía de México. 2d ed. Mexico, 1965.

Dobie, J. Frank. "Br'er Rabbit Watches out for Himself in Mexico." *TFSP* 27 (1957): 113–17.

———. "Catorce." *TFSP* 12 (1935): 194–200.

Dorson, Richard M. *Buying the Wind: Regional Folklore in the United States.* Chicago and London, 1964.

Elson, Ben. "The Homshuk: A Sierra Popoluca Text." *Tlalocan* 2 (1947): 195–214.

Escajeda, Josefina. "Tales from San Elizario." *TFSP* 12 (1935): 115–21.

Espinosa, Aurelio M. "Comparative Notes on New-Mexican and Mexican Spanish Folk-Tales." *JAF* 27 (1914): 211–31.

———. *Cuentos populares españoles, recogidos de la tradición oral de España.* 3 vols. Madrid, 1946–47.

———. "New-Mexican Spanish Folk-Lore, I & II." *JAF* 23 (1910): 395–418.

———. "New-Mexican Spanish Folk-Lore, III, Folk-Tales." *JAF* 24 (1911): 397–444.

———. "New-Mexican Spanish Folk-Lore, VII, More Folk-Tales." *JAF* 27 (1914): 119–47.

ESPINOSA, JOSÉ MANUEL. *Spanish Folk-Tales from New Mexico.* New York, 1937.

Folktales of the World Series, general editor Richard M. Dorson: *Folktales of Chile,* ed. Yolando Pino-Saavedra (Chicago and London, 1967); *Folktales of China,* ed. Wolfram Eberhard (Chicago and London, 1965); *Folktales of England,* ed. Katharine M. Briggs and Ruth L. Tongue (Chicago and London, 1965); *Folktales of France,* ed. Geneviève Massignon (Chicago and London, 1968); *Folktales of Germany,* ed. Kurt Ranke (Chicago and London, 1966); *Folktales of Hungary,* ed. Linda Dégh (Chicago and London, 1965); *Folktales of Ireland,* ed. Sean O'Sullivan (Chicago and London, 1966); *Folktales of Israel,* ed. Dov Noy (Chicago and London, 1963); *Folktales of Japan,* ed. Keigo Seki (Chicago and London, 1963); *Folktales of Norway,* ed. Reidar Christiansen (Chicago and London, 1964).

FOSTER, GEORGE M. "The Current Status of Mexican Indian Folklore Studies." *JAF* 61 (1948): 368–82.

———. "Mexican and Central American Indian Folklore." *The Funk and Wagnalls Standard Dictionary of Folklore, Mythology, and Legend.* New York, 1950. 2:711–16.

———. "Nagualism in Mexico and Guatemala." *Acta Americana* 2 (1944): 85–103.

———. "Sierra Popoluca Folklore and Beliefs." *University of California Publications in American Archaeology and Ethnology* 42 (1945): 177–250.

———. "Some Characteristics of Mexican Indian Folklore." *JAF* 58 (1945): 225–35.

FRANCIS, SUSAN. *Habla y literatura popular en la antigua capital chiapaneca.* Mexico, 1960.

GAMIO, MANUEL. "El material folklórico y el progreso social." *América Indígena* 5 (1945): 207–10.

———. *Mexican Immigration to the United States.* Chicago, 1930.

———, ed. *La población del Valle de Teotihuacán, México.* 3 vols. in 2. Mexico, 1922.

GARCÍA ICAZBALCETA, JOAQUÍN. "Provincialismos mexicanos." *Memorias de la Academia Mexicana* 3 (1886): 170–90.

GARIBAY K., ANGEL MARÍA. "Fray Bernardino de Sahagún: Relación de los textos que no aprovechó en su obra: Su método de investigación." In *Aportaciones a la investigación folklórica de México,* pp. 7–32. Mexico, 1953.

GATSCHET, ALBERT S. "Popular Rimes from Mexico." *JAF* 2 (1889): 48–53.

GAYTON, A. H. "The Orpheus Myth in North America." *JAF* 48 (1935): 263–93.

GÓMEZ MAILLEFERT, EUGENIO M. "Supersticiones de la región de San Juan Teotihuacán, Estado de México." *JAF* 31 (1918): 488–95.

GONZÁLEZ CASANOVA, PABLO. "Cuento en mexicano de Milpa Alta, D. F." *JAF* 33 (1920): 25–27.

———. *Cuentos indígenas.* 2d ed. Mexico, 1965.

GOODWYN, FRANK. "Another Mexican Version of the 'Bear's Son' Folktale." *JAF* 66 (1953): 143–54.

GUERRA, FERMINA. "Mexican Animal Tales." *TFSP* 18 (1943): 188–94.

HANSEN, TERRENCE LESLIE. *The Types of the Folktale in Cuba, Puerto Rico, the Dominican Republic, and Spanish South America.* Berkeley and Los Angeles, 1957.

HIESTER, MIRIAM W. "Tales of the Paisanos." *TFSP* 30 (1961): 226–43.

HUDSON, WILSON M. "The King and the Saurín." *TFSP* 22 (1949): 179–84.

———. "To Whom God Wishes to Give He Will Give." *TFSP* 24 (1951): 128–32.

HULTKRANTZ, ÅKE. *The North American Indian Orpheus Tradition: A Contribution to Comparative Religion.* Stockholm, 1957.

IBARRA, ALFREDO, JR. "El cuento en México." *ASFM* 3 (1943): 25–31.

———. *Cuentos y leyendas de México.* Mexico, 1941.

JANVIER, THOMAS A. *Legends of the City of Mexico.* New York, 1910.

BIBLIOGRAPHY   253

Jiménez, Baldemar A. "Cuentos de Susto." *TFSP* 31 (1962):
    156–64.
Johnson, Jean Bassett. "Three Mexican Tar Baby Stories." *JAF*
    53 (1940): 215–17.
Kelly, Isabel. *Folk Practices in North Mexico*. Austin, Texas,
    1965.
Law, Howard W. "Tamákasti: A Gulf Nahuat Text." *Tlalocan*
    3 (1957): 344–60.
León, Nicolás. "Foc-Lor Mexicano." *Memorias de la Sociedad
    Científica "Antonio Alzate"* 24 (1906–7): 339–95.
————. *El negrito poeta mexicano y sus populares versos: Con-
    tribución para el folklore nacional*. Mexico, 1912.
McAllister, J. Gilbert. "Kiowa-Apache Tales." *TFSP* 22
    (1949): 1–141.
Mason, John Alden. "Four Mexican-Spanish Fairy-Tales from
    Azqueltán, Jalisco." *JAF* 25 (1912): 191–98.
————. "Myths of the Uintah Utes." *JAF* 23 (1910): 299–363.
Mason, John Alden, and Espinosa, Aurelio M. "Folktales of the
    Tepecanos." *JAF* 27 (1914): 148–210.
Mechling, William Hubbs. "Stories and Songs from the South-
    ern Atlantic Coastal Region of Mexico." *JAF* 29 (1916): 547–
    58.
————. "Stories from Tuxtepec, Oaxaca." *JAF* 25 (1912): 199–203.
Mendoza, Vicente T. "Cincuenta años de investigaciones folk-
    lóricas en Mexico." In *Aportaciones a la investigación folk-
    lórica de México*, (1953), pp. 81–115.
————. "Visión general del Folklore." In *Nuevas aportaciones a
    la investigación folklórica de México*, (1958) pp. 9–29.
Mendoza, Vicente T., and Rodríguez Rivera de Mendoza, Vir-
    ginia. *Folklore de San Pedro Piedra Gorda, Zacatecas*.
    Mexico, 1952.
Miller, Walter S. *Cuentos mixes*. Mexico, 1956.
Moedano N., Gabriel. "El folklore como disciplina antropo-
    lógica: Su desarrollo en México." *Tlatoani* 2, no. 17 (1963):
    37–50.
Newell, W. W. "The Passover Song of the Kid and an Equiva-
    lent from New England." *JAF* 18 (1905): 33–48.

PAREDES, AMÉRICO. "Luis Inclán: First of the Cowboy Writers."
American Quarterly 12 (1960): 55–70.

——. *"With His Pistol in His Hand": A Border Ballad and Its
Hero.* Austin, Texas, 1958.

PARSONS, ELSIE CLEWS. "Folklore from Santa Ana Xalmimilulco,
Puebla, Mexico." *JAF* 45 (1932): 318–62.

——. "Zapoteca and Spanish Tales of Mitla, Oaxaca." *JAF* 45
(1932): 277–317.

PÉREZ, SOLEDAD. "Mexican Folklore from Austin, Texas." *TFSP*
24 (1951): 71–126.

PÉREZ SERRANO, MANUEL. "El duende y la matlacihua." *ASFM* 5
(1945): 35–40.

PEZA, JUAN DE DIOS. *Leyendas, tradiciones y fantasías de las calles
de México.* Paris, 1870.

PIMENTEL S., JACOB. "Creencias." *ASFM* 9 (1955): 147–63.

——. "El dueño de los venados." *ASFM* 9 (1955): 13–16.

——. "Miscelánea de creencias en la Congregación de Los
Angeles, Simojovel, Chis." *ASFM* 11 (1957): 207–24.

PINO SAAVEDRA, YOLANDO. *Cuentos folklóricos de Chile,* 3 vols.
Santiago, 1960, 1961, 1963.

RADIN, PAUL. "The Nature and Problems of Mexican Indian
Mythology." *JAF* 57 (1944): 26–36.

RADIN, PAUL, and ESPINOSA, AURELIO M. *El folklore de Oaxaca.*
New York, 1917.

RAEL, JUAN B. *Cuentos españoles de Colorado y de Nuevo Méjico.*
2 vols. Stanford, California, n.d.

——. "Cuentos españoles de Colorado y de Nuevo Méjico
(Primera serie)." *JAF* 52 (1939): 227–323.

RANGEL, NICOLÁS. "El teatro." In *Antología del centenario:
Estudio documentado de la literatura mexicana durante el
primer siglo de independencia,* 2: 1015–29. Mexico, 1910.

REDFIELD, MARGARET PARK. "The Folk Literature of a Yucatecan
Town." *Contributions to American Archaeology* 3 (1937):
1–50.

REID, JOHN TURNER. "Seven Folktales from Mexico." *JAF* 48
(1935): 109–24.

ROBE, STANLEY LINN. *A Dialect and Folkloristic Study of Texts*

Recorded in Los Altos of Jalisco, Mexico. Doctoral dissertation, University of North Carolina, 1949.

RODRÍGUEZ RIVERA, VIRGINIA. *Santa Bárbara: Estudio histórico y
geográfico de la oración de la Santa.* Mexico, 1967.

ROMERO, JESÚS C. "El folklore en México." *Boletín de la Sociedad
Mexicana de Geografía y Estadística* 63 (1947): 657–798.

SANTAMARÍA, FRANCISCO J. *Diccionario de mejicanismos.* Mexico,
1959.

——. *Diccionario general de americanismos.* Mexico, 1942.

MARTÍNEZ, CELEDONIO SERRANO. "Pedro de Urdemalas en la nar-
ración tradicional en Guerrero." *ASFM* 6 (1950): 415–28.

STORM, DAN. "The Little Animals of Mexico." *TFSP* 14 (1938):
8–35.

THOMPSON, STITH. *The Folktale.* New York, 1951.

——. *Motif-Index of Folk-Literature.* 6 vols. Copenhagen and
Bloomington, Indiana, 1955–58.

VILLA ROJAS, ALFONSO. "Significado y valor práctico del folklore."
América Indígena 5 (1945): 295–302.

WAGNER, MAX LEOPOLD. "Algunas apuntaciones sobre el folklore
mexicano." *JAF* 40 (1927): 105–43.

WHATLEY, W. A. "Mexican Münchausen." *TFSP* 19 (1944): 42–
56.

WHEELER, HOWARD T. *Tales from Jalisco, Mexico.* Philadelphia,
1943.

YOFFIE, LEAH R. C. "Present-Day Survivals of Ancient Jewish
Custom." *JAF* 29 (1916): 412–17.

ZUNSER, HELEN. "A New Mexican Village." *JAF* 48 (1935): 125–
78.

Index of Motifs

(From Stith Thompson, *Motif-Index of Folk Literature*, 6 vols. [Bloomington, Ind., 1955–58]).

A. MYTHOLOGICAL MOTIFS

Motif No.		Tale No.
A511.1.9	Culture hero born from egg	3, 4
A511.2.1.1	Abandoned culture hero captured by use of net	4
A511.4.1	Miraculous growth of culture hero	3
A512.1	Culture hero's grandmother	4
A521	Culture hero as dupe or trickster	4
A522.1.2	Rabbit as culture hero	1
A524.2	Extraordinary weapons of culture hero	3
A526.7	Culture hero performs remarkable feats of strength and skill	3
A527.3.1	Culture hero can transform self	4
A571	Culture hero asleep in mountain	3
A711.2	Sun (and moon) as a cannibal	34
A901	Topographical features caused by experiences of primitive hero	3
A972	Indentions on rocks from prints left by man (beast)	3
A975.1	Why stones no longer grow	4
A977	Origin of particular groups of stones	5
A989.4	Pile of stones marks site of battle	5
A1021	Deluge: escape in boat (ark)	1
A1145.1	Earthquakes from movements of subterranean monster	3
A1422	Assignment of edible animals	4
A1711	Animals from transformations after deluge or world calamity	1
A1724.1	Animals from body of slain person	4
A1730	Creation of animals as punishment	1
A1931	Creation of vulture	1
A2003	Origin of insects: released from sack (trunk)	4

E. THE DEAD

F. MARVELS

H. TESTS

J. THE WISE AND THE FOOLISH

L. REVERSAL OF FORTUNE

S. UNNATURAL CRUELTY

T. SEX

V. RELIGION

W. TRAITS OF CHARACTER

X. HUMOR

Index of Tale Types

(Type numbers are from Antti Aarne and Stith Thompson, *The Types of the Folktale* [Helsinki, 1961].)

I. ANIMAL TALES

II. ORDINARY FOLKTALES

Index

276

GENERAL INDEX

Hero (*continued*)
vives dead chickens, 15; transforms into ant, 71–72; transforms into eagle, 68–69, 73;
transforms into hound, 71; transforms into lion, 73; transforms
into tiger, 73; travels of, 8–11;
tricks *patrón*, 138–41; wins contest, 108–9; wins *hacienda*, 138–
41; wins king's daughter, 114–
15; wins princess, 137; works
five years for twelve cents a year,
134–35; writes on high rock, 10
Hiester, Mariam W., 236
Horse: as enchanted prince, 102–
12 passim; members of magician's family as, 82; becomes
church, 85; becomes lake, 86;
helps hero, 104–12 passim; knows
old saying, 51; travels at great
speed, 79
Hudson, Wilson M., 228

Ibarra, Alfredo, Jr., lxxxv
Illness: caused by evil eye, 32–33;
caused by witch, 26; cured by
magic flower, 125; of enchanted
prince, 100
Immortality, of hero, 11
Impersonation. *See* Deception;
Trickery
Incláre, Luis, lviii–lvix

Janvier, Thomas A., xiv, lvix
Jealousy: of girls of sister, 96; of
grandmother, 15; of ugly sisters,
91–92; older brothers of younger
brother, 125
Jiménez, Baldemar A., 219
Johnson, Jean B., 211
Journey: of hero, 8; of hero to
king's palace, 18; of *ranchero*,
128–29; of snake, 10–11; to
otherworld, 5
Jugnetetoqui. See Fire iguanas

Kindness: of enchanted prince to
girl, 96; of girl to bird, 96; of
hero to animals, 66; of hero to
mother, 8; of hero to old lady,
108; of hero to parents, 112; of
lady to children, 90–91; of magician's daughter to hero, 79–88
passim; of priest to hero, 65; of
mouse and dungbeetle to woodcutter, 117–22; of sexton to
drunkard, 175; of woodcutter to
mouse and dungbeetle, 115–18;
woodcutter frees snake, 50;
woodcutter helps serpent, 113

La Llorona, legend of, xvi, lxxii,
lxxx
Law, Howard W., lxxviii, lxxxiii,
199, 200
Leo XIII (pope), xxii
León, Nicolás, lx–lxi, lxiii, lxiv,
lxv, lxx
Linnet, 17; as hero's messenger, 18
Lizard: deceives hero, 17; is pun-
ished, 17
Lorenzo, Agustín, legend of, xxix–
xxxiii, xxxiii–xxxvii
Lying. *See* Deceptions; Trickery

McAllister, J.G., 225
Madsen, William (American anthropologist), xxviii
Magician: assigns tasks to hero, 80–
83 passim; becomes bird, 85;
wins wagers, 78–79
Magic objects: devil's ear, 76;
flowers cure sick woman, 125;
flowers sing, 126; glass of spittle, 83–85; guitar, 110; guitar
music cures prince, 101; gun,
28; hero's staff becomes tree, 10;
meat of cow enables eagle to
transport girl, 99; mirror, 113–
15; *morral*, 31; powder, 80;